the color project

the color project

SIERRA ABRAMS

Published by Gatekeeper Press
3971 Hoover Rd. Suite 77
Columbus, OH 43123-2839
www.GatekeeperPress.com

ISBN: [to come]

Printed in the United States of America

for my papa

i'm so glad we got to keep you

CONTENTS

Author's Note xiii

One: "Strawberry Swing"
    Coldplay 1

Two: "Crayola Doesn't Make A Color For Your Eyes"
    Kristin Andreassen 7

Three: "Moon"
    Sleeping At Last 13

Four: "Strange Attractor"
    Animal Kingdom 21

Five: "Dance For Me Wallis"
    Abel Korzeniowski 29

Six: "So Long, Lonesome"
    Explosions in the Sky 37

Seven: "I Wear Glasses"
    Mating Ritual 43

Eight: "Rustle of the Stars"
    A Silent Film 57

Nine: "Clouds"
Borns 65

Ten: "Beautiful World"
The Chevin 69

Eleven: "The Other Side of Mt. Heart Attack"
Liars 79

Twelve: "Quesadilla"
Walk the Moon 87

Thirteen: "Fall"
Cider Sky 97

Fourteen: "The Other Side"
Civil Twilight 107

Fifteen: "Count Me In"
Early Winters 117

Sixteen: "Young Hearts"
Strange Talk 129

Seventeen: "Say It Out Loud"
Katie Herzig 145

Eighteen: "Suspension"
Mae 157

Nineteen: "Stars (Hold On)"
Youngblood Hawke 165

Twenty: "Harbour Lights"
A Silent Film 177

Twenty-One: "Yes!"
Dario Marianelli.. 189

Twenty-Two: "Dopamine"
Borns 195

Twenty-Three: "I Lived Here"
Martin Phipps 201

Twenty-Four: "Tightrope"
Walk the Moon.. 207

Twenty-Five: "Guillotine"
Jon Bellion 213

Twenty-Six: "Shake it Out"
Florence + the Machine 219

Twenty-Seven: "On the Nature of Daylight"
Max Richter 225

Twenty-Eight: "Lay Your Cheek On Down"
Moonface 235

Twenty-Nine: "Runaway"
AURORA 243

Thirty: "Sugar"
Editors... 251

Thirty-One: "Tenderly"
Houses... 263

Thirty-Two: "40 Day Dream"
Edward Sharpe and the Magnetic Zeros................... 271

Thirty-Three: "Let Them Feel Your Heartbeat"
A Silent Film...281

Thirty-Four: "Winter"
Mree..295

Thirty-Five: "Ice Dance"
Danny Elfman 301

Thirty-Six: "Pressure Suit"
Aqualung..307

Thirty-Seven: "Creature Fear"
Bon Iver..319

Thirty-Eight: "Pieces"
Andrew Belle..325

Thirty-Nine: "I'll Believe in Anything"
Wolf Parade 333

Forty: "Lighthouse"
Patrick Watson 345

Forty-One: "Stainache"
Emmalouise..355

Forty-Two: "Til Kingdom Come"
Coldplay...367

Forty-Three: "Big Eyes"
Matt Corby..379

Forty-Four: "Over You"
Ingrid Michaelson 387

Forty-Five: "Our Voices"
Matthew Barber 393

Forty-Six: "Kettering"
The Antlers 399

Forty-Seven: "Ambulance"
Eisley.. 405

Forty-Eight: "The Crypt (Part 2)"
Abel Korzeniowski... 413

Forty-Nine: "Beginnings"
Houses... 421

Fifty: "Thousand Mile Race"
A Silent Film.. 429

Fifty-One: "This Is the Countdown"
Mae 441

Fifty-Two: "Tomorrow"
A Silent Film.. 445

Fifty-Three: "Story of an Immigrant"
Civil Twilight... 451

Fifty-Four: "All My Heart"
The Mynabird... 457

Acknowledgements... 463

About the Author 465

AUTHOR'S NOTE

Two and a half years ago, in January 2015, I sat down with a lone paragraph I'd written the year before and started the first draft of *The Color Project*. It was done in a heartbeat, messy and choppy, but oh-so-precious to me.

The thing was: it had turned out quite a bit sadder than I'd expected it to. At first I didn't know all the reasons why this was a good thing—I just thought I was staying true to the story. I'd set out to tell a story similar to my own, to write a heroine as awkward as me, to write about a good boy with a heart of gold, and to write about community in the way I'd seen it all my life.

But what I got was so much greater.

This book, I discovered in a later draft, was slowly helping me to overcome my fears about . . . well, several things, but two big things. One was an insecurity I'd struggled with for so long, an insecurity that had been layered with severe depression for five long years. The other is more difficult and complicated to explain, but you'll know it as soon as you get to it.

Fear is a terrible, tricky thing. Sometimes you don't even know you're afraid. And how can you overcome something if you don't know it exists?

I owe this book everything. For helping me *see* the fear, and helping me to overcome it afterward. I am not the same person today, because of this book. I am a kinder, braver, happier person. I am a better listener, a better fighter, and a better storyteller. I am unapologetic and critical and melancholy. I am a crier. I am hopelessly romantic.

I am on my way to becoming the last person I ever expected to become. I am on my way to writing stories I never thought I'd write. I am on my way to journeys I never thought I'd have.

All because there was a silly book in my head that taught me how to be brave.

So here's to books that change us, and here's to you, for trying this one out. I hope it's everything you need it to be.

XOXO,
Sierra

June 15th, 2017

chapter 1

QUEUED:
STRAWBERRY SWING
BY COLDPLAY

SOMETIMES I LIKE driving east when the sun is setting in the west. That way I can see all the signs as they're lit up in flames along the road, their words unreadable, all the buildings glowing in the evening sun. The sky is neither blue nor black; rather, it's a mix of in-between purples and pinks and oranges, and for just a few minutes the world shines like a bright star before it's plunged into darkness.

This—this moment of suspension—is what I love most about my drive home from work. Today, everything's like fireworks. A splash of color here, a blinding sunray there, the dark skyline bleeding into the rest. I'm enthralled at the sight of it all, basking in its beauty, with music blasting and the windows rolled down and my (too long) hair whipping against my glasses.

I am the most unsuspecting person, and all because of a golden sunset.

I'm jolted by two separate bumps, one right after the other, followed by the terrible yet inevitable noise: *Thump. Thump. Thumpthumpthumpthump—*

That's my only warning before my car jerks to the left, then to the right, then back again. There's a loud clunking noise that makes me want to shriek to the high heavens, but I can't, because my jaw has locked my mouth shut in fear.

For three-point-five seconds, I have no idea what's going on. My hands are shaking (*Is this an earthquake?!*) and my heart is pounding in my throat. Cars rush past me, way too fast (or am I just slowing down?) and their drivers are angry. Someone swerves around me while I try to get into the next lane to my right. I wait a few seconds, taking a deep breath . . . . . and a scraping sound comes from behind. The reality of what's happening hits me hard: My tires are indeed flat, my tailgate is dragging on the asphalt, and if I don't pull over soon I'm going to get hit.

It takes a lot of maneuvering (and telling myself out loud that I will not die like road kill) before I manage to make it to the sidelines without impact. California drivers pass me at speeds well over the 65 MPH limit, honking rudely and flipping the bird, all because they have places to go and people to see and *I* got in their way.

"I could have died!" I protest aloud. My voice comes out wobbly. I grip the steering wheel and gasp, blinking back tears. *It'll be all right . . . right?* I think. Almost hyperventilating, I turn on my hazards and proceed to stare at the blinking in my dashboard. It's like someone's holding a giant sign right in front of my face, with flashing letters that say, "WELCOME TO ADULTHOOD".

I am thoroughly unamused.

On my list of things I want to do during the summer after graduation, you might see the words *Go to the beach* and *Read ten books* and *Bake more*. Never ever would you see, *Run over something inconspicuous on the freeway and get two flat tires.*

But who cares about my list, anyway? Two flat tires are what I get.

It takes a few minutes, but I eventually calm down enough to call a tow. I probably sound pathetic because Jenny, the woman on the other end of the line, tells me to sit tight and not worry. How kind of her.

I make myself as comfortable as possible with a bottle of water and a book (which I always carry in my purse for emergencies just like these) while I wait. I can't concentrate on the story, but the smooth white pages and contrasting black ink have a way of soothing me. After about thirty minutes—five of those were spent staring blankly—I finally close the book and set it in my lap.

And take a good, long look at the tow truck as it slides into place in front of me.

Here we go.

When the driver steps out, my first thought is, *Oh, great.* He's big (about twice my size) and hairy (like a freakin' Yeti). He almost looks *mean.* I groan as I slip out of my car, the freeway wind hitting me. Suddenly, as my limbs stretch for the first time in over an hour, a dramatic growl echoes in my stomach. Of *course* I would get hungry *now*, of all times. All I want from life is an animal-style cheeseburger from In-N-Out, and, right now, that's the last thing I'm going to get.

Oh, just get this over with.

Thankfully the tow truck driver, Julian, is quick and efficient and hardly talks at all. I nearly laugh when I see his name tag. I always imagine Julians as lean, young men with good hair. Probably surfers. Definitely playing the guitar. It's totally inappropriate to laugh, however, so I stifle myself with two pieces of gum while he goes about his business.

Eventually, his business includes the official stuff. I hand Julian my driver's license and cringe, as I always do when I know someone's going to see my full name. All my important documents are a constant reminder that the truth is often a lot uglier than life's many facades.

Thing You Should Know About Me #1: My full name is Bernice Aurora Wescott, and I hate it. Who thinks of these things? Apparently, only my parents. And *only* my parents, my sisters, my best friend Gretchen, and my employer know my full name.

To everyone else, I am Bee.

I sometimes wonder if my mom went crazy in those very important minutes after my birth when she named me, and I think maybe my dad went with her. They did it again, with both my sisters, Astrid Jean (hers is the most tolerable) and Millicent May. Poor Millicent. Sometimes I think she has it harder than all of us, but at least we can call her Millie. There is only one child in our family who was spared eternal torment—our older brother, Tom.

All things considered, I know I have no right to think Julian's name is humorous, and watching him look at my driver's license sobers me greatly. After our brief interaction, when he hands back my documents, he gestures for me to sit in the passenger seat of the truck. I awkwardly climb in (I'm short; I can't help it) while he gets in on the driver's side. When he pulls into traffic, I flinch at the truck's protesting screech, as if my car could fly off at any given moment. But then we're driving, and the road is smooth beneath us, so I try to relax and trust that Julian-the-non-surfer-who-can't-play-guitar (okay, maybe he can) knows what he's doing.

That doesn't last long. Minutes later, when I can't bear the awkward silence anymore, I pull out my phone to call my mom. "You've reached Chloe Wescott," her voicemail practically sings to me. "Leave me a message at the beep."

"Hey, Mama," I murmur into the receiver. "Just calling to let you know—"

The line beeps. She's calling me back, so I click over.

"Hey," I say, falsely chipper.

"Hey," she replies. She's not even *trying* to be chipper. My mother, who speaks fluent Sing-Song and has the laugh of a hummingbird, sounds upset. Sad. Anxious.

I squint. "Sorry to call while you're driving the girls around—"

Her sniffle interrupts me. "It's okay, Baby Bee. Your dad took them to dance class today."

"Papa? But isn't he working?"

"He got off early." Her voice tightens, tone restrained. She doesn't offer an explanation, so I don't ask. "I'm just eating dinner. Want me to save you some?"

She sounds like she's trying to smile and is failing miserably. "Sure," I say. "Not sure when I'm coming home, though. I got two flat tires."

Beside me, Julian grunts. I start, having forgotten he was there in the first place. But then I just scowl. Is he laughing at me? I squint at him for an indecent amount of time before realizing my mom is asking me questions.

"Sorry, sorry, what?" I ask.

"You're okay, right? No injuries? Your car's okay?"

"Yes, I'm fine. Car's fine. We're headed to Mike's right now."

She lets out a deep breath. "Okay, okay."

"Mama?" I ask.

"Yes?"

I hear it again, the tightening of her voice, the sniffle, and I sigh. I want to ask her what's going on, what happened to make her cry, why Papa's taking time off to take my sisters to dance. But Julian's sitting next to me, we're almost to Mike's, and I'm feeling funny. So I blurt instead, "Can you pick me up if I need you to?"

She clears her throat. "Sure, that's fine. Just see if Michael can do it first?"

"Okay. See you soon."

"Love you," she says, her voice small.

"Love you, too," I say, equally quiet. I shake this strange feeling from my shoulders, straighten, and hang up.

I glance at Julian, who's studiously staring ahead at the road, both hands on the wheel. I say a quick thank-you to the heavens that he wasn't a weirdo or someone who wanted to talk the whole time (not that I gave him a chance) before he pulls into the parking lot at Mike's.

chapter 2

QUEUED:
Crayola Doesn't Make A Color For Your Eyes
by Kristin Andreassen

MIKE'S IS A car shop owned by a nice man named—you guessed it—Mike. But his son, Michael, basically runs the place, and he's the real reason my family comes here regularly. Tom and Michael have been best friends for almost sixteen years, as long as I can remember. I have *mostly* good memories of growing up with him around, but I tell him that I only remember him teaming up with Tom and not letting me play video games with them.

Michael sees me from across the garage and strides toward me with his arm raised in greeting. I return the wave and gesture with my thumb at my car behind me, rolling my eyes.

He laughs. (And I suspect it's *at* me.)

"*Bee*," he says teasingly, trying to hug me with his grungy wife beater and greasy hands. I close my eyes and wait for it to end.

I love hugs, but not from sweaty Michael. (You'd be surprised how many of them I've received in my life.)

Michael pats the hood of my car as two of his coworkers slide it onto solid ground. "Come on in. We'll take care of you."

"Thanks, Michael."

He nudges me into the small office building to the left of the garage, and when everyone inside turns to look at us, he shouts, "Look who broke her car!"

I halt fast, giving him a mean side-scowl. "*I* didn't break my car."

"Yeah, yeah." Greg, another of Tom's friends, chuckles from behind the computer. "Bee always says it wasn't her."

I harrumph. "Well, it wasn't."

"Come on, you guys," Keagan says, coming up beside me. His green eyes sparkle in that dazzling-Keagan way. He's not quite a pretty-boy, but he sure is nice to look at, with his thick, wavy brown hair and square jaw and a thin nose. "It was probably Tom's fault. Slit your tires or something."

"Finally, someone with sense." I grin at Keagan. Not for the first time, I wonder why Tom doesn't work here with all his buddies. He practically lives here when he's not working the night shift at the warehouse. (Or sleeping. He does a lot of sleeping.)

"Dude, Bee, we haven't seen you in a while," Greg says. "How are you?"

"Not so bad. New job and everything."

Keagan raises an eyebrow. "New job?"

I feel a sheepish grin covering my face. "Yeah, I'm a florist's assistant now. Today was Day Three on the job."

"Phew," Greg says. "What's that like? Sounds like an allergy attack to me."

I smack his arm softly. "It's a little shop called Tracy's Market Flowers, in Oceanside."

"That's a long drive," he says quickly. (Greg, ever the optimist.)

"Yeah, but it's worth it," I say. "So far." This job has to be the most interesting thing I've ever done for money. (Please don't take that the wrong way.) Giving flowers to surprised individuals, watching their faces fill with the most adorable confusion and delight, is my new favorite thing. "I keep the shop clean and help out at the front desk, but mostly I help deliver arrangements."

"I'm glad you like it, Bee," Keagan says, wiping his face with the hem of his shirt. It's not too grimy yet, but it leaves a trail of dirt on his forehead.

These boys, I think, affectionately. "What about you guys? How's your summer so far?"

"Nothing awful has happened," Greg answers. "Yet."

Keagan smiles. "Pretty good. Not as interesting as yours, though."

"Busy," Michael says. He drops some paperwork on Greg's desk and smiles ruefully. "Organize those."

With Greg grumbling about the messes everyone leaves for him to clean, Michael touches my arm, suddenly all business. "I have to leave in an hour, so we should get you sorted." He opens the door that leads from the small office to the garage.

My car has already been moved into the garage alongside three others. I try to keep up as Michael weaves his way through the ports, but I accidentally run into four men and a tire en route.

When I finally catch up to him standing by the hood of my car, Michael looks at me and shrugs. "Aside from the tires, how about I give you a full exam? While it's here."

"If you think she needs it," I say, pushing my hair out of my eyes. It's down to my waist now, and the constant fluttering and swishing around my face sometimes makes it hard to concentrate. (Thing You Should Know About Me #35: Because being bored with short hair is worse than being annoyed by long hair, I'll never cut it again.)

Michael nods. "Why not? It's been a while." He runs a hand through his ruffled blond hair. Now, Michael can surf *and* play guitar. *He* should have been named Julian.

I laugh. Quietly.

To myself.

Which is precisely when I discover someone looking at me.

The Boy is standing over the car next to mine, reaching deep into the hood. The first thing I notice about him are his clothes. In the grungy mess of the car shop, I would expect someone dressed exactly like Michael: black and other dark colors, complete with torn jeans and maybe even a bandana like Keagan sometimes uses to keep grease out of his hair. But no. The Boy is wearing a pastel yellow sweater, which I stare at for a second too long. Why on God's green earth would he wear such a lovely, light-colored sweater to work at a car shop when it's going to get greasy and torn?

I chide myself for staring at his sweater—so instead, like the social genius I am, I stare at his face. He reaches for something on the table beside him, then slips his hand back into the engine, lips puckered as he bites the inside of his cheek. He's got that thin, lean look, all high arches and sharp cheekbones. His dark blond hair is purposefully messy, swooping up in the front. (He could give Douglas Booth and Sam Claflin a run for their money.) I notice that his eyes are a light brown, almost golden . . . and then I try to un-notice because those eyes are looking right at me. Again.

Belatedly, I turn red like a blood moon, and he chuckles. *Chuckles*!

NOPE, I think to myself, mortally embarrassed and mourning the loss of my dignity. I turn back to Michael, who's fiddling around with something next to the engine, eyes squinting in concentration.

"So, what's up?" I ask, desperate to stop thinking about The Boy and whether or not The Boy is still looking at me and laughing at me, but Michael puts out a shushing hand. I roll my eyes.

Finally, after a few more minutes of muttering under his breath, he straightens and shuts the hood. "You probably need new brake pads, and I think you should have your transmission fluid changed. I can have it done in two or three days. Can you go without a car for that long?"

"I guess so... I mean, I have to, right?" I stutter, trying to imagine how I'll get to Oceanside.

"Considering I'm doing it for free—"

"Wait, what?"

"I mean, not the tires. But the other stuff is easy. So, yeah, I'm super nice, thank me later." Michael waves his hand. "If you can wait another hour I'll drive you home."

"I guess I have no choice. Have anything to eat?" I think my stomach is eating itself now.

Michael laughs. "Sure, check the office fridge. And Greg is probably hiding a bag of Lays behind the desk."

I peer into the office window. Greg, who was munching on a bag of BBQ potato chips, slowly takes his hand from his mouth, as if he knows I'm eyeing his snack. He shakes his head, I nod, he shakes his head, I nod, he shakes his head . . . But I know I've won because he quickly goes back to work. (I'm infamous around here for always eating the chips they have stashed.)

"Thanks, Michael!" I holler. I swoop into the office, where Greg is attempting to hide the bag under his desk. Laughing, I shake my head. "No, no, Greg, it's fine. I'll check the fridge."

Greg visibly relaxes, pulling his chips close to his chest, and I laugh harder. All that's left for me to do is pull out a yogurt and spoon, sit on the edge of the swivel chair across from Greg, and wait for Michael to take me home.

chapter 3

QUEUED:
MOON
BY SLEEPING AT LAST

THE HOUSE LOOKS dark from the outside; our small street has no lights to guide me to the door. Around us, the city of Escondido is quiet, getting ready to sleep.

I wave goodbye to Michael and hurry to the front door with my phone flashlight. I unlock it as quietly as I can so I don't disturb the movie I hear playing in the back room. I slip inside, lock up, and make my way toward the noise.

My mom is sitting alone on the couch. The girls and my dad obviously haven't come home yet, or else at least one of them would be sitting next to my mom. I can't tell if Tom is here or not, but his presence is everywhere as always: shoes by the door, a sweatshirt over the back of a chair, clothes folded by the couch and waiting to be put away. I scrunch my nose at his boxers lying flat on the top, the Superman logo staring up at me. (I am never watching any Superman movies with Tom *ever* again.)

I study my mom from the doorway, hoping she doesn't see me. She's crying; I can tell immediately by the way she lifts her thumb to her cheek and wipes at her cheekbones every twenty seconds. It's silent crying, but she hasn't stopped since I walked up.

My stomach sinks. I'm frozen, alternating between wanting to give her space and wanting to slip onto the couch next to her for some cuddles. Before I can make up my mind, however, the front door bursts open and Astrid and Millicent rush inside. They're yelling about some musical and arguing over who can sing the words with the most accuracy. Still in their leotards and tights, they push past me like two fierce winds ("Hi, Bee!" they shout) and sprint toward the couch.

Mama quickly hides her tears behind an award-winning smile while they tell her about their auditions at dance today.

I glance back at the door, but my dad hasn't come inside yet. I bite my bottom lip.

"Bee!" my mom calls. "I didn't see you come in!"

"Just got home," I say, and smile at them from the doorway. Millie (an old soul for her thirteen years) has her hand over her heart like she's telling an exciting story and losing her breath. Astrid glances at Millie and rolls her eyes. At fifteen years old, she's the cynic of the family. (I swear, getting a tear out of her is like trying to get water out of a long-dry well.)

The three of them look alike. My mom passed down her long, golden hair to all of us, but that's where it ends for me. The girls have the shape and color of her eyes, the oval face, the small nose, and the thin lips. I, on the other hand, got my dad's nose (let's just say it's not as small and dainty as my mom's), his round face, his green eyes, his full lips—and all his mannerisms, too. Everyone tells me I look like him, something that pissed me off when I was younger. *How dare they tell me I look like a boy?!* I'd rant. But now I understand what they mean, and I take it as a compliment. Papa has a kind, honest face, with eyes that literally sparkle. (And hey, he was pretty darn good-lookin' in his yesteryears, if his high school yearbooks are any indication.)

My mom sees my smile and smiles back. It's genuine, which puts some of my worries at ease. "How'd it go, baby? Want some leftovers?"

I shrug. "I'll have to pick it up in a few days. Michael's doing a full checkup."

"He's so nice." My mom waves me over. "Want to watch the movie with us?"

I almost comment that she's already cried enough for one day, but manage to hold the words inside. Instead, I say, "I'm not in the mood to cry right now. Thanks, though." (Thing You Should Know About Me #17: I'm a crier. I feel a lot of emotions, deeply and with abandon.) "But I *will* accept kisses goodnight."

"You're going to sleep?" Millie asks. She looks up at me with her big blue eyes as I walk over to her, and gives me a quick kiss.

Astrid scoffs. "She's not going to sleep. She's going to stay up all night reading and watching YouTube videos."

"I *am* going to sleep, actually. I'm tired." I kiss my mom on the forehead.

"Lies. You always say that, and then we see your light on at midnight."

I turn to Astrid and smack the back of her head before she can run away. "Which means you're up at midnight every night, too. Just kiss me."

She tucks her lips around her teeth. "I never loved you," she says in perfect old-lady-with-no-teeth character.

I raise one eyebrow, unamused. "Wow. I've never seen *that* one before."

She breaks into a smile, then, and lightly kisses my cheek. "Goodnight. I'm sure you'll sleep soundly tonight."

Her smile turns evil. I grab a pillow and whack her until she's cowering on the couch.

Laughing, I snatch up my purse and wave at them. "See you tomorrow!" I snag some quick leftovers—cold mac-n-cheese—before disappearing into the rest of the house.

My bedroom is down the hall, and I close the door behind me, sighing happily into the silence. It's really messy: unfolded clothes at the end of the bed, books lying on the ground because I don't have enough money saved for a new bookshelf, and three coffee mugs creating rings on my desk. I sling my purse onto its hook before taking the mugs to the kitchen. I rinse them out and hurry back to my room.

Taking one look at the pile of clothes on my bed, I realize I have no energy left. I grab my bowl of mac-n-cheese, shove the clothes aside, and sit down with an exasperated, "No way."

That's when I see there are *seventeen* unread messages from Gretchen. I check the clock. It's eight o'clock here, so it's eleven her time. I pray she's still awake as I stuff my face with mac-n-cheese and read her messages.

Gretchen

Daily song! Get ready. Are you ready?

. . . I don't think you're ready.

Well, I don't know why you're not answering me because Facebook tells me you're online. I think Facebook is lying to me. *shakes fist* ZUCKERBERG!

I laugh outright and continue to scroll.

Gretchen

Anyway, new song. GET READY.

Below this, there's a link for a song called "Moon". I press play and turn up my Bluetooth speakers.

Gretchen

ISN'T IT THE MOST BEAUTIFUL SONG EVER?! I AM SO IN LOVE.

                                       Bee

WHAT IS THIS MAGIC?! I am in love with it only twenty seconds in. Why haven't we heard this before?

I smile wide when the green light appears next to Gretchen's name. It takes a minute, but soon new words pop up on my screen.

Gretchen

I DON'T KNOW. BUT WE CAN DIE HAPPY NOW.

Dude, where were you all day? I miiiiiissssseeeddd youuuuuu!

I give her a quick update on all things Bee & Car. I think about the beautiful, yellow-sweater-wearing boy in the shop and nearly mention him, *nearly* say something about my rude staring, but then Gretchen's reply comes in, and I forget.

Gretchen

I'm shaking my head right now. Only you, Bee, would get two flat tires. Only you.

I take the last bite of my leftovers and set the bowl on the desk, right where the old mugs used to be.

                                       Bee

I know. But that's why you love me, right? Because I provide amusement and entertainment to combat the everyday mundane?

Gretchen

I love you; this is true, but not just for that reason.

Also, I hate to be rude, but I need to go to sleep now.
I've been staying awake just for you.

                                                              Bee

                                    Thanks. You're the best. Sleep well.

Gretchen

I think you're crap.

I smile. I've heard this a thousand times before—it's our way
of saying goodbye, because goodbyes are stupid, and we don't
like them. It's our coping mechanism for living three thousand
miles apart and missing each other every single day. (I love her
parents, but I also resent them for taking her away from me *all
the way to Pennsylvania.*)

Hearing Gretchen say "I think you're crap" makes me forget
that we're so far from each other.

It's the biggest lie ever, but I don't care.

Replying to her message with those same, sacred words, I
exit the app and pretend I'm not super-tired as I stand up and
start stuffing my unfolded clothes into my drawers. The mess
will still exist, but at least I won't have to look at it or sleep on
top of it. I'm folding up my favorite pink shirt when there's a
knock on my door

"Come in," I mumble, hoping whoever's there won't actually
hear me.

He does. My papa stands in the now-open doorway, hands
in the pockets of his paint-splattered jeans, his shirt equally
messy. The Flash lightning bolt logo looks sad with paint

splattered across it. I shake my head and tsk, saying, "You and Tom."

My dad ignores my teasing and steps into the room. "What? We love our superheroes. Just like you, so don't try to pretend you aren't as nerdy as we are." He looks pointedly at my Clark Kent t-shirt hanging half out of my drawer, then holds out his arms to me. "I didn't realize you were home and I'm offended that I didn't get a hug." He sniffs with pretend vexation.

I smile and hug him tight. "Sorry, I'm tired."

He raises an eyebrow. "Did you build an attic today?"

I groan. My dad loves to compare his job with each of his kids' to remind us that we don't work nearly as hard as he does. (I admit: It's true.) "No, Papa."

He chuckles. "I'm just messing with you."

I'm about to take a swing at his arm when my mom appears behind him and practically pushes me out of the way to hug my dad. "Matt Wescott, you have to come snuggle me—I've been crying over that movie!"

Ah, the aftermath of sad period dramas. This happens every time.

"Oh, baby," my dad says dramatically, "I'll snuggle you anytime."

Ew, gag me. I mean, I love my parents, and I love that they love each other, and I wish more parents loved each other like they do, but *really*? They're standing in my doorway, making out like teenagers.

"Um." I choke. "Um, please?" Then I realize I haven't actually asked them to do anything. (The struggle is so, *so* real.) I try again, much louder, in the sternest voice I can muster. "Mom, Dad, can you please exit the doorway and find your own secluded area of the house to . . . suck face?"

They stop and look at me, my dad wrapping his hand around my mom's. "You don't have to ask *me* twice," he says.

I raise my eyes to the heavens and close my door on them.

"Young lady," my mom starts, but then she breaks out in a giggle.

I lean against the door. It eases my worried heart to see them like this, as they usually are: totally in love, my mom happy, my dad there to catch her if she loses it again. I wonder, for the millionth time, how my parents can love each other like newlyweds after twenty-five years of marriage. It's like our own personal fairy tale; I'm constantly telling my sisters and Tom that we are the product of true love.

Thing You Should Know About Me #395: I'm a *hopeless* romantic. Any book with a love story in it is more likely to grab my attention. I love weddings so much that I crave them. I cry during most romantic movies. I even have my favorite engagement ring picked out at the local jewelry store. (Who am I kidding? I have an entire Pinterest board full of similar rings. My future man will *surely* get the hint.)

I look back at my closed door one more time, smiling to myself. I almost peek outside to make sure they've gone, but I think better of it. Then I pull on my pajamas and collapse onto the bed in a sudden wave of exhaustion.

I'm asleep before I remember to turn out the light.

chapter 4

QUEUED:
STRANGE ATTRACTOR
BY ANIMAL KINGDOM

I GET TO WORK the next two days by using my parents' extra car. I can't *really* complain, even though it's a minivan and I get strange looks from moms everywhere I go.

I'm at work when Michael finally calls. I can't answer with my hands full of peonies and roses, but as soon as I clock out for my break, I listen to his voicemail. It confirms exactly what I want to hear: MY CAR IS READY! I imagine colorful confetti raining down around me.

Excited to be back in Familiar Car Territory, I immediately call Tom. "I need a favor," I demand when he answers.

He clicks his tongue. "Let me think about it. Hmmm. No."

"Tom! I need you!"

"What's wrong?" he asks.

I hear giggling in the background. "Are you with Andrea?"

"Yes, obviously. Where else would I be?"

Ugh. "Tom, *really.* Will you be home tonight to take me to Mike's? My car's ready."

"I'll be home at nine. If they're still open, I can take you then, okay?"

I thank him quickly and hang up. After a few more phone calls, I get a hold of Michael to ask if I can pick up late tonight. (These back-and-forth phone calls are starting to get on my nerves.)

"Yeah, sure, you can stop by late," he says. "Levi will be there working overtime. I'll let him know you're coming."

I have no idea who Levi is, but I thank Michael anyway, "Are you sure I don't owe you anything?"

"Positive. You're Tom's little sister. I feel I owe it to you for all those times I stole your bras and put them in the freezer. Just don't break your car again and we can call it square."

I suck in a sharp breath. "I didn't break my—"

"Hey, Bee, gotta go. Levi's calling."

I hang up, ignoring the little voice in the back of my head that's wondering who Levi is, and why I haven't met him. I clock back in and reach behind my back to retie my colorful apron.

Around me, the shop is a bright world of petals and loose leaves on the ground and gifts and buckets and glass. From my vantage point, I can see the gift shop ahead, the cooler to my left, and the designer's workstation just behind me. Tracy is there, working away, her silver hair cut in a short bob and her reading glasses slipping down her nose.

I push up my own frames and reach for the nearest bucket of lilies to clean off the stamen. It's one of the things I find myself doing automatically in the shop, checking for orange pockets of powder in every bud even if I've already gone over the flowers. There's something therapeutic about the repetitive motions: squeeze, swipe, squeeze, swipe. After I toss the stamen in the trash, my palms are stained with orange, like splotches of sunshine.

Since the checklist for the day is completed, and it's nearly two o'clock, I stand beside Tracy for a few minutes and watch her work. The flowers she's using are bright, not a combination I'd particularly choose, but the arrangement comes together beautifully. The hot pink gerbera daisies and purple dahlias contrast with yellow carnations and white hydrangea to create something I would never have expected. Okay, I wouldn't put it in *my* house, exactly. But somebody ordered this, and it smells amazing, and I just know they're going to be pleased. (Tracy's customers are *always* pleased.)

I look at the clock. There are ten minutes till two, so I busy myself by cleaning up the mess Tracy just made, my feet constantly tapping or moving, my fingers always holding or snipping. I don't even mind when I trip over a loose bucket on my way out the back door, or that the minivan is stiflingly hot, or that it takes an hour and a half to get home instead of thirty minutes. I'm just so excited to pick up my car, to see new tires and feel new brakes.

And to never have to drive this minivan again.

The repair shop is dark when Tom and I pull up in his car. Everything is closed down except for one of the garage doors, where a single car is raised. Two legs stick out from underneath.

My brother parks in front and nods. "There's Levi."

I peer into the dim light of the parking lot, trying to better see the man under the car. "I'm rather put off that everyone knows him and forgot to introduce us," I say.

Tom snorts. "He's been at the shop for three months and you haven't met him?"

I'm about to retort, but then Levi is climbing out from under the car, standing, wiping his hands on his orange sweater—

The Boy.

I nearly shriek. "Tom, I can't go in there."

"What?" He looks rather alarmed. "What's wrong?"

"I was staring at him, oh dear God, I was staring *right at him* three days ago, and he smirked at me, and I feel *so awkward.*"

Tom looks at me, completely blank-faced for exactly three and a half seconds before he bursts out laughing. His buzzed head tips back with perfect glee. If it were possible to roll around in a car, Tom would be doing it right now.

"What?" I hiss.

"You think he's cute," he says between gasps.

It's not a question, not one bit. My brother knows me too well, and I swear I will punch him so hard if—

"Come on, Bee. He probably sees so many people come through here every day that he won't even remember."

"I'm not stupid. He knows Michael is my friend, he saw me talking with all the guys, and Michael told him I was coming tonight. He knows. *He knows!*" I'm hissing again, which means I'm about to overload on excitement. (Not the good kind.)

Tom gets out of the car and comes around to my side. He grabs my arm and helps—no, yanks—me to my feet. "Stop being such a wuss. He's just a boy. Since when do you give a crap about what boys think of you?"

He's right. I'm being irrational. I'm fine. I'm fine.

I'M FINE.

I straighten my coral cardigan and brush my hands down my dark wash jeans and take a deep, deep breath of serenity.

Levi greets us as we approach, his sweater and dirty jeans clinging to his form, hair mussed and twisted every which way.

He shakes my brother's hand like he knows him, like they've been friends forever. I'm tempted to shrink back behind Tom and just die, but then Levi is looking at me and holding out his hand, and his eyes tell me I was right: *he knows*. I probably look like a lost chicken, plucked clean of feathers, being placed on the chopping block.

I shake his hand anyway.

"I'm Levi," he says.

" . . . Bee." I manage to get the word out, chiding myself instantly for my ridiculous lack of control. But gosh-darn-it, he is beautiful. Even more so up close. (And I really want to touch his hair.)

"Your car is good and ready," he says, smiling. (Oh, yes, he has a brilliant smile.) "We took care of her. Michael said, in these exact words, 'Bee's very in love with her car.'"

I nearly whimper, but hold back the tiny sound before it comes out of my mouth. "He did?" I laugh, breathy and unsteady. "Well, I *do* love my car."

Do I sound like an idiot? Yes. Does Levi notice? I'm not sure. He just smiles at me and waves us around to the back, pulling my key out of his pocket. His nice sweater looks like it needs a good washing, and I'm seriously tempted to ask why he's wearing it. But Tom is here, and Tom doesn't seem confused or curious. I'd rather not be the one to ask a question when the obvious answer is lost only to me, so I press my lips together.

Levi unlocks my car and grabs some paperwork off the dashboard, then hands me my key. "Everything's set to go," he says. The light from the streetlamps along the road is a nice accent to the sharp features of his face. He grins.

"Thanks, dude." Tom shakes his hand again and pats my shoulder. "Bye, Bee."

When Tom is halfway across the lot to his car, I realize I'm still staring after him and that Levi is staring at *me*.

I face him, thankful for the semi-darkness to hide my blushing skin. "Thanks, Levi. I appreciate you staying late and everything."

He shrugs. "It's nothing. I was already going to be here."

I smile, hold up the key, and reach for the door handle. "I'll let you get back to it, then?"

He presses his lips together in a thin smile and doesn't let go of my gaze. "Do you have a name for your car?"

I am completely taken aback by this question. "Oh, um. No?"

"Well, good. We started calling her Sylvie around the shop—because she's silver. Just wanted you to know, in case she doesn't come when you call anymore."

It takes me a second too long to catch the joke.

Oh.

Oh, he's good. Really good. So charming that I'm lost to his actual words. "Well, I suppose that settles it?" *Bee, stop with the questions that are supposed to be statements.*

He nods with finality.

I roll down my window and close the door, but he hasn't left yet. I hook up my iPhone and ask, "So, how do you like working here?"

Look at me, making conversation with a cute boy all by myself!

"It's a good time. Keagan got me the job—he knows I grew up on cars."

"The guys are good company."

Levi's smile agrees with me (in more ways than one). "How come I've never seen you here?" he asks, as if he's genuinely interested.

"Oh, just, graduation and a new job." I smile at him as sweetly as I can, but inside . . . I swear there's an angry gorilla in my chest, pounding out a jungle rhythm. "Thanks again," I say. I need to get out of here. He's so *distracting*, dammit. Distractingly beautiful. (Beautifully distracting?) Besides, I talk way too much when I'm nervous. I'm about to start babbling, and that will be the worst thing imaginable.

He understands I want to leave (*Oh dear, I hope I'm not being rude*) and backs up. "See you around, Bee," he says, his voice lazy in that California way. I want to box it up and save it for a sad day.

Then, just like a snap of my fingers, he's heading back to the shop, and I leave him behind.

See you around, Bee.

chapter 5

QUEUED:
DANCE FOR ME WALLIS
BY ABEL KROZENIOWSKI

"BEE? DID YOU pick up the bill?"

These are the first words I hear when I get home from Mike's. I pause mid-stride, frowning, and backtrack. I put my head around the doorframe to find my mom sitting on the couch, checkbook in hand, her floral-patterned glasses falling off her nose. "What bill?" I ask.

"Didn't Tom tell you?" she inquires without looking up.

I shake my head. "No."

"He's so busted," Mama says, laughing, but I can tell she's only half joking. "I told him to tell you to get the bill from Michael tonight. Remember the little job he did for your dad two weeks ago?"

"Oh, yeah. He can't just mail it to you?"

"Well, he's going to have to now. Unless you can pick it up tomorrow?"

I swallow. "Pick it up? Maybe." I totally can, since I only work a four hour shift tomorrow, but the possibility of me making a fool of myself in front of Levi is *very* real. I already feel like I should be banned from spending extended periods of time with The Boy. If I can sneak in, grab the check, and get out before anyone can spot me, it will all be fine.

"Would you, please, baby?"

I swallow again—and nod. My social failures shouldn't stop me from saving my mother from Tom's lack of memory. "But only because Tom's sleeping all day tomorrow. I have a few choice words for him . . . "

She chuckles. "Just make sure they're nice. And Bee?" she asks as I turn again.

I smile at her over my shoulder.

She pauses over her work for a second, as if carefully choosing her words. "Do you . . . have any leads?"

My smile droops, because I instantly know what she's talking about, and I don't want to discuss it right now. "Um. No?"

Thing You Should Know About Me #601: I love a lot of things. I find genetics fascinating, and fashion trends, and gourmet cooking, and astronomy, and architecture and interior decorating and production. Which is why it is incredibly hard for me to figure out *what* to study and *where* to study. I decided shortly before graduation to take a gap year, which I think worries my mom. I'm pretty sure she imagines me homeless at twenty-five whenever this topic comes up.

"Are you doing research?" she asks.

I approach her and kiss her cheek. "Yes, of course," I say, and instantly feel guilty for the white lie. It isn't that I don't *want* to research, I just haven't had time these last few weeks. "I'll have a lead soon, I'm sure."

Possibly another white lie, but a very hopeful one.

My mom smiles. "Okay, Baby Bee."

I smile back. "Okay. I'm going to get some sleep."

She lets me go with another kiss and I hurry to my room. I try to shut my door behind me, but Tom appears out of nowhere and follows me in. He gives me a relieved look.

"What?" I ask as he leans against the doorframe.

"Thanks for saving my ass. I totally forgot."

I shake my head at him. "Don't you have to be at work?"

"I'm leaving in a few. Hey, I wanted you to know there's a party tomorrow night at Keagan's. You should come—it's the first party of the summer."

I raise both eyebrows. "Um . . . if I'm not too tired?"

"You can get the check from Michael, if you don't want to go back to the shop."

"Yeah, okay, probably."

He stares at me.

"Okay, I'll go." I laugh at his look of pure excitement.

He grins. "Excellent. Maybe I can get you to play pool this time."

"Don't press your luck. Now get out and go to work, you turd."

"Sleep well, Beef," he says, kissing my forehead.

I roll my eyes at his stupid nickname for me, watching him go, and shut the door behind him. Since he sleeps most of the time I'm actually home (stupid night shift), I miss him more than I expected I would when he first got this job months ago.

I pull out my phone and text Michael to ask if he can bring the check to the party. Then I switch apps. As expected, Gretchen has messaged me, and she's still awake—even though it's one o'clock in the morning her time.

Bee

I'm sorry I'm late. Long day at work, and then I had to
pick up my car.

Plus Tom was slow getting ready. He's a pain in the butt,
as usual.

Gretchen

Ha! But he's a cute pain.

Bee

Ew. We are not having this conversation. I have
something better for you. I met a boy today.

Gretchen

YOU MET SOMEONE? YOU. MET. SOMEONE. BERNICE,
PLEASE TELL ME YOU HAVE A DATE.

Bee

Please! Goodness, no. He's been working at Mike's for
a few months, apparently. I finally met him and OH MY
GOD he is so attractive. Annnnnd . . . well, I may or may
not have seen him before. When he caught me staring
at him at the shop a few days ago. It was incredibly
mortifying. I'm 1000% sure that he recognized me.

I describe Levi in detail, taking care to include his
amazing hair and the bright sweaters and how *freaking
tall* he is. I can practically hear Gretchen sigh in
response.

Gretchen

He sounds like a dreamboat! I'll sacrifice a goat so he'll ask you out, like, yesterday.

Bee

A goat? Really?

Gretchen

I'M FLUENT IN GOAT SACRIFICE.

Bee

Oh my God, I'm cackling.

Gretchen

Just try to sneak a picture next time. I want to see him.

Bee

You know I suck at sneaky pictures. But I can tell you this: his name is Levi.

Gretchen

OMG. Sexy.

Bee

Of course he's sexy. He has Douglas Booth hair.

Except . . . .bigger and better.

In the end, there is no comparison.

Gretchen

. . . .

. . . .

. . . .

Bee

What?

Gretchen

I hope you realize how many penis jokes I could make right now.

Bee

GRETCHEN!

SSSSHHHH

NO! NO PENIS JOKES!

Gretchen

Calm down, freak. I won't . . . .this time.

Bee

Never. Not a single penis joke ever or you're as dead as Jay Gatsby.

I can just feel your smug grin. It's disgusting.

Gretchen

Well, hurry up getting your claws into him.

(Oh, it's even more smug and disgusting than you're imagining.)

Bee

Shut up.

Hey, I have to go now. I'm falling asleep just thinking about what time I have to get up tomorrow.

And there's a *party*.

Gretchen

Ooohhh. Tom talk you into that?

Bee

Yes. He knows how to sweet talk me into almost anything.

Gretchen

LOL! I bet he sweet talks lots of girls into lots of things.

No worries, I should sleep, too. Talk to you tomorrow, ok?

Bee

Oh, gross, thanks for that mental image.

And yes, of course. Love you. I think you're crap.

I lock the screen and gaze at it longingly for a few seconds before setting it on the nightstand. I barely have the energy to change into my pajamas before I'm out, lost in dreamland. There are flowers, in this dreamland, and a beautiful boy named Levi wearing a bright sweater made of all different colors, all at once.

I swear he's smirking at me.

chapter 6

QUEUED:
So Long, Lonesome
by Explosions in the Sky

IT'S WAY TOO early for a Saturday, but I'm here at the shop an hour early for Tracy while she makes an emergency run to the market. My only instructions are on a small note in the back.

> Bee, go ahead and start cleaning up the mess I left. So sorry—I couldn't finish everything before I started falling asleep. I'll be there at eight forty-five, if I'm lucky.

I grab my ruffled apron and start washing buckets. This job takes a long time since Tracy left about thirty of them stacked together. It takes even longer than usual because I have to wrestle them apart. After a good forty-five minutes, I've washed them all, sprayed the insides with bleach, and stacked them upside down on the drying rack. The tower reaches well past my head, and I just pray and pray and pray there isn't an earthquake today, of all days.

After I set up the signs and filter through the cooler for any old flowers to throw out, I turn on the computer. I'm not dumb when it comes to electronics, but this computer is way too slow for its own good. Tracy tells me it's her next big purchase. (I'm counting down the days.)

I open the doors and let in the cool ocean breeze, then stand behind the counter at nine o'clock. It's my first Saturday to work, and I'm not entirely sure what to expect: the manic insanity that Tracy described in detail, or just . . . busy.

So I wait.

For exactly nineteen seconds.

Three women appear in the door, propped up on four-inch heels and hoisting bulky purses over their shoulders. When they ask for a bouquet for a birthday brunch, I point them to the premade section in the cooler. "And if you can't find what you want there, our designer will be in shortly and can create something for you." I glance at the clock. *Please, Tracy, hurry.*

Lucky for me, the women find what they want, pay, and rush out in a number of minutes. Not-so-lucky for me, however, they aren't the only customers to enter in the first twenty minutes. Before long, I'm rushing around, grabbing bags and ribbons and mugs and candles from the gift section.

And yes, I'm panicking. I'm trying my hardest to breathe deeply, trying not to count down the minutes until Tracy gets here, but—

My phone dings—a text from Tracy. I read it as I run to the back to grab a new vase to replace a broken one. (I'm amazed it didn't cut the elderly lady who grabbed it off the shelf.)

Tracy

Stuck in traffic. Be another twenty minutes.

My eyes widen and my breathing quickens, but there is absolutely nothing I can do about this. I trade the flowers from the broken vase to the new one, then I ring her up with a discount, and send her on her way with a smile. (I hope she believes the smile.)

Finally, the busy morning begins to slow down. I lean against the counter, running my gaze over the room to make sure nothing has been broken or messed up by grabby customer hands. But I only have a few minutes before the doorbell makes a terrible racket as yet another customer pushes the door open. I cringe inwardly, twice—once for my aching feet and a second time because this woman looks mad already.

"How can I help you?" I ask, with my biggest, friendliest smile. I adjust my glasses, which have been sliding down my nose all morning, and stand up straighter.

Her eye twitches. "I need an all-white arrangement for a funeral. Something big, showy, in a basket."

I nearly let out a squeak. We have absolutely nothing like that stocked in the shop right now. Bee, think fast! "Unfortunately, due to the expense of that kind of arrangement, we don't keep any premade in the shop." I'm worried I sound just as frazzled as I feel, but I press onward. "Our designer is currently on her way with a fresh batch of flowers—would you be willing to wait?"

She blinks hard, as if in pain. "Sure. Whatever. But she better make it good."

"Oh, she will," I say. My face hurts from smiling. "She's the best."

The woman mumbles something under her breath, but waits

by the front desk. It's almost like she's watching every move I make. It's terrifying, but I try not to think about it.

Ten minutes later, Tracy stumbles through the back door holding six dozen wrapped roses, three dozen under each arm. "Hello!" she cheers, laying the roses on the table. She laughs. "That was a nasty drive. Bee, can you get the rest in the back of the car and lock it? I'll help our *lovely* customers."

I take the opportunity, practically running outside. The car is wide open and full to the brim with flowers of all different colors and sizes. I pick them up, only able to carry four or five sets at a time, and put them with the roses. When everything is locked up, I head to the front of the shop—only to have Tracy call me back to the designer's table again.

"Help me here, sweetie," she whispers, when I'm close enough to hear. "I'm overwhelmed. Hand me that oasis."

I run to the sink and grab the soaking green foam and help Tracy cut it down to fit in the basket. She starts working on the funeral piece, her fingers skillfully placing each wide fern leaf (which Tracy calls "leather") into the green foam. I help her strip the white roses of their excess leaves and cut them down to size while she arranges them. I want to stand and watch her all day, but more customers have arrived, and I have to go on delivery soon.

I step up to the counter. A young woman approaches me, looking like she's about to burst into tears. She's holding a premade bouquet from the cooler, one full of white and lavender flowers that I haven't learned the names of yet. "I want something just like this. Do you mind making it larger? I have to take it . . . to . . . a funeral." She says the last words on a heaving breath.

I take the vase from her, nodding. "Let me take it to the back. How much do you want to spend?"

"No more than ninety dollars."

I smile sympathetically, but when I place the arrangement on the table in front of Tracy, she shakes her head at me. "I can't. You do it. Grab that vase there—" She points behind her. "And grab more leather and those lavender dahlias."

I stand there, gaping at her. "You want *me* to make it?"

"Why not?" She smiles. "You've seen me do it before, right? You know what it's supposed to look like. And I've seen the way you decorate the shop for me! I know you have an eye for color and order."

I whimper incredulously. "Okay," I say, and some part of me snaps and bursts into action. I hardly know what I'm doing as I grab the leather and three lavender dahlias. I cut and wipe the stems of the leather like I've seen Tracy do it, then set them in the vase so they make a circle around the rim. I add a few more layers, then pick up the original arrangement and place it inside the new vase. There's still room around the edges, so I fill it with white wax flower. Once it's full, I add the three dahlias and three stems of spray roses.

I step back. Tracy steps back. She looks at me. I blush. "Is it okay?" I ask.

She whistles approvingly. "It's more than okay. I know you had something to work with already, but I'm impressed."

I nod, completely uncertain, but something is buzzing inside of me as I head to the front counter to ring up our customer. I'm happy to see that she's no longer on the verge of tears. (I feel a bit like flying.)

chapter 7

QUEUED:
I Wear Glasses
by Mailing Ritual

DINNER IS SCATTERED that night. My sisters have ballet at seven, and my dad comes home from work late. By the time I'm hungry, my mom and sisters are gone, and my dad is sitting at the table alone. He's spooning cereal into his mouth (cereal for dinner; welcome, one and all, to my family) and reading the book that's propped up between his fingers. *Crime and Punishment*, the spine says.

Thing You Should Know About Me #104: I'm a book pusher, constantly telling people to read certain books, often to get them out of their comfort zones. I've been badgering Papa to read this book for ages, and it looks like he's finally taking my expert advice. It also looks like I was right to recommend it, because he's enthralled, his blue eyes focusing hard on the pages. It's only when I step in front of him that he looks up and scratches his short brown hair. "Hey, Bee."

"Hi, Papa." I lean down to kiss his cheek. "How's the book?"

"Good stuff. Raskilnikov is digging himself into a deep hole."

I sigh dramatically. "Ahh, Raskilnikov."

He leans back. His clothes are dusty from work, and his cheeks are unshaven. "Going somewhere tonight?"

"Out with Tom and some friends."

"Where is he?"

"Probably in his room."

"Hmm."

Papa seems a bit more tired than usual. I wrap my arms around his shoulder and give him a squeeze. "How was your week?"

"Good. I'm tired of working on this attic, though."

"Yeah?"

"Yeah. There was a problem with the electrical company, so now we have to wait until they rewire the entire second floor."

I pat his arm. "That's super annoying."

"Hmm," he says again. Then he rubs his eyes and grunts. "I'm going to watch some TV before I go to bed—want to join? I'm starting a new science fiction show."

I'm rather tantalized by this, but I give him an apologetic smile. "I promised Tom."

"Well, I suppose I should be urging you to go out more often anyway, so . . . good for you."

I laugh, high-fiving him as he heads into the living room. "Thanks, Papa. See you tomorrow."

It isn't until I get into my room that I remember that it's Saturday, and my dad doesn't work Saturdays. There's a split second where I wonder why he's so tired if he hasn't worked all day. Then I find myself staring at my closet, thinking about the party and the weather and what to wear (and The Boy), and that moment is past and forgotten.

I decide on jeans and my favorite blue shirt and polka-dotted sweater. My shoes match the blue on my shirt, and I've even put on my favorite pair of gold earrings. I pull my hair into a messy bun and apply lip gloss.

Thing You Should Know About Me #204: I don't wear makeup. My skin is sensitive and I'm too practical to spend more than twenty minutes getting ready. But every once in a while, when Tom convinces me to go out (or there's a wedding; these are the only acceptable times), I borrow some of my mom's makeup. Right now I'm looking in the mirror at my slightly-more-smooth face, and it surprises me. I look . . . older. It takes a few seconds, but the near-panic queasiness settles in my stomach with a whoosh. When did *that* happen?

"Hey, Beef!" Tom yells from across the house, rescuing me from my moment. "Time to go!"

"Coming!" I answer, grabbing my purse, and rush outside. Tom's already waiting by his car . . . and his *girlfriend* is with him.

Thing You Should Know About Me #70: I don't like Andrea. Now, I like mostly everybody, but Andrea is one of the few people I don't like without any particular understanding of *why*. There's just something about her that bothers me. And despite wracking my brain for a reason, I don't have one. Tom, however, is completely enthralled by her gorgeous blue eyes and candy-red lips and prim way of sitting and standing.

"Bee," she says to me. Her smile is not quite a smile.

"Andy," I say, because she's insisted I call her that. As if saying a nickname over and over again will generate some sort of familiarity between us. "I didn't realize you were coming."

"Is there a problem?" Tom asks, glancing back at me through the rear-view mirror.

"No, of course not," I say, shrugging. Then I notice the slight downturn of his mouth and the way his eyes flicker to Andrea briefly, as if he's not quite *looking* at her, and I want to ask. But I'm afraid he'll bust me for being nosy, so I move to something else. "I'm excited for tonight."

My words are genuine. As much as I'm not a huge fan of big, loud parties, I have hopes that I'll enjoy this one. After all, it's at Keagan's house, a place I'm comfortable with. I breathe in and out, steadying myself after my long day, finding some solace in familiarity.

Tom smiles. (Although his eyes maintain some wariness.) "Good."

The party is in full swing when we arrive.

I walk in first (bad idea), so I'm immediately hit by a wave of humans: Keagan, Michael (who slips my mom's bill into my purse as he hugs me), Greg, and some of Tom's old friends from high school. I hug Mariah and Trey, who both graduated with Tom last year, and Mariah introduces me to her friend. Because of all the noise, I barely register that her name is Casey. Behind me, Tom is shouting something about a video game, and the music blares, and the sound of cue sticks hitting billiard balls pops against my eardrums.

I awkwardly smile and nod at Mariah and Casey, even though I suddenly can't focus on either of them (oh God this party is already overwhelming me *helphelphelp*). I turn toward the game room, scanning for the pool table, and when my eyes find it, I nearly drop and cover my head. There stands Levi (OF ALL PEOPLE) making a perfect shot, his tall, lean body bent over the table, and I have to force my mouth closed. *Enough gaping at him, Bee.*

If I wasn't going to let Tom talk me into playing before, I'm sure as hell not going to now. And if I thought for one second that this party was going to get me out of seeing That Boy today, I was dead-wrong.

Levi straightens, his bright red sweater falling loosely across his shoulders and around his long torso. When he raises one hand in a triumphant fist pump, I can see the top button of his jeans, and the belt around his hips, and the sliver of skin and hip bones and muscle just above that.

Everything is beautiful. Everything is terrible.

I clear my throat. Once again I'm staring at him, and once again he's caught me. He knows exactly who I am and that we talked and that he named my car and that I'm an awkward human being, but he still smiles at me.

I nod in his direction, grinning a little too hard, thanking God he's too involved in the game to walk over to me. I wonder when he's going to start thinking I'm a creep for staring all the time. I need to compose myself, get my crap together.

He's just a *boy.*

(Who just happens to be everything I want, so help me.)

Tom slaps my shoulder, already holding a beer, and leans close to me. "Hey, don't take this the wrong way, but everyone can tell who you like."

I elbow him hard in the ribs. "I don't like him," I whisper harshly. "And you already know I think he's cute, so you don't count as *everyone.*"

"O-kay," he says lamely. I can't help but smile at him. "I won't let your secret out, then. Could be bad for you."

I purse my lips. "Tom, you're incorrigible."

"Come on, Bee," Andrea says, coming up beside Tom. "You don't have to show off with all your big words."

Her tone is decidedly teasing, like she's my older sister and she wants to mess around with me, but somehow her smile looks like a sneer. I wonder for the umpteenth time if I'm reading into something or if I'm actually right. "Incorrigible?" I ask. "It's not *that* big—"

Someone to my left interrupts me. "Unredeemable, incurable, habitual."

I suck in my breath.

"Come on, Andy," Levi continues. "If you don't know that word, then maybe you should retake fifth grade vocabulary?"

He's teasing, laughing like it's all in good fun, but now he's pissed off the Wicked Witch of the West. With a disgusted glance in my direction, Andrea shrugs and turns to my brother. I half expect her to hug him, to play the whiny girlfriend, but they don't even make eye contact. Tom grabs his beer bottle and tosses it in the trash, and Andrea heads straight to the drink table.

I don't know what's going on with them, but I brush off my concern and pivot to face Levi.

He's right there. Right behind me. *Too close too close too close.*

"You know her by Andy?" I blurt.

He shrugs. "She practically chewed me out the second time I met her and didn't call her Andy. I never forgot again." He chuckles, fingers wrapped around his cue stick, which rests chalk-end-up next to him. "But I'm sure you know all about that."

"Ha!" I laugh, a little too loudly. (*Tone it down, Bee.*) "Yes. Well. Tom must see *something* in her."

"Hmm." He glances over at Tom, who is purposefully avoiding eye-contact with us. "Maybe."

My shoulders relax. "You see it, too?"

"They've never been this weird."

I sigh heavily. "Right? I mean, I don't know her that well, but . . ."

"Yeah." Levi jerks his head up at the sound of his name being yelled from across the room. "One sec, it's my turn."

I follow him to the crowded pool table. It looks like Keagan and Michael have joined the game, as well as three new arrivals. To avoid being trampled, I sit down behind them on one of the kitchen barstools next to Mariah. I don't understand the rules of the game at all (I'm dreadfully confused), but I watch intently nonetheless. The room tenses when Levi knocks three of the balls out of the game. A cry goes up: anguish from Michael, triumph from Keagan.

It's Michael's turn, and then Keagan's (I'm starting to get the idea that they're playing with teams), and three other guys I don't know. When it's Levi's turn again, he saunters over—narrowly avoiding the foot Michael sticks out to trip him—and sets up his shot. We're all watching, holding our breath, and Michael is completely bitter that we're all rooting for Levi.

Of course, he strikes perfectly, and the balls fly just how he wants them to, and everyone jumps up wildly. Levi shouts something I can't understand and grabs Keagan's face in his hands. Laughing, Keagan slaps him on the back, raising their hands in the air between them like they've won some big championship. Everyone crowds around them and I'm grinning hard from their contagious joy.

Mariah leans in close, laughing over the racket. "Levi's been trying to beat Michael at pool for over a year. The tension's been high."

I laugh, knowing Michael's competitive spirit and typical winning streak. I'm happy he lost a game; he probably deserved it for something.

When things calm down (and Michael is only half-grumbling, and Keagan has stopped running around yelling "WINNEERRRRS!" in his loudest voice), I find my way back to the barstool. Before I can get comfortable, Levi sits beside me, his elbows resting on the bar behind us. I get a split-second thrill looking at him, admiring his well-cut jaw and shoulders and long legs. Then I snap myself out of La-la Land and realize he's said something.

"Wait, what?" (I blush. Profusely.)

He laughs, leftover flush from his victory on his cheeks. "Nothing. You look dazed. Are you tired?"

How to answer that question . . . " . . . Yes," I decide on. "A little."

"New job stuff?"

I smile—he remembered. "Mostly that. Also, parties wear me out."

"Why?"

"Nerves." I don't know why I'm telling him this. I'm headed straight for embarrassment.

He tips his head back. "You don't look nervous."

"Ha!" It's the second time I've burst out laughing at something he's said, and I want to tell him *that right there* is a sign of nerves. But that would mean admitting that *he* makes me nervous. No can do, Beautiful Boy. "Well, that's good to know."

Levi takes a sip of beer and sets his bottle on the counter behind us. "So what's this new job?"

I smile. "I'm a florist's assistant. The delivery girl—whatever you want to call it."

He returns my smile with his own. "That suits you."

"Really?" (*You don't know me*, I want to say. *Not yet, you don't*, I want to add.)

"You have that look about you. It's the long hair, I think."

I pat the bun on my head. For the second time, I'm thrilled

he remembered that detail from our meeting yesterday; I'd worn my hair down when I picked up my car. "At least it does *something*."

His expression asks me why: one eyebrow raised, the left corner of his mouth tightened in a quirk.

I sigh. "I once donated fifteen inches of my hair to Locks of Love. Great decision, don't get me wrong, but it was . . . not my best look. I couldn't do anything with it. I know I wear it up a lot now, but at least there's the option when I need it."

He nods. "Fair enough." He runs a hand through his own hair, ruining his perfect coif. His fingers are thin and smooth, but I remember their steady grip from our handshake yesterday.

At this sudden and vivid memory, my body reacts with a ruddy blush that lights up my face. *How nice. It was just a frickin' handshake, dammit.*

"What about your job?" I ask. Time for a distraction. "How do you know about cars?"

Levi takes another swig from his bottle and sighs. "My dad's worked with cars since before I was born."

I raise one eyebrow. "So . . . you grew up inside an engine?"

Levi is about to answer when Keagan pops up beside me, interrupting. "His dad practically owns Maserati."

Levi looks positively horrified. "He doesn't."

"He might as well," Keagan adds.

"Owns *a* Maserati, or . . . owns . . . *Maserati*?" I take a deep breath of realization, my head filling with seven and eight figure numbers and multiple dollar signs.

"Um." Levi spreads his hands and looks at me apologetically. "Both, actually. My dad grew up in a local shop, same as me, but then he invested, and hit the jackpot, and, well . . . he got really wealthy really fast. He owns some of the best and fastest cars in the world."

He looks so uncomfortable. I want to make him smile. "So you grew up inside a . . . very . . . expensive engine?"

I almost regret the dumb joke as soon as it's out of my mouth, but it makes Levi laugh. *He likes my dumb jokes!* "Yeah, basically," he replies. "It wasn't always what I wanted, but it's got me a good job now."

"Hey, Levi!"

All three of us turn toward the speaker: a girl with shoulder-length dyed-blue hair, standing on the other side of the pool table. She waves ecstatically at Levi.

"Elle!" Levi waves back, sliding off his barstool. "Stay here," he commands, catching me by surprise. I comply, even though I can't tell if he wants me to stay there because he wants to be alone with this girl or if it's because he wants to be able to find me after. He bounds toward Elle, wrapping his arms around her in an all-encompassing hug that makes me smile.

I lose the rest of their moment when Keagan stands directly in front of me, green eyes locked onto mine. "Little Bee, if you have the hots for my best friend, I swear I will—"

"Keagan, shut up and sit down," I interrupt, yanking on his arm. He sits on the barstool next to mine.

He laughs, shrugging. "I was going to say I will fully support the idea, but whatever. He's pretty nice, huh?"

"Yeah," I murmur.

"Actually, I take that back. He's not just nice, he's *the* nicest, a one of a kind rarity, almost extraterrestrial, full of brilliance unmatched by the world."

I laugh. "I didn't realize this. I'll take it into consideration next time I talk to him."

"Good. He'd never say it of himself, of course, but we all know it to be true."

"I suppose I'll see for myself soon enough." I furrow my

brow, trying to sort out their friendship. "How long have you known him?"

"Close to eight years, I think. I knew him when my mom lived in L.A. We kept in touch when I was in Colorado and then reconnected here."

I give him a smile, and hope it doesn't look like pity. His mother is . . . wild. He moved here to escape her, get a good job, and bring his sister here when he can get custody. "I'm glad you did." I glance over at Levi and Elle (sort of hoping he'll come back to talk to me again). "His family sounds interesting," I say, for lack of a more eloquent way to express what I feel. The type of people who have that kind of money don't really hang out with the Middle-Class People of Escondido.

"They are . . . um . . . well. Not really a family anymore." Keagan shrugs. "His parents divorced, a couple of years ago."

"Ah." I wonder if that's why he was so hesitant to talk about his dad. "That sucks."

"You have no idea," he agrees.

I want to be nosy, but I let it go. Across the room, Levi and Elle are standing closely, her white shirt contrasting against his red sweater. He's got the sleeves rolled up (the room *is* getting warm), gesturing, as if asking how tall something is. Elle nods and says something I can't hear. *Ugh*, I think, and then blurt, "Are they dating?"

Keagan nearly snorts out a sip of beer. "Levi and Elle? Ha! No."

Okay, then. I try again. This time, it's the question I really want to ask, the question I've been dying to ask since I first saw him. "Why does he wear those bright sweaters?"

This seems to get Keagan's attention. He looks at me, closely studying my face, for an uncomfortably long time.

"What?" I ask warily, leaning away from him.

"I'm just trying to figure out if you're serious."

An exasperated sigh escapes me. "I know nothing."

After a few seconds of thinking and more looking at me (I squirm) he says the five words I absolutely did not want to hear. "Why don't you ask him?"

"What? Ugh. Why can't you just tell me?" I try to picture myself walking up to him, asking that question. Would he laugh like he did a few minutes ago, like he's comfortable with me? Would he smirk, like that first day? Or would the question annoy him? Keagan seems to think there's something important about the sweaters, more important than just style, but I don't really want to ask *Levi*.

Keagan rolls his eyes at me. "Because, Bee. He wears the sweaters so people will ask about them."

"But you could just answer it for him."

"And steal all his joy? Nope." He drinks the last of his beer and tosses the bottle in the trash. "If you want answers, you've got to step it up. And trust me—you won't regret it."

I am saved from (possible) humiliation by my brother begging me to take him home. Andrea is already by the car, and they're both pissed—with alcohol *and* anger.

I can't believe I didn't notice that they were gone, that they'd gone off somewhere, arguing. No, not arguing—*fighting*. Tom's face is red, his hands are fists, and I don't know how to respond except nod and follow him. I say goodbye to Keagan as we head out the door, apologizing for the quick departure, promising, at his persistent request, that I'll come hang out at the shop one day soon. And as I put the key into the ignition and look back at the house and start the car, I can't help but feel like I left something unfinished. Like there was something *more* waiting for me inside.

Once I drive onto the main road, I roll down the windows to escape the stifling tension radiating between Andrea and Tom. I've seen them fight before, but never like this. Tom is fuming, and Andrea looks like she couldn't care less if he lived or died. I slip the charging cord into my iPod and start the music, hoping some happy songs will lighten the mood, and that I won't feel so stupid for not asking the one simple question I am dying to know the answer to.

chapter 8

QUEUED:
RUSTLE OF THE STARS
BY A SILENT FILM

O N TUESDAY, I end up working in the flower shop alone. It's *slow*, and there are too many loose flowers and no walk-in customers to take them off my hands. We don't even have deliveries—imagine that! And since no one is here to make a mess for me to clean, I sit at the front desk and twirl my newly trimmed hair in my fingers, messaging Gretchen, hoping that something will happen so Tracy has to come in to work.

I sit idly for an hour before my gaze is drawn to the cooler by three tiny yellow roses, the last of their dozen, sitting alone amidst a dozen red and a dozen purple. They're several days older than the rest, which means Tracy will likely throw them out before she can use them.

What's the worst that could happen? I ask myself. Tracy telling me off for using a few bad flowers? I'd never do it again and she'd forget about it in less than an hour.

I glance at them several times, my heart thudding, before taking matters into my own hands. Leaving the front desk, I enter the cooler and gather the roses hastily, along with some leftover stock, a couple of mums, and leather. I grab a vase to go with it, too, something tall and yellow, one of the mismatched vases somebody donated to the shop. Tracy won't miss it, and if she does . . . well, this arrangement is just an experiment. Tracy can dump the flowers if she wants.

Laying everything out on the table, I start by cutting the leather stems. The first time they're too tall, and the second time they're too short, so I grab another bunch and cut them to an *almost* perfect length. Because I don't want to try again and mess it up, I organize the leather into the vase around the edges to create a frame, and then start on the rose stems.

A few minutes later, I take a big step backward so I can see the full piece. As adorable as it is, I'm almost tempted to take it apart. What if it's not as good as I think it is right now? What if Tracy sees it and hates it? What if I come back to work tomorrow and want to pretend I never made it?

But . . . look at it, Bee, I argue with myself. I set the arrangement at the back of the cooler, away from customers but exactly where Tracy puts her ice coffee every morning. With any luck, it will make her smile.

With a glance at the clock, I realize I've spent an hour on this arrangement. I hurry to clean up the leaves and petals that now grace the worktable and floor, then finish the last items on the checklist. At six o'clock sharp, I lock the front door behind me, my hair whipping in the oceanside wind, my mouth curving with a smile.

I don't see Tracy at all the next day when I open the shop later in the morning at her insistence. I do see all the signs of her early morning escapades: freshly brewed coffee in the kitchenette, new flowers in the cooler, ribbons strewn across the tables. To my surprise, the arrangement I made is no longer at the back of the cooler, but in the front.

Tracy made a few adjustments, adding pink spray roses to complement the yellow—and she's selling it at a discounted price because the flowers are older—but it's there. And when the arrangement sells at noon, the buyer complimenting it again and again, I find the flowers I want next, make myself at home at the worktable, and I do it again . . .

. . . and again and again and again. Every new day, Tracy puts the arrangement at the front for a discounted price, and by closing it sells. On the fourth day, when Tracy comes by the shop in the evening for weekend wedding prep, she immediately checks the cooler's front display.

I know she's looking for my arrangement, but she won't find it. It sold twenty minutes ago to an elderly lady looking for something small to brighten her kitchen.

Tracy waves, but passes right by me. "Meet me in the back in five minutes, young lady."

Hands jittery, I close the cash register and finish hanging ribbons on their rack before joining Tracy at the worktable. She gives me a once-over, as if deep in thought, arms crossed over her chest. I take a drink of water while I wait, pretending I'm not vexed by her seriousness.

Then she asks, "Do you want a promotion?"

I almost spew water across the table. I choke it down, coughing. "Um." I cough again, covering my mouth until it passes. "What . . . what do you mean?"

Tracy taps her fingernails along the worktable. "You have a real gift, Bee. I want you to be my on-call designer. I need help with designing throughout the week so I can focus on weddings. I'd pay you more, of course. And train you."

"I don't know what to say," I whisper, split between shock and excitement.

"How about *thank you* and *yes*. Those will do the trick." She pauses, then adds, "If you don't mind."

If you don't mind. As if! But of course, I try not to seem too overeager. (I fail.) "This is . . . amazing." My eyes are bugging out, I just *know* they are. "Seriously, you think I'm that good?"

"You totally are, and I think you know that already. Take some time to study all the different types of flowers this week— I'll send you home with some flash cards—and on Monday I'll raise your pay."

I squeak out my thanks while she flips through the order pages for the wedding. (*Shh, Bee, shh. Stop talking.*) When she pauses, looking up at me expectantly, I lunge at her with a hug.

She pats my back, laughing. "Get back to work, Bee."

I let her go, fisting my hands around the hem of my apron, jumping once before heading to the sink. I'm too excited to care that there are a million buckets to wash.

I scrub quickly enough to blister my fingers.

I spill my news at the dinner table. My sisters don't have ballet tonight, my dad's off on time, and even Tom is home. But since we're all here for dinner, everything is *loud*. Chaos is our middle name. (Erm . . . something like that.)

After a few attempts to get everyone's attention, I clang my fork onto the edge of my plate a little too hard. It's like the butterfly effect: My mom stops talking to Tom, Astrid stops singing *Les Miserables*, and my dad stops flicking Millicent on the forehead while trying to steal her last piece of steak.

I grin, too wide to fit my face, and say, "Tracy's giving me a promotion. I'm going to design floral arrangements."

The babble that follows—oh, my gosh, now my ears really hurt, because it's worse than before. They're all congratulating me, asking a million questions about things I don't have answers for. Amidst it all, I see my mom's face light up as she listens in rapture. She squeezes my hand across Tom, who leans back to let us have a moment. "Bee," she says, "that's amazing. I'm so proud of you."

Those words mean so much to me, I could cry. But I'm distracted by Millicent asking, "Can you make me a flower crown? I've always wanted to wear a flower crown!" She slaps Papa's hand away from her plate again.

I laugh. "Maybe Tracy can teach me that next."

"Make one for me, too," Papa says, with all the innocence of a dog who's eaten too much toilet paper.

Everyone laughs, even though we're all rolling our eyes at him. Millicent is suddenly indignant about Papa trying to steal her food (again), so Tom uses the moment to lean in close to me. "You up for a little promotion celebration?"

I eye him with suspicion. "Um . . . "

"You should come to the beach with me tonight. Bonfire with some of the guys."

"Oh, really?"

"Yeah."

I squint at him. "Just . . . *the guys*? What about Andrea?"

His smile falters. "She's not coming."

I accept this with a shrug and start clearing the table with everyone else. Tom's on dishwasher duty, but with our combined force, we finish cleaning in record time. While he stacks the last of the clean dishes in the cupboards, I grab my purse, and then we both holler goodbye to our parents as we make our escape.

Outside, the sky is clear and full of a thousand stars, a perfect summer evening, with a slight breeze coming down the hill in our neighborhood. I laugh for no good reason and for every reason all at once. Something about today is just . . . happy. I'm not even mad when Tom pulls his car onto the main road (going in the opposite direction of the beach) and asks, "Hey, mind if we pick up Levi first?"

Of course, I have to *pretend* to be mad, as all good little sisters do. I groan, sinking into my seat. "You tricked me into this."

Tom pats my knee. "You've got to get over your fear of . . . whatever you're afraid of."

I don't deign to answer that, so instead roll down my window and let the night wind wash over me. (WhyamIblushingwhyamI blushingwhyamIblushingwhyamIblushing—)

It turns out Levi lives on 10th Ave., about two minutes from my house, and he's already waiting for us. He slides into the back seat and slaps Tom on the shoulder. "Great timing, man, my mom's baking again and—"

He sees me.

I smile.

He grins. It cracks his face in the most adorable way. "Bee! I was expecting Andy."

The way he says it--like he'd rather see me than Andy--makes me far happier than I expected. "Nope, just boring old me."

"Never boring." Levi gives Tom a sidelong look. "Where's Andy?"

Tom sighs and pulls out onto the road. "Not here." Levi and I exchange what (I think) could be called a "knowing" look, and—*fine*, I'll admit that it thrills me.

Eventually, Tom turns up the music, and we ride in silence for a few minutes. I lean with my left elbow on the console, my head tipped back, my eyes closed as I sing along softly. Then I feel someone tapping my arm. It's Levi, straining against his seatbelt to get closer to me, and he's pointing up.

The open moon roof displays a wide variety of stars. Out here on the highway, there are no streetlights or neighborhoods—it's just a straight shot around the mountain, on the side of the cliff over the reservoir, and then through the hills—so it's very dark and quiet. I look up with Levi, our heads semi-close, and smile.

He asks, "Do you know the stars?"

"Not really."

"Me, neither."

"It's a shame," I sigh.

"I *can* be rather stupid."

Embarrassed, I hurry to say, "That's not what I meant."

He laughs, and I laugh, and find that it is incredibly difficult to keep my eyes on the stars when Levi's sitting next to me.

"I meant," I add, "that I wish one of us did."

"Yeah."

I adjust in my seat, to make the conversation easier. "Stars are almost . . . like . . . moments. To me." As soon as these words come out of my mouth, I start to feel stupid. Do I *sound* stupid? I don't know where this is coming from; I've never consciously thought about it before. It's always been a thought at the back of my mind, like *I like chocolate ice cream*, and *I would marry Matt Smith if he asked me*, and *My mother wants me to go to college*.

Somehow, *The stars are like moments to me* fits on this list. "It's like . . . they're twinkling and staring us right in the face, but we have to be brave enough to grab hold of them. You know?"

Levi looks at me, then sits back in his seat, still looking, still studying. Like he's pondering. Somehow, this puts my nerves to rest.

"You're right," he says, finally. "You're absolutely right."

chapter 9

QUEUED:
CLOUDS
BY BØRNS

THE REST OF my night is split into tiny moments. Or stars, if you will.

I see Tom and Michael, going into the dark water in nothing but their underwear. (I'd rather stab myself in the eye with a hot poker than see their soggy asses again.)

I see myself, like an out of body experience, standing by Keagan, not doing the things I've dared myself to do.

I see Levi chatting with that girl Elle again, although this time they don't stand so close, and she's wearing a Hannibal t-shirt that matches her hair. (I think I'd like to meet her.)

I see Keagan stoking the bonfire to keep it going, warming his hands over the flames. His long, wavy hair casts a shadow over his face.

I see Levi, rolling up his jeans and standing with bare feet in the small waves. His sweater is yellow, like the first time I saw him, and I feel a pulse of boldness.

I see the tide, slowly receding, being pulled by the moon.

I see the moon.

I see Levi.

I walk across our little corner of the beach, in our corner of the country, in our corner of the world, and I smile at him. A little hesitant, a little uncertain. But I say, anyway, "Can I ask you . . . um . . . a kind of . . . strange question?"

He stuffs his hands into his pockets. "I like strange questions. Shoot."

I take a deep breath. "Why do you wear bright sweaters?"

I'm pretty sure his face glows, set off by the moon, or by his happiness, or by something magic in the air that's also affecting me, filling my heart. "I was just waiting for you to ask!" he says, laughing. "You kept staring at my clothes."

Me, internally: *I'm so relieved that you think I was staring at your clothes, of all things.*

Me, externally: "Well, everyone seemed to know why except me, but I didn't know how to ask without it coming off as weird . . . so . . . "

He smiles. "Will you let me show you?"

To this, of course, I nod.

"How about right now?"

There isn't a single thing I want more than that, but still, I raise one eyebrow. "It's almost eleven."

"Yeah, but if you come to the office tonight, you'll get to see everything all lit up."

He has an office. Of course he does.

After a pause, I nod. "All right, but this better not be a prank," I say, thinking of all the trouble Tom would get up to just for a scare.

Levi just laughs. I pretend I'm not affected by his laugh, that it doesn't make me want to laugh with him. "Okay then . . . " I say, but I'm still hesitant. "Not a prank?"

"No." He tilts his head to the side as if observing me, watching my expression change from worry to happiness. "Definitely not a prank." He blinks, eyes catching the moonlight. "Do you have *any* ideas?"

"Not one."

Levi grins, turning once more to the ocean, his shoulder brushing mine. "Good," he says. "It's better that way."

chapter 10

QUEUED:
BEAUTIFUL WORLD
BY THE CHEVIN

TOM DROPS US off on the corner of Escondido Blvd. and 10th Ave., which makes me suspicious. "I thought you said we were going to an office?" The only buildings I know along these roads are restaurants and thrift stores and hair salons. (And Levi's house.)

"We are," Levi replies, getting out.

Tom waves me out of the car. "I'll see you at home," he says, and the second my door is shut he drives away. Levi promised to take me home, and while I *mostly* trust him, it still feels a bit weird to be left alone with a Boy on a dark road at midnight. (Thing You Should Know About Me #33: I'm not a rebel.)

Levi motions for me to follow him, so I do—only a few steps down the block. He stops at a dark building, its glass doors and large windows completely black. Unlocking the front door, he holds out a hand to stop me from following. "Take a step back and look up."

I do as he says. He steps inside, folding into the dark building like he never existed, and I swallow hard. "Levi?" I call out.

A second later, I'm blinded. Colored lights brighten this corner of the street, bathing me in a rainbow. The sign across the top of the building reads THE COLOR PROJECT, in bright, curling, bold letters. It's shocking, mostly because I was not expecting this much light, but also because I've passed this place a million times and never thought about it once.

Now that there's some light, I can (sort of) see Levi inside: his outline, his yellow sweater, half of his face. He smiles, waving—or is that him gesturing for me to come inside?

"I've driven past this place before," I call to him, looking up at the bright sign again.

He steps into the open doorway, raising one eyebrow, and his mouth quirks in that way of his. He sweeps his wavy, messy, brilliant hair off his forehead. "Want to see inside?"

"Yes," I say, a little breathless, and join him. When he flicks the light switch, and all the fluorescents flicker into existence, I notice five things in rapid succession.

First: the enveloping brightness of the room, blues and greens and oranges, all swirling on the walls.

Second: the toys in the corner, organized inside wooden cubbies.

Third: the window to an office, and a closed door beside that, set up like a doctor's office.

Fourth: the flecks of glitter on the ground. It's not inlaid; rather, it needs to be swept off the floor. I wonder about it for two seconds before I'm distracted by Levi lifting himself onto the counter protruding from the office window. He kicks his legs out once and then crosses them at the ankles.

Fifth: Levi.

He just happens to be my favorite thing, out of all of this.

He's watching me closely, his expression equal parts pride and joy and contentment.

"Is this, like, a second job?" I ask.

He waves me over, grabbing my hand as I attempt to lift myself onto the counter. Considering my legs are not nearly as long as his, it takes more than one effort. Finally, when I'm firmly seated beside him, I cross my ankles like him and let go of his hand.

"The Color Project is . . . everything to me." His shoulders curve a little, in a humble way. "It's a charity. People in the community come here, apply for whatever they need, and we provide the money or help via our sponsors."

I make a choked noise as I turn my head so I can look up at him. He looks down at me, meets my gaze, and I try to shut my surprised, open mouth. "Levi."

The smile he gives me is the best one yet. "I love it here."

"I'm so . . . surprised. Amazed?" What is the right word I'm looking for? Looking around me, I ask, "How . . . how does it work?"

"You can pick up an application either from the box outside or the front desk. I have volunteers, ages fifteen to twenty-five, who come in at three-thirty every day and answer the phone, meet walk-ins, and sometimes conduct interviews.

"When someone applies, we look at how much money they need and figure out where they are on the waiting list. Well, first we do background checks. There have been a few sneaky liars, but for the most part, everyone checks out. Then we compare it with how much money we have coming in. We have a stable monthly income from consistent sponsors, plus extra donations that come from random people throughout the year. We never turn anyone down, of course," he adds, answering my next question, "but if there's ever a budget deficiency, we put the least pressing applications on a special wait list. Anyway, when we have the funds for the next applicants, we call them in for an 'interview'—" Levi makes quotations with his fingers "—and give them a check."

I let it all sink in, trying to close my gaping mouth. "I can't believe this," I say.

He looks sheepish. "I'm hoping for a bigger facility someday, but right now this is all we can afford. We're growing in sponsors every month, though, so that's good. More people are willing to give than I expected."

"Levi . . . you *run* this place." It's a statement, made purely out of awe and some disbelief.

"Yeah." He says it in an unassuming way, like he doesn't want that kind of attention. (I love him a little bit for it.) While I'm mooning over him like an idiot, Levi jumps off the counter. "Want to tour the back? It's just two rooms."

"You don't even have to ask," I answer.

Levi unlocks the door by the office window. The hallway behind it leads to a dead end with a door on either side. The left door leads to the office I saw through the window in the lobby, but I only get a quick peek in. "Sorry it's so disorganized right now," he says. I brush him off, catching sight of glitter on the round table at the back. I start to mention it, but Levi's already across the hall, opening the other door.

"This is where we have interviews." Levi turns on the light, and I step into a small, simply-furnished room. It has a desk in one corner, and a chair and love seat and coffee table in the other. To the left is a slightly open door that leads to what I think might be a bathroom.

There isn't much to take in, but I take it in anyway. "The Dreams-Come-True Room?"

He laughs. (He has so much laughter.) "Yeah, I suppose it is. I like that name." He sits on the arm of the chair, hands pressed flat between his thighs.

"So, how many volunteers do you have?" I'm bursting with questions, but this is the first out of my mouth.

"There are six, for now. Missy, Albert, Nikita, Suhani, Clary-Jane, and Elle. You saw Elle last night, yeah?"

I smile, recalling her Hannibal t-shirt and blue hair. "She's adorable."

He smirks. "Don't let her hear you saying that. She'll throw a fit."

"Good to know."

"Clary-Jane is the oldest volunteer, so she's who I go to when I can't conduct an interview or if something goes wrong. She takes care of things like a pro." He looks up at the ceiling, as if going over a list in his head. "Elle usually runs errands, organizes events, and talks to sponsors. She's tough and quick and . . . well, *mostly* professional.

"Then there's Missy, our front desk receptionist on most days. Her mom, Gabriela Alvarez, has always been a huge TCP supporter, which is great, but I think she *really* wants Missy to volunteer here because of her insane shopping problem. Just wait till you see her shoes." He makes a face like he swallowed something sour.

I laugh. "Are they that bad?"

"Ugh." Levi shakes his head. "They're horrendously bejeweled and expensive."

"Wait . . . her mom . . . you mean Gabriela Alvarez, the news anchor?"

"The one and only."

I raise an eyebrow. "So you're on first name basis with a celebrity, huh?"

Levi's gives me a mischievous grin. "If I told you some of the people who have sent checks to TCP, you wouldn't believe me." Then he cocks his head. "You can sit down if you want."

I don't want to sit. I'm bursting with energy—this place is

buzzing with it—but Levi is offering, and he's lovely, so I sit anyway.

Levi makes himself comfortable across from me. "Nikita and Suhani are here because their parents are monthly sponsors. They really love our community." He chuckles. "I dare you to ask them about their birthdays."

"Are they twins?"

"Just ask," he repeats. "And lastly, we have Albert, the youngest volunteer we've ever had—age fifteen. He's a good kid. His family moved here from Germany a year ago, and while he's adapting really well, they want him getting some cultural and language lessons after school. Oh, and, he's obsessed with throwing glitter at rude people, so let me warn you to never be rude."

"He likes . . . to throw . . . glitter?" I ask in disbelief. But now my question is answered—that must be where all the glitter comes from.

"Yes. I know. It might be the wildest thing you've ever heard. He says he thinks it will change attitudes, like it's a social experiment."

My laugh comes out as a cackle. "That's ridiculous."

"Trust me, I know. But just wait till you get a mouthful of glitter. Then it'll be *obnoxious*." He takes out his phone; I catch a glimpse of the numbers *twelve* and *seven*. Levi gives a small laugh, his eyes drifting back up to my face. "You know, this might sound crazy since it's midnight and all . . . but would you like to get donuts with me?"

The rest of our conversation goes a little something like this:

"But . . . it's midnight." (That's me.)

"So?" (Levi appears to be confused.)

"Is anything open?" (I am also confused.)

"Peterson's is open twenty-four hours." (He says it like I should know what this is.)

"I don't know what Peterson's is . . . " (I sputter a little, but only because he's pretty.)

"Bee! That's an atrocity!" (He grabs my hand.)

Which is how I end up in a very short line of midnight-snackers in front of a street corner donut shop with outdoor seating only. The store is lined with windows full of fluffy pastries, and we have to order through windows outside, like getting tickets at a movie theater. The whole street is wafting with the sugary-sweet smell of icing and sprinkles.

Levi looks down at me and says, very seriously, "Pick, and I'm buying."

"No, Levi—"

He gives me a fake stern look. "I won't have it."

I match his expression with equal determination. "I don't want you to pay."

"I'm going first so I can just tell them to put your order on my dime."

I glare.

He glares right back. "It's one dollar, Bee. *One dollar.*"

I sputter. "Fine. *Fine.* Surprise me."

He raises one eyebrow. "Stubborn, but I like your style. I'll order you my favorite. You *have* to try it, but you don't have to like it." Then he leans to whisper, "But trust me—you will like it."

I wave him off. "*Okay,*" I laugh. But no matter how distracting the frosting-and-pastry smell is, my mind is still on The Color Project. I put my hands out, palms up, and exclaim, "I just . . . can't believe you do all of this. Wait—how old are you?" (I'm totally *not* asking for my own benefit.)

"Nineteen," he says simply.

I laugh. (It's an incredulous laugh.) "You run a charity at nineteen. It's so . . . noble."

"Nah." He looks embarrassed, hands tucked into his pocket. "Not really. I love it so it doesn't count."

"Oh, believe me, it does."

He looks like he wants to change the subject, so I let him. His expression is thoughtful but teasing as he says, "Now it's my turn to ask *you* a question."

Oh no. I must look funny because he laughs.

"Don't be afraid," he comforts. "I just wanted to make sure . . . Your name: Is it just the letter 'B', or is it B-E-E?"

I smile in relief. "B-E-E."

"Is it short for something?"

"No," I say, a little too fast. I almost answered yes, but how could I betray my own principles? The lie, however, sits in my mouth like vinegar. I clear my throat.

He calls me on it instantly. "Liar."

"What?" I gape at him.

"You blushed. You cleared your throat. You even glanced around like someone was following you. You are *definitely* lying."

I groan in embarrassment.

"It's really that bad, huh?" He nudges me with his elbow.

"It's the worst."

"Will you tell me?"

"No."

Exasperated, Levi orders for us, and a moment later he hands me a donut in a little bag.

I accept it. "Before I try this . . . delicacy . . . answer me this: If you work at Mike's when you don't have to be at The Color Project, do you *ever* have time off?"

"Ha!" he laughs, then directs me across the street. I assume we're walking back to his house, and my ride home. (I don't want to leave yet, but I don't know how to tell him that.) "Sometimes. I mean, I don't come into the office on random days throughout the week, depending on the volume of applications and who's volunteering. Some weeks are busier than others, but that's just fine with me."

"Because you really love it," I murmur.

"Yeah. I really do." Levi gives me a look. "I answered your question, so now you have to try it."

Sighing, I reach into my bag, grab the donut and a napkin, and take a deep breath before my first bite.

Heaven. Just—heaven. "Oh, HOLY MOTHER," I exclaim, crumbs dropping from my mouth. (Gee, I must be a vision.) "What have you done to me?"

Levi's laugh is like heaven, too, but I don't comment on that. "See?" he teases. "I don't know how you managed to avoid Peterson's for this long, but now you can start living."

I take another bite.

"Hey, wait," he says, reaching for my donut. "You didn't want this, remember?"

I jump away, my laugh sounding like a shriek in the quiet of the neighborhood, but I don't care. I'm having too much fun. "No way! I'm finishing this one."

Levi shakes his head in exasperation and makes another lunge for it.

I jump out of the way again, shouting, "Donut thief! Donut thief!" down the empty street, and our laughter sends birds rising into the sky.

"Do you want to come back, sometime, maybe?" Levi asks. "To The Color Project?"

We're standing in my driveway at one o'clock in the morning. I'm leaning against his car, finishing up the last of my donut. He stands just in front of me, looking especially tall, making me tilt my head to meet his gaze. "Of course I want to come back."

"That's good."

"Mm," I say, stuffing my face with my donut.

"You could come back for an interview. I have one on Wednesday at five o'clock."

"I'll be there." (Some things in life are just that simple.)

Levi leans against his car next to me, hands in his pockets. He crosses his ankles, the bottom of his Chuck Taylors scuffing the concrete. "So now you know why I wear bright sweaters."

I hum in agreement, smiling as I wipe my crumby fingers on a napkin.

He continues, "People like you . . . .you ask questions."

"People like me," I repeat. Then I ask, "People like me?"

"You have a soft heart, you know? You seemed like the type of person who would care." He pauses, crossing his arms across his chest. "Tom is the same way. He pretends to be Macho Man but is, in reality, a softie."

I snort.

"Don't ever tell him I said that."

"Oh, never." I pull out my house keys. "Thanks, Levi. For everything."

"You're welcome, B-E-E." He spells out my name with the funniest look on his face, like he's trying to figure out what my real name is. He won't ever guess it. Not in a million years. (I hope.)

I grin at him. "See you Wednesday?"

"See you Wednesday."

Moments later I watch him drive away, before unlocking the front door and slipping in as quietly as possible. I like to imagine the world is somehow a happier place, because of today.

chapter 11

QUEUED:
THE OTHER SIDE OF MT. HEART ATTACK
BY LIARS

I T'S CHAOS IN my house.

Mondays aren't usually so hectic, but here we are: one sister singing musicals at the top of her lungs and the other telling her to shut up, my parents sitting in the living room discussing something important in hushed tones (their attempt at quiet makes them louder than usual), Tom and Andrea yelling at each other on the front porch.

And here I am, minding my own business, waiting for the storm to pass.

We've already eaten dinner, but even that was broken up by Andrea showing up to "talk". What's happening outside is not exactly what I would call talking, and I don't think Tom would, either.

After a half hour of texting Gretchen, I decide I can't take it any longer, so I plug in my phone and head into the kitchen.

Astrid doesn't pause her singing to say hi, but Millicent approaches me and buries her head in my shoulder, moaning in agony.

"Make her stop," she says, practically weeping.

"I wish I could. Only stabbing her will do the trick."

"No, that will make her wail louder." Millie moans again.

"Then there's nothing left but to bury her in the backyard," I tease.

This earns a laugh. "Think Mama and Daddy will miss her?"

"Nah. I bet that's what they're talking about in there right now."

We both turn our heads toward the sitting room, where my parents are bent over some paperwork. Looking at them—my mother, stiff and tight-lipped, and my father scratching his head—makes me oddly . . . dizzy. I glance down at Millie. "Any idea what they're actually talking about?"

"No. They look so serious. And Mama was crying earlier."

I shake my head. Millie looks so distraught that I know it won't do to wonder aloud, *What on earth are they so sad about?* So I think it instead. "Well, then. Are Andrea and Tom almost done?"

Millicent gives me a look. "I hope so. She's dropped the F-bomb, like, a million times."

"Seriously?" I pat Millie's arm. "Gunna go kick them off the porch."

Astrid sings over to us, "You do that, Bee."

I shoot her a glare before heading to the front room. I can see Tom and Andrea through the bay windows in the front room, their mouths open as they yell, their fingers close to each other's chests, accusing. Their eyes full of nothing but disgust (on Tom's part) and anger (on Andrea's part). I'm working up the nerve to go to the door and tell them to take it somewhere else, when Andrea shakes her head, drops her arm, and—walks away.

I'm as startled as Tom; Andrea is never the one to say goodbye first. She's too aggressive, too intense. She has too much to say. But now she's straight up leaving, waving her hand over her head as if to tell him not to follow. My heart breaks a little bit for him.

Behind me, Astrid stops singing, and I can hear my parents talking in a normal tone, although I can't hear the words. When I look outside again, Tom has disappeared, and without a second thought I bolt for the door.

He's heading toward his car, his stride sad and slow. (Andrea's car is already gone from our driveway; I can hear her angry tires screeching down the road.) I catch up to Tom, hands in my pockets, watching him from the corner of my eye. His jaw works and clenches. His hands fist and his eyes burn.

"Want to talk?" I whisper.

"No," he grinds out.

"Can I come with you?" I head toward the passenger side, whether he likes it or not.

He doesn't answer, so I sit beside him. He pulls out of our driveway and I lean back in the chair, soaking up the last pink rays of the sunset. Tom's driving is smooth and controlled, despite his mood, so I relax until he's ready to talk.

This turns out to be an hour later when we park in Ocean Beach right in front of the water. Tom drove around a bit, as though he wasn't sure where he was going, and by the time we stopped the sun had gone down completely. I spent the drive thinking about a lot of things, lost in my own little world, enjoying the silence. I thought about flowers and promotions. I thought about glitter and shoes and donuts. I thought about my parents sitting close together, their stressed expressions, and

Millie hearing my mother cry, and what I will ask them once I work up the courage.

Mostly, however, I thought about Levi. (But isn't that obvious?)

Tom's voice interrupts my thoughts of Levi's swooping hair and bright eyes and infectious joy. "Bee?"

"Yeah?" I whisper. My voice is weirdly hoarse. I clear my throat.

"Sorry. I can take you home if you want."

"I don't mind," I murmur. Goodness, he sounds so broken. I'm tempted to ask all my questions, but he's a thin pane of glass about to shatter anyway, so I wait.

"I was right," he says. He pauses, his breathing shallow, then says again, "I was right."

"About what?"

"She cheated."

I'm so angry I'm about to bust a hole in the car window. "With who?" I sputter.

"Some asshole her sister dated once."

God, I hate Andrea. I hate her so much. (I feel a rush of dark pleasure that I was right to hate her all along.)

Tom heaves a breath. "I can't believe I trusted her so much." Then he shakes his head, saying, "You know when you see things in hindsight, and you wonder how you didn't see the details when they were in your face the whole time? I was so blind to so many things. Especially," he adds, facing me, "how rude she was to you. To everyone. I let her do that, and I'm sorry."

I take his hand, holding his rough fingers in mine. "She was pretty terrible."

"Everyone kept telling me, but I wanted to believe that we could go back to normal. To *before*. That's stupid, though, because we've never wanted the same things. Not even in the beginning."

I bring my knees to my chest and lean my cheek on them. "You can't really go back to the beginning, though, Tom."

"I noticed."

"I'm sorry."

Tom's quiet a moment, his hand squeezing mine now, too tight for comfort. But I can't seem to move away. "I'm trying not to regret it, but . . . " He lets out a sort-of-chuckle, but it's completely mirthless. "What does that say about us, then, if we're already so ready to regret each other?"

"I don't know," I whisper. I feel an ache in my chest strong enough to break something.

"I gave her so much, you know? I went into our relationship wholeheartedly, and look where that got me."

"Don't," I warn, leaning my head on his shoulder. "We do things, and we learn from the bad and celebrate the good."

He huffs out a breathy laugh. "You wizened old goat."

"Wow, thank you."

"No, thank *you*." He kisses my forehead, like a sweet brother.

I close my eyes. The world around us is quiet except for the crashing of waves and the dim beating of our hearts. And my thoughts. Once again, my thoughts are quite loud. They overtake everything else in a way that I don't quite understand.

I'm thinking, more than anything, about my first kiss. It wasn't anything spectacular, but I guess that's the point. It wasn't special, and neither was the boy. Karl, in tenth grade, with his long-ish pale hair and his freckles and his cute smile. We weren't popular kids, both lost in the terror of high school, not sure what the hell was going on—so he kissed me. Somehow, those two facts are always linked in my mind.

We dated. For two weeks.

It wasn't the kiss that turned me away, or any of the kisses after. It wasn't even Karl. Instead, it was the way we were around each other—intimate, but not. We were so close, our mouths and our hands and our hips and yet, it was the way I wanted to be with someone . . . not Karl.

So while the rest of my classmates were attaching themselves to someone the moment they had the chance, I was holding back. I was seeing things I liked and things I didn't like, making mental lists and compartmentalizing everything.

Thing You Should Know About Me #5: I made the decision, one month after breaking up with Karl, that I wanted to wait until I was married to have sex. It wasn't out of fear—nothing like that. It was because the memory I had of my time with Karl was incomplete, like I had done something with no meaning. I wanted the next kiss to mean *everything* to me, and someday I'd marry someone who meant even more than everything.

I still want that. Call me a romantic, call me unrealistic all you like. Of course, now, sitting here in the dark, it has me thinking about Levi and how much I like him, and how one day I'll like a guy enough that it will turn into love. (I don't think, *What if that guy is Levi?* Because at the moment, it would be too unbearable if he wasn't "that guy".)

Tom brushes my forehead with another kiss and puts his car into gear. "Let's go home," he says quietly.

I nod, saying a silent goodbye to the ocean and the clean line of sand and the pier (and a cluster of Ocean Beach hobos). "Thanks for letting me come with you," I say.

He glances over at me, his arms resting lightly on the steering wheel. "I take that back. Let's not go home—let's go get ice cream."

"FroYo?"

"Nah, I'm talking real, good ole fashioned Cold Stone."

"Bravo," I say, and make sure he knows he's paying.

We sneak back into the house at midnight, rushed with sugar and trying to laugh quietly. We fail, our laughs coming out as snorts that are nearly as loud as the door that we accidentally slam behind us. (It sounds suspiciously like we've consumed copious amounts of alcohol instead of ice cream.)

Tom changed over the last hour, from hurt and angry to soft and laughing. I was beginning to suspect he didn't miss Andrea at all. Maybe he will tomorrow; maybe he'll cry over her next week. But for now, I've made him happy. (Me, and ice cream.) For now, he could think about everything *except* Andrea.

Looking at Tom in the dimly lit hall, I realize how much he's like our father, warm and welcoming, with broad shoulders and strong arms. When we say goodnight, trying to catch our laughter before it escapes *again*, I force him into an embrace. But then it's not so much forcing because puts his chin on my head, running his hand up and down over my hair, tangling it in a truly brother-like fashion.

Then he says, "Don't ever change, Beef."

I smile and tell him I won't. He leaves me standing in the hallway, where I lean against the wall, immersed in the sudden quiet.

Then I hear, "Bee?"

"Papa?" I gingerly step into the dining room.

He sits at the table, his hands in his pockets, and he looks up at me like he hadn't spoken my name in the first place. "Hey. Did you have fun?"

"Yes." I stand by the opening, still unsure. "What . . . What are you doing awake?"

He shrugs. "Just couldn't sleep, is all."

I nod. "Okay."

"You work tomorrow?"

"Yeah."

"Good. Keep up the good work, Baby Bee."

"Thanks, Papa."

He stands up, scratching his head like I saw earlier. To me, his head-scratching has always been associated with nerves, which he usually hides tremendously well. But here it is, twice in one day, *and* he's up late.

So is my mom, who I hear sniffling in the other room. I look at Papa, and he looks at me, and we both pretend we can't hear her. He nods, shuffling out of the room. Confused, heart pounding, I turn and head in the opposite direction. I shut my bedroom door behind me and pray it keeps out that sad, quiet noise.

chapter 12

QUEUED:
QUESADILLA
by WALK THE MOON

I DRIVE TO THE Color Project first thing after work on Wednesday, my fingers tapping against my steering wheel to the beat blasting through my speakers. I feel a strange sense of calm, almost like my brain has shut off due to overwhelming excitement. (And probably a fear of me puking.)

I get to see Levi today. I've been counting down the *hours*.

Even though I park directly in front, four feet away from the door, the sun blasts me so hard when I get out of the car that I'm starting to sweat by the time I'm inside. (It's the end of June, when dry California briefly turns humid.) Inside the office, the air conditioner is blasting at full force. I stop at the window, where a young girl sits, chewing her nails and texting. She's got her dark hair in a high ponytail, glitter on her eyelids, and even more on her shoes, which are propped up on the desk between us. Even her arms, chest, and neck shimmer with glitter lotion.

I stare blankly. *So* this *must be the infamous Missy Alvarez.*

"Hi! Is Levi here?" I ask, tearing my eyes from her shoes. They're the kind of footwear you'd expect to see on Beyoncé during a red carpet event—not on a girl wearing jeans and a t-shirt in a charity office in Escondido.

But, here we are.

Missy smacks her gum. She's about to answer when The Boy sticks his head into the room behind her. He smiles. "You!"

My lips break apart in a wide grin. "Me."

Levi stands behind Missy's chair. "Missy, meet Bee. Bee, this is Missy."

"Hi," I say. "Nice to meet you."

"Is she a new volunteer?" she asks Levi, and then blows a spectacularly large bubble. It pops perfectly, as if she's practiced this moment again and again.

He looks at me for a second, then at Missy. "Not unless she wants to be." His words are loaded with invitation and (I think) hope, but his tone is unassuming, letting me off the hook.

Missy groans. "You should get someone to take over some of my hours. I just don't have enough time in the day, you know?"

I swear Levi's eye twitches. He opens his mouth, as if to say something—and then blows out a deep breath. "I'll open that for you," he says, nodding to the door on my right. He disappears, and a few seconds later it swings open.

"Bethany?" he asks.

I shut the door behind me, a little too hard. "Bethany who?"

His face falls. "That's not your name?"

"Oh, um, no?" I laugh out loud. "Of course it's not. I would be relatively happy if my name were Bethany."

He harrumphs, but his eyes tease me. "Well, I was going to *say.* Bethany is a beautiful name, and you looked like you might be one."

"Thanks, but no. I'm not."

I follow him into the interview room, where Levi heads straight for the desk and grabs three pieces of paper, stapled together. Then he ushers me over to the sitting area. "Ready to see what we do up close?"

I'm so awkward; I don't know what to do with my hands or how to sit (I feel like a stiff board). But for once, I do know what to say. "I'm so ready."

The corner of his mouth shifts upward. "You're not a Bonnie, are you?"

I almost choke. "Bonnie? No."

He looks at me directly in the eyes and says, "Hmm. I guess not."

I want to tell him to stop trying to guess when there's a knock at the door and Missy stomps inside on her four-inch pumps. She steps to the side to allow someone in, a woman around twenty-five-years-old. Her hair is light blond, cut to the shoulders, and she has blue eyes that *actually* sparkle. I'm struck immediately by how happy she looks, shaking Levi's hand.

Then he's turning to me, and I snap into focus. "Stacey, this is Bee, one of our volunteers."

I shake the woman's hand, smiling at Levi's words. I'm pretty sure he's said this for Stacey's benefit, because explaining my presence would be complicated otherwise, but I like how it sounds anyway. I think Levi knows this, the same way he knew I would care about The Color Project in the first place.

After the introduction, Levi and I sit on the love seat together. (I don't think about this too hard.) He hands me the paperwork and points to the main paragraph in the middle of the first page. I read over it, barely listening to their conversation so I can catch up on Stacey's story. She was recently diagnosed with breast cancer, the paper reads, an early stage the doctors think will be easy to control, but her treatments are going to be harsh.

By the time I'm done reading, it's only been a few minutes. I look up at them, captured by how they're laughing and talking. It makes this seem more like a coffee date with a friend than an interview with an applicant.

After another minute or two or maybe thirty (this place is like a time vortex), Levi stands and approaches the desk, digging through a small box of envelopes. He finds what he's looking for and, without preamble, holds it out to Stacey.

She accepts the envelope, very warily. "What's this?"

"Your check." Levi sits next to me again, putting his arm around the back of the little couch.

(So, essentially, around my shoulders. Ha. No big deal.)

"What?" Stacey asks, her voice tight.

"That's how it works," Levi says. "You apply and come in for an interview. I meet you, talk with you, and send you home happy. I always like to tell our applicants in person that they've been accepted."

Stacey holds back tears, just barely. "Thank you," she whispers, pressing the envelope to her chest. "This will take care of so much."

"That's another thing," Levi adds. "If it's not enough down the road, come back and let us know."

"I don't know what to say," she whispers, standing, letting Levi hug her. Then she reaches for me and engulfs me in an embrace, her arms tight and warm and oh-so-grateful. "Thank you so much," she whispers, to me.

To me.

I just grin, not sure what to say. It's not my thanks to receive, but I can't tell her that. By then I have to say goodbye, so I stand back as Levi leads her out of the office.

After a few seconds of staring at the closed door, I slump heavily back into my seat and go over the papers in my hands. I glance at each page, trying to find a dollar amount. It's on the next page—I see it instantly.

Ten thousand dollars.

TEN THOUSAND DOLLARS.

Levi returns to find me gaping. Leaning against the arm of the chair across from me, he's got his hands in his pockets, shoulders slightly shrugged, and he looks nervous. "Well?" he asks. His voice is soft, bordering intimate. "What do you think?"

"Levi." When I stand up, my legs are a bit wobbly. I hand the paperwork to him. "I don't know what to say." I'm whispering because I may or may not be on the verge of tears, and I really (really, really, really, *really*) don't want to cry in front of him.

His gives me a smile like he knows I'm on a precipice—like he knows he put me there. It's like he's experiencing the same level of emotion that I am, but he's used to it, he can rein it in. "Feels good, doesn't it?" he asks.

"Yeah," I say, but it sounds more like a breath than a word. My mouth won't move like I want it to. Why can't I say the words that will tell him how badly I want to be a part of this? I know he already knows, to a certain extent. He made me a part of this, after all. But I want to say it. I want him to hear me say it.

He tips his head back. "Thanks for letting me show you. I thought you'd want to be in the loop from that first time I talked to you."

I blink at him. I'm thinking about that first evening I met him, when he dazzled me with his charm. Which leads me to think about the other day, when he told me he thought I had a soft heart. Everything in me is warm except my words—those are frozen inside my mouth. Nothing I can say will compare with the compliments he's given me, and the good he's done here with The Color Project.

But, as it turns out, he doesn't need my words. He gestures for me to follow him into the hall—where Missy surprises us, hands on her hips.

She is *dazzling*. And when I say dazzling, I mean even more than just her shoes. "*Albert*," she seethes. "He threw glitter all over me because I called him a turd, and now it's all over the mess that Nikita and Suhani left *this morning*."

"Missy," Levi says, placing his hands on her shoulders, "I don't really feel bad for you. You unleashed the monster."

"I DIDN'T MEAN TO. THE WORD JUST CAME OUT." She isn't just upset: she's furious.

Levi's smile is something mischievous. "I know. Just clean up the glitter and I'll have Clary-Jane do the rest of the organizing on Friday. I'm coming back in thirty minutes. I want your checklist *done*." He walks away, with me following close behind, and calls back over his shoulder, "And Missy? *Freaking answer the phone* when it rings. Remember what we talked about."

We head out of the lobby and into the warm evening air. I pull out my keys, trying to figure out what to do (how to say goodbye).

"Do you want another donut?" Levi asks.

My heart thuds, a caged animal. I try to make my smile not-giddy. "So long as you don't try to steal it."

He laughs, stepping to the left so we can walk side by side.

I clear my throat. "So . . . am I going to meet them? The rest of the volunteers?"

We're both facing ahead (studying the menu as if we're *not* completely focused on each other) but I can feel his smile radiating off of him. "If you want."

"Yeah, I do." (*Levi, you know I do.*)

"Good."

We order and sit down at Peterson's outdoor tables, our fingers already sticky with donut glaze. Levi passes me a napkin from across the table.

"So what about you?" he asks. "I've shown you all the things I like to do—now it's your turn."

Whatever I'd expected him to say, it wasn't this. "Oh, um . . . You don't want to hear about my boring life."

"No, really. I do."

I bite my lip. "I . . . I guess there's not much. I just graduated high school. I'm taking a gap year. I told you about my job, right?"

He nods. "Florist's assistant. Delivery girl."

I grin. "Right. Well, now I'm also part-time designer."

Levi raises one eyebrow. "That's pretty rad."

(I'm blushing.) "It's been fun. She says I have a natural eye. My designs have turned out nice enough, I think, even though sometimes I can't be sure if she's just being nice or . . . what." I shrug.

"You'll get the hang of it," Levi says. He looks me over, like staring at me is the most normal thing in the world. (I wish I could look at him with as much confidence.) "I'd love to see something you've made."

"Yeah, I will." I take a deep breath in, let it out, and give him my most confident smile. (I probably look ridiculous.) "Hey, I have a picture on my phone of something I made earlier. If you'd like to see." I don't know why I'm doing this—why I'm not nervous about showing him my designs—but I whip out my phone and . . . Panic rises. "Oh no. *Shoot.* My mom called me, like, seven times."

He grimaces like he understands. "Do you need to call her back?"

"Yeah, probably." I click on my mom's name; she answers after one ring. "Hi Mama," I say quietly. "Sorry, I forgot to text you."

"Bee, where are you?" She doesn't sound angry, just . . . weary. I think about her crying the other day and mentally kick myself for forgetting to tell her I wasn't coming home after work.

I breathe out. "I'm sorry, I'm, um . . . I'm with a friend."

I glance up at Levi, only to get distracted by his delighted expression. I shake my head to clear it. "He works at Mike's. He helped fix my car."

"Oh, okay."

I sigh at the disappointment in her voice. Thing You Should Know About Me #3493: I've never, ever—not even once—worried my mother with my activities outside the home. I'm the model child for punctuality and phone calls and check-in texts and safety. She probably thought I was dead in a ditch somewhere, because if I don't alert her of my whereabouts, it means something's awfully wrong. "I'm sorry I forgot to call. I'll be home soon. I'm at an, erm, a charity organization."

She makes a surprised noise. "What?"

"Can I tell you about it later? I need to say goodbye."

Levi gets my hint and stands up. After tossing our empty wrappers and napkins in the trash, we take to the sidewalk.

My mom sounds much more relieved. "Sure, baby. I'm just glad you're safe."

"No, I'm fine. Love you, Mama."

"Love you, too."

She hangs up. I give Levi an apologetic, *I'm-so-embarrassed* look, but he shakes his head, smiling. "You need to go," he says. "I understand. I've had my fair share of worried-mom phone calls."

I stop at my car, retrieving my keys from the bottom of my purse. "Thank you, Levi. This was so fun."

"You're welcome," he says, a tad quiet, but his face is so happy that I don't know what to do about it, or what to say, or how to process.

I raise my hand in farewell as I get into my car, tucking my purse under the tray between seats, and back out of the spot. I'm gone, too far gone, by the time I realize I forgot to get a phone number or an email address. I left Levi standing there, watching my car disappear around the corner, and I know I'll have to come back a third time—a fourth, a fifth, a tenth, a millionth—because I can't just *forget* about all this. I can't forget about Levi, not ever.

chapter 13

QUEUED:
FALL
BY CIDER SKY

MY DAD SITS quietly at the dining room table, eating fried chicken (his true love after growing up in the south) and reading *Crime and Punishment* again. He's made very little progress, but I—the annoying book pusher—have to content myself with the fact that he's made any progress at all.

"Did you just get home?" I ask, because he's still in his work clothes and has (long-dried) paint on his cheek.

"Yep." He stands, places his plate in the sink, and washes his hands. "Long day today."

I frown. "I haven't seen you, like, all week."

He also frowns, an exaggerated version of mine. "I know. How's work and your promotion?"

"It's . . . actually really fun. Nerve-wracking, sometimes, but fun."

He nods in understanding. "You'll have to make something for your mother and bring it home."

I smile. "When I get really good at it, I will."

"And what about this afternoon? Did you have fun, wherever you were?" I assume he heard my phone call with my mom because his eyes are twinkling, teasing.

"Yeah, it was a lot of fun, actually," I say, hoping he doesn't bring it up. "Did Tom tell you about this local charity organization?"

"He did not."

"One of Keagan's friends runs it. Levi." I quickly explain TCP while I still have my dad's full attention. "He's such a neat guy, Papa. I think you'd really like him."

"I see. Why didn't you tell us about this before?"

"Daaaad. I haven't seen you all week, remember?"

He smirks at me. "Just be thankful you don't have a criminal record, Bernice."

"Shh," I whisper. "Don't call me that."

"If that's the only punishment you get for scaring your poor mother, you deserve it."

I stick out my tongue at him. "Fine."

He taps my nose, smiling, despite the exhaustion I see creeping into his eyes. "See you later, Bee. I'm going to bed early."

"Sounds good. Love you, Papa."

He hugs me quickly, then leaves to find my mom. I hurry to my room, passing Astrid in the hall. Her smile is fit for the Grim Reaper. "You almost got *so* busted, Bee. Mom was, like, so close to crying."

"I wasn't almost *busted*," I argue.

Astrid follows me back to my room and leans against my door frame. "So, a charity, huh?"

"Yeah. You should come with me sometime."

She shrugs. "Yeah, maybe." So like Astrid. So . . . dry.

"I'll tell you when I go next."

"All right."

"Okay, Astrid. Time to close the door."

"I wasn't even here," she says with an air of mystery. "I'm a ninja."

Then I watch as she pushes off the door, turns around—and runs smack into the doorframe. I burst into a cackling laugh (it rivals the Wicked Witch of the West's), while Astrid rubs her forehead.

"See? I'm so ninja that the wall didn't even see me coming."

I gasp for a full breath amidst lingering giggles. "Go away, you dork," I manage.

She complies, still rubbing her forehead, huffing an indignant breath.

I shake my head, coming down from the high of laughter, and pull out my phone to check for messages.

Gretchen

You disappeared again.

I hope aliens haven't invaded California. Let me know if you need me to rescue you.

If I don't hear back from you in 24 hours, I will DESTROY this planet to find you.

Bee

HA!

Thanks, but there's no need.

Gretchen

That'd better be because you were on a date with that delectable boy of yours.

Bee

I just snorted out my water, thanks for that.

He's not my boy, okay?

But.

Gretchen

I WAS RIGHT?!?!?!?!!?!?!?!?!

Bee

I was with him, yes.

Gretchen

HURRAAAAAAAAY! Is he still as delicious as last time?

Bee

Gretchen, you're hopeless. He's not food.

However, I will begrudgingly admit he is delicious. I spent an hour with him, and every moment of it was wonderful.

Gretchen

I seem to be missing something here. So basically . . . you're saying it was a date?

Bee

You hush. I went back to The Color Project, to see more of what he does there.

I'd explained TCP to Gretchen over the weekend. While she'd seemed thoroughly impressed, she was far more interested in Levi, which is also probably why she listens eagerly to me explaining what I saw in the interview room today. My fingers hurt from typing everything out, but Gretchen's reply is worth it.

Gretchen

WHY THE HELL HAVE YOU NOT MARRIED HIM ALREADY?

Bee

Because that's a bit unorthodox, don't you think?

Gretchen

He sounds like the most unorthodox nineteen-year-old I've ever heard of. Just make a move already. Please. You're killing me.

Bee

Not happening. Besides, he probably has a girlfriend already. Wouldn't want to face that humiliation.

I pause. Oh. I really don't like that thought, not at all. I groan.

Bee

You know what? I hadn't actually thought about that
before.

. . . .

I don't like it.

Gretchen

Yep, you're a goner. Nice knowing you, Bee.

Bee

Wow. Gee, thanks.

Gretchen

I was teasing you, dork. You'll be fine. When will you see
him again?

Bee

When do you think?

As soon as I possibly can.

That evening, when I'm helping to clean the kitchen after
dinner, I finally get to tell my mom everything about TCP. She's
fascinated, and I think it puts her at ease. (I'm not sure if the
worry lines on her face are from me or whatever was bothering
her the night I heard her crying. I hope neither.)

"Mom, can you believe he's nineteen?"

"What?!" She gives me a sharp look. "Is he lying to you?"

I shake my head. "I don't think so." Shrugging, I pour the leftover noodles into a Tupperware and slide it into the fridge. "I'm excited to maybe . . . I don't know . . . maybe volunteer a couple of hours a week."

"Okay honey, I love the idea. Just don't overwork yourself, especially if Tracy keeps bumping up your hours."

"I'll be careful, I promise. But I think it will be a nice way to spend the summer. I don't know . . . I think, maybe, TCP could become important to me."

My mom slips her arm around my waist and hugs me. She's so short that her head rests on my shoulder. (And I'm usually the short one.) I smile as she says, "Don't let any pretty boys get you in over your head."

"Oh, Mama," is all I say because, honestly, I don't know how to respond. Anything else would be useless arguing and lies. He really is a pretty boy, and I'm already totally in over my head. "You should come visit with me, sometime."

"Okay. Sounds like a plan."

Millicent pops her head into the room. "What's his last name?" she asks.

"Were you eavesdropping, M&M?"

She gives me her most innocent smile, batting her eyelashes. "No, really. What's his last name?"

"I . . . actually don't know."

"I think it should be Berenstein."

" . . . why?"

She heaves a romantic sigh. "Bernice Berenstein," is all she says, and it's all she has to say. I lunge at her, a teasing snarl on my lips.

She screeches and jumps back. "Don't kill me!" she shouts as she runs, a squeal escaping her. "Don't kill me don't kill me don't killllll me!"

I tackle her on the couch, pinning her down. "I'm not going to kill you, but I *will* take my sweet time torturing you."

She screams and laughs as I run my fingers up and down her ribs. "STOP! STOP! BEE, STOP IT!"

I finally get off her, adjusting my t-shirt and my glasses, which tilted awkwardly in the fray. "Millicent May, be thankful I'm not a terrible person."

She giggles, standing up again, backing away. She opens her mouth like she's going to say something, then closes it. Then says with an accompanying giggle, "Mrs. Berenstein."

I laugh, a little too loud, but I can't help it. "God, that is awful."

"I know," she says, grinning like she's told the funniest joke in the history of jokes.

I roll my eyes. "You should get out of here before I bury you in tickles."

She shrieks one last time before darting out of the room. I glance over at my mom, who is squinting at me, a tiny smile on her pretty lips. "What?" I ask.

"Nothing. Nothing." And she turns back to the stove.

But I'm still thinking about Levi, and his eyes on me, everything about him made from pure joy and delight and I just want to wrap myself in it, in *him*. I have to remind myself to breathe. "Mom?"

"Yeah, baby?"

"Would it be weird if I liked him?"

She glances at me. "No, not really. *I* like him already, and I haven't even met him. He's a potential Precious Heart, you know?"

"You're not allowed to like him. You're too old *and* you have Dad." I sigh. "And yes, yes I do know."

She sticks out her tongue at me.

I laugh and slump against the fridge door, staring blindly at the back of my mom's head as I wonder: What if some things are unavoidable? What if this is the ebb and flow of destiny?

If it is, destiny doesn't sound half bad.

My mom has this Thing With People. There are Precious Hearts, and then there are . . . Regular People.

She can spot these Precious Hearts instantly, smell them a mile away, because she is one. (She'd deny it to her grave, but . . . case in point.) The group consists of people like Florence Nightingale, Martin Luther King Jr., Mother Teresa, Anne Sullivan, Marie Curie, Denzel Washington, and Lin-Manuel Miranda. They are people who give and teach and express love in ways that inspire the rest of us to do more, to be better.

I cannot deny that Levi could easily make that list.

(If I'm really honest, he already has.)

I lie awake in bed that night, eyes on the ceiling, my mind not-so-far-away in TCP's office, imagining meeting the rest of the volunteers. And even though Missy's a drama queen, I wouldn't mind working with her.

I roll over onto my side with my arms tucked around my pillow like it's a lifeline. Even as I mull over everything . . . serious Grown Up Things like my future and college . . . despite it all, I fall into a deep sleep.

Behind my eyelids, I dream of Missy and Levi arguing over the last donut in a once-full box. Uneaten, it frowns at them, clearly unamused. Then it bursts into glitter just before I wake up.

chapter 14

QUEUED:
The Other Side
by Civil Twilight

HERE'S THE THING about fighting: In my house, unless it's between us siblings, we don't hear it much. My parents, while far from perfect, don't fight all that often. When I look at them, I see exactly what I want to have with someone, someday. They argue and have their moments, but I believe, in the end, their love is what counts the most.

So when I hear them fighting later in the week, I halt in the middle of the kitchen so I can listen. (Thing You Should Know About Me #249: Sometimes I have no qualms about eavesdropping. It might be terrible, but hey, at least I'm honest about it.)

My parents, I discover quickly, have locked themselves into their bedroom, conversing in loud whispers and rushed words. Even though I put my ear by the door for a few minutes, I can't make out a single thing they say. I leave when my mom starts crying, her sobs creating an ache in my chest that makes me feel hollow.

So I do the first thing I can think of—I get in my car. I drag my sisters with me, too, and I text both of my parents to let them know we've gone out. The girls protest—Astrid because she's stubborn, and Millicent because she's crying.

"They're going to get a divorce. I just know it!" Millicent wails.

Despite my own worry, I almost laugh. Meet Millie, the resident Drama Queen. "What makes you think that, Millie?"

She wails some more. "First last week, then the other day, now today—I just know it!"

"Would you calm down?" Astrid scolds against the sound of Millicent sniffling.

"Millie, I highly doubt they're getting a divorce. All parents fight." I don't admit to her that I'm also upset by what I heard. Or, in this case, what I didn't hear. Being left in the dark about something so tense makes my nerves go haywire.

"This is the fourth time in two weeks!" Millie protests, as if that proves everything.

I shake my head, feigning control, and buckle my seatbelt. I don't respond until I've pulled out of the driveway. I'm trying to remember the last time my parents fought so much. "Stop, Millie," I finally say. "You're not helping anything."

"Where are we going, then?" she asks, still through tears.

"I don't know," I answer, but really I do. I want to check if Levi is at TCP, even though there's a chance he's working at Mike's. Still, I want my sisters to see the place, to meet him, to see what I saw. I think that—with a little change of scenery—Millie will grow back her usual smile and Astrid will lose her bad attitude.

It's not going to be easy. Astrid lets out a low groan when I pull up to the building a few minutes later. "Are we *seriously* going to see your boyfriend?"

I groan as I exit the car, realizing that I'm going to have to change tactics if I want this to work. "No, because I don't have a boyfriend. I'm taking you to get donuts down the street. And then I'm going to take you to The Color Project to see if I can get a phone number from Levi."

"You can't just go to the car shop and, like, ask Keagan?" Astrid points out.

I bite back a retort. "No. I don't have the energy to deal with those boys today. I just want to relax. Besides, don't you want a donut?"

"I do!" Millicent pipes up, no longer crying, though her voice still sounds a little frail. "I want one. Can I get one with pink sprinkles?"

I smile and hope it doesn't look tired. "Sure."

She tosses her thick blond hair over her shoulder. "Good."

Astrid rolls her eyes again but says nothing. She's quiet and contemplative as we hurry along the sidewalk. I lean into her. "Don't worry about it, Astrid. It can still be a good day."

My words don't inspire me like I'd hoped, but Astrid brightens some. After we wait in an extraordinarily long line, I order for Millie and myself, let Astrid place her order, and pay. I'm grabbing the box of sugary sweet donuts when—

"Bee?"

No.

Nonononono.

NO.

I want to drop and play dead, but I can't pretend like I didn't hear him. I turn slowly, feeling like a very creaky tin man. Levi is standing in the line beside me, hands in his pockets, looking happy as usual. He probably just made someone's day and is still high from the rush.

"Hey!" I exclaim. (*Great. Super awkward. Now fix it, you idiot.*)

He laughs. "Did you come back for the good stuff?"

I nod, embarrassed. Something about him catching me here after the last two times I've been here with him makes me supremely uncomfortable. It's like I've broken some secret pact of friendship. I also don't want it to be obvious that more than half of my reason for coming back was to see him. (I'm a hot mess.) "I brought my sisters," I say by way of excuse, waving them over. "I figured they have to try this as much as I did."

"Heck yeah, they do." Levi quickly orders his donut and pays. When he has his bag, he comes to stand beside us. He shakes the girls' hands, very politely. "I'm Levi."

"Millie," my youngest sister says, blinking incredibly fast, eyes glued to his face.

"Astrid," my other sister mumbles. She isn't nearly as impressed, but Levi takes no notice.

"Nice names." He sounds genuine, but I wonder if he's trying to get me to spill the beans on my name. *Hell no.* He must see my expression, because he grins. "Want to come back with me? I have to grab some paperwork, and then I'm off for an evening shift at Mike's."

I nod. "Sure."

Millie and Astrid have no choice but to follow. Levi is the first one to talk, walking so close to me that our elbows touch. "I'm glad I caught you before I left. Did everything work out okay? With your mom?"

"Yeah," I say. "Thankfully, I have a good track record."

Laughing, he opens the door to TCP, ushering us inside. I don't see Missy, but rather a girl in her mid-twenties with short brown hair and misty blue eyes. She's talking to an applicant, but quickly stands to open the blue door for us before disappearing back into the office.

Levi lets us into the interview room. A boy is sitting on the loveseat, staring lazily at the pile of glitter specks in his palm. "Hello?" he asks, very politely, a light accent lilting his voice. "Levi, what's going on?"

"Want to meet Barbie?" Levi asks the boy, who I assume is Albert.

There are a few moments of silence. Then I realize he's referring to me, and everyone is glancing with uncertainty in my direction. Levi, because he expects a reaction; my sisters, because they have no idea what the heck is going on.

The sound that escapes me is practically a snort. "Nice try."

That damn smirk again. He runs a hand through his hair and nods. "I was close. Wasn't I?"

"Not even a little bit." I turn back to Albert. "I'm Bee."

"Nice to meet you." He's looking at Astrid intently. "You?"

"I'm Astrid Jean Wescott," she says, lips tight, wary.

"And I'm Millicent." Millie frowns when Albert doesn't look at her. "Excuse me, what's your name?" she prompts.

Albert lifts his hand—palm flat—and blows, hard, into Millicent's face.

Millie sucks in a sharp breath—and instantly regrets it. "There's glitter in my nose!" she screams, and runs straight through the open bathroom door.

I laugh, but quietly, so I don't feel like a terrible sister. Levi, on the other hand, looks terribly vexed. "Albert, please go get the vacuum."

Albert sighs. "Fine. Goodbye, Astrid Jean Wescott," he adds. Then he scurries from the room.

"Whoa." Astrid is staring at the ground where the glitter lies in a heap. "He is *so* cool."

Levi puts his hand over his face. "Don't say that. Albert's glitter problem might just break me one day. I have recurring nightmares about it. There's a vacuum filled with glitter, and it explodes, and I can never ever clean it up no matter how hard I scrub and how often I sweep." Here he gives Astrid an exhausted smile, as if his dreams are actually sucking energy from him.

Astrid crosses her arms. "I don't see the problem."

Okaaaay, time to change the subject. "Thanks for the other day," I say, abruptly, to get his attention off Astrid.

Levi looks up sharply. "Who should be thanking who?"

"Definitely me thanking you."

He shakes his head. "No."

"Yes."

Shrugging, Levi says, "I don't fight about stupid things," before turning to the bathroom. "You all right in there, Millie?"

My sister comes out with her hair and eyelids sparkling, but her nose seems all clear. "Fine. Fine."

Levi nods gravely. "Albert gets to the best of us, Millie."

She brightens. "Okay."

We leave when Albert returns with the vacuum and Levi grabs his laundry from the bathroom. Albert stares at Astrid for a bit longer, his blond hair flopping into his eyes. When we close the door on him, Astrid's cheeks are bright red. "He is *so* cool," she repeats.

The brunette at the front desk stops us on our way out.

"Is this the famous Bee I've heard all about?" she asks, extending her hand to me over her desk. "I'm Clary-Jane."

Levi gives me a shifty look, like he's embarrassed.

He's been talking about me, I think. I choke on my words as I shake Clary-Jane's hand. "Hi, yeah, I'm Bee." I clear my throat. "Nice to meet you! And these are my sisters."

Clary-Jane shakes their hands, smiling. Then she continues

her work, stapling papers together and organizing them in a filing cabinet to her right. "I heard you had the tour last week."

"Yeah," I say, sneak a glance at Levi. His cheeks are red.

"Isn't it awesome?" Clary-Jane asks.

The genuine excitement of her tone gets me. "Yes! I love it here already."

"Good." She glances at Levi before saying, "You should come to the fundraiser we're hosting in a couple of weeks."

"Clary-*Jane!*" Levi exclaims in a pathetic voice, pouting his bottom lip. "*I* was going to invite her."

I glance between them. "What fundraiser?"

"Basically," Clary-Jane goes on, "we're a bunch of artists are donating their paintings so we can host a gallery. People bid on the art, and the money we raise goes directly to the community."

Levi leans against the wall beside the window. "That was the original reason I named it The Color Project; I wanted to use art to help the needy. After a year, we're finally getting to that point." He gives Clary-Jane a withering look. "Don't steal my thunder. *I* want to do the inviting."

She smiles with feigned innocence. "Sure thing, boss."

"Good. Now." Levi frowns at the clock on the wall. "I have to be at work in ten minutes."

"Oh, gosh. I'm sorry," I say. "We'll leave now."

"I'm not kicking you out or anything," Levi says. "Just letting you know I have to leave. I'm covering Keagan's shift today."

"We'll go with you, anyway. We should get home." It's nearly four o'clock and I have dinner duty tonight.

Outside, the girls say goodbye to Levi before getting in the car and closing their respective doors. I linger outside a little longer. "Thank you for the introductions," I say. "I think it's incredibly amazing what you're doing here."

He grins as if that's the best thing he's ever heard, as if he doesn't hear the praise all day long already. "I'll send along an invitation to the fundraiser, okay? Which reminds me . . . " He reaches into his pocket for his phone. "I need your info."

He holds it out to me. I take it. (Read: I have to physically restrain myself from excitedly ripping it out of his hands.) "Of course."

"Phone number and email, if that's all right."

I give him my phone to add his number to, and add myself to his contacts as "B-E-E". When I hand it back to him, he laughs.

"Thanks, Bailey."

I shake my head no. "You're really off track, you know?"

"Well, how am I supposed to make any real guesses if you won't give me any clues?"

"You're not." I smile mischievously. "That's the point. I know how to play this game."

He squares his shoulders. "I'm not giving up. Not now, not ever."

"That's nice," I say, distracted because Astrid is waving at me from the car, her phone in her hands. "What's wrong?" I call out.

"Mom called!" she yells through her window. "She said we should come home. The storm blew over."

I nod and wave in response, but when I turn to Levi, he's got a question written all over his face. "A storm?"

I swallow. "My parents were, um, fighting earlier," I admit, although saying it out loud sounds a little silly. "Millie started panicking, so I took them out of the house. I told her it's normal for all parents to fight, but our parents do this so little that I think it's just weird for us all."

Levi, I realize, suddenly looks pained. Whatever I've said has set off a nerve, *and* I'm babbling. "I'm sorry," I add, quickly.

He shakes his head. "No, don't be sorry." He shrugs, his shirt moving with his form. "My parents are divorced."

I wince. "Oh, yeah. Keagan mentioned that."

"I'm okay with it, now. I live with my mom, and she's great. I'm happy I only see my dad once a month, if that."

"Gosh." I open my mouth, close it, and open it again. I don't know what to say.

The smile starts to come back into his eyes. "Don't be flustered. It's not a big secret or anything."

(*Don't be flustered*, he says. But I am, and it's not *just* because I unwittingly brought up a rough topic.)

He takes his keys from his pocket and loops them around his fingers. "I'm sorry I have to leave you, Bee, but I'm going to be late. Keagan will kick my ass for screwing up his shift."

"Oh, right! Yes! So sorry."

He shakes his head, reaching out to touch my arm. His thumb lingers on the skin above my elbow. His skin feels cold, but maybe that's because in .5 seconds my body managed to retain the heat of a thousand suns. "You're always sorry, Bee. Stop that."

Then he drops his hand and backs up a few steps, slowly.

I grin, despite myself. I'm still thinking about his hand on my arm, and how even though he's held my hand before (and shook it, and bumped my arm with his, and put his arm around my shoulder), this was far more intimate. This was deliberate. "I'll try."

"Good. See you later?"

"Of course."

"Good," he repeats, and after looking at me for a moment longer, we part ways on the sidewalk, sunshine stretching between us.

chapter 15

QUEUED:
Count Me In
by Early Winters

THE THIRD TIME I hear my mom crying, I'm walking into my house with one arm around my most recent floral creation (which I loved enough to purchase for myself). My stomach instantly clenches at the sound, every part of me going still, with my foot keeping the door half-open behind me.

"Hello?" I call out.

No answer, but the crying fades into soft sniffling. Whatever's going on, she doesn't want me to know about it.

I close the door and tip-toe toward the living room, where I'm surprised to see my mom and dad sitting on the couch together. The mood is different this time, raw. They sit on opposite ends, my mom with her face in her hands, my dad leaning back with his eyes on the ceiling. I've never seen that expression on his face before, so I don't know what to call it.

My throat grows tight, eyes clouding. I don't want to see this.

I don't want to know—not right now, not today. Today has been a *happy* day.

Swallowing hard, I head to my bedroom, placing the flowers on my desk. I shake my head, ignoring the tension creeping into my shoulders, and pull my phone out of my pocket. There are the expected messages from Gretchen, of course. But there is also a text from Levi, to my surprise and delight. It's the first text I've gotten from him, and it's been almost a week since we exchanged numbers. (If you guessed that I've been dying of suspense this whole time, you're right. It's been a terrible week of waiting.)

Levi

Don't be a stranger, Bianca.

Bee

Not sure who you think you're texting, but my name isn't Bianca. :P

Levi

You can't stop me! I'm a name-finding machine.

Bee

You'll never guess it! Mwahaha!

I immediately regret sending that. "Oh, God," I groan.

I switch to Gretchen's messages while I wait for his reply, my fingers fidgeting over the keypad.

Gretchen

My dad has a business trip out to Arizona next week and I am so upset. Because this means he will be so close to yoooouuuu and I can't go with him.

Bee

UGH. Why can't you go?

Gretchen

I wouldn't be able to get off work. Besides, he wouldn't drive/fly me out to CA just for a brief meeting. He's too busy for that right now.

Bee

I'm thoroughly disappointed in him.

Gretchen

I know, right? I thought the parents are supposed to be disappointed in their children's life decisions, not the other way around.

I almost reply that I'm laughing, but I'm *not* laughing. I'm not happy at all, and when not even Gretchen can cheer me up, I know it's serious. On the other side of my bedroom door, I have a crying mother and a concerned father, and I can't breathe when I think about it.

So I tell Gretchen. I tell her about the quiet talks and sniffling behind closed doors, and what feels to me like well-kept secrets and sadness.

Gretchen

Yikes, Bee. You okay?

Bee

I'm sure it'll all be okay. They'll be okay, I'll be okay, etc., etc.

Gretchen

Please call me if you need to.

Bee

I will. I guess I'm just worried about them, like
something unfixable happened between them. I don't
remember the last time they fought to the point of
tears. I might have been, like, twelve.

Gretchen

Can't you just . . . ask them? Ask them what's wrong?

Bee

Working on that one. I think I'm just gunna go to TCP
this afternoon. I brought home an arrangement, but
maybe I should take it to them. And last time I got out
of the house, it really helped.

I take a picture of the arrangement to send to her, but as soon
as I do, I get the nagging feeling that this is a totally dumb idea.

Bee

Dude . . . I dunno. What if they just smile and nod, but
secretly they think it's ugly?

Gretchen

I'm rolling my eyes at you so hard right now. TAKE
THEM TO HIM. He said he wanted to see something
you'd made, right?

Bee

UGH. Why are you always right?!

Gretchen

Because I'm the best. Now GO GO GO!

There's a text from Levi when I switch apps.

Levi

I'm seeing a maniacal side of you I didn't know existed. It terrifies me.

Bee

I am no damsel in distress.

Levi

Now that I know, I won't try to cross you. It might be dangerous.

Bee

Very, very dangerous. Also, I am coming to see you.

Levi

R U REALLY?!

Bee

Yes.

Levi

Sheesh, don't get excited or anything.

Bee

Ha ha. See you soon!

If only he could see my smile, my cheeks flushed with red, and hear my swiftly beating heart.

My chest loosens as soon as I pull up to TCP, parking in the last empty spot. My hands, however, are still jittery as I grab the vase of flowers from the passenger seat and head inside.

There are more people in the lobby than I've ever seen at once, and they all look a little like parents waiting for the doctor to tell them the sex of their baby: both excited and terrified. Missy is at the front desk, appearing as lazy and disinterested as ever. Behind her are two Indian girls, one with thick, straight hair, the other with a short, curly bob. They don't look like twins, but their mannerisms are so similar it's uncanny. The one with the short hair is talking on the phone while the other goes through files, standing back to back, moving in tandem.

I approach the desk, tapping the counter to startle Missy into action. She clacks her manicured nails on the desktop and glares up at me. "What?" she snaps.

"Missy, come on," I say, my words bouncing off the wall of her attitude.

She rolls her eyes. "Looking for Levi?"

"Yeah, actually, I am. And I brought these for the office." I set the vase on the counter. "Can I leave it here?"

"Sure. Whatever." Missy watches as I set up the vase to the side, near the window into the office.

"Is something wrong today?" I ask.

Missy lets out an exaggerated groan. "Yeah, my dad is a jerk."

I wince. I know for a fact that I've opened up a can of worms I did not want to open. But it's too late to close it now because

Missy keeps going. "He took away my shopping privileges. How am I supposed to buy those Christian Louboutin crystal-embellished pumps on sale next week if he doesn't let me have the card?"

I raise one eyebrow. (How the hell am I supposed to answer that?) "Um. How much are they on sale for?"

"Twenty-seven hundred dollars. Originally almost seven thousand! You *do* realize how important this is, right?"

I choke. As in, I actually choke. I turn away from her, hacking into the crook of my elbow to mask the sound. It makes sense now, why she's here. To redefine the word *important*.

"What did I say?" Missy asks, over the racket I'm making. Everyone in the lobby is looking at me.

I might die.

A new voice interrupts, lightly but distinctly tilted with an accent. "Here, give her some water. Missy, please answer that phone."

I take the water that one of the twins offers me, the one with short hair, and swallow it all in three gulps. The girl smiles up at me as my coughing subsides.

"I'm Suhani," she says, holding out her hand.

I choke-laugh and set down the water cup. "I'm Bee."

Suhani laughs with me. "Nice to meet you. Levi told us you would be in. Glad you didn't die on account of Missy." She whispers this last part as if we're privy to some secret.

I laugh again, still shaking with aftershock coughs. "I'm fine, I'm fine. Thanks for the water."

The other sister, who I assume is Nikita, comes through the blue door, followed by Levi himself. He's shaking hands with another young woman (an applicant, I'm guessing) who looks incredibly sickly. She wipes her eyes (I see people doing that a lot these days) and at the last second, Levi pauses and pulls her into a hug.

Feeling intrusive, I look away until I hear the front door shut behind the woman and Levi calling my name.

(Cue: Breath hitch.)

"Hey!" He looks like he's about to hug me, but then he stops short and raises an eyebrow. "Are you okay? Your face is . . . erm . . . red."

I clasp my hands over my cheeks. "Um, I'm fine. Just . . . choked."

"You choked?" He rubs the back of his neck, obviously confused. Nikita whispers something to him and he laughs. "I see," he says. "Guess what, Bee?"

"What?" I say.

"Nikita and Suhani aren't actually twins."

They both whack him hard on the shoulder. At the same time. (Very twin-like.) This, of course, only makes Levi grin wider.

"We are, *too*!" Suhani says in a harsh whisper.

"Are not," Nikita counters. "I was born December thirty-first at eleven fifty-three at night, and Suhani was born January first, twelve ten in the morning. We were born in different *years*, which makes me older by far."

I laugh in surprise.

Suhani hangs her head. "It's not fair. Not one bit." Then she raises her head, meets Levi's gaze, and her mouth sets into a grim line. "You!" she accuses, poking her finger into his chest. "You promised you'd never bring this up, again!"

Levi raises his hands in mock surrender. "It's payback for yesterday."

Crossing her arms, Suhani juts out a hip. "Oh, right. When I called you a noodle-headed chicken man?"

I almost choke again. "A what?!"

Nikita wraps one arm around her sister's waist, her expression all innocence. "Actually, I think you said he was a cowardly grandmother."

"Are you sure?" Suhani asks, practically gleeful over Levi's confused expression.

He sighs. "Come on, just t—"

"Oh!" Nikita interrupts, raising one hand in the air. "I think I hear the phone ringing. I should get it because we all know Missy won't."

"And would you look at that," Suhani mutters. "The fax machine is flashing lights at me. If you'll excuse me, boss."

Levi throws his hands up, looking hopeless and exasperated. "I can never win."

"What the heck is going on?" I demand, trying to hold back a giggle.

"They like to say things about me in Hindi and then never tell me what they've actually said. It's exhausting. DOES EVERYONE HERE ENJOY PICKING ON ME?" he yells.

The entire staff—literally all six people in the office—yell back, "YES."

Levi rolls his eyes. "Want to come back with me? I have a few more interviews."

I nod, probably too vigorously, but my enthusiasm only seems to spur him on.

"I think you're going to like this couple I have next," he gushes shutting the blue door behind him. "Augustin and Ivanka. They moved here a year ago from the Czech Republic and are applying for the funds to get married. They need help organizing and planning as well, which is something I've never done with TCP, but I figured, why not?"

Levi ushers me into the Dreams Come True Room and continues, talking quickly. "I'm having them here a second time to finalize details. Their dilemma is that their family is flying in from Europe and that's all they could afford. They're currently living with a very low budget and need help to pay for and organizing everything. I'm also trying to see if I can gather enough funds to send them on a honeymoon, but that all depends on the fundraiser."

I stare at him. (It's hard *not* to stare at him.) "They are going to be so happy."

"I hope so." He sits on the loveseat, looking over the paperwork in his hands, absently patting the cushion next to him. "The only problem is, we have a clashing of dates. Their family bought tickets for a date I approved, but then the fundraiser got moved to the same weekend. It was out of my control. So now I have to figure out how to do both. In one day." He laughs—a very pained laugh.

I grab the papers and scan over them. "You can get away with it, right?"

Levi bites his bottom lip, then says, "I don't know. I think it might be too much in one weekend. I may have a lot of sponsors, but I'm doing most of this on my own." He gives me a nervous laugh. "It's times like these that my small number of volunteers seems *painfully* small. Maybe they'll have perfected cloning by then. Think they can crack the code in a few weeks?"

I want to laugh at this, but he looks so . . . lost. I've only known Levi for a few weeks, but I don't want to see him looking lost ever again.

"Look, we can figure it out," I begin, but I'm cut off by the door opening. Nikita leads in a man and a woman I vaguely remember passing in the lobby. They're young, only a few years older than me. The way they grasp each other's hands and stand shoulder to shoulder and gaze at us with hopeful, happy eyes . . . it makes my chest squeeze. Levi looks genuinely happy to see them, but I can also see the distress in the curve of his mouth. He's worried he can't follow through, that he might disappoint them.

This kills me. I don't want him to even *mention* the complications, and I especially don't want him to tell them he can't help them in all the ways they need. They deserve their happily ever after as much as anyone.

Levi hugs them both before inviting them to sit down. He stands there in front of them as if uncertain what to say, shuffling from foot to foot with his hands stuffed in his pockets. When he opens his mouth to speak, I panic. He's going to tell them he can't do it, that he has to change plans, that something's wrong. Ivanka, with her long brown hair and round eyes, is grinning like she can't stop, and Augustin has his arm around her shoulders like he won't let her go.

They can't know something's wrong.

I grab Levi's arm, hooking him close. "Will you excuse us for two seconds?" I ask them—then drag Levi into the bathroom and lock the door.

"What are you doing?" he demands, completely confused, shoulders slumped as he stares at me. I wonder if he's starting to regret his decision to invite me back for interviews. I probably look crazy.

"You absolutely *cannot* let them know that something is wrong," I say in a whisper.

Shock registers on his face. "What else am I supposed to tell them?"

"That everything will work out just fine."

"What if it doesn't?"

I put up my hand to shush him. "I'll *make* it."

"What?" He stops short, squinting at me, and I realize I'm still holding his arm.

I don't let go. "I'm going to help. I'll do whatever I can to make sure they get their wedding on the same weekend their family visits. I'll organize it all, Levi. I know you're stressed from running this place, and you have a lot going on with the fundraiser, so you need someone to come in and help with more than just office stuff. I want to do it. I'll get the other girls to help, and we'll put everything together. I'll even arrange the flowers myself if I need to. But you cannot go out there and tell them anything except that you're so excited for their wedding and you can't wait to meet their families."

I'm breathing hard, my fingers digging into his skin, my heart about to jump out of my throat. I've never been this close to him, and it makes me feel . . . alive. Like I'm all blood and veins and pulse, and I'm not going to stop, not ever. His surprised expression, his breathlessness, are like a bolt of electricity to my heart. I'm lost, so hopelessly lost, and then, *and then*—he takes my face in his hands and grins.

He takes my face in his hands. Suddenly, every doubt I've ever had about this, about *him*, disappears. I need this. I need it badly.

"Yeah," he says, while I'm totally helpless to do anything but look at his face, which is much, much closer to mine than it's ever been. "Yeah, okay. If you're up for it."

I make myself speak. "I'm totally up for it. I wouldn't have offered otherwise."

"Okay." He drops his hands. "Don't let me stand in the way, boss."

Laughing quietly, I point to the door. "Now get out there and congratulate them. I've got a wedding to plan."

chapter 16

QUEUED:
Young Hearts
by Strange Talk

SEEING IVANKA'S FACE as we discuss her wedding, watching Augustin's eyes grow warm with thanks, is probably the greatest thing I've seen since I discovered Henry Cavill. (Levi tells them my name is Bonita, but I think I can live with that. I *think*.) At the end of the meeting, the bride hugs me tightly, her thin arms wrapping me close, and Augustin kisses my cheek like a true gentleman.

"Thank you, Bonita," Ivanka tells me, hands clasped around mine.

Just behind me, so close that only I can hear him, Levi chuckles. I'm tempted (oh, so tempted) to turn around and hit him square in the chest. But instead I smile at Ivanka and say, "You know, everyone calls me Bee."

"Bee is lovely." Ivanka pulls me close again. "Will we exchange telephone numbers for contact?"

"Yes!" I exclaim, grabbing for my purse. I pull out my phone, quickly reading over a short text from Gretchen (*I miss you!* it says) and hand it to her. "Will you put your information here?" Then I give Levi a snide look that clearly says, *You suck.*

He chuckles silently, shaking his head, as if to tell me, *I'm not going to stop.*

We say goodbye to the happy couple at the door to the lobby—and that's when I realize how long we'll be here. The crowd of people here has just gotten bigger, which means we have a lot more work to do. Over the next hour, Levi invites three more applicants to the back, and all three leave with checks in hand. Four others turn in their applications and background check information, then go over specifics with Clary-Jane. Two more are sponsors who've come to check up on the place personally, make sure it's running smoothly, and that their money's being put to good use.

I sit back on the couch and watch it happen, completely in awe.

Eventually, after the last client is gone, Levi comes back into the interview room alone and slumps onto the couch beside me. "You good?"

I sigh loudly, feigning an attitude. "I'm good, but I can't believe you're still trying to guess my name."

He scoffs. "Out of everything that just happened, *that's* what you're thinking about?"

I scrunch up my nose at him. If I counted the inches between our faces (which I'm not doing at *all*), the number would be five. "Bethany, Barbie, Bailey, Bianca, Bonita . . . What's next?"

"I don't know. I'll have to think about it. This is very serious business, you know."

"Apparently."

Levi's phone rings (it's a song I recognize but can't quite place), and he pulls it out of his pocket, swiping right.

"Hey, Mom," he says, leaning forward, elbows on his knees. "Yeah, I'm at the office." A pause. "Sure I can. Mind if I bring a friend?" Another pause. (I'm pretty sure *I'm* the friend.) "I might have a job for you, too, if you can spare the time. I'll have Bee talk to you about it." He laughs. "Yeah, that's the friend. You'll love her, Mom." Levi twists at the waist and pats my knee. I jerk.

"Ready?" he mouths to me.

"Where are we going?" I whisper.

"My mom needs eggs," he whispers back. "Yeah, Mom, I'll be there in thirty minutes. Make sure you have enough for us. Okay, bye."

I laugh. "What was that?"

"My mom needs eggs because she's baking cookies and I think you should come with me."

Just like that, huh? But it makes me smile. If he wants me to join him, I am *not* going to say no. "Your mom is baking cookies at . . . " I check my phone. "Eight o'clock?"

He nods, heading into the hall. The office is terribly empty compared to the last few hours. Levi turns off the lights and locks up. "My mom needed something to help her cope, after the divorce. We quickly found that she gets sad later in the evenings, so one night, about a year ago, she tried baking a cake. It became a sort of calming ritual, except she changed it to cookies because those are easier. It usually works, although she needs to listen to copious amounts of Paula Abdul for it to work *perfectly*."

"Your mom sounds awesome." I step up to my car. "I'll follow you, okay?"

"I'm just up the street, remember?" He nods toward the street. "We can drive together."

I don't hesitate. (Inside, I'm shrieking.) "Sure."

Levi unlocks his car. As soon as we get in and the doors are shut, his phone goes off again, the same song as before. He screens the call (I see the word "Dad" pop up, even though I'm 100% not looking) and turns it off, shoving it back in his pocket. "Sorry," he says. "My phone doesn't normally ring this much in the evening."

"It's fine. I don't mind if you take the call."

"I don't want to," he says between his teeth. He's trying to smile, but it looks like a grimace.

"What song was that?" I ask, instead of all the questions I want to ask about his dad.

He backs out onto the road. "My ringtone?"

I nod.

"'Guillotine', Jon Bellion."

"Oh! I knew I'd heard it before."

He squints at me suspiciously. "I was starting to worry about you."

"Excuse you!" I retort, rolling my eyes. "I don't live under a rock, okay?"

He glances at me, mouth twisted like he's trying not to laugh. "Fine, fine. How about Florence + the Machine?"

I nod.

"Walk the Moon?"

I nod again.

"St. Lucia?"

"Yes, Levi."

"But here's the real question: Do you know Bon Iver?"

I groan, my shoulders sinking. I've had this argument with

other Bon Iver fans before, and it's not pretty. It never ends in my favor, either. "Yes, but I don't . . . really . . . like them."

"Bee, I don't think we can be friends anymore. Justin Vernon is my favorite. Ever." He feigns a wounded expression.

"Sorry," I say, cringing. "You can show me some songs if you think you can win me over, but my best friend has been trying to get me to like them for forever . . . "

"I like your best friend already. What's her name?"

"Gretchen."

"Gretchen can be my friend."

I laugh. "She'd love you."

Levi grins at me and parks in front of Major Market. He makes a quick job of this shopping trip, grabbing two dozen eggs and heading to the front. My short legs can barely keep up with his long ones.

Penis jokes, Gretchen's ever-present spirit whispers into my ear, as is common for best friend spirits to do. *Ugh, no, NOT NOW,* I reprimand her as I wait for the cashier to ring us up. Grabbing the eggs at the end of the line, I ask, "What about *my* favorite bands? Have you heard A Silent Film, San Fermin, or Blindside?"

"Love the first two, but I've never heard Blindside."

"Well, then. You're going to hear them tonight."

"Oh, it's *on*, Bridget."

"WRONG!" I shout, yanking open his car door. I love the sound of his laugh as it follows me. I buckle into my seat and hold the eggs on my lap. "Speaking of names—"

Levi turns to me with hope in his eyes.

"I'm not going to tell you. *Chill*—"

He taps the side of my head with one finger. "*Beeeeee,*" he pleads in a sing-song voice.

"Shh, Levi!" I swat his hand away. "I was going to ask what you named your car, since you took it upon yourself to name mine."

He drives through a yellow light to get out of the parking lot, then glances at me with a wary smile. "I've never actually named my car."

"Oooohh!" I practically jump in my seat. "I nominate myself to do the honors!"

He chuckles, indicating that he understands: I've won this war already, and there's no use arguing. "Dear God, what have I gotten myself into?"

I give him a taste of his own medicine: a smirk I hope shoots his nerves right in the heart. "Well, he's dark green, but I feel like calling him Forest would be way too obvious."

Levi laughs again, like he can't help it. His sharp features are lit up by street lights and signs on buildings and the red lights of the car in front of us. "Bee—"

I shush him vigorously and keep going. "He's super soft, like velvet." I pat the leather seats. "Older, but taken care of. Refined."

"My car is refined." He smirks, and I laugh because it does sound rather ridiculous. "Okay then."

"So," I announce, "his name is Maximillian. Obviously."

Levi laughs, so hard and so suddenly that he presses a hand to his stomach. "Okay, okay," he concedes, turning onto his street, breathing hard as he tries to control his laughter. "Maximillian it is. Can I at least call him Max, if I need a break from the mouthful?"

"Well, duh. Any self-respecting Maximillian needs the nickname Max. It is the Way of Things."

His smile never breaks, and I am happy. I adore that smile.

Levi's house is small.

I guess I didn't notice this factor the last two times I saw it, but now it's obvious. Unlike the last time I was here, lights illuminate the windows, contrasting the night. I like it immediately, with its shutters and gables and white siding. It looks inviting and warm, and I'm bombarded with an image, one I'll never, ever be able to forget: Levi and me, sharing a perfect kiss on the patio, my hands on his shoulders as he hooks his arm around my waist and dips me backward.

I stop in my tracks. I just thought about me and Levi kissing. The real Levi, the one *not* kissing me, is staring at me from the patio, waving me to him.

I'm frozen.

"Come on, Bee!" he calls out.

That's what does it: His voice (and his hair) and his welcoming smile as he sweeps open the door. I pick up my pace, entering his home. A delicious smell hits me, like oranges and cookie batter and summer. It also smells like Levi. (But let's pretend I never noticed, for the sake of my sanity.)

The front room consists of a brown leather couch and a TV mounted on the wall, as well as a bookshelf stashed with self-help, cooking, and gardening books. Around the corner I hear Paula Abdul singing away, her voice echoing in the small space. I slip off my shoes and place them beside Levi's, put my purse by the door, and follow him inside.

Levi's mom stands at the kitchen sink, her back to us. She's singing with Paula, voice rising as the song's emotions heighten. Levi clears his throat loudly, making her jump and turn, glasses askew on her face, bubbles coating her hands.

"Levi, dear." She pauses the music by touching her elbow to the pause button on the iPad. "I didn't hear you come in."

"I wonder why," he teases, letting her kiss his cheek. "Mom, this is . . . " He shrugs, pauses, and shrugs again. "I don't know. I don't know her name. She won't tell me."

I gape at him, but it quickly turns to a smile. "Oh, so you're trying a different tactic now? The guilt trip?"

Levi's response is to stick his tongue out at me. His mom laughs, reaching for me. Her hug is warm, her hands still soapy. She holds them away from my body so as not to get suds on my hair. "That was his favorite as a little boy, the guilt trip. He's quite good at it actually. This young man's charm is unreal."

I shake my head, pretending to be exasperated. "My name is Bee. Nice to meet you."

Her smile is just like Levi's. "Bee, I'm Suzie. You're welcome in my house any day."

"This nameless creature," Levi interrupts, "has been helping out at TCP for a couple of weeks."

"It's only been a few days," I protest, but Levi's words strike me. It feels like I've been a part of this for a lot longer. Like I've always belonged here. (I think I like this.)

"Welcome to the Project, Bee!" Suzie waves her hands in the air. "You want to stay for cookies? They'll be done in about twenty minutes."

"I'd love to."

She claps. "Goodie! Levi, get our guest comfortable, maybe with some coffee or tea or juice or *something*, and I'll bring the cookies to you."

Levi salutes his mom. "Thanks, you're the best, love you, all that mushy stuff."

"You know you love it, Levi Brenton Orville."

"Have fun with Paula," he says over his shoulder, ushering me toward the back of the house. There's a sitting room and a small hallway that leads to the bedrooms. Levi opens one of the two doors in the hall and disappears inside.

I hadn't thought about what his room looks like, but when I see it, I know I wouldn't have expected this. It's nearly bare, with white walls and navy bedding and books that evenly line the baseboards of one wall. The sliding doors to the closet are closed. I stare for a second too long into the full-length mirror at my frizzy hair and reddened face. I've been thinking about him too long, obviously.

"What?" he asks, stirring me from my trance. "Is something wrong?"

"No, no." I shrug. "Just . . . thinking." I hope he can't see the lie.

He reaches into his closet and pulls out an iPod and headphones. "We're going to need these," he says.

Once we're in the sitting room at the back of the house, Levi stands in front of me, feet planted, unraveling the ear buds. "You're going to listen to 'Michicant'. I'll be disappointed, severely, if you don't like this song."

I sit down on the couch. "Are you threatening me?"

"Yeah, with a life without cookies."

"Ah!" I gasp.

His smirk is very satisfied. (I think about kissing him again.) "Here, have these."

The song that plays into my left ear (Levi has the right ear bud) is . . . not exactly what I expected, but it's not my favorite, either. I can't see myself listening to this on a daily basis, let alone it becoming my favorite song. But I sit through the whole thing, shoulder to shoulder with Levi. His eyes are closed, and he looks so peaceful I almost don't say anything when the song is over.

He sits up and takes the bud out of my ear. "Well?"

I smile sheepishly, shrugging my shoulders. "Well." I clear my throat. "I *really* want a cookie."

He rolls his eyes.

"But it wasn't . . . terrible?"

"That's all you've got?" He sighs loudly and heavily. "I suppose that's all I can ask of you."

"I didn't love it, but it didn't make me cringe like the last song I heard by them."

"Which was?"

"I can't remember."

"Hmm." His humming noise is full of disbelief.

"Here," I say, pulling out my phone. I find my favorite Blindside song and hook up the ear buds. "You get both ears, and you have to listen to the whole thing."

"Yes, ma'am," he says, laughing.

I flick his arm, then immediately pale. I touched him. On my own. Without thinking about it. Sitting back on the couch, I try to calm myself. *It was just a flick, Bee. Chill.* And yet, all I can hear is Gretchen's voice, buzzing inside my brain, saying, *You're a goner, Bee. So far gone.*

Mortified, I focus on the sound of Suzie and Paula's duet with enough energy to power New York City.

When the song finishes, Levi hands me my phone, movements lethargic. His eyes are sort of glazed over. "That . . . was beautiful."

"I told you."

"But I feel incredibly slighted. Or, just . . . not good at this. Now I have to show you a song you'll really love." He wraps his headphones as he studies me. "I must think about this in depth."

"We've got all the time in the world," I say, wanting this to be true.

"That's a lovely thought." He grimaces. "Speaking of time, I should probably be going over flier layouts right now, but here I am, listening to music and eating cookies."

"Well, you're not eating cookies *yet*, and remember: Now you have me to help you."

"I'm glad you want to help, but . . . be honest . . . you're here because you feel bad for me."

"Nope. What's there to feel bad for? I'm here because I love a good happily ever after story." (It's not *completely* a lie.)

He leans a little closer to me, our shoulders brushing. "Then, thanks. I think I might be a little lost without you."

Can't breathe can't breathe can't breathe can't breathe— "You could have done it."

He shakes his head vigorously. "I wasn't thinking straight today. I almost made a total idiot of myself."

"You're not an idiot," I whisper. "Not even close."

Gretchen is right, as usual: I *am* a goner.

"Do you want milk, my dears?" Suzie asks, interrupting us. She peeks her head around the corner.

"That'd be nice," I say, but my eyes are still on Levi, and his eyes are on me, and poor Suzie is ignored.

Suzie is still there a few seconds later when she asks, "And you, Levi?"

"Oh." He turns to his mom. "Definitely—wait, what was your question?"

Suzie smirks, her mouth looking incredibly like Levi's, and repeats herself.

"Yes," he decides. "I want milk."

I haven't moved when he turns back to me, and his expression is amused. "Sometimes I tune her out."

"Actually," Suzie interrupts again, stepping into the room with a tray of cookies, which she sets on the coffee table. "He's usually such a good listener. I wonder why he's so spacey tonight."

"Mom." He grabs a cookie and his glass of milk, giving Suzie a sideways glance.

"Goodness, Levi, you should get a girlfriend," she continues. (Her words cause me to choke on a chocolate chip.) "I'd love to do this more often, you know. It's nice to have another girl in the house."

She's staring at him pointedly.

"Mom," he says again, at a loss. His hair is ruffled, his eyes alarmed.

"Yes, dear?"

He shakes his head and changes the subject. "Do you . . . want to help plan a wedding?"

Wrong question.

"Are you getting married?!" Suzie shrieks. "Grandchildren, here I come!"

"MOM." Levi has to laugh at this, despite the pink that flushes his cheeks. "Please. Calm down. We're funding a wedding and part of the deal is that we have to help them set up."

"Now *that's* exciting." Suzie settles deep into the plush armchair across from us. "When is it?"

"It's . . . .the same day as the fundraiser. Bee—" he gestures at me "—stepped in and took charge like a boss, but we still need help. Is there anything you'd like to do that will make things easier? I'll email you budget details later."

"Hmm. Not as exciting as grandchildren, but I'm still happy to help." She winks at me, adjusts her glasses, and offers, "I can cook."

"I'll ask what they want at the reception. I'm getting the final details tomorrow."

"How many people?"

Levi thinks for a second. "Around fifty, I believe. Mostly their extended family from Prague, but some local friends as well."

"Oh, Levi! I could bake some traditional Czech pastries!" she exclaims, rather adorably.

Levi grins. "We'll see. Anything else you can do? Anyone you know?"

"I'll think it over. But, Bee, if you need *anything* at all, you just ask me, okay?"

I nod fervently. I love this woman so much already, despite

how badly I'm still blushing at what she said before. (*So he doesn't have a girlfriend.*) "Absolutely."

"Good, good." Suzie leans forward, eyes suddenly alight. "Levi, I have an idea!" Standing, she hurriedly puts on her shoes and rushes toward the sliding glass door to my right. "Come on!" she gasps.

"Your mom's amazing," I whisper to Levi as we follow.

"Thanks. I'm glad she hasn't scared you off yet." With a few long strides, he's out the back door. "Mom," he says, running a hand through his skewed hair, "you're a genius!"

"Yes, dear, I know."

As I look at the backyard, a sense of nostalgia comes over me. It's landscaped with rose bushes and pathways, and plenty of room for people to dance and talk and eat. There's even a little patch of grass that could hold fifty chairs, if we arranged them the right way. I'm looking at a tiny wedding venue, tucked away in the backyard of this beautiful boy and his wonderful mom, and I suddenly want to cry. They're happy tears, but they're hot on my heels, and I so badly want to have a switch installed on the back of my head that will allow me to turn them off whenever I want to.

"What do you say, Bee?" Levi asks. Then he pauses, as if he senses what I'm feeling, his smile soft.

I hold back a sniffle. "I love it so much. Really, this is incredible. Suzie, did you do all this?"

"Yes! I'm out here every day, my dear. I think it will be more worth the work now than ever."

"This is so awesome," Levi murmurs, arm around his mom's shoulder.

"Now," Suzie says, kissing his cheek. "I'm going to clean up. Lock the door behind you when you come inside." She presses my hand when she passes and disappears inside.

When we hear muted-Paula and the banging of kitchen utensils, Levi leans closer to me. "Are you all right?"

"I'm fine," I say, but I'm so not fine. I put my hands on my face.

He smiles at me. It's a sad smile. "What's up?"

"This." I shrug. "It's so beautiful, and it's been a long day for me."

"Your parents," he guesses.

I nod slowly, hesitant. "I left the house because I couldn't stand being there." I tell him about how I found my parents earlier, the way they sat and how my mom cried. And Levi—he seems to care. Genuinely. Then I realize that he's got one arm around my shoulder.

The Boy is touching me, and I didn't even notice it. I feel suddenly lightheaded.

When I'm done with my story, he looks down at me thoughtfully. "I'm probably going to sound like a cold-hearted bastard but . . . what if it's nothing?"

Actually, I hadn't thought about that.

"What if it's just a bad day?" he continues, seeing me pause. "What if your mom heard a sad story and she wanted to tell your dad?"

I want him to be right, but I just can't shake that something deeper is happening. Every time I've heard her crying is starting to add up, starting to make the world sullen and gray. But I nod anyway.

"Have there been any other signs?" he asks. "Of . . . well, anything?"

I shake my head no. I have no proof; everything is in my head, driven by emotion and fear. It really could be nothing.

"Then all you can do is wait it out." His quiet voice comforts me. "And you *can* ask them, you know? There are a lot of times

I wish I would have asked my parents about what was going on. Just . . . don't let it get to you, at least not yet."

"I won't." Nestled against his side, I tilt my head upward. "Sorry I'm a mess."

"And I'm sorry I'm in your personal space," he says, stepping back.

"You're fine. It's no big deal." (*Too soon! Come back!*) "Anyway, I feel better. I think that counts for something."

"I'm glad," Levi answers, grinning at me with straight teeth and lips that I want to touch. (I want to run the pad of my thumb over the soft skin there, and I want to see his face when I do.) "I think it counts for everything."

chapter 17

QUEUED:
Say It Out Loud
by Katie Herzig

Levi

Hello, good morning, I hope the ten hours we've
been apart have treated you well. If you're sure about
this—sorry I keep asking—I have a list for you. Ready
for it?

I squint at the text, then rub my sleepy eyes, blocking out
the intense sunlight barging into my room. My clock reads
10:03, but Levi sent this text hours ago. The promise I made
yesterday—my evening with Levi and Suzie and cookies—fills
my head. I feel my body surging with energy as I make myself
sit up and reply.

Bee

Don't you ever seel?

Sleep. I mean sleep.

Anywhoooo. Dude I totaly want to d this! Stp asking nd send over the list.

Im in suspne

No. Sspene

DAMMIT!!!

Suspense.

I just woke up. Pleas forgve me.

Groaning, I click the lock button and slide out of bed, already feeling the heat of the day in my bedroom. My eyes still won't open all the way from exhaustion. "Hey, can someone turn on the AC?" I shout to the rest of the house, pulling my pink summer dress over my head.

No one answers, but when I head into the kitchen, everyone's there, even Tom, and they're laughing like it's a party.

"Just wake up, sweetie?" my mom asks me.

I rub my eyes, realizing too late that I didn't even look at my hair. (I probably look like a ferocious lion with The Worst Case of Bedhead Ever.) "Yes. Did you know that it's really hot in the house and I feel gross?"

"The AC broke," Astrid explains. "Papa's getting someone to fix it tomorrow. Millie and I are going swimming later, wanna come?"

"No, thanks." I put my hair up with a leftover band around my wrist. "I'm busy today."

"But it's Sunday," Millie whines. "Come play with us!"

"M&M, I'm planning a wedding that takes place two weeks from now, and today is the start of everything. No buts!"

"A wedding?" Mama asks, handing me a plate of waffles. The scent of syrup and strawberry jam hits me hard and my stomach grumbles.

"Yeah. I offered to take over this project because Levi was stressed out."

Astrid's grin is quick. "Of course you'd do that for your boyfriend."

My dad smacks her gently upside the head. "Now, Astrid, no need to state the obvious."

"Yeah, Ass-trid," I chime in, emphasis on the *ass*. But then I register the rest of my dad's sentence, and all I can do is glare.

Millie sticks her tongue out at me. Papa shakes his head, like he's going to scold me for cursing before noon, but my mom saves me by putting her arms around his waist. I hold my breath, seeing them like this. In fact, we all pause.

I don't think my parents notice how we're all looking at them, watching to see what they'll do. They're talking and teasing as if nothing has been wrong the last few weeks. Mama says something snarky that I don't catch. My dad gasps and, without warning, starts to tickle her. At that, my siblings and I release a collective breath, laughing with them, thankful that whatever was going on between them seems to have passed.

I glance up, meeting Tom's gaze across the kitchen. We nod at each other. I haven't seen him much since the breakup, but he looks better now than he did last week, like he's been getting more sleep. I stride over and smack his arm affectionately. "Hi, loser."

"Beef," he says with equal affection. "So, The Color Project, huh?"

"Yes."

"Getting really involved, yeah?"

I squint at him. "Ye-es." I draw out the word with hesitance.

"That's cool." Tom squints back at me. "Levi's pretty great, huh?"

"Yes, but—" My phone dings.

Tom looks down at the screen in my hands. Levi's name pops up next to the text icon. "Speaking of," he says.

Looking at his eyes, the way they sparkle with purely evil delight, I instantly know what he's getting at. "You're just as bad as the girls, making fun of me! Would you be mature, *please*?"

Tom puts his hands up defensively. "Bernice, I've done nothing to offend," he says in his most innocent tone.

"Shush, Tom. I come over here to ask you how you're doing and you tease me."

His eyes laugh, but he keeps his mouth in a straight line. "Fine, I'll stop. And I'm good, thanks for asking."

This has me smiling. "Moving on okay?"

He shrugs. "I think so."

I take the moment of vulnerability to kiss his cheek. "Good."

He brushes me off, feigning disgust. "Just go text your boyf—" He makes a little surprised O with his mouth, jumping out of the way of my protesting swats. "I'm just—I didn't mean to—stop, Bee! Just text him back!"

I shake my head at him like he's a hopeless case (well, he *is*) and finally sit down at the table with my waffles.

Levi

I may need a PhD in linguistics to translate those texts, but I'll do my best.

Frantic, I scroll up. Now that I'm more awake and *aware*, I instantly see that there are close to a million typos in my previous texts. I groan.

Bee

Not my best work, I admit.

But I can assure you that, despite what you've just witnessed, I did indeed graduate high school.

Levi

I believe you. But only because you listen to good music. (People with good taste in music are the only people you can trust.)

I emailed you the list. The girls' numbers are all at the bottom, in case you need help with anything. They know to be as on-call as they can.

Bee

Awesome!

I'll talk to Tracy about flowers tomorrow, and market prices, and if she can help out/donate some of her time.

Levi

Great! You can use the office as much as you like. I'll give you a key.

Bee

No worries!

I can do almost everything from my house.

Levi

☺

Oh, and I forgot to tell you, the flowers you designed
look amazing. Your boss was right to take advantage of
your talent.

                                                    Bee
                                        Really? Thank you!

Levi

I'm not kidding/exaggerating, in case you're wondering.

                                                    Bee
                                                  I was.

Levi

Stop that. It's as bad as you saying you're sorry all the
time.

                                                    Bee
                                                  Sorry.

Levi

Ha. Very funny, Banana.

                                                    Bee
                                        God Almighty.

Levi

Okay, that was sort of a joke guess. Kind of. Who knows? Maybe your mom really craved bananas when she was pregnant with you. Besides, fruit names never stopped celebrities! Apple Martin, Banana Wescott, etc.

Also, did I say thank you yet? If not, thanks.

Bee

NICE TRY! My mom craved peanuts and ice cream when she was pregnant with me.

I don't remember if you thanked me, but it doesn't matter. I'm so excited to start.

Levi

You're the best.

I feel my breathing pause and my stomach coil up—without permission, might I add. Lord help me. I write back, a simple response, the only one I can come up with, and immediately get to work on his list.

Bee

Oh, hush.

It's amazing what can happen in a week, using the power of a list and a budget and a company to back you up. Here's an idea of what it was like:

- Ivanka chose all her colors and flowers.

- We've attempted to pick the right dress, with no luck. *Yet.*

- Tracy has agreed to teach me how to arrange centerpieces, as well as boutonnieres and flower crowns. (And to help with whatever I can't finish in time.)

- My mother and Levi's mother met, and you could say it was love at first sight. One moment, Suzie was handing over a box of vases ("From Ivanka," she said. "She wanted to know if you could make the arrangements in these."), and the next she was talking to my mom about gardening. I don't really know how it happened; the moment is a blur in my memories.

- My mom, Suzie, and I set up a faux wedding ceremony and reception on Friday night—exactly eight days before the big day—and popped a bottle of champagne to celebrate our accomplishments.

- I Skype Gretchen approximately four times to update her on the happenings while perusing the internet for tutorials on arranging centerpieces.

It is now Monday, which means I have not seen Levi in exactly five days, and this frustrates me. (*Unlimited* frustration, I say!) I'm leaving Tracy's to meet Ivanka for our second round of dress shopping—in exactly thirty minutes. As I rush to hang up my apron and gather my purse, Tracy calls after me. "Don't forget to bring the vases on Friday morning! I need to go over the basics with you!"

I wave to her over my shoulder in response, shooting out the door. Thirty-seven traffic-filled minutes later I burst through another door, into the boutique dress shop in Del Mar. I spy Ivanka to the side, looking at two dresses set up for her on the rack. A few feet away from her is a girl around my age, wearing a gold, shimmering shirt and torn jeans, with thick hair that turns to waves at the bottom. (It's dyed blue.)

I smile when she notices me and shake the hand she sticks out to me.

"You must be Bee," she says. "I'm Elle."

"Nice to finally meet you," I say. "I think you're the last of the volunteers I've met."

Elle nods, passing her wallet back and forth in her hands. "I was out of town last week. Levi told me all about you, how you stepped in for the wedding. Awesome job you've done so far."

Her words make me feel warm and fuzzy. "Thank you."

Ivanka looks over her shoulder. "Bee, what do you think of these?"

I put my arm around her in a quick hug and say, "These are stunning. Have you tried them on?"

"Not yet." She looks worryingly at the price tag. "But it is too much—"

"Nonsense." I take both dresses off the rack and start toward the back of the store. "Don't worry about that, remember?"

As I'm getting her set up with an employee near the dressing rooms, Levi calls. "Hey," I answer, turning toward a quieter spot of the store.

"Hey, Brennica."

"I'm sorry," I drawl, with what I hope is an extra dash of attitude. "You have the wrong number."

Levi chuckles. "No, I'm pretty sure this is Brennica. Long blond hair, glasses, wears jeans every day, likes to smile, is very short."

"Oh!" I gasp, faking a sudden realization. "I think you mean Bee!"

"No, I mean Brennica. I definitely mean Brennica."

"Okay," I say, finally losing it to laughter. "Cut the BS, Levi. What's up?"

For a second I think he might cooperate, but then he says, "I wanted to let Brennica know that she'll need to wear something more formal to the fundraiser on Saturday. Something not-jeans. If this is a problem, I can fund a nice dress."

"Shut up. You'll do no such thing. What are you going to wear?"

"It's easy for men. We only have so many options."

"So, should I wear a dress or a skirt or like . . . a *formal* dress? Are you asking me to prom?"

This gets an outright laugh from him. "A dress would be fine, and no, this is not prom. My mom tells me Anthropologie is a good fit for these things, although I have no idea what that means. Is she talking about a major in anthropology? If so, we don't have that kind of time."

"It's a store, Levi."

"Right, right." He's driving now—I can hear a little echo from his headphones and the white noise from passing cars. "Will you be sure to pass this information on to Brennica?"

I groan, but I also can't help the laugh that escapes me. "Sure, Levi, I'll tell Brennica."

"So you concede!"

"No. But nice try. Your persistence is admirable."

"Bee!" I look up at the sound of Elle's voice. She points to the platform in the middle of the dressing room area, and there stands Ivanka, a perfect little fairy in white. The dress is dazzling, strapless and falling well past her feet, the train flowing behind. The entire skirt is laced with beads that catch the sunlight streaming through the front windows.

Ivanka stares at herself in the three mirrors, glimmering and ethereal and fighting back tears, and clasps her hand over her mouth.

"This," she says, choking on the word.

"Hold on, Levi. I'll call you back." Slipping my phone into my pocket, I step onto the platform with Ivanka. I whisper her name in awe, staring at her reflection with everyone else in the store. "You are such a beautiful bride."

"Is it good?" she whispers.

"It's freaking perfect. Ivanka, you're the Czech princess." I smile and wipe away the two tears that are slowly sliding down her cheeks. "If Augustin doesn't faint from your beauty the moment he lays eyes on you, I will be thoroughly disappointed."

Ivanka laughs. "He is a strong man. He will pretend he is not crying."

I laugh with her, my arm around her shoulder. "If you're sure, we can buy it today. Elle?" I ask, just to be sure she has the company card.

"Yep." Elle nods, her expression appraising. "It really is great, Ivanka."

The bride hugs me again, the beads on the dress making the prettiest clinking noise, and then heads back into her dressing room. With the bright lights of the dressing room beating down on my head, I prop my shoulder against the wall and dial Levi. "Sorry to leave so suddenly. Ivanka found her dress," I say when he answers.

"Good!" There's a smile in his voice. "Hey, Bee, tell me you're free tonight."

"Um, maybe?" Thud-*thud*, thud-*thud*, thud-*thud*, goes my heart.

"Come over. Mom's making her famous chicken and dumplings for Ivanka and Augustin. We'd love to have you with us since you've been such a big part of the wedding."

"I don't think we have any family plans tonight, so it should be fine."

"Yes!" he exclaims, making my heart leap. And when he says goodbye, part of me wishes I'd told him that my heart is a wild creature and that I want to have dinner with him every night and that I love his mom and that today feels like flying.

chapter 18

QUEUED:
SUSPENSION
BY MAE

IT'S BEEN A while since I last ate chicken and dumplings, but I'm pretty sure Suzie's are the best in the world.

I'm sitting beside Levi under the stars in his backyard, laughing at the stories Augustin and Ivanka tell about the first time they met, how they fell in love. Levi laughs as well, and when his head moves his hair bounces with a life of its own. He's relaxed, and I'm smitten. It's no longer just a possibility; I'm well aware that I'm falling hard. I might try to pick myself back up, but let's face it: I like it here. From this angle, I can see the stars and the sky spinning around me, and the universe doesn't feel so large, and I think I might know myself in a bigger way.

But in the same way that everything feels good, it also hurts. My chest aches and my heart is a little too big, and when Levi puts his arm around my shoulders and leans in to ask how my food is, my throat strangles, and I don't know how to speak.

(What are words, anyway?)

After barely getting myself together, two seconds too late, I smile up at him. (*Oh, God, no, not the dazzling eyes. DON'T LOOK AT HIS EYES, BEE.*) "It's delicious." I only *just* manage to not say something stupid. (Like, "You're delicious.") I fixate on Suzie so I don't fall into the abyss. "Suzie, really, you're amazing."

Suzie winks at me. "I'm glad you could make it tonight," she says.

"Me, too."

Ivanka puts her hand over her fiancé's, grinning. "Augustin has already asked four times to see the dress. I tell him 'no', but he does not listen!"

I laugh. "Come on, Augustin. Play fair."

"I am too happy," he protests. "Was she the most beautiful creature you ever saw?"

"Yes," I say, although I'm lying, because Levi is the most beautiful creature I've ever seen. "She's an angel." I take the last bite of chicken and set my spoon down. "When does your family get into town?"

"Friday morning, early," Ivanka says. "I miss them very much."

I smile sympathetically, trying to imagine moving so far away from my family. "I'm excited to meet them."

"I've already told them about you, the girl Bonita who likes to be called Bee. They cannot wait to see you."

I am so glad I don't have food in my mouth right now—I would have choked. Suzie puts her head in her hands, as if sharing in my exasperation. And Levi . . . well, I've never seen him look so smug.

I realize, with my stomach clenching tight, that there are a lot of things I haven't seen him do, a lot of things I don't know about him—and I want to know them all.

"Thank you, Ivanka," I say, giving Levi the Death Glare. "Your wedding will be a great success, thanks to everyone giving their time and energy. I'm so excited for you both."

"Would you like to stay for dessert?" Suzie asks, staring to clear the plates.

"Thank you, but we should leave," she says, and nods at Augustin. "I have to hide my dress from this one."

We say our goodbyes at the front door. I'm watching them drive away, getting ready to grab my purse and leave, when Suzie drags me back into the house. "*You*, at least, must stay for dessert!" she tells me.

I smile and nod in assent. "Okay, if you insist."

"I do," she says with finality.

"As do I," Levi adds from the kitchen. I find him standing at the sink, sleeves of his orange sweater rolled up to his elbows, scrubbing away at a plate. He grins at me over his shoulder. "Just so you know, your phone rang."

I excuse myself to the front room and dig through my purse. Gretchen called twice in the last three minutes, probably because I texted her before dinner—with all the calm of a hysterical puppy—to tell her where I was going. And since I hear Levi and Suzie talking, their voices quiet, I click on Gretchen's name and put the phone to my ear.

She answers in two seconds flat. "Bernice, you better have good news for me."

"It's just dinner with his mom and Ivanka and Augustin," I whisper, trying not to sound exasperated. I suddenly feel exasperated. (I think this is what comes with wanting something you cannot have.)

"So what?!" she squeals. "Are you still there?"

"Bee?" Levi's voice scares me. I jump, heart thudding, and face him. (His eyes are laughing at me.) "You okay?"

"It's Gretchen," I mouth.

"Let me talk to her," he says, just as Gretchen screeches into my ear, "Is that him?! Let me talk to him!"

I laugh, overwhelmed, and hand him the phone. "The feeling is mutual."

He puts the phone to his ear. "The famous Gretchen!" He smiles at me and continues, "It's good to put a voice to the name. Now I just need a face." He pulls the phone away and looks at the picture I have of Gretchen in the background. "Ah, got it," he tells her. He's silent for a few moments, his eyes still laughing. "We're about to have dessert." Another pause. "I heard you love Bon Iver," he says finally, and laughs. (I just *knew* that was coming.) "Yeah, I've been trying to get her to love them, but she's stubborn."

I roll my eyes at him.

He smirks. (Dear Levi, could you please stop giving me heart palpitations? Sincerely, The Nameless Creature) "Yeah, she just did."

I gape. "What are you talking about?"

"Gretchen predicted you'd roll your eyes."

I shake my head. "This is hopeless."

He's back to Gretchen now, so I sit down on the couch and listen. "What has she told you about me? I assume since you know who I am that she's talked about me," he says, a bit quieter.

I sit up straight. Levi's nodding his head into the phone, grinning, laughing at his own jokes, at hers.

I want to die.

"Oh, you know, that you're best friends and all that. That she misses you every day. That you're practically twins." Levi pauses again, his face growing serious, eyes narrowing.

Without even a glance in my direction, he turns away from me.

"Hey!" I protest. He holds up one finger, so I sit back and watch him, all tall and lean and pretty as he rests against the door frame that leads to the kitchen. Eventually, after a few mumbled responses and nods, he turns back to me.

"Nice to finally talk to you, Gretchen," he says, and hands the phone back to me.

Yep, I'm dead. "Gretchen, what on earth?" I meet Levi's gaze, surprised to find him already looking at me. No, more than that: He's studying me. Not smiling, but happy. Curious, but not invasive. His lips part like he's contemplating saying something, but then he turns away from me.

My whole body is one giant, pounding heartbeat.

Gretchen's laugh rings in my ear, but I can barely hear it over my rushing blood. She says, "It's nothing, really. Just . . . talking."

I want to strangle her. "As dead as Jay Gatsby, Gretchen," I threaten.

"Your attempts to terrorize me are futile because you love me too much. Now, go. Be charming. And snatch him up, because if you don't, I will. He likes *Bon Iver*. Also, I think you're crap."

And just like that . . . she hangs up.

Levi comes back into the room to find me staring at my phone, shocked. "Here, have some pie."

I take the plate from him absently, but his laugh brings me back. "Sorry," I say. "She drives me crazy, but I love her."

He nods, as if completely understanding, and then motions toward the back door. We walk, past the patio table and onto the path that curves around the yard, coming to a little double-seated swing, between two looming rose bushes. I sit down, and he joins me, scooping a fork-full of pie into his mouth. "So. Gretchen. How'd you meet her?"

I shrug. "She lived here, for a long time. My parents knew her parents. And then her dad had to move for his business. It wasn't until then that we realized we couldn't live without each other. Like soulmates, but . . . not?"

Levi laughs. "I mean, I only just met her, but I'd say she's a keeper."

You're a keeper. "What about you? Your friends?"

"I have a lot of good friends now, but . . . " He shrugs. "This might sound stupid, but it's hard for me to make friends."

I scrunch my nose up at him. "Lies."

"I promise it's not. I'm only just learning how. I didn't do much friend-making in high school. Everyone around me was a little like my father: insincere, arrogant, self-centered. Maybe it was just the school I was at . . . I don't know. But if there's anyone I don't want to be, any type of person I don't want to hang out with, it's my dad." Levi studies me from the corner of his eye. "It's not that he's a terrible man. He's not the monster under my bed; I'm not afraid of him. He just . . . he breaks hearts, you know? He broke my mom's heart and said nothing, did nothing. He broke my heart and he didn't even know."

I breathe out heavily. "Where is he now?"

"Malibu, in a huge mansion, with however many girlfriends he wants. It's like he turned fifteen and then never aged mentally."

I fake-gag. "Do you see him often?"

"He comes to TCP events." Levi sets his empty plate on the ground. "You should know something, Bee."

I lean forward, hands on my knees, the empty pie plate in my lap. I'm stuffed and comfortable and the air is cool. I don't want to move ever again.

Levi takes a deep breath in and says, "I didn't found The Color Project, Bee."

I turn in surprise. (Although it's hard to look at him and I want to close my eyes or disappear or make him disappear. His hair is so touchable and his lips are pursed like they want to be kissed and they want to be kissed by me.) "You didn't?"

"I mean, it's mine now. But my father started it, years ago,

before the divorce. It was under another name, Orville Center
for the Needy. He totally sounds like an arrogant jackass, huh?"

I bite back a laugh. "Yeah, he kind of does."

"When my dad told me about the divorce, he tried to bribe
me into 'being okay' by offering me anything I wanted. I took
my time . . . . I dunno, maybe I just wanted to mess with him.
There wasn't much I wanted, anyway. Especially not his typical
rich divorce bribes—a shiny car, a yacht, a new gaming system.
I wanted something that wouldn't remind me of my dad and
his money every time I looked at it. Something I could make
my own."

I stare at him, openly. (I'm too impressed to care.)

"I didn't have a single idea what I wanted until the week before
the divorce. My mom was on her last few days volunteering for
the original charity, and I guess . . . I guess that made us realize
we didn't want him to ruin a good thing with his selfishness and
greed. So I asked him for the charity, and he gave it to me. It's
under my mom's name, but she put me in charge of basically
everything. We did everything we could to keep the original
sponsors and donators. My dad pays rent every month, but
as soon as we're independent, I'm moving to a bigger facility.
Somewhere we can have our fundraisers *and* our interviews, if
possible."

I'm still gaping. I shut my mouth but continue to stare.

"I hope that doesn't . . . I don't know . . . make things weird,"
he adds.

I laugh outright. "That doesn't make anything weird. You
turned down everything else in the world to run a charity.
Do you know how much I respect you for that?" I'm mostly
whispering now because I can't believe I said the words out
loud. (*Is* this *that thing they call confidence?*)

"You respect me?" He laughs. As if this was *funny*.

"Duh, of course I do. Who wouldn't?"

"Um, my dad?"

"But we already established that he's an arrogant jackass. Do I seem like an arrogant jackass to you?"

He chuckles. "No."

"Then you have no choice but to believe me."

"Fine." His expression changes then, but I can't quite pinpoint it. Then he says, "Can I tell you something?"

I nod.

"I feel like I've known you longer than most people in my life."

"I know," I whisper.

"It's kind of weird."

"And yet," I say, looking at the stars above us, thankful that Levi is on this spinning planet with me, "it's not weird at all."

He sits back, the swing moving with him, and looks up with me. "The stars again."

"Yeah. They're always the first thing I think about when I go outside. Even in broad daylight."

"Same here. After our conversation, I did a little bit of research. That one right there is Orion." He points, tracing the constellation, and when I scoot in close to him, I can see it.

"Ah! With the line of three stars?"

"Yeah."

"Any others?" I don't want to move, with my shoulder pressed up against his chest and my elbow against his thigh and our faces angled just right so that they're not touching (but they might as well be).

"Don't remember them." We laugh, and he drops his arm, and I regret not paying more attention in astronomy last semester. "One day, maybe, I'll learn them well enough to teach you."

I nod, not thinking about the stars anymore, and dare enough to lean my shoulder against his. *I'll be here*, I think. I close my eyes and try not to dream about stealing kisses in a world made of flowers and stars.

chapter 19

QUEUED:
Stars (Hold On)
by Youngblood Hawke

On Friday morning, eight o'clock sharp, I deliver the vases to Tracy. She's drinking coffee from a massive mug, a green-and-blue-striped shawl covering her shoulders. She looks up at me, raising her arrangement recipe book in salute. "Good morning."

"Morning," I say, pushing my glasses up my nose once I set down the box. "Here they are. How long until opening?"

"I set it back to ten so we can get everything done." Tracy taps the glass edge of one vase. "These are pretty. Want to grab the flowers at the back of the cooler and then we can get started?"

I nod, grab my apron, and get to work. I'm unusually jittery, rushing with nerves and excitement. I want to create these centerpieces, and I want them to be beautiful. I want them to make Ivanka smile. (Also: I want to impress Levi.)

I drag out the wedding flowers. Pink peonies—the last of

the season; wax flower; lisianthus, in lavender and white; pink spray roses; bright orange dahlias. There is also white misty and some leather. I stand back and watch Tracy as she looks over everything, as if trying to decide what to grab first.

She finally steps up to the worktable with two peonies, one lavender lisianthus, a handful of wax flower, and misty. I lean over the edge of the table, watching as she cuts them down to size—expertly and on the first try—and places the flowers in the vase at an angle. When she looks up at me, I'm already desperate to try it out.

I fill the first vase, my fingers learning the curve of the petals and the different feel of each stem. The textures relax me, and the sensation of the knife in my hand as I slice off the old ends makes me feel like I'm in control. I lower the flowers into the vase at the approximate angle Tracy did, gauging the weight of the peonies and the feathery buds of the misty to see where they will fall. I stuff it full of filler and leather, make sure it's tight, and then turn to Tracy with the vase in my hands.

She tsks. "Stunning, Bee. Really. Just move this one here," she adds, grabbing the peony and adjusting it ever so slightly, "and add a spray rose here." She grabs and cuts a spray and puts it into the corner, where it fits perfectly with all its little buds. "Perfect. You're a natural."

"Really?" A bubbling sensation lifts my chest. "Are you serious?"

"What?" She grins, stepping backward, out of the way, as if she wants to give me room. "Doesn't it feel natural when you hold the flowers, the way the knife curves against your palm?"

"Well." I pause, gaping at her. "Actually, it kind of does."

"Don't let me keep you," she says, her smile softening into something like pride.

After Tracy escapes into the back office to do paperwork, I busy myself making four identical arrangements. All of them beam at me on the table as I finally take a breather and a drink of water. "Eight more to go," I call back to her.

She peeks around the corner, grinning. "They look excellent. Remember you have to learn how to make boutonnieres today so you can make them at home later. Remind me an hour before your shift is up."

I finish two more arrangements before it's time for me to open the shop. I begrudgingly drag myself away from the work table. Tracy's promise to teach me something new is what spurs me on the rest of the day, through cleaning and broken buckets, grumpy customers and shattered glass. I don't get why today had to be the busiest of the week, but with every new flower I trim and customer I help, I'm reminded of why I'm here. It brings a sort of comfort to me. I want this; I want to learn.

The crowd finally lulls around two o'clock. Tracy wraps up her current arrangement, sets it on the cooler rack, and sits beside the ribbon table.

The process for boutonnieres, while time-consuming, is very straightforward. There is a lot of wire, ribbons, and green tape. I twist the ribbons to make three loops on each side, using thin wire to hold it in place and create a tiny bow. Everything revolves around the little rose bud, popped off the stem and stuck through with another wire. The other pieces—the bow, the filler, and the greens—are wrapped with tape and into a little curly-Q at the end.

I leave at three, my fingers sore from ripping tape and folding wire. I have four more boutonnieres to make when I get home, so I put all the supplies into the back of my car and close the trunk. I'm getting into the driver seat when I see Tracy running after me, another bucket of flowers in her hand.

She comes to a stop by my door, huffing and leaning against it. "I forgot—I need you to make the bride's bouquet."

"What?!" I suck in a breath. "I've never made—"

"No, I know. If I see it tomorrow and it doesn't look good, I'll fix it. But I need you to try tonight. I already have to make the flower crown because we didn't have time for me to teach you, and you have five more centerpieces to make tomorrow. Unless you can get them all done tonight."

I push down my sudden outbreak of panic. "Okay, okay, I'll try."

She breathes out deeply. "Thank you. I'm just too busy with the other wedding."

No kidding. I smile thinly, putting my car into gear. "Thanks for your help, Tracy. I know Ivanka is going to be so excited."

"I can't wait to see pictures," she says, and moves out of the way so I can back out.

I wait until I'm stuck in ridiculous traffic before I pull out my phone to call Levi. "Levi, I think I'm dying," I say, so fast I don't even think he said hello. "Is there anyone who can come over tonight and help me? I have a billion things to do before tomorrow."

"I can help you," he says. "I got the catering for tomorrow fixed—did I tell you about that? Big fiasco. Anyway. I'll just pick up my dry cleaning and come over."

I breathe out. "Really? Are you sure? Tomorrow's a big day and I don't want to bother you. I thought you might be at the office and could send someone over. I just got stressed . . . and there were a bunch of upset customers ordering for *funerals*, which made everything worse. But I don't know why I'm freaking out because it's not that big of a deal. I can get it done, I just . . . " I shrug to myself in the car and then realize Levi can't see it. "I don't know," I finish. "I'll just call one of the other girls, it's no big deal. Sorry to bug—"

"Bee!" he yells over my rambling, and then I realize he's been talking to me this whole time. "Don't you dare call the other girls. I remember recently a certain someone stepped in and helped me when I was stressed, so now I'm going to return the favor. Where should I meet you? And what do you need help with?"

I smile. I can feel the warmth spreading under my skin. I want to hug him. Indefinitely. (Forever.) "I'll be at my house if that works. Otherwise, I can drive to you."

"No, that works. Text me your address."

"I will. And it's to do with the table arrangements, the bouquet, and the boutonnieres. I just need someone to stand with me and fold ribbons and cut wires and hold things. I'm still new to this, so I'm afraid I'm going to screw everything up."

"Bee, stop." His voice is so commanding that I do. I stop. He clears his throat. "You've got to take this one thing at a time. We'll start with what's most important, and work our way down. I can hire another florist if we run out of time."

"Okay," I say. I take a deep breath in and breathe out. "I'll be home in thirty minutes. See you whenever you can get there."

"See you soon."

Thankfully, I'm able to get home five minutes earlier than expected. (A miracle.) I pull into the roundabout and wave to my sister, who's sitting on the front porch with a book in her hand.

"Hey, Astrid! Will you help me?"

She lopes over to me. "What's up?"

"I need you to carry these two buckets in." I open my trunk and set the buckets into the crooks of her arms. "Send Millie out here, too, will you?"

Astrid wanders off, watching her step so she doesn't splatter peony blooms all over the porch. A few moments later, Millie runs out of the house. "Hey Bee! Guess who's here!"

I look up quickly, brushing my (bothersome) hair from my eyes. Millie streaks past me, grabbing the basket of supplies I hold out to her. Levi's on my front porch, hair a mess, hands in his pockets. He starts to walk toward me.

(*Oh, God.*)

"Oh, hi," I say. "I didn't even see your car." But when I look around, I see it right on the street, as obvious as the GIANT palm trees in our front yard.

He shakes his head, half a smile lifting the corners of his lips. "No need to stress, Bee. We'll get this done." And he hugs me, as if that's super normal, as if it isn't going to squash my lungs and paralyze my limbs. I lean against him like the helpless child I am and heave a sigh.

"Thanks," I say. I grab the remaining bucket and the second supply basket, but he takes them from me. I just look at him in response. I'm afraid if I open my tired mouth, I'll blurt out something stupid (like, "I kind of love you"), or if I try to grab them back I'll trip over my own feet. So I let him go and shut my trunk and follow him inside.

I shut the front door behind me, and when I turn, Millicent is smiling dreamily at Levi. "Levi met Dad," she says to me.

"Oh?" This news wakes me up. "And how did that go?"

Levi cracks a smile. "He told me he was disappointed that I haven't seen *Back to the Future*, but he was pretty impressed with my knowledge of Adam Ant and Danny Elfman."

I roll my eyes. "He's my sci-fi buddy. I get all my nerdiness from him."

Levi follows me out to the backyard, where I set everything on the patio table. "I'd like to watch *Back to the Future* now. I'm feeling . . . out of the loop."

"Don't worry," I reassure him. "Don't say anything, but . . . I haven't seen it either."

Levi clears his throat. "Speaking of . . . "

"Hey, Bee." My dad puts his arm around my shoulder. "How was work?"

I hug him tight around the middle. "Really busy, actually. Aren't *you* supposed to be at work today?"

"Nah, I got the day off." He ruffles my hair.

"Papa, please." I duck my head. "It doesn't matter how old I get . . . "

My dad winks at Levi—*winks!* "You'll never get out of the hair-ruffle," he says to me.

Levi smiles at me, eyes lit by the pretty sun. (Or maybe it's that his pretty eyes are lit by the sun?) "It makes you look like a wild pixie."

I reach up and flatten my hair. "Gee. Thanks."

Papa puts his hand on Levi's shoulder, glancing between us. "You want anything to drink? Root beer? Orange juice?"

"Only if you put it in her sippy cup," Astrid comments, passing through the room. Her grin is smug.

I choose (with some difficulty) to ignore her. "I'll have a root beer, if there's enough."

Levi nods. "I'll have one, too."

I set up the buckets, my dad brings root beer to us in the mason jars my mom saves as cups, and Levi sits patiently, waiting for my instruction. I take a sip of the cold drink and sigh happily. "Okay. Levi. First, I need to teach you how to make bows."

(Ah, the smirk. It returns.) "How manly," he says, deepening his voice an octave.

"I know," I say. "You should feel *so* privileged."

"Dude, yes."

I laugh, holding up a bow for him to see, and launch into an explanation. I show him an example and watch closely as he tries his own. Soon he has the hang of it, making the eight bows I need in rapid succession. While he's busy, I pop four rose buds and loop a wire through each one. Levi sets down the ribbon and, catching on, starts to copy me with the wires, the leather, the green tape.

And so it begins. It takes us half the time to get through the boutonnieres, but we slow down again when I get to the bridal bouquet. My fingers, while accustomed to working with flowers, are not used to holding the stems like this. My wrists start to ache after a few minutes. Levi puts down the ribbon and tape and reaches for the buds, lightly covering the tops of the flowers, keeping them steady for me.

"Damn, Bee. I don't know much about bridal bouquets—"

I give him a look.

He grins. It's a sheepish grin. "Okay, I don't know *anything* about bridal bouquets. But this is really beautiful."

I fumble. "Thanks." My vision narrows as I add flowers and filler inch by inch. With Levi there to hold everything down and fix strays, however, my load becomes lighter and I'm finished in two minutes. I grasp the stems as Levi ties everything off and cuts the stems down so they're even. Then I hold out my arm and we look at my newest "masterpiece".

"Wow." Levi sits back on the bench and whistles. "Bee. I think we have something here."

"What?" His words distract me from my (relatively pleased) inspection.

"I mean, like I said, I know nothing about this stuff—I work with cars, you know?" He laughs. "But." He lifts a finger to make his point. "I *know* when I'm seeing talent."

"Thank you," I say quietly, but I'm grinning. "A-ny-way," I say with emphasis, setting the bouquet in its square vase. There's a bit of water at the bottom, just enough to keep it alive and healthy, but not enough to seep into the ribbon. "Will you put this in the fridge? Erm, the extra one in the garage. Millie can show you."

My sister pops her head around the corner upon hearing her name. "Yeah, I sure can. Right this way, Mr. Orville."

He grimaces. "Don't even go there, Millie."

She laughs and flounces her hair as he follows her into the house, out of sight. I stare after them, half thinking about Levi in the sunshine, half thinking, *Oh my gosh, my sister is going to be such a flirt.*

While I wait for them to come back, I start on the rest of the centerpieces. I sense my dad watching from the door, and after a few moments, he joins me.

"Bee, is there something going on?" He clears his throat. "Between you two?"

I blush. "No," I say, because it's the truth.

Dad looks at me pointedly. "But you want it to."

My fingers idle, and I drop my hands to the table in a gesture of surrender. "Am I really that obvious?" I whisper.

"Maybe not to him. But I know my little girl. You look at him the same way you look at Henry Cavill on the TV."

"*Ohmygosh*, DAD."

"What?" He laughs when I punch his arm.

"I'll stick you with these pins—just try me!"

He sticks his tongue out. "No thank you." Then he nudges my arm. "Just be sure to tell me if something happens. I want to be *in the know* so I can kick that boy right in the baby-maker if he tries to hurt you."

I laugh so hard at this, I feel my face getting red.

My dad raises one eyebrow. "I was serious."

"I know, Papa. I know." I wipe my eyes free of tears.

"What's going on?" Levi asks, coming outside again. He looks at me curiously. "I keep finding you with your face all red."

I gasp out a ridiculous sort of squeak and say, "Um, my dad was just . . . being weird." I put both hands on my dad's back and push him toward the door. "He was also just leaving. Go on, shoo-shoo. I need to work."

Papa shrugs, patting Levi's arm on his way back into the house. "Don't let her eat you alive," he whispers at the last second.

"Whose side are you on?" I shout, then drop my head in my hands, listening to Levi's quiet chuckle. The door shuts but I'm still hiding. (And I'm still reeling from my dad using the words "baby-maker" in reference to Levi.)

Speaking of . . . He puts his hand on my shoulder. "Bee," he says, and when I don't move, he drapes one arm around me. (Nonononono noooooooooooo.) (But also: YES.) "You look embarrassed," he says, teasing in his voice.

"Let's just say my dad has no shame, living in a house of mostly girls." I look up and grin. I can't help it. Smiling is my mouth's automatic response to seeing his face.

"Oh, it's the same with my mom, having lived with only boys for nineteen years."

"I'm glad someone shares my pain."

He smiles and nods at the work table. "Can I do anything else?"

Just like that, I'm back in stress mode. I reach for one of the last buckets. "If you could cut three of each of these flowers to the same length as my examples, that'd be great."

He gets to work, his fingers quick with the knife. I arrange the flowers as he passes them to me. Eventually, I break the silence between us. "How are things coming along for the fundraiser?"

"Great, actually." Levi passes me a stem of hot pink sprays. "Aside from the catering mix-up." He glances at me. "Seriously, dude, you have no idea how easy you've made this for me."

"It's my pleasure."

He cuts two more stems down before saying, "Did you figure out what to wear?"

"Actually, I have two dresses I'm deciding between." I set the last flower into the last vase and sigh happily. "Done!"

Levi stands back and looks at my handiwork. "Ivanka is going to love this." He pauses, his thumb brushing a tiny spray rose. When he opens his mouth again, his words surprise me. "Once we put these away, can I see the dresses?"

"I mean . . . um . . . " I clear my throat. "Yeah. Sure." I gather two vases and gesture for Levi to do the same. We put them in the garage fridge (which barely closes, it's so full) and head back inside. "Here, I'll grab the dresses." I reach my door, opening it, about to let Levi in when—

I jump back. "Um, I forgot to clean my room. You can't come in."

Levi shrugs. "I don't care."

"Well, I do."

"You've been busy lately. It's understandable."

"Yes, but I still don't want you to see it. It's . . . *awful.*" Okay, it's not really, but it's bad enough to be embarrassing. "I'll be right out."

He stays obediently in the hallway. I grab the dresses on their hangers, and a few seconds later I'm standing in front of him, holding them up for him to see. One is navy blue with an empire waist and loose pleats in the skirt. The other is green and fitted, patterned lace forming to its shape. It's a total hip-hugger, and when Levi immediately points to it, I blush. (*Why am I blushing?!*)

"This one. Absolutely, one hundred percent."

"Really?" I squeak out.

"Yeah. That green will look beautiful on you."

I think my throat is closing, but I force words out anyway.

"That's . . . sweet." *Oh gosh, Bee, keep it together. He just called the dress beautiful and you're acting like he proposed.*

"Trust me?" he asks.

The question tugs at the corners of my mouth until I'm grinning. "I think so..."

"Good. Because if you don't wear it . . . " He gives me a pointed look.

"What? Are you threatening me?"

He laughs. "God, no. I'm just . . . well, yeah, actually. I am. Watch out—you don't want to incur my incredible, overwhelming, and absolutely terrible disappointment when you show up in a dress just as beautiful."

I roll my eyes, but I'm laughing, too. "You're the worst at threats, you know." I dodge his hands, which are—to my absolute horror—reaching out to tickle me. "Don't!"

"You're no fun, Bambina."

"Stop!" I shriek as he reaches for me again. I've cornered myself, but I'm quick to open my door and rush inside, shutting it in his face. "My name," I yell, "is NOT Bambina!"

I soak in his laugh through the door as I lean against it and hug the dresses to my chest. In the heat of the evening, with sunshine littering my room, I imagine that his laugh commands the sun's rays, and the sky is bursting with our joy.

chapter 20

QUEUED:
HARBOUR LIGHTS
BY A SILENT FILM

IT'S NINE O'CLOCK in the morning and I'm late for work.

Scratch that: I'm late for everything. Since I've pushed work back by a half hour, I'll be not-so-fashionably late to the fundraiser. My dress is hanging in the back of my car, and I turned off the music a long time ago because my head is pounding. I hardly slept at all last night, stuck on the wedding, bursting with ideas and the WORST headache ever. I even *dreamed* about destroying the wedding.

So this day is off to a fabulous start.

I pull into the parking lot and run like a madwoman into the shop. I gasp out insane-sounding apologies about traffic and the zipper on my brand new dress, but Tracy just waves her hand at me. "Be quiet and work."

I smile nervously, grab a bucket from the cooler, and start.

The morning goes by much too quickly. Between managing

the front desk and changing out the buckets and loading up my car with the arrangements I made yesterday in the shop, I can hardly breathe. I think it's my clothes, despite the fact that I chose sweat pants and a loose T-shirt. (Actually, they chose me. They're what was left of my clean clothes. Somebody help me.)

Tracy kicks me out of the shop at eleven-thirty, exactly fifteen minutes after I was *supposed* to leave. "Get out of here, crazy. You're going to miss everything."

"Thank you, Tracy," I say, my body filling with relief, even as I think, *Tell me something I don't know.*

I drop the vases and flower crown and boutonnieres and bridal bouquet off at Levi's house. He's already gone, as I expected, but Suzie and Elle and my family are in the back, setting up.

The whole place is coming together like a beautiful dream. Lights are strung. Tables are set up by the back door. Tom is helping unfold chairs and place them in a line. It's really nice to see him focusing on something that makes him happy. (Read: Anything that's not Andrea.) He smiles as Elle attempts to open a chair that doesn't want to budge. She curses loudly and colorfully, eliciting a gasp from the corner of the backyard.

Suddenly there's Albert, practically leaping across the grass, pulling glitter from his pockets and tossing it into the air over Elle's head.

She sputters, waving her hands around. "Aaaallllllbbeeerrrt!"

Tom gapes. "What the hell?" Then Albert scampers off, and Tom's laughing, taking the chair from Elle. He yanks it open.

Elle sputters again and blinks hard. "Thanks."

"Yeah," he says.

I roll my eyes and set the three vases on the closest table. My mom and Suzie are there, wrapping silverware in napkins. My mom kisses my cheek.

"Just set them on the front porch," Suzie says, giving me a quick hug before bustling away. "I'll bring them out back. I know you need to go. And you can change here, too, if you need to."

After a few trips back and forth, I set the last of the flower-related items on the front porch, grab my dress and makeup bag and shoes and jewelry, and dash inside. I find the bathroom empty. (Thankfully.)

I lock myself inside.

Take a deep breath.

And another.

You're late, I tell myself. *Hurry, Bee!*

But I just stand there, staring at my red face, puffy with dehydration, and my heaving chest.

I realize, a little too late, that I am terrified about the fundraiser.

Terrified I'll make a fool out of myself in front of all these wealthy, refined men and women who are willing to drop thousands of dollars on a painting.

Terrified to wear this pretty dress in front of a pretty boy. (My pretty boy.)

Terrified my feelings will take a swan dive off a cliff without my permission.

What do *I* know about these things?

So I call Gretchen. (Obviously.) She answers so fast I wonder if she's been waiting by the phone. "Dude, you better not be calling me from the fundraiser."

"I'm not," I say. And, of course, I start to cry.

"What's wrong?" Gretchen's voice is instantly soft. "Bee?"

"I'm freaking out, okay?" I sniffle. "It's ridiculous, I know it is, but I'm totally panicking. I've never done anything like this before, and the little sleep I got last night was filled with terrible dreams about the wedding failing, and I'm so nervous I'm going to trip or say something stupid. Levi is in charge of these things, people are going to be around him *constantly*, and I have nowhere else to be, so I'll be with him, too." I'm not making sense, but Gretchen doesn't seem to mind. She lets me talk, as if I'm giving a grand, important speech, rather than sniffling through a half-coherent rant. "He told me last night he thinks this green dress will look beautiful on me and I don't know what to think about that."

Gretchen sighs. "Bee, you have to keep moving. This is *vital*. Breathe. Drink water. Stop thinking about him like that. Think about the fundraiser and the amazing things you've done to get everyone to the wedding."

I sigh, painfully heavy. It wavers. It overwhelms. And then it happens: The stress glides out of me on that sigh.

Not the fear, though. The fear is still there, trapped inside my heart. (I really hope it decides to make an exit soon.)

"Okay," I say, wiping tears away. Now my face is even redder. "Can I keep you on the phone?"

"Duh." Gretchen yawns. "Don't know why I'm tired right now, but this phone call will help me stay awake while I wait for my mom to pick me up."

"Talk about work," I say. "Distract me. I need it."

So she does. I laugh at her stories of her coworkers as I pull my dress over my head. I powder my face, put on blue eye shadow and pink blush. I adjust my glasses, wipe off the excess makeup dust, and start on my hair. Gretchen's voice soothes me—even though I eventually lose track of her story—and I have no more trace of tears. I can do this. It doesn't change my fears, but I can forget them, at least for now.

Miraculously, I'm only fifteen minutes late to the event.

Everyone is already inside the auditorium, taking their seats and whispering. I flash my invitation and rush in, but there are absolutely no seats left, so I follow the usher's directions to the back. There are a few people there already, frowning at me as I stand in front of them. At least I'm short and they don't have to strain to see over my head.

Before I can even set my purse down, Levi is on stage, tall as ever, hair hastily brushed back so it doesn't flop onto his forehead. He's wearing a gray suit, one that is obviously *very* expensive and tailored to fit him perfectly. I blink. Hard. Gretchen told me to control it, to not let my stupid feelings get in the way, but I absolutely *cannot* ignore how handsome he is. That suit was made for the gods, and yet here he is, just a regular boy from Escondido, pulling it off like a pro.

He's magnificent.

At first I don't hear a single word he says. (It's the aforementioned magnificence, clouding my vision.) But then (with my eyes closed so I can *focus*) I hear about his mission and his goals, about TCP's current clients. He lists off everything he loves about his volunteers. He names them all, thanking each one individually.

But then . . . he starts talking about me.

Oh no. Absolutely not, *Levi.*

"I met a girl a few weeks ago, friend of a friend sort of thing," he begins, "and I introduced her to The Color Project. She seemed to have an interest, and I wanted to include her. I was pretty sure she would have great ideas, but in the end, she exceeded my expectations. She saved me when I thought I was going to have to say no to a couple who really just wanted to get married.

"But this girl . . . she didn't take no for an answer. She made that wedding happen. Tonight, Ivanka and Augustin are getting married, with their entire family here from Prague to celebrate with them. All because Bee, our heroine, gave up the last two weeks of her life to plan a wedding for a couple who couldn't. That's the spirit of The Color Project—that's why you're all here today."

He thanks the audience, stepping off the stage, and I'm crying (for the SECOND TIME TODAY). The lights go up, people are moving, but I can barely see through my tears. I wipe them away as best as I can and let the crowd take me.

The main room in the building is covered in art pieces, placed on the walls and on easels. People flock to them, pointing and talking and writing on the auction papers hanging beside each frame. I'm curious to see more, and also to eat (I don't remember eating today), but more than anything I need to find Levi.

He finds me first. He calls my name, his voice almost lost in the crowd, but I hear it. (Oh, I hear it.) I turn, bumping into someone, my legs threatening to twist into a pretzel and tip me backward. Levi grabs my arm, smiling, eyes alight, and tugs me into a hug. "You okay?" he asks, somewhat alarmed when he sees my face.

"No," I moan. "You made me cry." I pat my cheeks lightly, as if this will get rid of the possible tear streaks through my makeup. "Do I look terrible? Is my mascara running?"

He shakes his head. "No. You look so beautiful, Bee." He runs his thumb over my cheek (this closeness burns me) and nods. "Your mascara is fine, and I'm sorry I made you cry."

"It was beautiful. It was a good cry." I laugh, a little shaky.

His smile touches only his mouth; his eyes are searching,

uncertain. "I'm . . . um . . . I honestly don't know what to say to that."

I laugh. "Trust me, I love a good cry. I'm honored by what you said," I whisper, not sure how else to tell him.

(What I say: I'm honored.)

(What I want to say: I'm totally falling for you, you ridiculously wonderful boy.)

He's so obviously relieved by this that I laugh again. He lightly touches my shoulder. "Want to get some food? Or do you want to look at the art? I can introduce you to a few people, or we don't have to, whatever . . . " He shrugs. "Up to you."

"Food," I say. "Definitely food."

Five minutes later I'm holding a plate piled high with a sandwich and salad. I'm too jittery to sit down, so we wander among the paintings. They are beautiful, masterfully crafted, the different styles and colors calling to different parts of me. I find one toward the back of two ballerinas in dark red tutus, wrapping their laces. It's close to an impressionist style, but with a touch of modernism I can't quite place. "Levi, this is beautiful."

He smiles. "Patrick is one of our regular donators and a personal favorite among these artists."

"He's already my favorite and I'm not even halfway through."

"If you like this one, let me show you something." He takes my arm as if he's about to lead me onward, but then stops, and stands very still.

His eyes, I discover, are focused on a man. He's holding a glass of wine and flanked by two women showing so much boob that I'm afraid of accidentally seeing a nipple. I focus on the man instead, going cold when I realize how much he looks like Levi, but twenty-something years older, silver streaking his hair. His suit is fine, a dark shade of gray, almost black. The shirt beneath is red, making him look exotic with a dash of pompous.

"Levi, is that your dad?"

He groans. "Yeah. Let's go."

But Mr. Orville spots us—he's looking right at me—and smiles broadly. He's insanely handsome, the type of man you realize will always be gorgeous, no matter his age, like Brad Pitt or Jon Hamm or Hugh Jackman.

Mr. Orville pats Levi's shoulder. I want to smile at him, to make myself approachable, but I don't like his eyes, how cold they are, how . . . devouring.

And then he says, "The event turned out, son."

Turned out how? I think. *How about amazing? Or fabulous? Or extremely wonderful? How about, "You're an excellent young man, and I'm proud of you."* A scowl threatens my lips when Mr. Orville turns to me, but I manage to turn it into a smile. (I hope.)

"I'm Bee," I say, shaking his hand. His palm is dry, but his touch makes me want to shrink back. I don't like how he's looking at me.

"Bee, the famous Bee? The one I keep hearing all about?"

The fact that Levi has talked about me to his dad, the dad he doesn't even like, makes me panic. *Of course,* I remind myself, *he did just tell an entire fundraising event about me. So. There's that.*

"I . . . guess that's me," I say. "Nice to meet you." (I hope I sound convincing.)

"You like art?" he asks.

"I love it," I say, "although I can't draw or paint or sketch to save my life."

"Let's hope it doesn't come down to that." Mr. Orville pats his stomach. "I think I'm going to take advantage of the food now. Nice chatting."

He's gone before I can say another word to him.

I turn to Levi, mouth agape. He runs a hand through his hair nervously, messing with it the way I like best. "Before you say anything," I say, "I must admit that, to the naked eye, he *is* charming."

"Sure," Levi replies, practically spitting. "And he'd like to charm the pants off every girl here. I mean that literally."

I sputter a laugh. "That's a terrible thing to say."

"Sometimes true things are terrible. I choose to ignore him." He turns his back to his father, putting one hand on my shoulder and nudging me forward. "See? Totally ignoring him flirting with one of our artists. Look at me, I'm a pro."

Laughing, I step out of the way of two men covering the nearest painting with a sheet. They carry it off, weaving through the crowd. Inside the auditorium, a man calls everyone back to their seats.

Levi grabs my hand. "This is my favorite part. Sit with me?"

If I were bold and witty, I'd say something fabulous. Something Marilyn Monroe would be proud of. Something flirtatious and irresistible. But because I'm just Bee (who thinks of witty things to say *after* the moment's gone), I answer with, "Oh, sure."

It turns out this is when they announce the winning bidders. Someone brings the paintings on stage, one by one, and the man with the microphone announces each winner and the amount donated. I become a little lost in all the large numbers— thousands of dollars are being donated by the second. I'm thankful for the distraction when Levi reaches over . . . and grabs my hand.

It's an unobtrusive move on his part, but every inch of me is aware of him, and in a moment of happy panic I squeeze his hand. He leans in close to me, his shoulder meeting mine, and whispers (very close to my ear), "Do you have a pen?"

I want to ask why, but it's too quiet in the auditorium, so I grab a pen from my purse. I think he's going to, I don't know, write a check or something. But then he grabs my hand, bends over my open palm, and begins to etch ink onto my skin.

It startles me, but I don't move away, even though I have no idea what he's doing. (I immediately realize I don't care.) After a few minutes, when my palm itches from the ink, he turns my hand over and starts writing on the back. I don't do anything, say anything; I don't move or even let out the breath that I'm holding. I realize that he hasn't looked up in minutes, hasn't laughed at a single joke made from the announcer on stage, hasn't clapped at all.

I keep my face forward, not daring to look down, not ready to be surprised by whatever it is. I don't look down when he's finished, when he sits back and drops the pen into my purse. I don't even look down when the fundraiser comes to a close and we walk outside. I wait until I'm in my car and Levi's in his and we're ready to drive to the wedding.

I start the car first, taking a second to breathe in deep. Then I hold up my hand, the back of it tattooed in swirly, looping designs, and small, even letters that are *so* Levi.

Songs that remind me of you.

I whimper, turning my hand to see the palm. The list is short, three songs, but I cannot breathe from happiness.

Harbour Lights
Anastasia
Lamplight

And below that, in smaller letters and parentheses: *(All by A Silent Film, of course.)*

I sit back in my seat, finally relaxing my shoulders. I've never before had a beautiful boy write about my favorite songs by my favorite band on my palm, and I'm pretty sure it's my new favorite thing. Ever. I turn my hand over, again and again, to be sure the pretty design is still there, and the words, and the trace of Levi that I wish was permanent.

He remembered. He always remembers.

Smiling, I drop my hands on the steering wheel and pull out of the parking space, moving up behind Levi's car at the stop sign.

I follow him home.

chapter 21

QUEUED:
YES!

BY DARIO MARIANELLI

IT'S NEARING DARK when we pull up to Levi's house. Lights have been strung over the porch and draped over the bushes, and two men stand out front, hands in their suit pockets. They see us drive up and go inside, as if they've been waiting.

I hope we're not too late.

Levi grips my hand—the hand covered in ink—before I can leave him behind. I don't know what to say to him right now; I think running into the house will solve all my problems. But it turns out Levi doesn't want to talk. He just wants to hold my hand.

That, I'm totally okay with.

The house is empty, but the backyard is so full of people it's almost as tight as the fundraiser. We break our hands apart when we step onto the back patio. Suzie runs toward us, exclaiming something about the fundraiser, clasping Levi close as she kisses his face.

"Was it amazing?" she gasps. "Did you have the best time?"

"Yes, we did." He flinches at her last big kiss to his forehead, then laughs. "It was a huge turnout."

Suzie claps her hands. "Good!" She pulls me in for a hug and asks, "Did you have fun, Bee?"

"It was awesome," I say, kissing her cheek.

"I'll try to come to the next one, I promise."

Levi puts his hand on her shoulder. "You don't have to, Mom."

Suzie shakes her head. "No, no—" Someone calls her name. Without warning, she makes a quick dash toward the center of the aisle, leaving us stranded.

I turn to Levi, confused.

He shrugs. "She doesn't come to events. I told her I didn't want her to if it would make her feel uncomfortable. She wants my dad at some things because she thinks it will be better for me to have him there. It's one of the many sacrifices she's making because I know she would rather kick his butt all the way to the middle of Kansas than miss all the important events."

I don't have the right words to answer, so it's a good thing we're interrupted. I'm pulled into introductions: Ivanka's mother and father, her cousins and her young brother. I meet Augustin's father (his mother passed away four years ago) and five sisters. There are others as well, but too many, too scattered, for me to meet in the allotted ten minutes I have before the wedding starts.

Soon Tom finds me, his smile wide. He looks nice in his slacks and polished shoes—I haven't seen him wear this nice of an outfit since our estranged older cousin got married three years ago. He gives me a quick hug, shakes Levi's hand, and says, "Bee, will you find Elle and tell her that the littlest sister confiscated her seat because she was too slow?"

"Why do I have to be the errand girl?"

"Because I'm pretty sure she went where no man can follow."

I laugh. "Fine, fine. I'll tell her."

I manage to sneak into the house without getting caught for conversation and find Elle exactly where Tom assumed she'd be—in the bathroom. She cracks open the door as soon as I knock, her eyes shifting back and forth down the hall before pulling it open wider. "Here. Quickk."

I'm ushered into the room, tiny as it is, and run smack into Ivanka. She's wearing her dress, with the train curling around her feet, her veil pushed back. She smiles at me, pulling me into the tightest hug. "So happy, Bee." She laughs, but I hear the half-sob underneath. "I feel so beautiful."

"You *look* so beautiful." Tears start in my eyes as well, but I wipe them away, turning Ivanka toward the full-length mirror. "Ready to show your man?"

Ivanka grins. "Yes. I am."

Elle claps her hands, all business, but her eyes are growing misty. "No crying, please. Save it for the ceremony. Did Tom reserve my seat?"

"He did, but he wanted me to tell you that the youngest cousin confiscated it. I doubt there's much hope for you."

She laughs. "Fine, I'm coming to steal back my land. In a few minutes. After we've finished her makeup."

I smile, nodding, kissing Ivanka on the cheek, turning toward the door. "I'll see you both in a few minutes, then."

I shut the door behind me—and bump into a tall figure in the hall. I know instantly by the gray suit fabric in my face that it's Levi, and suddenly my heart is no longer in my chest. "Levi."

He looks down at me. "The one and only. You okay?"

"Fine, and I found Elle."

"In the bathroom?"

"Helping Ivanka."

"Aha!" Levi pushes past me, the slyest of sly smiles on his lips. "I want a peek."

I gasp. "Not a chance!" I push him back with a (probably) ridiculous but (hopefully) fierce look on my face.

He laughs at me. It takes a few seconds to register that I have him pressed against the wall, my fists bunched around his lapels. His knees are bent so that he's just a little bit taller than me, and my legs are pressed against his, much too close.

"Remind me to never again call you a lady," he murmurs, eyes twinkling.

I let go, mortified, but he catches me. In the dim hall, he lifts the back of my hand to his lips. He presses a light kiss there, on the words that he wrote earlier.

"I thought you said you weren't going to call me a lady." I find the courage to smile at him, even though I'm completely devastated.

"I didn't, Brittany."

I hold back a groan of frustration by biting my tongue inside my mouth. I have never ever wanted to kiss a boy as badly as I want to kiss Levi right now.

I have to get away.

But he doesn't let go of my hand, and his gaze doesn't leave my face. "Did I guess it right?" he whispers.

"What?" I whisper back.

"Your name. Is it Brittany?"

I smile. "No, sorry."

He is quiet for a moment, and very serious. "How can I guess?"

"You can't."

"Is it an actual name or something your mom made up?"

I hesitate. "It's . . . an actual name."

"I'll keep searching, then."

"You do that."

"Bee," he says, and I realize we're still whispering in the tight hall, pressed close. It feels so natural, like I was always supposed to stand like this with him.

"Yeah?" I ask.

He shakes his head. "I thought of another song."

I narrow my eyes, letting him stand up straight, and look up at him. I'd almost forgotten how tall he is. "What is it?"

After a pause, after he licks his lips and lets out a small puff of breath, he says, "I'll tell you later."

We stand there, looking, searching, for at least another thirty seconds. Then he turns, dropping my hand, and takes three long strides out of the hall.

I'm left alone, a beating, bleeding heart in an open ribcage, not certain of anything, ready for everything.

chapter 22

QUEUED:
DOPAMINE
BY BØRNS

WHOEVER COINED THE term "a vision in white" must have had a vision of Ivanka. She is the prettiest bride I've ever seen, bar none. With the tiny lights strung above our backyard world, the soft instrumental music drifting over our heads, and every eye turned to the aisle, this wedding is absolutely perfect.

I find a seat next to my family, Astrid and Millie on either side of me. Levi smiles at me across the aisle, a light in his eyes (as always). I'm focused on the wedding, of course, but there's a part of me that's still thinking about the moment outside the bathroom, and his lips on my hand, and our legs touching. It leaves me twice as breathless as Ivanka's walk down the aisle.

The overall conclusion: I'm not breathing.

I'm the first to look away from our staring contest when Ivanka passes me. She reaches out her hand, touching mine, squeezing briefly. Then she smiles at her mother, who sits in front of me, and kisses her cheek. The photographer's flash goes off, catching these priceless moments, keeping them boxed in, safe and sound.

The ceremony is a breeze, inciting laughter and tears. I grip Astrid's hand too hard, eliciting harsh whispers about her fingers going numb. I notice, finally, how well the flowers mesh with the colors and theme of the wedding, and I feel a surge of pride lift me in my seat.

In the end, Ivanka and Augustin exchange vows and rings and a sweet, gentle kiss, and everyone stands to clap. Music starts again, a song about romance and a forever kind of love. *I'm absolutely going to cry*, I think, following the line of the crowd as we progress toward the food tables. Behind us, Levi and Tom and Ivanka's brother start to turn the chairs around and fill the backyard with tables. Ivanka stands beside her new husband, grabbing family members as they pass, hugging everyone. She's the sweetest little darling, and when I hug her, I feel warmth spread in my chest.

"Thank you for the wedding, Bonita," she says.

I laugh softly, squeezing her to me. "You were ravishing. It was perfect. Everything is perfect."

We're all full after dinner—traditional Czech food catered by locals—but it doesn't stop us from dancing.

We've moved all the tables and chairs to the side yard and set our shoes by the back door in a giant pile. I'm almost certain I'm never going to see my silver flats ever again, but at the moment I couldn't care less. I've got Astrid and Millicent on either side, the three of us holding hands, arms raised high, practically floating amidst the lights and sweet-smelling night air, the dry California grass against our bare feet.

I turn Millicent under my arm, then Astrid under the other. Astrid laughs as she and Millie trip over each other, falling into Agustin's youngest sister. She laughs and shouts something in Czech, her golden bobbed swaying with her movements. We laugh with her, shrugging, shouting back in English. There's no way we understand each other, but the sentiment is there. Sometimes obvious joy says more than words we can understand.

I spin, taking a peek at Levi, who's dancing with his mom. They're laughing at some private joke, moving to the music with equal parts jumping and dancing. He whispers something into Suzie's ear, leaning close, and her eyes go wide with her grin. She slaps his arm. Levi pulls away, laughing loudly enough that I can hear it. Suzie grabs his face and kisses him twice, as if she's congratulating him.

I turn away, feeling (only slightly) ashamed that I spied on their little moment. I peer through the crowd ahead, trying to find Tom. I spot him dancing at the edge of the group with Elle; her hands are in the air, her blue locks flying. Tom shakes his head like he's a little bewildered by her wild nature, but there's a smile on his mouth that's been there for hours.

A hand clamps down on my shoulder, bringing me out of my thoughts. Suzie dances close to me, grabs both of my hands, and drags me to Levi. He's standing with Ivanka, who's joined their little group. I wave at her, falling into step, raising my hands, until suddenly it's no longer Suzie and Ivanka and Levi and me. It's Levi. It's me. *Us.* An inescapable laugh falls from my mouth as he grabs me and spins me. I twist in his arms, letting him pull me a little bit closer, swinging to a song I don't recognize but want to remember forever.

Then it slows—the song, the dance, the atmosphere. Levi

doesn't let me go, doesn't step away. In fact, we're closer now, with his arm wrapped around my waist and his free hand entwined with mine. I sway in a moment of dizziness, but he holds me up, tucking me against him. I love this, the way I can practically feel the earth spinning under my feet. Our planet is flying at a million miles per hour and so are we.

"What do you think of the wedding?" Levi asks. His voice sounds a little hoarse. (*It's from talking and laughing all day*, I tell myself.)

"I think it turned out perfectly." I glance around and up at the lights hanging above my head. "It's dazzling."

He meets my gaze. "You pulled it off," he murmurs. "Actually, I'd say you more than pulled it off—you nailed it."

"I had the help of everyone in TCP. I had our moms. I had Ivanka. I had *you*."

(*I don't have you but I wish I did. I wish you were mine.*)

"True, but you planned it. You set everything up. You got the ball rolling."

"If you hadn't worn that yellow sweater . . . " I shrug.

He tips his head back, studying me. "How have you liked being called Bonita all evening?"

"It's actually kind of nice. I like it much better than my real name."

"Oh, gosh. Is it really that bad? I'll have to scrape the bottom of the B name barrel next time."

I want to pretend I'm offended, but all I can do is laugh at him. "You thought you were close, huh?"

He smirks. "Someday, I will be. I'll get close enough that I can really feel its presence, like a beast in the dark—because apparently it's just that ugly. And then I'll nail it right in the heart, and Bee?"

The answer on my lips sounds more like a squeak than a word. "Yeah?"

He spins me slowly, turning me so that I'm dancing with my back to his chest. I roll my head to the side so he can whisper in my ear, "The discovery will be my victory."

I laugh at this, to disguise the fact that I'm shivering, my stomach fluttering, my head spinning with the light. I can't see him, but I can feel him, warm and real behind me.

The song comes to an end, and we part—there are several inches between us, and we don't look at each other—but my heart is still beating, thrashing like a storm. I think, *Walk away, Bee, walk away.* But I don't know how, so I reach out my hand instead.

He takes it, just like I hoped he would.

chapter 23

QUEUED:
I LIVED HERE
BY MARTIN PHIPPS

I'M LYING ON the grass, face to the stars. My hair splays out behind my head like an extra-large halo, complete with a spray of sunrays.

The lights have been taken down. It's nearing midnight, but Suzie and my mom are still laughing loudly. My mom and I have the same loud cackle-laugh when we're tired—it reminds me of a machine gun—and my mom's machine gun has been going off consistently for the last hour.

Of course, this only makes me smile.

Everything makes me smile right now.

Ivanka and Augustin are gone; they climbed into their car amidst laughter and the dried lavender buds we tossed at them. They kissed once before driving off, a happy couple, hitched at last.

I helped make it happen.

God, it feels good.

Since there is no more light left in the backyard, I can see the stars pretty well from this angle, just like I could two weeks ago when I sat out here with Levi. Except now there are even more, filling the sky to the brim. I see Orion again—but like Levi, it's the only constellation I can remember.

I lift my head, sensing a pair of watchful eyes. The Boy himself stands by the back door, leaning against the frame, arms crossed, studying me.

"Hey," I say.

"Hey," he replies. He lies down beside me, our hands touching in the middle.

I grab his wrist before I can talk myself out of it. "Do you see all these stars? So many more than last time."

"Yeah."

"It's like they came out just for the happy couple."

Levi slides his hand up so that our palms are pressed together. We sit in comfortable silence for a few minutes, several minutes, hours, days, before Levi turns his head toward me. "Tired?"

"Not really," I answer, looking at him directly. (If only we weren't so close, I could breathe easier.) "Just . . . content."

"Happy?"

"Yes."

"Ready for adventure to take you?"

"Obviously." I chuckle, squeezing his hand. His long fingers squeeze back, then lace through mine. "What were you going to tell me? Before the wedding?" I ask.

He looks at me for a long moment, then up at the sky again. "It's . . . I just . . . can . . . " He clears his throat. "I found another song that reminds me of you."

"If it's a Bon Iver song, I can't guarantee a positive response."

Levi laughs. "It's not Bon Iver." He grabs my hand, the one

unmarked, and pulls a pen out of his pocket. "This is for you to listen to when you get home."

I'm full of light as he takes the pen to my hand. There are no frills to this drawing, only his even handwriting, and the words *I Lived Here by Martin Phipps*.

"Who is this?" I ask.

"An amazing composer. You'll love him."

"I hope so."

"Hey, Levi," Suzie yells from the house, "we need your help with the chairs."

Levi stands up, brushes his hands together, and helps me to my feet. "Duty calls."

I drop my gaze to my hands, lingering on the new song title written there.

"Thanks for your help, Bee," he says, quietly. "Today wouldn't have been . . . well, *today*... without you."

"Shut up," I say, teasing, but really my heart is in my mouth.

"No, really." He runs his hand up my arm. I freeze, my breath caught, and his palm stops on my shoulder. My bare skin feels like it's been set on fire. "Come see me at the shop on Tuesday, okay? I get off at three."

I nod. "Okay," I whisper. "I'll be there."

He waves once before disappearing into the house, and I'm alone in the yard, thinking of everything I want to say to him, and want to hear him say to me.

I wait until my family is asleep, the house comfortingly quiet, before I pull out my iPod and hook up my headphones. I scroll through Spotify for the song, and when it starts playing, my heart pounds so hard I can barely sit still.

Thing You Should Know About Me #83: I believe every person interprets music and lyrics differently. Which is exactly my fear when I hear the first notes. What if I don't understand what he's trying to tell me? What if I read into it?

But then the slow build of the beginning eases into a sweeping crescendo, and I just know I can't mess this one up. It makes me ache—the same ache I felt when I held his hand lying in the grass earlier. The same ache I felt in the hall outside the bathroom, when Levi kissed my hand, when I suddenly couldn't breathe and that was perfectly all right with me.

Levi.

He said this song reminded him of me. He said it—I heard him. He can't take it back. I won't let him.

The song ends, and I have no idea what I'm supposed to do next. This is what he wanted to tell me? The song is stuck in my head, replaying again and again. I want to see him now, to ask him if I got it right. I want to make sure that my overly-romantic self isn't wrong or disillusioned, that those moments were real.

With the headphones still plugging my ears, my heart jittery, my chest full and aching (just like the song), I wonder if he is falling asleep with that same ache right now. And then I wonder if I could call him, because I have no shortage of insane, crush-infused ideas.

My phone tells me it's one in the morning, but I have no self-control and my fingers are drawn to his name in my contacts without my permission (okay, that's a lie). I click on it, Levi, the name that now means everything to me, and lift the phone to my ears.

"Bee?" he answers after one ring, and there is no denying it—he's quiet, but not tired. He sounds as excited (and awake) as his mother baking cookies at night.

"Levi," I whisper. "I'm so glad you answered."

"You're not asleep?"

"No. I thought *you'd* be asleep."

He chuckles. "Nope, couldn't."

"But you must be exhausted."

"I am. You've been keeping me up."

I'm indignant. "Ex*cuse* me—"

"Did you listen to the song?"

I smile. "I did."

"Good."

"I loved it."

"Also good."

"I'm starting to trust your taste in music again."

"Don't insult me."

"I'm not. I'm insulting Bon—"

"Don't *even* say it," Levi hisses.

I burst into laughter and receive a loudly whispered, "Shut up, Bee!" from Astrid in the next room. "But Levi," I say, growing serious again. "*Levi*," I repeat, because I'm an idiot.

"Yes, Bee," he says softly.

I love that tone. (I only ever hear it when he says my name.) "About the song, okay?"

"Okay."

"You can't just—I don't know—what did you—"

He laughs.

"Leviiii. Don't laugh."

"I want to laugh—I'm happy."

"You need to be very, very clear about what you meant when you told me to listen to it." (I'm totally hyperventilating now. Great.)

"I really like you, Bee." There. It's out in the open, and his voice is quiet, and reverent, and lovely. "Look, I talked to Gretchen, remember? And she told me something that wouldn't stop pestering me."

"What. Did. She. Say?" I ask, grinding out each syllable. Gretchen is so busted.

"She told me she knew I liked you and that I'd better ask you out soon or she'd blow my cover."

"What?!" (SO BUSTED.)

"And so all along I was trying to think of how to do it but, like . . . I don't know how to do—" He swallows. "I didn't know how to ask you. And that song . . . Well. It said exactly what I wanted to say."

All I can do is sigh. Aside from wanting to strangle Gretchen, all I can think of is kissing Levi.

"Bee?" he asks.

"Yes?"

"Will you go on a date with me?"

"Only *one*?" I blurt. *Smooth.*

I hear his laugh and imagine him smiling in that big way of his. "I mean, I'm not picky."

"Tomorrow *is* Sunday, you know."

"I do know. And I'm all yours, if you want me."

I nod, and then I remember he can't see me. I lick my lips and close my eyes and say, "Yes. I definitely do."

chapter 24

QUEUED:
TIGHTROPE
by WALK THE MOON

MY FIRST THOUGHT the next morning is, *Oh, my God. I get to go on a date with Levi.*

My second thought is, *Why is the sun so bright this early in the morning?*

My third thought: *Why does my face feel swollen? WHY CAN'T I BREATHE THROUGH MY NOSE?!*

Frantic, I roll over and check my phone. It's 10:52, and Levi is supposed to pick me up at 11:00, and I've slept through all my alarms. Not only that, but my nose is stuffy, my head is pounding, and my skin feels sensitive to the touch.

I call Levi, but after a few rings it goes to voicemail. I know him—he's always on time. He's going to be here in five minutes whether I like it or not. But I don't want him to come over because I'm sick and he'll catch whatever I have. He doesn't have time for that in his busy schedule.

I call him again. No luck.

I groan. I sneeze. I sneeze again. I drag myself into the bathroom for tissues. I blow my nose—

Levi rings the doorbell. My heart both leaps and breaks. What is he going to think of me missing our very first date? Surely he'll be gracious, but I feel so bad I'm sick to my stomach. (At least, I'm pretty sure it's not the flu.)

Throwing my hair into a messy bun, I trudge to the front door. I can see Levi's spastic hair, the straight line of his nose and jaw, through the small square window. I turn the handle and let the door swing open, the sun immediately blinding my poor, sickly eyes.

"Bee?" he asks, and even though I can't see him clearly, I can tell he's bewildered by my appearance.

I groan. "Levi," I start, and have to pause to sneeze into my sleeve. "I slept through my alarms. I think I'm sick."

"Oh my God, Bee."

He reaches for me. I should be the better person and tell him to stay away, and that maybe he should throw some garlic and holy water at me before he leaves. But I can't resist when his fingers gently caress my neck, pulling me close. One hand remains on the back of my neck, and he uses the other to secure my arms around his waist.

When he kisses the top of my head, my whole body melts. "Levi, I don't want you to catch this."

He tightens his arms around me. "We've been breathing on each other for the last week. If I'm going to catch it, I already have."

I sigh. He really wants this, then. "Okay. I'll get ready," I say, and step back into the house.

"No way," he protests, following me in and locking the door behind him. "We'll just hang out here today. We can watch movies and, like, I dunno. I'll make you tea or something."

I gape at him.

"Is your family here?"

"What?" I snap out of my trance. "Um, no, they're all out today."

"Goodie. I say we watch *Back to the Future*."

I blink at him. "Are you sure? I mean, seriously—aren't you worried about catching this?"

His eyes practically have stars in them, they twinkle so brightly. "Who cares?" He stands with his hands in his pants pockets, eyes drifting slowly over my face. "I've wanted this for too long, Bee."

I let out a heavy breath. "We've known each other for a month."

"I know. Like I said, too long."

"Fine, then. You asked for it." I'm a bundle of nerves and fear and joy and pure amazement. I push all that down, however, and hold out my hand. As sure as the stars in the sky, his fingers wrap around mine, and my heart is calm.

We start watching the movie in the living room, but the surround sound almost bursts my sensitive eardrums, so we move into my bedroom. I thought this would be weird, but now that I'm sitting beside him on a pile of pillows (and under a pile of blankets) I'm incredibly comfortable. Too comfortable to move, in fact, which means Levi keeps getting up to get more tissue, or tea, or toast. (Toast is the only thing I can eat today; everything else sounds disgusting.)

Tom comes home at the end of the movie, to find me curled up in bed with Levi. He's taken completely by surprise, and despite having been Levi's friend for a while, he looks suspicious. Levi, on the other hand, looks completely unperturbed.

"Hey, man! What's up?" Levi reaches out his hand, which Tom hesitantly grabs.

"Um, just wondering what you two are doing in bed together. But no biggie, I'll just—"

He starts to back up, so I say, "I'm sick, you loser, and Levi's helping me."

"Like, how much?"

Levi looks at me like he'd like to know, too. (He's not taking Tom seriously *at all*.)

"I'm ready to tell both of you to leave if you don't quit this."

Levi smiles. "Should we tell him?"

I tilt my head back and meet his gaze for a second, my insides briefly melting at the expression on his face: pure happiness, and hope.

I nod. "Okay."

We both turn to Tom. "We're dating now," I say.

"She's pregnant," Levi says at the same time.

I hit his chest as hard as I can with the flat of my palm. "Don't."

Tom raises his hands in surrender. "I'll just back out of here until you decide you want to tell me what's really happening."

And just like that, he's gone.

"Wow," I say, drily. "That's going to scar him for forever."

Levi looks incredibly pleased with himself as he closes the laptop on our legs and places it on my reading chair. His eyes catch my new bookshelf and all the glorious books inside, and he smiles. "You're a reader?"

"Yeah."

Still sitting with his arm around me, his gaze drifts from the top to the bottom in slow motion, as if reading every title. "I'm surprised," he says finally. "I would have pegged you as a romance reader, but I see absolutely no romance titles on your shelf."

I feign a gasp. "I read far classier novels than Harlequin, thanks."

He laughs and nods at my top shelf. "I see a lot of John Green. And Maggie Stiefvater."

"As one should see on every shelf."

"I'll get on that as soon as possible."

I smile and sink down into the bed, my head resting on my pillow. Levi keeps his hand on my hair, stroking softly.

"You don't have to be here, you know," I wheeze. I'm on a high with him here, but he has to know I'm not going to keep him prisoner. He has to feel free to leave whenever he needs to. I'd expect this from a doting husband, maybe, but this was supposed to be our first date and—

"I know that, Betty." His fingers dig a little harder, turning what was a light caress into an incredible massage that sends tingles all the way down to my toes.

"You're good at that," I say, and blush for absolutely no reason other than that he's touching me with kind, loving fingers while sitting on my bed. (Take *that*, romance novels.)

"It comes from spending one too many nights with a stressed out, cookie baking mom."

He's so good, this pretty boy I've caught and captured inside my heart. I think about all the things we have to learn about each other. All the secrets we have yet to tell. (*Sex*, I think, *and girls and past relationships and* sex. *Ugh.*) I tuck these topics into an ask-when-necessary file in my brain. All the while I'm gazing at him dreamily, which I don't realize until he looks down at me.

"What?" he asks.

I shake my head, biting the inside of my mouth to keep the stupid words inside.

Levi takes a deep breath, and I think he's going to argue, but instead he says, "Is your name Benedetta?"

He asks this with such conviction that I almost take him seriously. But then I snap out of it. "BENEDETTA?" I gasp.

He cringes. "I take it that's worse?"

I laugh at him. "You're so far off."

"Well I don't think it's fair that you know my full name, and I only know one-third of yours."

"Too bad."

"Come on, Belladonna. Just tell me your middle name, for starters."

I squint up at him, hesitating.

"You can't deny me this. You're sick on our first date—you *owe* me!"

I can tell he's joking (his eyes sparkle and his mouth quirks and then he's laughing at me), but I feel bad. I do owe him. So I reach up and run my hand through his frazzled hair and pull him down so his ear is by my mouth.

"My middle name is Aurora," I whisper.

"I like that name," he whispers back, and I feel his breath on my neck.

It makes me warm. "Thank you."

He catches my hand that's woven into his hair, pulls it down to his chest, and holds it there. My other hand drifts around to the back of his neck, making sure he doesn't move. Not quite yet. I'm not ready.

With a sigh so quiet it's like a breath catching in his throat, Levi closes the gap between us and kisses my temple. My pulse thuds so wildly I'm pretty sure he can feel it, beating right against his soft mouth. And this is how we stay, him curled over me, our faces touching, our hearts like a broad river running between us.

chapter 25

QUEUED:
GUILLOTINE
BY JON BELLION

"**G**RETCHEN, I KNOW what you did," I say, very seriously. I flop onto my back on my bed, one hand holding the phone to my ear, the other tucked under the pillow at my head.

Gretchen squeals. "I sure as hell hope that means he finally asked you out."

"Your smart mouth is going to get you in so much trouble!" I shout. "How could you do that?!"

"HE ASKED YOU OUT, DIDN'T HE?" she yells back.

"YES, BUT I DON'T KNOW WHAT TO DO WITH MYSELF." I groan. It's been a few days, but the fears have already begun to settle. (What if I'm a terrible girlfriend? How does one average human rise to the occasion of dating the world's prettiest boy?)

"Just accept this gift I've given you," Gretchen argues.

"It's too much, too awesome."

She snorts. "Get over yourself." A pause, and a very suspicious *hmmm*. Then, "Has he kissed you yet?"

I groan again. "Dude, we've been on one date and spent the Fourth of July together. This hardly calls for kissing. Besides, I'm not ready for it yet."

I can just *feel* Gretchen's eye-roll. "You. Are. A. *Liar*."

"I am not."

"You *so* want him to kiss you."

"Yeah, but not *now*."

Gretchen makes another humming noise, this time disbelieving. "And how is he going to feel about your, um, unusual but honorable conviction? You know, your most important decision ever?"

"Shhh!" I blush. "We'll cross that bridge when we get there."

Gretchen snorts. "Whatever. I'm just happy you're finally together. Guess what? I'm sending you a letter in the mail."

"What?!" (Thing You Should Know About Me #12433: I like to write and read handwritten letters. I even hang the most special ones on my wall because I'm a sentimental old goat.)

"Yeah, I found this old stationery in a recently unpacked box from the garage, and thought I'd make your day."

I'm about to answer when my bed dips. I whip around, shouting incoherent nonsense in a brief moment of terror before realizing *Levi* is lying down beside me. He almost falls off from my jostling.

"Shit! Bee!" he exclaims, but he's laughing.

I scramble, realizing I've lost my phone in the fray. I find it—right as it slips into the crack between my bed and the wall. *Thump*.

"Leviiiiii," I groan, smacking him on the arm as he clumsily gets off the bed. "You made me drop Gretchen."

"Sorry, sorry." He leans over the crack where the phone fell. "Sorry, Gretchen!" he shouts.

I yank the bed away from the wall, he pulls the phone out, and before I can take it, he puts it to his ear. "Sorry, Gretchen," he repeats. "Totally my fault."

I sit on the bed, heaving a breath. When I look up, I find my sisters standing in my doorway, their mouths and eyes open wide.

Astrid's lips shape into a wry smile. "We'll be watching you two."

I run a hand over my face. "Goodbye, Astrid."

She and Millie turn on their heels and run, down the hall. Levi puts my phone back in my hand and sits beside me on the bed. When he kisses my cheek, I feel myself automatically leaning into him.

"Sorry I scared you so badly," he whispers, his chuckle tickling my ear.

I lose it, then. I break into laughter so hysterical I'm pretty sure I'm going to cry. I press the phone to my ear, lying back on my bed, legs dangling off the edge next to Levi's. (Although *his* feet actually touch the ground.)

"Gretchen?" I gasp into the phone.

She's laughing just as hard as I am. "What just happened?"

"Levi . . . erm . . . surprised me."

"Oh, my gosh! All I heard was screaming and then muffled talking and then a loud bang, and terrifying laughter."

Levi lies down beside me, still chuckling. I move so he can tuck his arm under my head. "Sorry Gretchen," he whispers again, his mouth close to the speaker on my phone (which means it's also close to my mouth). I push him back a little, rolling my eyes.

"She forgives you," I say, poking his ribs.

Gretchen protests, "I do not. Tell him I don't forgive him! Oh, just let me talk to him."

I turn on the speaker and Gretchen's voice comes blaring through. "LEVI! I don't forgive you."

Levi gives me a bewildered look. "I'm sorry I interrupted."

"Well." Gretchen *hmphs*, like she's blowing out a deep breath. "At least you're treating my girl right."

"I'm trying. I mean, I've only had a few days to get it wrong."

I smile at this. "I can get off the phone," I whisper, "if you want."

"No, no. She was there first," he says. "I'm fine hanging out here."

My smile turns to a grin. "Okay."

Gretchen, still on speaker, sighs heavily and says, "Levi, please tell me your hair is as glorious in real life as Bee makes it out to be."

I stop. I freeze and squeak and *oh my goodness* Levi is looking at me, confused.

"What?" he asks. "What about my hair?"

Gretchen snorts. "Bee obsesses over your hair. She thinks it was made from gold when the gods fashioned it on Mount Olympus."

"Bee likes my *hair*?" Levi sounds incredulous.

I want to dig my own grave right about . . . five minutes ago. "Gretchen, can you just talk about normal things, please?"

Gretchen laughs so loud it's like she's laughing into a microphone. "You miss me, Bee. Admit it."

I'm a little sullen, about to reply that yes, I miss her very much thank you, but Levi gets there first. "Billie misses you all the time. It's like the plague."

"Billie?" Gretchen asks. "Is that a new nickname?"

Sudden terror grips me. "NO," I say, too loud and too fast. "Levi's trying to guess my name, but SHH GRETCHEN PLEASE DON'T TELL HIM!"

Levi grabs the phone from me, looking so suddenly vexed that I'm worried he'll burst a blood vessel. "She knows? Gretchen, you know her name?!"

"Of *course* I know her name, I'm her best friend." Gretchen sniffs.

"Gretchen, tell me," Levi begs.

I gasp. "Gretchen Taylor McKenzie, if you betray me I will . . . do something horrible to you."

Gretchen grunts. "I won't betray you, Bee, just *calm down*. I just . . . can't believe you haven't told him."

Levi pouts at me but speaks to Gretchen. "I'm her boyfriend now. I deserve to know."

"One day, Levi, you'll be promoted to Bearer of the Name." Gretchen laughs. "It won't be half as awful as you think."

Levi thinks this is *hilarious.*

When the phone call is over, I lie next to Levi with his arm beneath my head and my arm slung over his stomach. I play with the seam of his shirt, feeling the soft fabric between my thumb and forefinger, my head nestled into the crook of his shoulder.

This is so new. So raw. I feel like I'm opening up, piece by piece. Showing myself to the world. And it's all Levi's fault.

So I let him hold me, in this new way that feels like he's drawing me out. He's searching, reaching; I'm the one he wants. His finger—just a single, soft finger—runs up and down my arm. I resist the urge to shiver and lean into his touch, but it's a losing battle. He laughs, quiet like a breath, and pulls me in tighter. It's like he's trying not to break the moment, same as me, and I thank him silently for it.

Of course, this is the exact moment that a blast of music from the *Into the Woods* musical hits my ears. We sit still, waiting for it to pass, but then it gets louder and *closer*. Astrid suddenly bursts into my room, iPod in hand, the song playing at full volume. She sings along with it, waving her hands in the air as she interprets the lyrics with her own dance. Levi sticks his leg out, trying to trip her, but she just flashes him a venomous look and keeps on dancing.

Astrid's out of breath when the song comes to a clashing end. She bows like a performer and squeaks out, "We're watching *Into the Woods* tonight after dinner if you want to join us." Then she skitters out of the room and slams the door behind her. (I hear my mom yell, "Don't shut the doors so hard! They're too old for your abuse, Astrid!")

Levi huffs out a long-held breath. "Was Astrid talking to me or you?"

I love that he doesn't comment on Astrid's ridiculous performance. "Um, both, I think."

"Well. We'd better join the party, then."

I feel a giggle escape my mouth. (I did not endorse the giggle, but that's the way these things work, apparently. The boyfriend and the giggles are a package deal.) "You're very nice to put up with her."

"Astrid's crazy, dude. I want to be just like her when I grow up."

I wiggle out of his arms, pulling him up with me, but when he makes a move for the door, I stop him. This time, *I'm* the one who leans in close. He holds my arm just below the elbow, my own hand resting on his stomach. When he turns his head, just an inch, I plant a kiss right on the hollow of his cheek, my nose against his cheekbone, and feel the caged butterflies in my stomach flap their wild wings in the beautiful agony of our close proximity.

chapter 26

QUEUED:
SHAKE IT OUT
BY FLORENCE + THE MACHINE

L EVI SITS BESIDE me at the dinner table that night. Millicent sits on his other side, batting her eyelashes. "Hi, Levi," she says.

He pats her head. "What's up, Millie?"

"Oh, nothing." She giggles, observing, "You're here a lot."

(How dare she? Those are *my* giggles.) I roll my eyes and point to her plate. "Millie, just eat your food."

"Of course I'm here a lot," Levi says, ignoring me. But he squeezes my hand under the table as he leans close to Millie, whispering a little too loud, "I reeeeeeally like your sister."

She makes a face, like pure disgust and discomfort, but not without a sprinkle of jealousy. "That's disgusting."

Levi nods. "Very."

Dinner progresses as usual (with loud singing and arguing), and when my sisters get up to put the food away and the dishes in the sink, Levi turns to me in his chair. "Bee," he says, and then stops. "You have something. On your face."

I sit up straight. "Where on my face?"

"On the right side of your lip." Levi smiles.

I wipe my lips with a napkin. "Better?"

"You missed it."

"Levi, you're not—"

He leans in . . . and kisses the spot. It's more on my cheek, really, but it's close enough to my lips that my breath hitches and I close my eyes in response.

"—helping," I finish, when he leans away.

"Got it," he says.

Then I realize *something*. My parents are across the able, glancing at us, slightly embarrassed (but apparently not enough to leave). They hurriedly look away, pretending they've been talking this whole time.

I know, for a fact, they have not. In my absolute mortification, I whisper, "My mother! My father!" I can't get the words out right; I don't know what I'm trying to say.

"What? They love me." Levi shrugs.

"I know, but—"

"No, I mean, your dad likes me," he says, quietly, standing up and pulling me with him. Only I can hear him because my parents aren't paying attention to us now. (Thank God.) "But your mom *loves* me. Have you heard her talk about how gorgeous I am?"

My nervous giggle sounds incredibly high-pitched. My mom has talked about how gorgeous she thinks Levi is, numerous times, but I had no idea *Levi* heard her. "Yes. Yes I have."

"Oh, come on," he teases. "You're not embarrassed, are you?"

"Me? Never!" I return, rolling my eyes, but I'm lying. I'm totally embarrassed.

"Well, good, because I'm not either. I think your mom has good taste."

"Thank you, Levi," my mom pipes in, because *of course* she heard him. OF COURSE SHE DID. And she kisses his cheek for effect as she passes.

Levi's eyes are laughing at me. There's *so* much laughter in them, like he's caught a spark of magic inside.

Well, with this guy, I wouldn't be surprised.

The sky is a deep and brilliant midnight blue, and I'm sitting beneath it. This feels like a privilege—not because of the sky, exactly, but because I'm sitting next to Levi. Our front porch steps creak a little every time one of us moves (to laugh or grab our root beers on the ground or when Levi kisses my cheek) but we are comfortable here.

"This was fun," Levi says suddenly. He tips his head back to take a swig from his bottle. "You should have me over for all your family movie nights."

Except it wasn't just a movie night. We shared music and played card games, and I proudly schooled everybody during Dutch Blitz. I glance at him sideways and grin. "We seem to have them more often now. I think it's a ploy to get you to come over."

He smirks. "They don't need ploys. Just you."

"Well, if it starts to feel like you're dating my family and not me, I'm sorry. I warned you."

Levi's smirk turns into a full-on grin. "You're ridiculous. Did you know that?"

I toss my hair, making sure the ends hit him square in the face. "Who, me?"

We're interrupted when Levi's car pulls into the driveway, Keagan at the wheel. He waves to us, pointing to the headphones in his ears and the phone on the dash. He doesn't make a move to get out, so Levi stands, patting his pockets. "I guess that's my cue—" He puts his hands in his pockets, a quizzical expression on his face. "Hmm. I must have left my phone inside," he mutters.

I jump up next to him. "I think I saw it on the computer desk." We head back inside, motioning for Keagan to wait. The house has gone dark, with my sisters already in bed, so we tiptoe on the wood.

But in this quiet, I get the sense that something is wrong even before I get to the living room. My heart is beating too fast, and everything I'd thought was over, every fear I'd thought was gone, returns. I cower by the open doorway, not going in but not leaving.

It's my mom. She's sobbing, and I hear my dad talking to her with whispered words I can't understand.

A knife in my gut: that's what this feels like. They were faking it this whole time, hiding in smiles and false joy, while underneath—behind our backs—they were doing this. *They waited*, I think. *They waited until they thought no one would hear.*

I blink, tears clouding my vision. The happiness I'd felt a moment ago now seems like a daydream. All I want is to know, but the unknown already scares me. How much worse will it be when they tell me—us—what's going on? Every possibility rushes through my mind: an affair, divorce, the house, his job. Was there been a death in the family? Will we have to move?

"Bee?" Levi whispers. I turn, and he's standing by the table with his phone in his hands. "It was right here." His voice is like porcelain.

I nod. "Okay."

He holds out his hand, which I take, pretending like I wasn't just about to cry. (We both know I was.) On the porch again, with the front door shut behind us, he puts his arms around me, squeezing tight. The pain almost starts to dissipate. Almost.

"You okay?" he whispers, chin resting on my head.

"Sure," I non-answer. My voice sounds brittle in the cool California night.

I hear his unspoken words: *But your parents?*

I don't address this, because that's exactly how I want to keep it: unspoken. At least for now. He respects this, of course, because he's Levi and he's always respectful.

So I just hug him. I soak in his embrace like the first sunny day of summer, even though he hasn't quite warmed that cold spot, deep inside me, that doesn't seem to want to thaw.

I sleep pitifully that night, or maybe I don't sleep at all. I do my best not to cry, hoping that tomorrow I'll wake up and it will all be a dream. But when I open my eyes in the morning (the last time I checked the time was at four o'clock), the sheets are twisted around my legs and my head is turned at an awkward angle.

My neck isn't the only part of me that aches.

That morning is the start of a routine, one that lasts for a week—but it feels like a year. I put on a smile for my sisters and laugh with my mom and hug my dad and go out with Levi and conduct interviews at TCP. I talk to Gretchen, and even then I keep my smile. I tell myself I'm doing this because there's nothing truly wrong and I'm reading into things, but I know that's a lie.

I know it's a lie because sometimes my mom still cries. Sometimes, my dad sits with her.

Sometimes, he cries, too.

They don't know that I know, and I'm terrified to tell them. What if everything I know about them, their marriage, our lives, is turning on its head? What if I'm standing in a house made of stilts, and asking the unaskable will kick it out from under me?

So I don't ask. I don't tell them I know they're hiding something. I don't ask questions.

I find out by accident.

chapter 27

QUEUED:
On the Nature of Daylight
by Max Richter

Levi

Hi beautiful. It's Friday and we're both off work and I have a hankering for the beach. Come with?

Bee

I love being called beautiful so early in the morning.

Levi

It's not early.

Bee

Here I should introduce you to my stance on mornings: they shouldn't exist before 9:00.

Levi

I'd be okay with that, actually.

                                              Bee

          Also, in answer to your beach question – I'd love that.

Levi

Ten?

                                              Bee

                              Yes please! I'll get ready now.

I add a smiley and, like, a million hearts—just because. Then I'm up and pulling on my pink sundress. I know my hair is going to get whipped around, so I brush through it once and leave it. (Some days, it's too long to take seriously.)

Levi finds me thirty minutes later, painting my nails at my desk. I never do my nails, but it's a nice day. I'm inspired. (I blame The Boy.)

Levi notices, of course. "Nails, huh?"

"Like the color? I borrowed it from Astrid." I wave the bright pink in front of his eyes.

"You could wear dull brown on your nails and I'd still think it's pretty."

"Oooh," I say, batting my lashes as he kisses my forehead. "Good answer. Ten points for Gryffindor."

He grins. "Those are great movies."

My smile quickly dulls to a frown. "But they're even greater books."

He looks very worried, very suddenly. I immediately grasp what he's not telling me.

"You haven't read them, have you? *Have* you?!" I gasp.

His expression immediately grows wary. "Nooooo?" he lilts, and I have to admit it's kind of cute. (Despite feeling like he's violated everything sacred in this world.)

I turn my back to him, grabbing the first book in the series off my shelf. "Looks like you have some catching up to do."

He raises one eyebrow, accepting the book that I've thrust against his chest, and looks down at it. "You want me to read? At the beach?"

"*I* want to read at the beach. *You* might as well join me."

Levi isn't convinced. "I guess I can try . . . "

I nod. "You'll love it. I'm full of great ideas."

He takes the bait. "Obviously."

Another good answer. I blush.

He sees.

The blush deepens.

Levi grabs my hand, laughing, and yanks me out of the room. "Let's go, crazy," he says, and I pretend I don't hear "Let's go crazy," because that would make me burn.

As it turns out, I don't have to do anything to convince Levi of his folly. He lies in the sand beside me, book in hand, open to the seventh chapter, his shirt mercilessly thrown aside as he tans. I say mercilessly because, oh my GOSH, my boyfriend has very, erm, nice, um, muscles. And now I'm not at all focused on my book, of course, because his profile is distracting me. I read a sentence, glance over, read, glance, read, glance. It's never-ending. (And, I repeat, merciless.)

Eventually, I nudge his side. "Levi?"

He grunts, turning the page. The skin where I elbowed him

turns white, reminding me that we've been in the sun for hours with no reapplication.

"You're going to burn, Levi." God, I sound like a mother. I don't want to sound like a mother. (*Shut your face, Bernice.*)

He doesn't answer in words and instead grabs the sunscreen at his side and hands it to me, not once taking his eyes from the page. I resist the urge to laugh maniacally as I squirt sunscreen into my hands.

"Enjoying that, much?" I ask, and look down at his back.

Now I'm going to have to touch him.

I squirm. I'm not nervous—I'm squirming because I *want* to touch him.

. . . okay. Maybe I'm a little nervous.

(*Merciless, merciless, merciless.*)

"Shh," he says, and is quiet for the next several moments while I whip up the courage to lather the sunscreen all over him. But as soon as I actually do it, the rest comes easy. It's nice, actually; as nice as I imagined it would be. Soothing, as if someone were doing it to me. I like being this close to him, and I like that he wants me to do this.

Or maybe it's the book. (Damn Harry Potter for making me doubt.)

Finally, I lie down next to him on my stomach, elbows propping me up. I lean my head against his shoulder, and he leans his head on mine. "I'm going to pretend," he says, "like that *wasn't* the best thing I've felt in a while."

My heart thrums like crazy. He's so cute, it's killing me.

I tell him this.

"Gee, thanks. I always wanted to be a lady killer."

I roll over onto my back, squinting into the bright yellow sun. "Didn't you though?" But he doesn't answer because he's back in the book. I grunt. "Levi, what part are you at?"

He turns the page and grunts in reply. I wait a minute before asking again. He finally shouts, "The sorting hat!" and smashes his lips closed, as if to tell me he's not going to speak again.

I laugh so hard that I roll back into him. Before I know what I'm doing, I've kissed the side of his mouth, my lips puckered.

This gets his attention, and he raises an eyebrow at me, very slowly. "What are you asking for?"

"Your attention."

His eyebrow goes up a little further. "You give me a good—nay, great—book, yell at me to read it, and then as soon as we sit down you want my attention?"

"One," I count, "I didn't yell. Two, we've been here for hours. Three, you've read over one hundred pages. Four, if you're going to leave me for Harry, you should do it now, instead of leading me on and breaking my heart."

Levi blinks at me. Then he tosses the book into the sand (I'll admit it—I cringe) and grabs me. I have no idea what he's going to do, so I wait. But he just holds me close to his chest, our warm bodies practically molding together. After a moment he says, quite dramatically, "I could *never* leave you for Harry."

I laugh. "Good to know."

"I could never leave you for anyone, Bambi."

"Ugh," I say. But it's quiet, hardly a noise at all, and he smiles slowly. Then I whisper, "Good," and let him tuck me against him, my bare cheek against his bare chest, our fingers entwined on his stomach.

We're both a tad burnt and completely exhausted when we get home, but I'm still smiling. I haven't stopped smiling since The Sorting Hat Incident. Levi's quiet, his hand tucked into mine the entire drive back. His silence is contemplative. I have a feeling he's thinking about exactly what I'm thinking about: today and our relationship and the way our hands are pressed together. His fingers are so much longer than my stubby ones (my fingers match my height and my hips), but they still fit in the best possible way.

He lets go once when we get out of the car—only to snatch it up again right away.

We stand on the front porch for a moment, faces close, bracing for my loud family inside, the people who will shut off any sort of lingering glances or laced fingers or caressing of knees and wrists and necks. The moment grows between us, cinching us together, making me hyper-aware of his smooth palm and his slight smirk and his hair that clings to the nape of his neck with sweat and salt water and sunscreen, and the way his eyes are so obviously on my lips.

Before he forgets where we are, before I forget who I am, I break contact and slide the key into the lock.

When it clicks open, I find the house surprisingly empty. "Hello?" I call.

The first thing I hear is my dad's phone ringing, somewhere in the kitchen. I go toward the noise, thinking I will find him. Instead I find his phone, alone on the counter, the number unfamiliar but the area code from San Diego. "Dad! Your phone!" I yell.

There's no sign of Papa anywhere, so I click on the green answer button. When a woman's voice responds to my hello, my stomach immediately grows queasy.

"Hello, is Matthew Wescott available?"

There he is—my dad is coming up the path from the backyard onto the patio. "Yes, may I ask who's speaking?"

"I'm calling from Scripps Green with a reminder for his appointment on Monday."

Scripps Green.

A hospital.

This woman is calling from a hospital, a very renowned hospital, one that covers an entire realm of treatments and operations, from plastic surgery to chemotherapy.

I was wrong. I was so wrong.

My dad, stepping into the house, sees his phone in my hands and the expression on my face and looks at me warily. "Bee? What's up?"

"Papa," I say. I can barely hold out the phone to him. My fingers don't want to stop shaking.

He squints at me, taking the phone, putting it to his ear. "Hello?"

The woman on the other line, faceless and nameless, speaks to him. And he immediately knows—that I know, that I'm putting the pieces together. He turns around and walks into the other room, shoulders hunched. I follow, tugging Levi behind me, every step uncertain and every breath more painful than the last.

When my dad looks up at me, hanging up on the receptionist, I shake my head. "What's going on?" I whisper.

My dad's sigh is heavy. "Bee."

"What's. Going. *On*?"

Levi squeezes my hand once. "I can go, Matt, if you want?"

"No, you should stay," Daddy says, and waves us to the couch. "You have a right to know. You'll find out soon enough, anyway."

I watch my father lower himself in his red recliner, and I wait. I wait for him to speak, to do something, do anything.

"It's stage 3C," he says, so quiet, and I'm completely undone. "It's in my brain."

Levi is as still as I am. I can feel his heart beating in his chest where it's pressed against my back. Yet, I can't feel my own heartbeat.

"*Papa*," I breathe.

"They can't perform an operation because of where it's at—too dangerous. I could lose a lot more than my life. So chemo and radiation, and whatever other special treatments we can try . . . they're all we've got." He clears his throat. (I can hardly see him. Why can't I see him?) "Bee, you can't tell your siblings yet. They don't know, and I wanted to tell you all after my first round of chemotherapy—"

"How long have you known?" I whisper.

"A few weeks now. They predict I have three months left, unless the chemo does something. A miracle."

The way he says it, so factual, so nonchalant—as if he's *used* to this news that *he's going to die*—makes me furious. I'm boiling over, red beneath my skin, pulling into myself. "How dare you," I say, because it makes more sense than anything else I want to say.

"What?" he asks, surprised. I never talk to him this way.

"I thought you and mom were getting a divorce. I thought you'd cheated on her or that something had happened with the house—or maybe you'd lost your job. I thought so many things, and I've spent so many weeks fighting these thoughts because I just wanted it to be okay. But this is worse. This is so much worse!"

He stands. I can see tears forming in his eyes and that's when I know it's too late for me. I begin to cry, letting him embrace me, but crying on his shoulder doesn't make me feel any better. I try to wrap my arms around him. I try to push my face into his cotton t-shirt.

I try to shut out the absolute agony inside me. It's like being ripped to shreds.

And when it doesn't work, I push him away. I don't want to hug him, even though I *do*, I desperately do. I accidentally hit Levi's shoulder with mine as I leave the room. He tries to stop me, but I am the Unstoppable Force. I wrench my hand away, turning the corner, and head for my car.

Minutes pass while I sit in the driver's seat, my chest hollow, my breathing deep and uneven. It isn't until Levi gets into the passenger seat that I realize I haven't driven away, and I immediately shove a shaking hand toward the ignition.

His hand covers mine, stopping me. "Bee, please."

His pretty eyes, round and blue, have never looked so sad.

"Levi," I grind out. My voice is gone.

"Bee, *please*," he begs. I relinquish my keys. He sets them in the cup holder and opens the space between us so I can climb over. I sit on his lap, my head on his chest, not hearing a word he's saying. His fingers brush through my hair.

(It reminds me of my father, combing his fingers through my hair, through Astrid's and Millie's. We all have such long, beautiful hair. He learned how to braid so well, just for us.)

I want to scream, to spit, to fold myself into the tiniest ball possible. I want to shout at my father for absolutely no reason, other than that he's dying and I can't change it. That is an unbearable truth, more unbearable than anything I have known in my small life.

(The world is so much bigger now.)

I can't do any of the things I want to do. All I can do is cry, and all Levi can do is hold me.

The world spins, and I feel pain everywhere, and I die a little bit inside with every tear I shed, so that I'm left feeling like a husk: empty, ruined, devoured.

chapter 28

QUEUED:
Lay Your Cheek On Down
by Moonface

WHATEVER ROUTINE I had before (with my parents, with Levi, with my siblings) is shattered. In its place grows a creature—a morphing, changing monster that disrupts every single day.

My father comes home from his first round of chemo, three days after I found out, and I can barely look at him. His face is puffy, his walk is slow, his eyes squint in exhaustion. There's one thing that isn't different: his smile. And he's smiling at *me* like he doesn't care about the last words I said to him three days ago. Like he understands.

This makes me feel incredibly guilty, so I sit beside him when my mom takes a nap and my sisters start their chores. (Millie and Astrid still just think he's sick, and I don't know when he'll tell them that he's dying.) Tom drifts in and out, claiming he needs a nap to recover from his shift, but he looks wary. (I wonder if he's already pieced together the puzzle.)

Sitting on the sofa, I put my hand on my papa's, feeling his pulse so faint beneath his skin. I don't look at him. I can't.

"You need anything?" I ask eventually, gripping his hand tighter.

"I'm fine. Thanks, Bee."

I shake my head. "I'm sorry," I say simply.

He nods. "I know."

My breath shudders. "No, I'm sorry about what I said—"

"I know," he repeats.

(Oh, how the heart aches.)

"Where's The Boy?" my dad asks.

I can't even laugh at this. "He's at the shop today, then TCP until eight tonight."

"Hmm. He should come see me."

"Why?" I ask.

"Because." He shrugs. "He should hang out with our family more, just in general."

"He's here all the time, Papa."

"Not all the time."

A sense of dread wells in my heart. I know what he's doing. He wants Levi around all the time in case he dies before he can see us with what we all hope will be a future together.

(1. The fact that he likes my boyfriend this much makes my heart sing.)

(2. The fact that he's preparing for what he thinks is the inevitable makes my heart weak.)

"I'll let him know," I say, acting like my voice isn't husky and that my eyes aren't full of tears. I am such a pretender. (I'm only half sorry for it.)

"You'd better." He squeezes my hand. "Will you read to me?"

I smile a little. "Sure. What book are you reading?"

"*Crime and Punishment*," he says. "Haven't been able to read much lately. Bad headaches."

I close my eyes, briefly, before grabbing the book off the computer desk. I don't want to think about his headaches. I don't want to remember him as the dad who had headaches so often that he couldn't read my favorite books.

So I read *for* him, picking up where he left off, and immerse myself in Raskilnikov's path to self-destruction.

"Does he get redemption?" my father asks at one point, interrupting me.

"Say what?" I ask, coming out my reading marathon in a fog.

"Raskilnikov. Does he redeem himself?"

"I'm not telling you. That's the whole point of the book!"

Papa frowns, but nods and tells me to keep reading. What I don't think about: the fact that there is over half the book left, and the fact that my father has three months of life in his bones. I don't think about it because it scares me, like a fist around my heart that is slowly squeezing, slowly and painfully and with certainty. I can only scream silently behind my eyelids, and read, read, read.

Later I find Levi in his room, putting clothes neatly into his dresser. His door is wide open, so I let myself in and sit on his bed.

"Want to talk about it?" he asks. It's like he senses me, because I haven't made a sound.

"Hell, no."

"You have to talk about it eventually."

"Eventually doesn't mean today." I pat the bed beside me until he joins me. He tucks his arms around my middle and lays us backward, his nose pressed to my shoulder. My eyes are level with his wild hair, but I can hardly see it through my tears. So instead I thread my fingers into it, my lips on his forehead, waiting as teardrops silently drip onto his skin.

He only squeezes me tighter.

"He wants you around the house more," I eventually say, sniffling wetly.

"That's . . . possibly the best thing I've heard in a long time."

"Why?"

"It means your dad likes me more than I expected."

"What did you expect?"

"I don't know. I'm the one who had a shitty dad all my life—what was I *supposed* to expect?"

I shake my head, lips rubbing gently back and forth across his hairline. "I don't know. I don't know what to expect from all this stuff, either."

"What . . . stuff?"

"Dating."

He puffs a breath onto my shoulder, leaving chills to crawl their way up and down my spine. It feels altogether *too* pleasant. (I don't have the emotional capacity to think about that.)

"Well," he says, quietly. "I can stop by once a day if that will make him happy."

"I'm sure he'll be way too happy for his own good." (I say it as an act of rebellion; I know there's no such thing as *too happy* for someone who's dying like my father is dying.) "But are you sure you can fit it in?"

"Bee," he says, in that gentle tone reserved for me. "Of course."

"Well, do what you can. He'll be happy either way."

My ears are hit with a sudden wave of "Forever Your Girl" by Paula Abdul. We sit listening, silent, for a whole minute before we burst into laughter. Levi rolls onto his back so we're both looking up at the ceiling, our legs dangling off the edge. Once again, his feet touch the ground. Once again, mine do not.

"You'd better not be laughing at me," Suzie says, entering the room. Her hands are covered in flour.

"Oh," Levi says, laughing harder. "Not at all."

"Levi Brenton." She says it with such severity that we both stop and lift our heads to look at her. Then she grins. "No more tears tonight, Bee. Let me teach you my ways, with the help of a personal favorite."

I smile. "I'll be right in there. Thanks, Suzie."

She leaves us alone, dancing off to the beat of her music. Levi stands up, hands anxiously adjusting his plain gray tee by pulling on the hem. I totally notice the gray accentuating his form, how lean he is, how nicely toned his arms are, and I want to pull him back to me.

I stand instead. "Hey, Levi?" I ask, tentatively.

Levi takes my hand. "Hmm?"

"I haven't told Gretchen yet. I just don't know...how." I'm whispering, even though there's no reason to. I know I should feel ashamed for not telling her, but my fear of what she'll say, of her sadness mirroring mine . . . I'm not ready for it.

He nods and swallows hard. "It's not going to be easy. Want me to be there when you do tell her?"

"I just don't want to talk about it, remember?"

"Oh, I remember. And *I'm* just reminding you that your denial has to come to an end soon."

"I'm not in denial," I protest, slightly hurt by his (all-too-true) accusation.

He shakes his head. "You're not talking about it because you hope you'll wake up tomorrow and it will all have been a lie."

He's hit the problem in the head, but I'm not ready to confess. I shrug it off. "It'll be hard no matter what, when, or how."

"I know," he whispers. "But for now, let's bake. Pauluzie is waiting for us."

I laugh (half-heartedly) at this name combination, taking his hand. "We wouldn't want to disappoint," I say, even though my feet are stuck to the floor and my will to move is weak.

Levi seems to notice my hesitation, because he grabs both of my hands and, walking backward, starts to dance. I roll my eyes (my way of getting rid of tears), but his movements pull me in. The beat of the music carries me, and Levi knows all the lyrics (of *course* he does), and hearing him sing the words "forever your giiiirl" makes me laugh.

"Don't laugh at me," he says. "I had no choice but to memorize this song."

"You can't even blame this one on childhood," I say, lightness coming back into my step. "This is all since the divorce."

Laughing, he accepts the bowl of unmixed ingredients Suzie hands to him and lifts himself up onto the counter. The heels of his Chuck Taylors hit the cupboards, hard enough that his mom says, "Levi, don't kick the cupboards—you'll scuff them up."

"Mom, *Mom*," he says over the blaring music. "I will repaint them if I have to. Just let me live a little." Then he winks at me, pulling me into the little spot he's made between his legs. I rest my head and shoulders back against his chest, elbows on his thighs. He brings the bowl around to my front so that he's mixing the dough *and* holding me. It feels so good to be here that I could cry in relief.

"Hey, Mom, how about a song we all know?" he asks.

Suzie obliges, and after a second of silence from the iPod, Freddie Mercury starts to sing, mournfully and soulfully.

"Now, Bohemian Rhapsody I can *definitely* do," I say, and start to sing the next part of the verse. Levi joins in, chuckling, and after one more stir he gives the bowl to his mom and lets me lick the spoon. All I can think is, *Levi*, like his name is a blessing, like it's a kiss or a lifeline or a photograph. I'm also thinking, *So the baking thing really does work*, as I lean into Levi's embrace.

I let his warmth envelope me.

I stay one more hour, which means I get sent home with a warm plate of cookies. I bring them into the kitchen with me, feeling lighter than I have since my beach day with Levi. I set the plate of cookies down on the counter. "Astrid, Millie?" I ask, but when I turn, I realize they're already there.

I also realize they've been waiting for me, and that they're crying. Millie leans against Astrid for support, but Astrid doesn't seem too strong, either.

"Hi, girls," I say quietly. What else am I supposed to say? They know now; there's nothing for me *to* say.

Millie bursts into tears again. I'm carried into their arms by my own need for comfort, wrapping myself around them and into them until we're entwined, a sister-pretzel, all of us crying over our father. Our tears mingle and mix; our hiccup-sighs are almost a harmony. Then Tom joins us. He wraps his long arms around all three of us girls, kissing my forehead. His sigh is heavy, and it shakes, and that hurts me more than anything.

Not for the first time, I wonder when our hearts will break, or if they're just dissipating, inch by inch, until there's nothing left.

chapter 29

QUEUED:
Runaway
by AURORA

I STARE AT THE phone in my hands, blood pulsing.

Gretchen called me yesterday, but I couldn't bring myself to answer. I didn't text her back, or check Messenger, or listen to her voicemail. Yesterday was, in fact, one of three days since the beginning of our friendship that we haven't spoken. Everything inside me hurts and I don't know how to deal with it.I don't know how to bear my own pain and everyone else's, too.

What I do know: A week was far too long to keep this secret.

Sitting on the swing hanging over our back porch, I listen to her voicemail first, to see if it will bring me some courage and comfort. "Hey, Bee," she says, happy as a bird in the spring, "I hope everything's all right. Miss you bunches! You should call me back tonight sometime. I think you're crap."

I swallow hard. *Hi Gretchen, I'm sorry I didn't tell you about everything going on, please forgive me for being such a terrible friend, and for betraying your trust. Please know that I love you and can't live without you.*

That's what I mean to tell her. But when Gretchen answers the phone a few moments later, my mouth opens and I say, "Hey, sorry I couldn't call you back yesterday."

"Where've you been?" she asks, not unkindly. "I missed you!"

"Just . . . super busy at the shop." I bite my lip in disappointment. (*Seriously, Bee?*)

It hurts. It hurts. It hurts.

Gretchen sighs. "I can't wait to see the shop, someday," she says wistfully. "Whatcha doin'?"

"I'm relaxing outside. It's so hot here." I glance up, kicking our porch swing back and forth to catch the breeze. It's nine o'clock on Saturday, and I'm still in my pajamas.

"Sounds nice, actually." She clears her throat. "So . . . how's Levi?"

"He's really good," I say. I feel awkward and overheated and ridiculous. *This is your best friend—get a grip, Bee.*

"Mmhmm. Has he kissed you yet?"

"Gretchen."

"It's a legitimate question, Bee."

I roll my eyes. "No."

"Shouldn't be that hard—"

"Gretchen."

"What?"

"I'm *working* on it."

Gretchen says something, but it's drowned out by the sound of Levi asking, "Working on what?"

I jump, twisting to look at him where he stands behind the swing. "Nothing," I say, too quickly, almost like a warning.

"Is that Gretchen?" he asks.

"Yeah."

"Tell her I said hello," he says, but his eyes ask if I've told her about Papa.

I ignore this and relay his message. Gretchen grunts loudly. "Tell him to kiss you *soon*, or *else*."

I make a pitiful noise. "No, absolutely not."

Levi snatches the phone from me before I even realize he's moved. He sits by my legs on the edge of the patio and says, "Hello, *Gretchen*. What do you want to tell me that she doesn't want to say out loud?"

I tip my head over the back of the swing, making a face at the sky. I'm contemplating all sorts of things—such as what I'm going to eat for breakfast and when I can get to the gym and where my lost t-shirt went and oh, *all right*, I'm thinking about kissing him, too—when I hear him say, "I was already planning on it. Don't panic."

I jerk forward, staring at the top of his head, which now rests on my knee.

"Are you threatening me?" he asks Gretchen, sounding very serious.

She says something loudly and passionately on the other line. "Just give it back to me," I groan, thoroughly embarrassed.

He holds up a hand. "Excuse me, what?" He laughs. "All right, all right, don't worry about it, okay? I get it, you care *so much* and all that, etcetera, *etcetera*."

Despite myself, I laugh.

"Here you go," he adds (after Gretchen has the last word) and passes the phone to me.

Gretchen immediately says, "I'm not telling you what we talked about, so don't ask. Just go about your day like nothing happened."

"I can't now. You've ruined everything."

"Well, that's okay because I've made you laugh."

I look down, running my hand through Levi's hair, unable to stop myself. "That's all that matters, huh?"

"Yeah." She sighs. "I have to go to work now, okay? But you will call me later?"

"Okay," I say, heavily, and hope she doesn't notice.

She doesn't, because there are three thousand miles between us. "I think you're crap."

"I think you're crap," I reply, and hang up.

Levi turns his head so his cheek rests against my knee. He reaches up, wrapping his hand around mine, touching my pulse where it flutters under my skin.

"What are you doing here?" I ask quietly. He lets go of my hand, our fingertips just grazing each other, a new kind of torture. He must feel it, too, and drops his hand to his side.

"I came to see your dad."

"Thanks," I choke out, rubbing my eyes. I won't cry. I *won't.* "Want to do something for lunch?"

He nods his head. "I don't have any plans. Erm, actually, there's an interview later. But that's it."

Astrid calls my name, rushing out onto the patio, mouth open to say something else. Then her eyes narrow and she shakes her head. "You two."

I give her a very pointed expression. "What's up?"

"Don't make those eyes at me," she says.

"What are you talking about?"

"The 'I'm so in love, please leave us alone' eyes."

"I didn't know that was a thing."

"It is. You created it. When you started going out with Dufus over here."

Levi raises his hand. "I am Dufus."

Astrid cracks a smile at that. "It's all right, I mean, because he's pretty cool and all." She shrugs, as if she's the Queen of Benevolence to give us her blessing.

"Gee, thanks. What did you need, Astrid?"

"For you to come to do the dishes." She starts to leave. "Oh," she adds, turning back to us, "and put a bra on. Much appreciated."

I look down. I'm wearing a baggy t-shirt, one of my dad's old work shirts, and Astrid is right. Thinking of where my clean bra hangs on my doorknob, I press my palm against my face, mortally embarrassed. Levi acts like he hasn't heard (probably to spare me pain) and stands, grabbing my hand to help me up. He doesn't look at my face, just runs his hand over my arm, up, up, past my elbow, touching all my skin. His palm stops on my shoulder, his thumb resting on the soft spot by my collarbone. It brushes back and forth twice, his gaze locked there, mesmerized by something I don't understand, something that both terrifies and thrills me. I study his face as he does this, so thankful and scared.

(Thing You Should Know About Me #83: If you didn't *already* know, I love his face, with his adoring eyes and angled features and kind mouth.)

Finally, Levi shakes himself out of whatever trance he's in. "See you in a minute?"

I nod, letting him walk into the house. I see him sit down beside Millicent on the ground, his hair flopping into his face, and I take a deep breath in. *Steady, Bee.*

I take the other back door inside and run to my room, where I throw on actual clothes. (And a bra. Thanks, Astrid.) I wrap my hair into a bun atop my head and hurry back to the main part of the house.

Astrid stops me in the kitchen, handing me the sponge. "Mom said it's your turn." Her smile is persistent, clearly adding, *I'm going to tell her you're a disobedient brat if you don't.*

I raise an eyebrow. "Where's Levi?"

"Dufus?" Astrid grins. "He's sitting with Daddy."

"Okay. Don't make him work—"

"And he's helping Mama rearrange her jewelry box."

I rub a hand over my eyes, shaking my head. She leaves, and I hurry with the dishes, not wanting Levi to feel obligated. But when I get into the living room fifteen minutes later and sit beside him, I find he's having the time of his life, safekeeping the three pairs of earrings my mother has bestowed upon him.

His grin, meant only for me, bares all his teeth. "Next job: Jewelry organizer for the wealthy."

"Oh, *really*," I say, amused.

"Yep. We'll move to L.A. and buy a huge mansion once I've saved enough money, and we'll get a dog and a fish and have a really great swimming pool and invite all my celebrity friends over for a party."

"The American Dream," I say drily, but in reality, I'm brimming with joy because he said "we".

"Absolutely, honey." He pats my knee.

"That's nice, dear," I reply, in all seriousness.

Astrid pretends to gag, but Millie is smiling at us in rapture. "You two," she says. They're the same words Astrid said earlier, but they sound completely different coming from her. Less cynical, more romantic. I reward her with a smile and a kiss on the cheek.

"Yeah, *you two*," my dad says from his recliner. "So ooey-gooey."

"Dad," I say, very seriously. "Don't invite Levi over and expect us to never look at each other."

He winks at me. "Of course not."

I smile, even though it hurts.

Levi places the earrings in their new spot in the box and grabs the next pair from my mom. "Hey, Matt, mind if I borrow your daughter tomorrow? We probably won't be back until late."

Papa's eyes narrow. "Um." He looks uncertain, but not

because he doesn't trust Levi. He's confused about the question because Levi borrows me all the time.

I nudge Levi. "Meaning . . . ?"

"There's a TCP event in Malibu, and I have a plus one."

My dad makes an "ah" shape with his mouth. "Well, sure. That's fine."

Levi looks at me, as if waiting for an answer. Does he think I'm going to say no? Ha! I rest my chin on his shoulder. (Our faces are touching in a lot of places but not enough places. Not the *right* places.) "That sounds like fun! What kind of event?"

"Silent auction. One of our sponsors is putting it on, actually. I've been talking to ehim about the TCP building, and he's interested in discussing his properties with me."

"You're moving TCP?"

"I have no plans yet, but if he can offer me something better than what we already have, I'll take it. He owns, like, ten houses and several office buildings."

"Sounds . . . rich."

"Oh, believe me, he is." He kisses my nose. The fact that he can do this in front of my whole family without getting scolded means he's scored some serious points. "And I'm taking you to dinner."

I give him my best skeptical look, but I'm actually hyperventilating inside. "Where to?"

"Somewhere awesome. Duh. Dufus knows best."

I make a strange giggle-hum in the back of my throat. It sounds awfully giddy. "Whatever you say."

"So long as you keep your cell phones on you," my mom says, "I have no problem with it."

I grin. "I'm excited. What time should I be ready?"

"One o'clock."

I nod excitedly. "It's a date."

Once again, Astrid makes a gagging motion, and Millie is in

the clouds. But they're both smiling, and my parents are, too, and that makes everything a little bit more bearable.

I spend the evening with Papa.

My mom and sisters leave for ballet class, so it's just me and Tom and my dad. The last time this happened was . . . well. I don't remember the last time this happened.

I sit on the couch, my legs curled under me. It's nearing dinner, so Tom is heating up some leftovers. Papa has his legs up on the recliner, listening intently while I explain the process of creating a Zen Artistry arrangement. As I pause to show him a picture of the orchid with its wide petals and the long, skinny shoot of horsetail, he says, "Will you read to me again?"

I look over at him and instantly forget about the picture. His eyes are closed and his chest is rising and falling in regular, even breaths. Tom hands me a plate of food and sets Papa's on the coffee table. "When he's ready," he whispers to me.

I nod at Tom and say to Papa, "Of course I'll read to you." I grab *Crime and Punishment*, opening to the bookmark.

It takes me a moment before I realize this is where we left off, nearly a week ago, and that he hasn't picked it up since. I glance at the table, noting that the book was exactly where I set it down last Monday. The cover has even gathered a bit of dust.

My heart is breaking, breaking, every inch shattering. (But what did I expect?) "Daddy," I murmur.

"Yes?" He doesn't open his eyes.

I don't know what to say. "Okay. I'll read now."

He smiles, warmly.

I hide my tears from him and Tom (and myself) and start to read.

chapter 30

QUEUED:
SUGAR
BY EDITORS

IT'S SUNDAY AFTERNOON, the silent auction looms ahead, and I feel compromised. "I can't believe you made me leave the house like this."

From the driver's seat of his car, Levi casts me a brief look and frowns. "Why? You look beautiful."

I let out a howl of laughter. My face is flushed, my hair is greasy from the heat, and I'm wearing the sweatpants I wore yesterday around the house. I suddenly feel warm—and it's not just from all the sun. "Shut up, Levi."

He gives me a mystified look. "I'm not lying to you."

"Well, you're delusional."

"We're going somewhere casual for dinner, so relax," he says, and for some reason, this surprises me. He explains, "I figured we could only handle so many snooty rich people in one night."

I laugh again. "Right. Well. I still could have just slipped the dress on before we got into the car."

"What dress?"

It hits me like a freight train: absolute panic. "What *dress*? WHAT DRESS?! Levi, the dress I'm supposed to wear tonight, *that* dress!"

I look over at him, and he's trying not to *smile*. As if he's got all the secrets locked inside his mouth. I blush. (*Shh, forget about that, Bee.*) "I knew we forgot something," he says.

I turn sharply toward the back seat. My dress, which I expressly put on the seat, is nowhere to be seen. "Levi. Why are you . . . *happy*? This is terrible!"

He breaks out into a full grin. "I'm happy because I told Astrid to hide the dress inside. I was distracting you with that long and very excellent hug. Remember?"

Oh, I remember. "Why?" I wail.

"Because I have something better."

I'm silent, looking at him incredulously. Then I explode, "You bought me a dress?!"

"Good job, you caught on."

I give him the Devil's stare. "Excuse me, Levi, how dare you," I say. "I protest—I'm going naked."

Levi chokes on nothing but air. He hacks a couple of times, hand over his chest. His expression is one of complete surprise and . . . well, I immediately regret saying what I said.

"I take that back," I hastily amend, because now he's glancing over at me, probably imagining the scenario I so stupidly presented. I sincerely hope that, in the aforementioned imagined scenario, I am standing behind some strategically placed leaves. "I'm wearing my sweatpants, and you can't stop me."

"Don't be difficult," he says. His cheeks are pink with embarrassment.

"Too late."

He laughs, making a smooth right turn into a parking lot that comes out of nowhere. It belongs to a fish and chips place, a tiny little shack nestled into the side of the mountains. There's only outdoor seating, because in California (where it never rains and you're across the freeway from the Pacific Ocean) you never want to sit inside.

"I found this place a couple of years ago when my dad moved up here," Levi explains as we hurry out of the car and get into the line. After driving for two hours, I'm thankful for a minute to stretch my legs. "I've wanted to bring you here all summer."

I don't answer right away, just enjoying the view. He looks down at me, sudden panic crossing his face. "What?" I ask.

"Do you not like fish and chips?"

Oh, Levi. "Of course I love fish and chips! It's seafood and French fries—who do you think I am?"

He puts a hand on his chest, as if in relief. "Oh good."

Together we step up to the open ordering window. Levi orders our food, but when the lady asks for his name, he says, "You know what? Put it under Barbie."

The woman in the window looks at me. I look at her. I challenge her to say something.

Levi walks away.

I smile my best fake smile, then hurry after him. "That's *it!*" I yell—and in front of whoever happens to be watching, I run at his back, fling my arms around his neck, and lock my legs around his waist. "You're not allowed to do that ever again!"

His laugh catches on the hills behind us. He hefts me up, walks a few feet, and plops me down on the last open table. "Then just tell me."

When he turns around, I grab the front of his shirt and pull him in. "Maybe."

He raises an eyebrow. "That's the closest you've come to a yes."

"Don't press your luck." I move to my seat, and he sits across from me, and I feel my chest constricting. For a moment I wish he would ask me why I won't tell him, but then I'm thankful he hasn't because I have no answer for him.

Suddenly, I feel small and young and a little bit helpless, because I'm head-over-heels for him and I still don't know how to just open my mouth and say my name.

"Trust me, I'm not pressing anything." His smile catches the sun, and he places his hand over mine, gently and with certainty. "I'm just thankful we can cross Barbie off the list."

We arrive at the silent auction with just enough spare time to get ready. The house is massive, tucked into the hills above the cliffs, complete with a roundabout driveway, pillars, and land to spare. The valet takes Levi's car (a freaking valet!) after Levi grabs his suit and my new dress from the trunk. (He put in a bag so I can't see it. Rude.)

The man who meets us at the front door is younger than I'd expected, maybe in his early thirties. He looks as brilliant as John Legend at an awards ceremony, with his hair buzzed close to his scalp and his elegant beige suit complimenting his dark skin. When he smiles, it's warm and kind and immediately puts me at ease amidst all this grandeur.

"My friend," he says, and brings Levi in for a tight hug. "Good to see you."

I step inside behind Levi, who puts his arm around my shoulder in that reassuring way of his. "This is my girlfriend, Bee. Bee, this is Felix."

I pass my makeup bag from one hand to the other so I can shake his hand. "Nice to meet you."

"The pleasure's mine. I've heard wonderful things about you," Felix answers, and shuts the door behind us. The foyer is immense, with marble floors, columns, and two sets of stairs— one to the left and one to the right. Felix nods at the staircase to the right, and the woman who stands at the bottom. "Julia will show you to a guest room where you can get ready. I can give you the rest of the tour when you're done."

"Thanks, man," Levi says, shaking Felix's hand again. When our host disappears down the stairs into the rest of the house, we follow the maid up the stairs. She takes us down the grand hallway marked with huge paintings to one of the guest rooms.

"Let me know if you need anything," Julia says, and closes the door.

It's a huge room with wood floors, a massive king-size bed, and beautiful lace curtains. There's a bathroom to our right, but all I can see of it is the giant porcelain tub. "Wow," I muse. "Nicest guest room I've ever seen."

Levi faces me. "You get the bathroom," he prompts as he hands me the dress bag. "I'll wait for you out here."

I bite my lip, accepting his gift with hesitant hands. "Okaaay."

He touches my shoulders and nudges me backward. "Don't keep me in suspense. I'm freaking out."

"You don't look like you're freaking out," I say, but then I make eye contact. He is, indeed, freaking out. "Never mind. But you're cute, you know."

He growls. "Bee."

I smile innocently. "Going, going, gone."

And I shut myself into the silence of the marble bathroom.

For a second I just...stare. This bathroom is the size of my bedroom, and the bathtub is the size of my bed. It's beautiful (like Michelangelo-painted-my-ceiling beautiful) and daunting. The same kind of daunting as opening this bag to see the dress inside. But I can't let it stop me—not when so much of Levi's happiness is riding on my shoulders.

I strip down to my bra and underwear first, taking my hair out of its messy bun, and remove any and all rubber bands from my wrists. Thing You Should Know About Me #48132: I'm the queen of procrastination when my nerves settle in. So I know I'm really and truly nervous when I'm staring at my mostly-naked self in the mirror for five minutes, deciding what to do. *What if I hate the dress? What if it's a beautiful cut but a terrible color? What if it doesn't fit?*

I brush these thoughts aside when I realize Levi is probably already dressed and ready to go. So I grab the bag and untie the bottom, and out spills the edge of the dress—no, it's a *gown*—and another, smaller bag. Hyperventilating, I grab the smaller bag and open it up first.

Inside there's a small piece of paper that reads, *My mom says you'll need these. I didn't look. Swear on my life.* Laughing—and realizing too late that he can probably hear my laugh and *oh gosh what if he thinks I'm laughing at the dress*—I pull out a strapless bra, a pair of silver heels, and a small box. I lay the bra on the counter and the shoes on the ground, and I open the box.

Inside is a dainty necklace, made of thin metal and pearls strung at intervals. I immediately think of Suzie, and how she must have slipped this in from her own collection. It looks like something she would wear.

I hardly know what to do. I'm numb and surprised and overwhelmed as I lay the necklace on the counter and switch out my old bra for the new one (my boobs do not like strapless bras, but I will survive). Then, heaving, I finally pull the dress all the way out of the bag.

It's blue—that's the first thing I notice. It's blue like midnight, my favorite blue. It's strapless, draped in tulle that wraps across the bodice. The bottom half is also tulle: one side dropping to the ground, the other side open to just above the knee to show off a little bit of leg, wrapped in such a way that will hug my hips.

But what gets me is the fabric from the knee down. It looks as though it has been dipped in glitter of all different sizes, and I'm suddenly thinking of the stars that drift above our heads, and every conversation we've ever had about the constellations.

Bee, don't cry, you ninny. Thankful I haven't put makeup on yet, I unzip the side, careful not to pinch the tulle, and pull it over my head. I can tell from the moment it is around my chest that it will fit like a glove, so I pull the zipper back up, put the shoes on, and wrap the necklace around my neck.

It isn't until I look in the full-body mirror that I have to remind myself to breathe. Just the dress alone makes me look five years older. My hair sits in uncharacteristic waves around my face, and the necklace is dainty, and the shoes are sexy. (Am I allowed to use that word right now?) I stare and stare and stare, and it only makes me feel stranger and younger and older all at once, and my heart is beating so hard I can't breathe.

Is this what Levi sees, when he looks at me? Is this what he *wants* to see? Is this the way he wants me to dress? I turn, my right leg showing through the slit up to my lower thigh. I look beautiful, but something about it feels strange.

A knock at the door startles me, a squeak strangling my throat as Levi says, "Bee?"

I heave a breath. "Coming, just a minute."

"Okay."

Oh, gosh, he sounds so cute, waiting for me to come out and show him, all nervous and cooped up and one-hundred percent handsome. I should want to get out there and grab his hand, to thank him and kiss his cheek. But all I can think is that this—the hair and the shoes and the strapless bra and the *dress*—this is all Bee.

This is not Bernice.

I close my eyes, but I still can't breathe. I don't know how to do Bernice. It's like Bernice is hidden deep, and I'm pretending to be this girl, Bee, who laughs and flirts and creates and plans, but who isn't really like that at all.

I blink hard, swallowing. There has to be another time to think about this, when Levi isn't waiting for me and there isn't a party downstairs and I can cry if I need to. I take a deep breath, and then another, and head toward the door.

In the bedroom, Levi stands by the glass door, lace curtains on either side of him, looking out over the ocean. His hands are in his pockets, and his hair is sticking up straight, as if he's been tugging on it in nervousness. He turns, saying, "I heard you laughing and—"

He sees me, his smile plastered to his lips like he doesn't know how to fix his mouth, like he doesn't know what to do. I can't find the words or the breath to say them. He's not even looking at the dress; he's looking at my eyes and my lips, and I see his desire. He is a reflection of me.

He crosses the room, hair beautifully askew, hands still pocketed in his gorgeously chic suit. It's light gray, contrasting perfectly with my dark look. I panic and say, "I love this dress." I mean it, even though I still feel queasy with nerves.

But then he's stopped in front of me, and he's actually looking, eyes crossing the length of my body. I've never felt so hot and cold and everything in between, all at once, like it will never end and I never want it to. "It's incredible, Bee," he says, his voice quiet.

I look down at the dress, at the starry, glittering edge, and I whisper, "It reminds me of the constellations. Did you plan that?"

He smiles with one corner of his mouth. "Would you break up with me if I lied and said that I totally did?"

We laugh, but it's stilted by whatever's happening inside both of us right now. He touches one strand of hair lingering on my cheek, his finger grazing the corner of my lips. Then his *mouth* is suddenly very close. His warm breath mingles with mine. There's a moment of us breathing together and not touching anywhere and just *being*, before he takes the next step and presses his body to mine and his lips are a whisper.

But they're there. They're an agony I've never experienced before.

Levi walks me backward until I'm against the wall and his hands are all palms against my stomach and hips. I shiver. He presses his lips to my cheek, sweet and gentle. A huff of breath escapes his nose, and a helpless noise at the back of his throat makes my knees wobble.

I tilt my head back, so he can see me, that I'm ready, that I can't breathe and neither can he and we're both starving for each other so he might as well just do it.

This is the kiss that means everything, I think.

And then his lips are on mine, awkward at first and so uncertain. I'm not sure what to do either, with my breath whooshing out of my chest and my hands splayed in the air because I don't know where to touch him. Our noses brush, his lips so foreign on my skin—and yet, I want them there. I want them there until they're no longer foreign, until we've memorized each other so thoroughly that my lips are imprinted on his and his on mine.

Then, he stops.

"Levi," I say, eyes still closed. When my lips move, I can feel his right there, just above mine, waiting.

"I want to do this right," he answers.

This time when I say his name, it's a whisper, a tiny moment of breath, and I put my hands on his cheeks. "Levi, Levi, Levi."

As if my touch has given him boldness, his arms encircle me

so that I am completely against him. My chest arches into his. He takes it slow, tasting my lips eagerly but gently, waiting for me to let go. The second my body softens and my arms slide around his neck and my mouth opens, he kisses me furiously, warm and strong and all kinds of delicious.

Yeah, I think. *This is* definitely *that kiss.*

There's something so terrifying about standing here with him, so fully invested, neither of us willing to leave the other. I forget everything: my papa, my fears, the fact that there's a castle surrounding us and anyone could knock on the door. And I don't want to go back—I don't want him to let me go. To make sure he doesn't pull away, I wrap my fingers in his hair and tug, deepening what we already had, making him hum. All I want to do is jump up and wrap my legs around him, let him hold me, but this dress is too snug around my hips.

His hands run along my hips and try to lift one leg, but it's awkward and fumbling and restricted. I let out a single huff of laughter, but that's all I can do before we're kissing again. He manages to pick me up with his arms around my waist, my shoes two inches off the floor, and I feel a little bit like flying and floating and growing wings.

Suddenly, an unbidden thought hits me. "I still have to do my hair," I whisper into his mouth. Then I go on with kissing him, because who cares about my hair? I sure don't.

He chuckles. "What? Don't want everyone to think we've been making out?"

I groan. "Does it look horrible?"

His lips graze mine, so beautiful and much too far away for me to be perfectly happy. "We'll have to see." He sets me down, holding me still while I catch my balance, and straightens. His lips are red, and I touch them, my hands on either side of his face, both thumbs trailing over where I was smashed against him only a few seconds ago. Levi closes his eyes. "Bee."

I look at him in wonder, that sharp face and lashes like silk and sensational, crazy hair that *I* made crazy, and I murmur, "We *kissed*."

"I know," he says, opening his eyes, and swoops in for one last peck before letting me go completely. "There's no going back now."

I can't believe what just happened and I have no idea what to say, so I grab his hand and tug him into the bathroom. "Come here, you have to fix your hair, too."

He lets me drag him along, but the moment we see *us* in the mirror, we stop. Levi's suit looks like he just rolled around in it and his hair sticks up straight like there's no gravity. My own hair is tossed around my face. My lips look darker.

Both of our cheeks are pink.

But despite our ridiculous appearances, neither of us can laugh. The desire to kiss each other senseless is still strong, and seeing us like this, beautiful and embraced and *loved*, makes us want to do it all over again.

Levi steps up behind me, wrapping his arm across my chest, his other arm around my waist, and kisses the side of my neck. I shiver, lifting my hands to touch his hair again. He nudges me with his nose. "Do you know what time it is?"

I check my phone on the counter. "Thirty till."

Levi sighs. Then, reluctantly backing up, he grabs his hair gel from where it sits in my makeup bag. "Better get going, then."

I watch as he unbuttons his suit jacket and takes his gel-covered fingers to his hair. He's done in a single minute, whereas I'm still figuring out how to style the jewel-studded clip in my hair. He waits patiently, sitting on the counter while I apply foundation and eye shadow. He talks about tonight, and the people coming, and the money he hopes to make for the charity—all the while watching me closely, studying my hands and my lips and my eyes. I can tell he's paying more attention to my every move than he is to his own words, and it makes my heart pound almost as fast as it did when he was kissing me.

It isn't until I'm done, standing up straight and wiping my powdery hands on a towel, that he reaches for me and kisses my cheek lightly. "All I can think is that the sooner we get this over with, the sooner I can mess up your lipstick."

I resist the urge to smother his cheek in pink. "Sounds like the best plan we've had all day."

"Ready?" he asks.

"So, so ready," I answer.

He takes my hand in his, heated by his heart pumping blood and some wild affection for me that's written in the stars, and I feel like he's holding my heart instead.

chapter 31

QUEUED:
TENDERLY
BY HOUSES

THE FIRST SILENT auction I went to with Levi consisted only of wall art, but this auction is bigger and brighter and is made up of everything colorful. There is art, of course, but there are also bursts of fashion, and musical instruments, and furniture designed by men and women with foreign-sounding names. The room, set at the back of the house with wide, bay windows to give us the perfect view of the ocean, is empty of people—but that will change soon. I can hear cars outside, expensive engines revving, a man laughing, a woman shouting.

I predict correctly: As soon as the front door opens, admitting the first guests, they don't stop pouring in. They're all dressed in clothes that far surpass mine in quality, but at least I feel as fancy as they look. Levi smiles as he shakes each hand offered to him, genuinely happy everyone could come, and makes it a point to introduce everyone to his "very beautiful girlfriend." (*That's me,* I keep reminding myself.) I smile, shake hands, make small talk . . . and all the while I wonder if I can do this, if I can be this person without falling apart. I think about our kiss, the way he touched me, and hold onto that image like a lifeline.

That is who I am. That is what we are.

For a while, there is nothing but the sound of laughter and clinking and too many footsteps. Everyone has come; the filled rooms echo and swallow me whole. But then the door opens again, and it's like Levi has frozen beside me, his breathing hollow. I look up from my appetizer, sensing his alarm.

Oh, hell no.

Levi breathes, "Dad?" and sets his glass down on a tray and drops my hand and escapes up the stairs into the foyer to where his dad is taking off his coat.

I decide, very stupidly, to follow him. "Levi," I interrupt. Already he looks pissed, and neither of them has spoken yet.

"Bee," Levi says, voice a little harder than usual, but I can tell he's trying to keep it under control for me. (Although, *why* he is so angry is a little lost on me.)

Mr. Orville smiles at me. "You look gorgeous tonight, Bee."

I hate his smile, so slimy and catching. "Thank you. Levi has good taste."

Mr. Orville gives me a once-over. His gaze stops on my neck and the pearls around it. "Who . . . where'd you get that?"

I touch it gingerly, thankful when Levi puts his hand on my back. "Mom let her borrow it," he says, the defense in his voice like a shield around me.

"It looks nice," Mr. Orville says, but his gaze lingers. "I remember it from our wedding."

I suddenly feel warm, in a very not-so-good way. In an embarrassed way. In a very angry way. (Thing You Should Know

About Me #2,201: I have never wanted to suffocate someone before, but they say there's a first time for everything.)

Levi shakes his head, as if unbelieving. "Dad, could you just drop it?"

"What? I'm only reminiscing. It's a happy memory." His smile, vicious and cold, tells me otherwise. "If you'll excuse me, I have some goods to bid on."

Levi breathes out as Mr. Orville glides past us, his arm brushing mine. I shudder, then put my head in my hands. "Ugh, Levi. I'm sorry—I can take the necklace off."

He grunts. "The necklace is not the problem—*he* is. He wasn't invited—I don't know who told him to come."

I take Levi's hand in one of my own, reaching to turn his face toward mine, so he can see my own doubt and anger. I should give him comfort of some kind, but I can't seem to find a single thing to say, so I just lift myself on my toes and kiss the very top of his lips.

"Thanks," he says, and even though he's unconvinced, I gather a little thrill from kissing him here, around all these people. It grounds me in a way I had not realized it would, and that keeps me from doubting myself for the millionth time tonight. Together, we turn and watch the progression of people, the way they group together and write on cards and drink champagne. The way Levi's dad saunters through the crowd and stares at the women and makes them laugh too hard and touches them too much.

I want to throw up.

"God, he makes me sick," Levi says, echoing my thoughts. "This is exactly why I told Felix not to invite him."

"There has to be a mix-up. You know, Felix probably has a secretary who does these things for him—maybe a note was misplaced?"

Levi shrugs, sullen. "Can't do anything about it now."

"Right. Good attitude."

He gives me a sidelong look. His expression is *almost* laughing. "My attitude is *terrible* right now."

I kiss him again, a little harder this time, and have to wipe the lipstick off his face with my thumb. (Not that I mind touching him.) "Sarcasm, Levi. Sarcasm."

Levi is only required to stay long enough to collect the money. We're invited to stay for the after party, but there are other things we'd like to do this evening. (Like kissing.) So we spend our last half hour in Felix's home listening to the host calling out names, watching men and women walk to the front of the crowd with checks in hand. Levi shakes his head, like he can't believe it, but I can. Everyone loves Levi. They love what he's doing, too, and I'm sure they look at him and his smile and feel his warm handshake and think, *What a standup guy.*

It's just the way the world works. All I have to do is stand by his side, hold his hand, let him drape his arm around my shoulder or waist. Sometimes I even let him kiss me, soft and warm and light, which helps me forget about how strange it feels to be here.

It's been dark for two hours by the time Levi collects the check from Felix, and it's folded neatly and placed in his wallet with the words "The Color Project" written across the front. We say quick goodbyes to Felix, thanking him again and again, before sneaking back upstairs to gather our things.

The bedroom immerses us in quiet; we can barely hear the sounds of the party below us. Levi squeezes my hand as we stare across the bed and out the glass door, lingering on the ocean that goes on forever.

"Hey," he finally says, walking to the window. "I think there's a lookout over there."

I stand beside him, putting my arms around his waist. He points toward the north, where the cliffs jut out over the ocean and there are no houses or cars. "We should go," I say. "We've got time, right?"

He nods. "It's only ten."

"Then let's do it."

Levi turns in my arms, kissing my forehead. He rests his chin on the top of my head and inhales. "I'm glad you're here."

"Me, too." I turn my head, tilting backward, and it's like he just *knows* I want him to kiss me. He lowers his mouth to mine. It's different this time, knowing what to expect, but no less exciting or wonderful. He squeezes my waist, then his hands are rising toward my hair, and he releases the clip so it falls loosely around my face. Instantly, his fingers get caught in the tangling waves, and he has to carefully—awkwardly—extract himself.

Laughing, I lean back and pull my hair to the side. "We should go," I whisper.

He touches my nose, softly, the pad of his finger trailing from top to bottom. "Okay."

I gather my old clothes and stuff them into the dress bag, as well as my shoes (I think the straps might be cutting into my skin by now) and my makeup bag. Levi stuffs his clothes into his own bag, shouldering it.

I glance out the window one more time.

"Ready?" he asks, holding out his hand to me.

I do more than that—I slide in for a hug. "Want to say goodbye to your dad first?"

He gives me a look that says *Ha ha no*. He tugs on my arm. "He didn't say hello, so he doesn't get a goodbye. Come on."

We wait for the valet to bring his car, but we only make it one block down the road before Levi's phone rings. He hands it to me as he turns onto the side road that leads to the lookout.

"Hello?" I answer.

"Hey, Bee, it's Felix."

I glance at Levi. "Hey... did we leave something?" I ask, my first guess. I take inventory, trying to remember if I left my shirt on the bathroom counter or my tennis shoes under the sink.

"No," Felix reassures, "I was just wondering if Levi knows where his dad is? We found his coat and wanted to return it to him."

I relay this to Levi.

"Seriously?" He scowls.

I nod.

"I have no idea where he is."

Felix tsks when I repeat this. "Well, if you hear from him before I do, let me know. And I'm sorry he showed up— Penelope was supposed to cross him off the list."

"It's all right," I answer. "Levi figured it was a mistake."

Felix sighs. "Thank him for me, and again, send his dad this way if you find out where he went."

I hang up, and Levi swings into the lookout parking lot (which consists of a few dusty spaces right before the cliff's grassy edge). He holds out his hand for his phone, and the second the car jerks to a stop, he's dialing his dad's number.

"Dad," he says. There is nothing but irritation in his tone. "Where the hell are you? Felix is looking for you—you left your coat." A pause. "Seriously? Where are you?" Levi puts his head in his free hand, grumbling something under his breath. "How many drinks have you had?" Another pause. "You need to pull over right now—Dad, don't give me shit. Pull over and park by the beach or something. Drop a location pin and send it to me. We'll come get you." His dad says something else, loudly, but I still can't hear him clearly.

Levi hangs up. He lays his phone between his legs and drops his head to the steering wheel—which lets out a bothered honk. He groans. "He said he lost count after drink four. And if I know anything for certain, it's that my dad is a lightweight."

I sigh. "Where is he?"

"About an hour north of here."

"Is he with someone?"

"Yeah, and she's just as drunk as he is. She was practically shrieking in the background." Levi looks up, out the window, at the cliff and our lookout and the moment we'd wanted to share here. He looks like he's about to apologize, so I stop him.

"You need to go get your dad, Levi. Don't worry about this."

"I can't believe him."

Frankly, neither can I, but this is important. Levi needs to know that I'm here for anything. "Let's go," I murmur. "We only have so much time."

Before he puts the car into reverse, Levi angles his body toward me, grabbing my face in his hands, and kisses me hard.

"I'm sorry," he gasps, in between bursts of kisses. "We'll come back here, I promise."

I smile and poke his cheek to make him face forward. "Don't get distracted now. You'll never get anything done."

"Right. Well, I can only think of one thing that *might* be as exciting as kissing you by the moonlit sea."

"What's that?"

He grins devilishly as he pulls back onto the road. "Borrowing one of my dad's *excellent* sets of wheels."

chapter 32

QUEUED:
40 DAY DREAM
BY EDWARD SHARPE & THE MAGNETIC ZEROS

LEVI LOOKS INCREDIBLY scrumptious in the front seat of his dad's matte gray Maserati GranTurismo. So scrumptious, in fact, that I have to stand back and gape at him for a second.

"Get in, Bee," he prompts, fiddling with the radio. With the flick of his wrist, the top of the car goes down, and I'm looking at a convertible that's almost as gorgeous as my boyfriend. He looks up at me when I don't respond. "Speechless?"

"No," I lie.

He calls my bluff. "It's kind of badass, right?"

I pretend to be unimpressed as I climb in. "Nah."

Levi laughs. "There's just no way in hell I'm paying for the gas to go get him, and he's not going to remember any of this in the morning anyway, so we might as well."

"Sounds reasonable." It's ten thirty now, which means it will be nearly midnight when we get to Mr. Orville. Wherever he's stopped. I silently thank Tracy for letting me take the late shift tomorrow.

Levi follows the map on his phone, which directs us to the Pacific Coast Highway. It's a drive I've always thought of as beautiful, but now I'm stunned. Looking out of this roofless car, I feel like I can see everything and touch all the pieces that make up the mountains and the ocean and the sky. My dress swirls around my legs, picked up by the wind, and my hair is never going to calm down at this speed.

Levi switches on a mix CD and turns it to a low volume that I can barely hear over the rushing and the sound of tires on asphalt and the ocean waves against rocks. We talk sparsely (Levi: *If we were stranded on a desert island, who would eat who first?* Me: *Sh, don't even think about that.* Levi: *It's important.* Me: *It will never happen.* Levi: *I'd let you eat me. I'm probably delicious, but then again, I hope no one ever knows for sure.*), mostly just holding hands between us, watching the small beach cities and mansions in the hills as they pass.

We reach Mr. Orville's awkwardly parked car at 11:44, and by this time I'm yawning and stretching and shifting uncomfortably. Levi makes a U-turn and pulls up behind his dad's sleek, black car—yet another convertible, this time a Jag—and flips off the lights. The beach is to our right, across the freeway; the little town we've parked in is called La Conchita.

That is, until I hear, "Son!" Jerking my head toward the sound, I catch Mr. Orville practically springing out of his car. His date is primping herself in the passenger seat, her skimpy purple dress showing me a lot more of her boobs than I ever wanted to see.

"Dad," Levi answers, and if I didn't know him so well, I would have missed the underlying relief in his tone. While Levi steps out to talk to his dad, Miss Purple Dress closes her mirror, collects her things, and saunters over to the Maserati in her four-inch pumps. She doesn't acknowledge my presence, just opens the back door and sits behind me.

Good, I didn't want to talk to you anyway.

After speaking quietly to his father by the car, Levi turns to look at me. "Bee, you feel comfortable driving one car?"

I immediately shake my head no, and Levi sighs and turns off the other car, the one we're going to leave here.

Mr. Orville fumbles with the handle on the Maserati for a second. Then he looks up at me, catching my attention only because I can feel his stare. "You," he says, as if he's only just seeing me.

I raise an eyebrow. I have no response for this idiot.

"I met you earlier?"

I can't hold back my laugh, but I still don't answer. *Yeah,* I think, *and at the last fundraiser, too. Nice to see you again. I'm your son's girlfriend. No need to remember me, though.*

"You're wearing my wife's necklace," he adds, his face darkening. From behind me, his purple-clad date makes a sound of protest. "Ex-wife," he amends, and finally manages to open the door. He gets in the vehicle (*jumps* is a more appropriate word), landing beside his girlfriend with a plop, and (I kid you not) grabs her boobs to catch himself.

"AuGUStus!" she shouts, laughing.

I turn to Levi as he gets in the driver's seat again and just stare at him, waiting for him to say something, anything, because I'm speechless.

He shields his eyes from the backseat and says, "If I wasn't wearing this suit, I'd probably puke."

"Son, did you meet Penelope?" AuGUStus! yells from the backseat, even though we're, like, a foot away.

Levi and I exchange a glance. "Ah," he says. Then he turns around. "Yep, we did. Buckle up, please, or you'll fall out onto the freeway and I won't be able to come back for you until tomorrow, and by then you'll already be a street pancake."

He mumbles the last bit, making me laugh loudly, over the sounds of AuGUStus! sloppily smooching Felix's (probably fired) secretary, over the music and the wind. The only thing left is Levi, and just as the rest of the world world disappears, he is everything.

We pull up to AuGUStus's house a little over an hour later, music blaring to keep us awake. I've yawned once a minute for the last half hour, and Levi's eyes look a little bloodshot. But the massive house looming ahead of us, even with its seven garage doors and palm tree collection and glass roof, provides a sense of calm. In my mind, House + Bed = Sleep.

Until I remember that we have to drive home, of course. "Who's on drive home duty?" I ask.

"If I have anything to say about it, neither of us." He inches into the Maserati's assigned garage and closes the door behind us. With one shared look, we seem to come to the agreement that neither of us wants to drive at this hour, so staying here is our only option. He nods and pulls the key out of the ignition, and at the same time we turn to look at the back seat.

AuGUStus! is passed out with his head in Penelope's lap, and she looks incredibly annoyed. Levi, in all of his wild-haired glory, shoots her his most charming smile. "Thanks for taking care of that," he says, climbing out of the car and closing his door behind him.

"Aren't you, like, going to help?" Penelope whines.

"Oh, I'm totally sure you've got this all under control,

considering how well you probably know him by now, in these, like, four days you've been dating him. Or should I say nights?" Levi walks around to my side (I'm staring openly like a shocked four-year-old) and pushes on my back with two fingers, toward the door that leads into the house. He glances back at Penelope one last time. "Peregrine, right? Have a *great* night," he adds, and shuts the door behind us.

I plaster my hand over my mouth, a giggle escaping. "That's not the first time you've had to do that, is it?" I say beneath my fingers.

"Nope." He flicks on the lights. An expanse of kitchen spreads out before me, so massive that it's like there's an entire canyon between me and the other side.

I make a sound of pure awe.

"It's butt ugly," Levi mutters.

"It totally is not. It's just . . . excessive."

"Okay, fine, it's gorgeous," he grumbles. "But I reserve the right to call anything and everything in this house gross any time I want, okay?"

I practically snort. The house is immaculate, down to the mahogany cabinets and giant sink and wide island tabletop. Everything sparkles. I take Levi's hand, following him first to the fridge (because he guesses I'm hungry and tells me he's starving), where he procures yogurt and water for us, and then out into the rest of the house.

I don't have much time to pay attention to the massive rooms I'm passing. I focus solely on Levi's hand and his long stride and the sleep that awaits me on the other side of the house. I might cry from sheer exhaustion and emotional discovery and happiness.

Levi first stops by his bedroom, which is set up like his room at home: organized, minimalist. He puts his backpack and yogurt on the bed and sighs down at them.

"What's wrong?" I ask.

"The day's over, that's what's wrong." He rubs the back of his neck. "There's an extra bedroom for you, down the hall—"

I act quickly, grabbing his hand before he can move. "Um, no." Suddenly I'm nervous, because I know that I don't want to sleep by myself in this gigantic, strange house where Levi's drunk dad could be lurking at any moment in time. But I also know that asking to sleep in his bedroom, where there is only one bed and a lot of floor, might open up a can of worms, and I will have to do a lot of explaining.

About sex.

Out with it, Bee. Just tell him.

My jaw is frozen shut. I don't want him to think it's stupid, or lame, or pathetic, because it's not. It's important to me, and I want him to know.

Levi raises an eyebrow at me, as if he's trying to give me the impression that he's clueless, but I know from the way his skin color deepens that he's thinking the same thing I am.

"I can't sleep here," I say, but since I mean in this house, it only confuses him more.

"Okay," he deadpans. "That's why I'm giving you your own bedroom."

"No, no, I mean, I can't sleep *here*, as in, the house, because it freaks me out a little bit—okay a lot—no offense."

"So you *want* to sleep in my room?"

"I do—I mean—" I whimper, hopeless. "I really want to, but if I do, I have to tell you The Thing."

This is not how I planned to do it. In fact, I hadn't *planned* to do this at all. In the several weeks of our dating life, I'd been so preoccupied with everything else (I'm looking at you, cancer) that I'd only thought about this *once*. I hadn't thought about Levi's expectations, or what his past love life looked like. He's probably had a ton of girlfriends—oh my goodness, this makes me feel even worse—and probably has experience, because he's Levi, and look at that beautiful face!

"Bee? What thing?" He's watching me, eyes traveling back and forth with me as I pace incessantly across his room. I'm pretty sure it's driving him crazy. *Three. Two. One—*

"Bee—" He puts his hand on my arm to stop me, running his fingers down my bare skin to tantalize me, bringing me in close to hold me. "What's this Thing you want to tell me that's making you so nervous? You're shaking," he adds, and it's true. My hands, especially, are wavering where I have them pressed to his chest.

"Okay, so, like, I've never had to explain this to anyone except my mom and Gretchen, and especially not to a boy, and *especially* not to my boyfriend, because, you know, I've never had one of those. One of you. You know?"

He nods, like this makes complete sense. (He's an angel.) "All right. Go on."

I wiggle out of his arms and sit on the edge of the bed, my hands fumbling in my lap. "I have this thing," I begin, and instead of continuing I just stare at his expectant face.

He nods, slowly, like he's trying to be patient. "You said that already."

"Okay, and, well. I wasn't really going to tell you like this. I just don't know what you expect and what you want but I have made a promise to myself not to have sex before I'm married because I want it to be the most special thing in the world, and I figured out when I was with Karl that it wasn't going to be special if we stayed together. That's why I broke it off with him, actually. And now I'm here and we're a thing and we kissed, naturally my next question is *what on earth is Levi going to think about this* so I'm asking you here, now, what you think MMPH—"

He smashes his whole mouth on mine, sudden and a little violent, but it's all the better for it. I grab his face and squish it between my hands because I am a lot panicky and he's here to make it better.

"Bee," he says quietly, and chuckles, and presses a few smaller kisses to my lips and nose and eyes and cheeks. "You're the most wonderful creature."

I whimper. "But what about your past girlfriends and experience that I don't have and do you want that from me and—"

"Bee! Bee. Calm down." He puts a finger on my lips and stands up straight. His hand curls around my head, pulling me close, so that my cheek rests against his stomach. I wrap my arms around his waist, squeezing a little too tight, but he doesn't seem to mind. "I was only just grasping the fact that we kissed, to be honest, but I'm glad you brought it up."

"Okay," I whisper, waiting for him to continue.

Levi's hands glide through my hair, soft and comforting. "I like more than your pretty face, Bee, so if you want to wait, then so do I."

"Levi," I say, but it hurts to speak.

"I've only had two other girlfriends," he adds, and heaves a breath. "They were shallow and nasty and liked that my dad had money, so they got on my bad side pretty quickly." He takes his hand and presses it to my cheek, which I'm sure feels like the surface of the sun. "Which would, you know, make me a virgin, too."

Um, Levi, I must have heard you wrong. I want to say this, but my mouth isn't working.

"Besides, I didn't work so hard at not turning into my dad for nothing." Levi gives the back of my head a playful nudge. "So, stop worrying. I mean, who do you think I am?"

I laugh, clinging to him as he pulls me upright. He grasps my chin with one hand, gazing at me in a way that makes me shiver and hope and wonder and dream. I'm full of constellations;

they burn, exploding and remaking me. Then he kisses me, sighing as my mouth opens to his. He touches my neck, my hip, fingers tangled in my hair, and my heart expands and bursts.

I am light and stardust in his hands.

chapter 33

QUEUED:
LET THEM FEEL YOUR HEARTBEAT
BY A SILENT FILM

THE ROOM IS quiet, Levi is asleep, and my head is spinning a million miles per hour. I'm resisting (with everything in me) the urge to roll over and curl up against his side and throw my leg over his. Doing so would surely result in the unraveling of everything we just discussed.

I consider, briefly, stealing his comforter to sleep on the ground. But then I just make myself turn my back to him and pull the covers up around my neck, and close my eyes tight.

I must categorize things, or else I'll go crazy.

One: I'm wearing his sweatpants (they're tight around my hips but I can't complain) and an old shirt of his. He picked it for me because it has Superman on it. I love him dearly. (Levi, not Superman.)

Two: Everything here smells like a musty version of him, probably because the room is hardly ever used, but it's still incredibly distracting. I probably sound like a dog sniffing for its bone as I bury my face in his pillow.

Three: I feel infinitely more comfortable than I did an hour ago before I told him The Thing. Now that I *have* told him, there's a weight off my chest, and a sort of happiness—no, *contentment*—sits in its place. He accepted it, no questions, and I have every reason to believe he's telling the truth. If it becomes a problem later, we'll deal with it then.

Four: I think about that, the deal-with-it-then, the possibility that one day there will be something we *can't* deal with. I think about him leaving me, us parting ways because of a disagreement too big to overcome. I think about never kissing him again and the hole in my heart that will eat away at the rest of me.

It's this thought that gets me most, because it's sharp and raw. What was life like before Levi? What did I do every day? What filled my time and my thoughts and my heart?

I flop onto my back, hand reaching over to grab his. (Levi sleeps like a starfish: arms and legs wide.) I pray I won't wake him when—

Like a tornado warning, my phone starts to ring. "Dammit!" I whisper harshly, jumping out of bed and flying across the room. I silence it, shocked to see my mother's number, and answer. "Hello?"

I'd sent her a text before bed, letting her know what happened, that we were safe, that we'd be home in the morning. It was too late to worry about whether or not she approved, but at least if she got the text in the morning, she'd know where I was.

But this! Hearing her voice say my name on the other end makes my knees wobble. Moving quietly so as not to wake Levi (he hasn't flinched once), I hurry to the bathroom and shut the door. I try to stay calm, for the sake of my sanity, and for sleeping Levi. There are a lot of reasonable explanations for my mom to be up so late (or early) that don't necessitate panic.

"Mom? What's going on? It's almost two in the morning!"

"Oh, baby Bee, I'm all right, but your papa fell in the bathroom—"

Too late. Staying calm is out of the question. "*What*?!"

"—and we had to run to the ER to make sure he's okay. The doctor says he's fine, just an external bump on that hard head of his, but they want him to stay a couple of nights in the hospital to be sure."

A wave of guilt hits me. I've been in Malibu for the past several hours, dressing up fancy with millionaires and kissing my boyfriend in nice cars and sleeping (trying to sleep) in his gigantic bed, while my mom is at home dealing with *this*.

I struggle to regain my composure. "Is he really okay? Truly?"

"Yes." She sounds so tired, I want to hug her. And I can't. Because I'm *here*. She continues, "I got your text just now because I finally have a moment to myself. Are you all right? Are you safe?"

"Yeah, Levi's asleep and I've been trying to."

"Okay, good. I wasn't worried, I promise."

I smile half-heartedly, even though she can't see me. "Mama, I talked to Levi today. I told him about everything." I put emphasis on *everything*, so she knows exactly what I mean.

"Aahh," she whispers. "What'd he say?"

"That it didn't matter. That he likes more than just my face." I'm blushing just remembering those words.

My mom sighs happily. "I told you he was a Precious Heart, didn't I?"

I sigh with her. "Yeah. He's the best."

She is quiet for a minute, and I can only imagine the things she must be feeling: the doubt and pain and anger and exhaustion at seeing my dad, her husband, in a hospital bed. The guy she was once getting giddy over with college roommates and her own mom, perhaps. Then she says, a little too chipper, "Well, I feel better now that we talked, and I'm so tired I'm going to fall asleep standing up. Call me tomorrow on your way back?"

"Of course."

"Come see Papa before work tomorrow, if you can. He asked for you tonight. I think he thought you were coming home earlier."

"I'll stop by, and maybe Levi can come with me."

"He'd love that."

"Hey, how are the girls?" I ask before she can say goodbye.

"They're all right. A bit shaken, but good. Your friend Elle came over to watch a movie with them because they couldn't sleep."

"Elle? Really?"

"Tom asked her to."

I open my mouth, then close it. Well. There's that. "Okay. I love you, Mama."

"Sleep well, Bee."

I press the red button and rest my head against the hard cabinets behind me. My hand drifts to my chest, which hurts like hell. I can't shake the feeling that I should have been there, even though I know I should also be here with Levi, supporting him. And his dad . . . that was an emergency.

Feeling cold and upset, I stand up and look in the mirror over the sink. It's modern, with a simple white frame; I feel like it shows too much of me. I don't know how to see myself when I feel pulled all directions, when there isn't a single thing I can do to help.

I open the door quietly, thankful Levi hasn't moved, and put my phone back on its charger. Then I stand by my side of the bed with my hands on my hips.

Levi's wide open arms look too comforting, too real, too wonderful. And I am in need of comfort, of reality, of wonder. I don't want to be here, not now, but I *do* want to be with Levi.

I lift the covers and slide in, scooting my hips closer until they are an inch away from his. This is practically unbearable, so I lay on my side and put my head on his shoulder and my hand over his stomach and my leg on his. He stirs and turns, and suddenly our feet are tangled, and both of his arms are around me. He turns so that my face is against his chest. I breathe him in, asking, "Is this okay?"

"Yeah . . . sss . . . okay . . . " he mumbles in reply. At least, that's what I think he said. I'm not sure how awake he is right now, but it doesn't matter. It's like he was holding out his arms just for me to roll into them, and that's all I need in order to finally fall asleep.

Levi's ringtone wakes me at the crack of dawn.

I roll over, reaching for him, mumbling that he should answer it or I'll kill him because *why would anyone call so early in the morning*. But then I realize he's not there. I'm grasping at empty sheets, and I haven't actually opened my mouth yet. Or my eyes.

I crack them, just a little bit, and see Levi rushing across the room to his phone. (I find it adorable that our phones are plugged into the same outlet, lying side by side. I realize this sounds ridiculous, but it's too early to care.) "Hello?" he whispers. He sees that I'm awake, and makes an *I'm-so-sorry* face.

I muster a smile, and he goes back to his conversation. I hear snippets of "What?" and "Are you serious?" and "When?" before he hangs up.

I push myself up to a sitting position, watching him pocket his phone in his sweatpants with a look of complete surprise and adorable wonder. "Who was that?" I mutter, rubbing my eyes.

"Felix." Levi runs a hand through his sleep-skewed hair and says, "Oh, my God. He said one of his friends at the auction last night lives in Carlsbad and wants to host an event for potential sponsors. He also wants to help us get an official building."

"Levi—that's crazy," I say, a little more awake, and push the covers off my legs. "Did he say when?"

"He's going to call me in a couple of days with more details, but I think . . . soon."

My sweetheart Levi looks like a deer in headlights. I smile, but not just because of his news, which must make me a terrible girlfriend. "That's amazing." I pause to yawn. "What time is it?"

"Almost eight. Sorry that was so loud—"

I wave him off. "I need to get up anyway."

His signature smirk takes over his face. "You slept so hard; you didn't even move when I got up. We were face to face, and I'm pretty sure our legs had become a pretzel. I didn't realize I'd been promoted to full-body pillow."

I snicker. "You offered yourself up for the job, so don't blame me." Suddenly, I remember why I slept so close to him in the first place, and my mood drops. "I got a phone call at two in the morning, from my mom."

He pales. "Please tell me it's not as ominous as it sounds."

I rub my eyes again, frustrated that I can't truly see, before realizing that my glasses are still off. "He hit his head in the bathroom, and they had to take him in. He's fine, but . . . " I shrug.

Levi huffs, standing at the end of the bed. "Okay. We can leave right after we eat, promise."

I nod, studying him and his hilarious hair that stands on end. *That's it.* I stand up on his bed and walk toward him. One of his eyebrows shoots up in question.

"Dammit," I say when we're two inches apart. "I was hoping to be a lot taller than you, but this is, like, only four inches."

"My bed's low to the ground."

"Dammit," I say again.

"Um, Becky, who said you could walk around on my things?"

"Um, Levi, shut up," I reply, and wrap my arms around his neck and kiss him deeply.

He tries to protest, but I keep kissing him, despite his frantic attempts at speaking. "I can't . . . you can't . . . abuse me . . . like that . . . there are . . . boundaries."

I pull back. "Like what?"

"Like . . . "

I roll my eyes. "Just kiss me."

He does, pulling me close with one hand on my lower back, the other curling around my neck. His lips press hard enough to open mine, and he kisses me so thoroughly that I don't notice his hand moving to my legs—which he then proceeds to swipe out from underneath me.

I shriek, falling backward, landing hard. "Oh. My. God."

He crawls onto the bed, one leg between mine, hands on either side of my shoulders. He kisses me again, smooth and comforting and *warm*. I can hear our breaths like little gasps between kisses, faster than normal, our heart rates skipping sky-high. The kiss lasts forever and is over too fast at the same time—fulfilling and wonderful but still not enough. It's like he knows this, and understands the boundaries I've set, because when I start to slow down, so does he. With a last peck on my nose, he stands up, grabbing clothes from his dresser, and heads into the bathroom. "I'll be out in a minute."

It takes only a moment before his phone rings again, almost painfully loud. "Dude, your phone's ringing again," I say over the noise.

"Yeah, I can hear it," he yells from the bathroom.

"Want me to answer?"

"No, let it ring."

His ringtone, as usual, is a jumpy, dancing song, and I'm feeling ornery, so I stand up again and start jumping around. "Levi, guess what?!"

"What?" he shouts back.

"I'M JUMPING ON YOUR BED!"

"Bee!" He sounds exasperated, but then there's a trickle of laughter that comes after. "I'm going to—" He bursts out of the room, wearing a yellow t-shirt and his boxer shorts. Which, adorably, are covered in rainbow stripes.

I laugh again, still bouncing, and ask, "Is *that* what you wear under your jeans?"

He looks down. "Uh, yeah?"

"You're cute." I bounce again, and this time he doesn't seem to notice or care.

"As long as you like them," he says, backing up into the bathroom.

"Not that I'll be seeing them much," I remind him, then jump off the bed and land with a thud. "What's for breakfast?"

Levi leaves the door open as he pulls his jeans on. He brushes back his hair and tosses his laundry into the basket by the door. "Let's find out."

Levi sets a plate in front of me. "Fresh cinnamon rolls, straight out of the oven."

My mouth waters at the steamy goodness in front of me. I kick my feet at the rung of the barstool beneath me, glancing up at Levi who is grabbing his own plate of cinnamon rolls. "Who made them?"

"Dad's maid."

I take a bite and immediately melt, just like the frosting on my tongue. "Wow. She's good."

"She's *damn* good."

I look over. "You've got some—" I lean in and kiss the top of his lips, where there is some lingering cinnamon and frosting.

Levi groans. "You can't do that."

"Why not?"

"Because, you minx, you—"

"Levi," a sharp voice interrupts.

I jump back, embarrassed, as AuGUStus! walks into the kitchen, sans Penelope. (*And good riddance*, I think.)

"Dad," Levi says, bristling.

AuGUStus! nods, noticing that we're eating the breakfast that was probably for him. "Did your friend meet Julia?"

I assume Julia is the maid, but I'm focused on the fact that he called me Levi's *friend*.

"Dad," Levi says again, this time as a warning.

"Sorry, sorry," he says, waving his hand like we're flies and he's annoyed. "Your *girlfriend*. I have a massive hangover."

"Dad, she's sitting *right here*."

"Hi," Mr. Orville says to me, like he's four years old, like he has no manners or training in social awareness.

"Hi, Au—" I swallow the unfinished word and my laugh. (*Oops.*) "Mr. Orville."

"Did you sleep well?" He pours himself a glass of orange juice and slips a cinnamon roll onto a plate. "I trust Levi gave you a tour?"

"We haven't gotten to that yet," Levi answers for me.

"You should have done it at sunrise," his dad continues. "Best time of day."

Levi's expression burns; he's not even trying to hide it anymore. "You think we were actually going to be up at sunrise after the night we had?"

I'm frustrated because I can't quite put my finger on how to help him. He looks so irritated, like he's lost his will to persevere. I remember what he said about his dad before we started dating: "He's not the monster under my bed." And I wonder if that's true. I wonder what Levi would say right now if I asked him about it. Maybe he isn't afraid, but everything I've seen so far has brought me to one conclusion: Augustus Orville *is* a monster.

Mr. Orville looks at his son closely before shrugging. "Why'd you take the Maserati?" he asks. I can't tell if he's put off or genuinely curious.

Levi's eyes widen in disbelief. "If you have a problem with me using your gas and miles to go pick you up an hour away, then you're going to have a problem for a long, long time."

"Seriously, kid? I'm messing with you."

Levi's jaw tightens. "Whatever."

"Whatever?" Mr. Orville smirks. (It's the nastier version of Levi's.) "Okay."

As if to give himself something to do, just for the sake of distraction, Levi puts our empty plates into the sink. Then he asks, "How's Patricia?"

"Penelope." His father looks down into his empty glass. "It's not that hard to remember, Levi."

Levi doesn't answer.

"And she's good," Mr. Orville finishes.

"Where is she?" Now Levi's just asking for a fight—it's in his eyes when he looks at me. I also see his apology, and I squeeze his hand sympathetically.

"She left early. She had to pick up her husband at the airport."

And just like that . . . everything in the room goes still as death.

"Hey, Dad?" Levi's livid, barely under control. "Can I speak to you in another room?"

Mr. Orville says nothing as he turns and walks out. Levi

follows without even looking at me. I know I'm not supposed to butt into their private discussion, but I can't help it: I wait for them to close the door before I stand just outside, ear pressed to the wood. (Remember what I said about sometimes not feeling bad about eavesdropping? Well, this is one of those times.)

"This *has* to stop." Levi's tone is muffled, but I can hear each word.

"I'm a grown man. I don't need my own son to tell me what to do like I'm a child."

"I'm not telling you what to do." Levi says it like he's trying to keep his voice level. "I'm asking you to respect some boundaries—boundaries that are important to me."

"I didn't know you had any," Mr. Orville snorts.

"Well, since the basic boundaries for any human being are unclear to you, I'm putting some up right now. Call my girlfriend by her name. It's Bee, okay? Think about me calling your girlfriend Patricia—I *know* her name is Penelope. It's a million times worse when you refuse to acknowledge Bee, who actually means something to me."

"Oh, Penelope means something to me."

"You're sick." Levi's starting to lose it, and he's not the only one. My fingers itch with anger; I want to do some damage.

"You think Bee means something to you? You're nineteen. You've got a lot of life left to live, a lot of people to meet, and you think you've struck gold."

"Oh, I definitely have. Bee's the best thing that's ever happened to me."

"You think that girl is going to make you happy? Keep you happy? I thought that about a girl named Suzie once, and she did nothing for me."

"That's *exactly* the problem!" Levi says, a little too loudly. (I'm cringing so hard that my face hurts; I've never heard Levi yell before.) "It was all about you. It was never about me, or

Mom, or our lives together. It was about you and your money
and your girlfriends and wanting a bigger house and nicer cars
and wealthier friends."

"Shut up, Levi."

(Oh, I'm definitely going to kill him.)

"I'm in love with Bee," Levi says, and suddenly the breath in
my lungs whooshes out. "I love that girl so much, I don't think
she even knows *how* much yet. I'm just figuring it out and I'm
glad I have a lifetime ahead of me to discover it."

I'm in love with Bee. It takes me completely by surprise. I know
we love each other like friends do—best friends, inseparable.
But *in love* is different. *In love* is big and loud and new and it
makes my knees wobble and my hands shake.

He continues. "I don't want you around her if you're going to
act like an asshole about . . . everything. It's one thing when it's
just me; I can ignore it. But I'm drawing a line when it comes to
Bee, and I don't want you to cross it."

His dad is quiet for a moment. "I can't believe you—so naïve.
I definitely didn't raise you."

Now it's Levi's turn to be quiet. "Maybe I am," he finally says.
"Naïve. I'd rather be simple and be like Mom than have no heart
and be like you. Excuse me."

I hear his footsteps headed toward me. I scramble backward,
but I'm too slow, and he sees me standing there like a lone
animal on a highway. He sighs.

"I'm sorry," we say at once.

"What did you hear?" he asks, clearing his throat.

"Everything," I blurt. (I may be an eavesdropper, but at least
I'm not a liar.)

"Okay." He rocks back on his heels and stuffs his hands in his
pockets. "Then I should probably explain some things."

"No, there's no need."

He glances at me.

"Unless you want to tell me just how much you love me." I attempt to smile, but *oh*, my face hurts as much as my heart does.

"A lot." He says it like he's reciting his favorite lyrics, with care and emotion, like he can't quite explain how they truly make him feel. (I'm crumbling.) "More than I expected or imagined." (I'm breathless.) "You've surprised me in every possible way."

I don't touch him. I want to, but I don't.

"We've wasted a lot of time here," Levi says, and holds out his hand for me to take. "Come on. Let's go see your dad."

chapter 34

QUEUED:
WINTER
BY MREE

THING YOU SHOULD Know About Me #293: In my mind, hospitals are one of two things. Either they're yellow and brightly lit with fluorescent lights and balloons, filled to the brim with loud, happy people. *Or* they're dim and dismal and quiet, sparsely populated by the dead and waiting-to-die.

In the evening, when the sun is just starting to set, the latter is what Levi and I walk into. I didn't get to go to the hospital earlier because traffic was terrible and I got to work with only five minutes to spare. So now, finally, we're heading toward my father's room, hand in hand, whispering about the delivery I had this afternoon. (A very grumpy woman working at a bar did not want to receive flowers from her ex-boyfriend in front of all her old man drinking buddies, who'd clearly been there since eleven that morning.)

Papa's room is toward the back of the third floor. It's a long and quiet trek, one we do not rush, because that would mean there's a *reason* to hurry to my father's bedside. When we stop to survey the room numbers, I cannot miss the fact that the rooms on either side of his are empty. Possibly because someone was released in happy, healthy condition, but also possibly because of something terrible.

I push down the heaviness in my heart and pull Levi inside behind me. "Papa!" I exclaim, a little too happily.

He looks up at me from the bed and smiles, and my mama, who is lying beside him all snuggled up, mumbles something. "Bee!" Papa says, reaching for me.

I hate seeing him like this, in a hospital gown, with those thin hospital sheets thrown over his legs, his body attached to machinery that's on the wall behind him. It hurts my heart, but I'm not about to show him that. "How are you feeling?"

"I'm all right. You know me and my hard head." He shakes Levi's hand, nodding with a wink.

"Um, yeah, Mom said something about that last night." I grip his hand.

"Did you have fun this weekend?" he asks.

I nod vigorously. "Want to see a picture of us at the party?"

"Sure," Papa says, leaning in close.

"I want to see," Mama gasps, sitting up. Her hair is wild on one side. "Oh, Bee, you look so beautiful. *Levi*, did *you* pick that out?"

Levi beams. "Sure did."

My mom is so obviously floored that it's almost funny. "She looks absolutely stunning."

"Doesn't she, though?" Levi places a chaste kiss on the side of my head.

"Levi's the real show stopper, though," I say, to divert their attention. "I mean, look at that suit."

Now Levi's blushing, but I ignore his awkward protests and study the picture with my parents. In the picture we're standing at the center of Felix's marble entryway, pillars on either side, my arms around his middle, bunching up his perfect suit. He's laughing about something Felix said as he took the picture, and my nose is scrunched up all goofy. Somehow this makes the picture perfect. More . . . accurate. It makes me feel less self-conscious about all the fanciness. All the expectations.

My dad hands my phone back to me. "Was it a good turnout?"

"Better than expected," Levi says, "and we walked away with more connections than we've ever had."

"Good for you, son," my dad says.

I squeeze Levi's hand. He's got this sad sort of smile, and I know he's thinking about the conversation he had with his own father today. AuGUStus! told him to shut up, told him he was naïve and ridiculous, and never once did he call him son.

"Thank you," Levi finally gets out.

My mom stands up, fixing her wrinkled shirt, and sighs. "I'm going to get ready for bed early, but you can stay as long as you want."

"Actually—" I begin, surprising myself. "I'd like to stay here tonight. You can go home, Mama."

She looks at my dad and then back at me and shrugs. "You sure, baby? You had a long weekend."

"It's all right, really. You've done this more times than I have."

"Thank God not too many so far." She shrugs. "Okay. You can borrow my pajamas if you want."

I nod. "Thanks. Did you bring *Crime and Punishment*?"

She waves at the table, where I see the book lying on a pile of magazines. I turn to Levi. "Can you take my mom home instead?"

"Of course," he says. "Good to see you, Matt," he adds, shaking Papa's hand. "Glad you're okay."

Levi and I head into the hallway while my mom gathers her things, and he doesn't waste time. He immediately kisses me, hard, on the lips. I slip my arms around his neck, desperately holding on to him, not wanting the moment to end. But I know it has to. "Levi," I whisper fiercely. "My *mother*. Oh-my-gosh-awkward."

He chuckles. "Okay. All right." He drops his hands to his sides, but his eyes are still holding me there, with my hands at the back of his head, digging into all his glorious hair, and I am so tempted to kiss him again. "Love you," he says, quietly, and my stomach does this little flip-flop thing. It's like my heart is being squeezed, and it can't pump blood like it's supposed to, and that's suddenly perfectly fine with me because *Levi*.

"Love you," I reply in a strangled voice. Then my mom is closing the door behind me and it's time to let Levi go. "Thank you."

He shakes his head like I have nothing to thank him for, but it's the truth: I have him to thank for *everything*.

Papa, it seems, has already fallen asleep by the time I get back inside the room.

I stare at him from the end of the bed and sigh heavily, and for two seconds my gaze strays to *Crime and Punishment*, halfway read, sitting neatly. I grab it, lying down on the makeshift bed on the window seat, and clutch it to my chest, my heart beating against its battered cover.

I return to staring at my dad and watch his chest rising and falling, and I have never been so thankful that I have him here. That he is alive.

The hospital no longer feels so bleak. It doesn't seem so dark, either, and I think it's because Levi was here, leaving his mark of joy. With this in mind, I pick up my phone. *Thanks for all the little pieces of you*, I text him.

I fall asleep like this, a book to my chest, phone in hand, glasses askew, newly kissed and very in-love.

chapter 35

QUEUED:
ICE DANCE
BY DANNY ELFMAN

WHEN LEVI TEXTS me cryptic things like, *Get your butt over here* and an address, I find it hard to resist. Which is how I end up parked on a neighborhood street in Escondido, my AC blasting on high.

I sit in my car for a minute longer, because Gretchen's on the phone. Her voice is filled with a level of excitement that would make me laugh if I didn't feel so guilty. I haven't told her about my dad yet, despite the fact that it's been a week since Malibu, two weeks since I found out about the cancer. I still can't open my mouth and force the words out. Every moment seems wrong because each time I imagine how our conversation would go, my heart twists painfully.

So I leave it in the dark. (I've never felt more like a coward.)

"Hey, Gretchen—" I hate to interrupt her hilarious rant about her coworkers, but I see Levi's car. (I need to go before I tell her everything and break her heart.) "Can I call you back in a little bit? I'm here."

"Hey, of course. Tell The Boy hello from his favorite person." Gretchen snorts. "Ah, LAK, what a time to be alive."

LAK stands for Life After Kissing. It's the new B.C. and A.D., according to Gretchen.

"Thanks, Gretchen. I'll tell him. And remind me to call you later if I forget."

She laughs and hangs up. I slide my phone into my purse and turn off the car, bracing myself for the heat wave I know will flatten me as soon as I step outside. But when I close my door behind me, pocketing my keys, I see something that I don't expect, and it distracts me from my grumbling.

Levi stands in front of one of the houses, legs spread, hands on his hips, looking up. It's an old Victorian-style home, probably built in the seventies, with white siding and a cute, wrap-around porch. There's a giant FOR SALE sign out front, complete with flyers. A picket fence lines the front and sides of the yard.

"Levi," I say, a question in my voice. "What are we doing here?"

He doesn't turn around. "I'm proposing to you and this is where we're going to raise our twelve children."

I wrap my arms around his waist and squeeze his middle. "Okay."

He closes his arms over mine and brings my hands to his lips. I sigh happily against his back.

"You're too easy," he says. "But for real? I think . . . I might want to move TCP here."

"Excuse me?" I stand next to him, one arm still around his waist. He tucks his thumb through the belt loop of my jeans.

"I told you about this," he says.

"I know, but, like . . . "

Levi pecks my temple with a kiss. "I talked to Felix yesterday, and he seems to think we'll like this house. I mean, I'm already inclined to think he's right."

"You like it enough to move everything here?" I'm not surprised, just wary. This could be just another massive project to overwhelm us. Or maybe that's just my own stress level beeping at me as it overloads.

Levi rubs my arm as if he understands my worry. "He thought we could work out a deal: a fair price and a fair mortgage, an easy move-in date, some time to get things fixed up . . . ."

Now, of course, I'm studying the house, imagining the whole thing: the sign along the second story beneath the windows, a new color for the front. Suzie could use her green thumb to freshen up the yard. The house is on the edge of a neighborhood, close to the main street, but still tucked away so it seems homey and warm. I'm suddenly as in love with the vision as Levi—and just as sold.

"I'm thinking about painting the front with stripes," Levi says. "A new color every panel, all the way up."

"Oh, my gosh," I say. "Are you allowed to do that?"

"Don't know. I'm going to find out, though."

"At least you can paint the inside. But Levi—what about the lease on the other place?"

"It's up in three months. Just enough time to place an offer and make the move. We could have a grand opening." He faces me and takes my face in his hands, excitedly. I'm reminded, for a second, about that summer party at Keagan's place, and the memory (of happier times) warms me. "Do you realize what this means? We'll have more room, cheaper rent. Like, my dad can finally stop paying the rent and TCP will be completely mine. I won't feel like I owe him anything. And Felix had an excellent idea, that I could start housing people who need it here in the bedrooms and pay them to help with TCP while they get back on their feet with a new job or new house. This means more help and bigger business, which in turn means helping more people."

I smile at him, my hands wrapped around his wrists, and lift onto my tiptoes. "This is a perfect idea."

His smile is radiant, of course, because his smiles always are. "Do you like it?"

"I love it," I say. "Now kiss me."

He dips his head. I'm lost to the rest of the world as he kisses me tenderly, appropriate for the side of the road where everyone can see, but just enough to make my toes curl in my shoes.

When he lets go, he kisses my nose and wraps me in a hug. "How's your dad?"

I sigh, relaxing. "He's fine." Papa was released from the hospital early, making us all happier and infinitely less scared. Somehow, him being under a doctor's scrutiny twenty-four hours a day made everything worse. Ignorance really *is* bliss. If they'd found something else wrong with him, I'm not sure how I would have responded.

A car pulls up to the curb behind mine and a man steps out, wearing a suit and looking very official. Levi lets me go, our hands joining between us. "Aha, it's Felix's realtor. Want to see the inside with me?"

I kiss his cheek. "I'm already sold, but of course."

There's a certain musty quality to the house that makes me nostalgic—although for what, I have no idea. Grandmother's house? (Thing You Should Know About Me #213: My parents aren't close with either of their parents, who live in Florida, so I have a very distant idea of what *grandma* must be like.) All

I know is that I want to see Suzie moving around the kitchen, baking cookies, and Elle writing out her to-do list at the dining room table, and Missy and Albert sharing the front desk (her shoes propped up and his glitter raining on her head). I want to see this front sitting room filled with applicants and I want to see Levi in the hallway, handing checks to clients.

I want to stand beside him.

It all feels very official, which freaks me out a little, but Levi's excitement is contagious. At the end of the tour we shake hands with the realtor, and when he drives away, Levi and I stand against my car, looking up at the house.

"This is the one," he says, and takes my hand.

"Have you seen the other houses?"

"No. But I don't think I need to."

"I agree." I squeeze his fingers. "Celebratory dinner?"

He makes a disappointed humming noise at the back of his throat. "My mom's making dinner tonight and I promised to be there. Annnnd . . . I would invite you over but she made an underhanded comment the other day about me ignoring her, so I feel like I should give her my full attention." He smiles as he taps my nose with the pad of his finger. "You, my love, are distracting."

I smile sweetly. "You'll have to make it up to me, then."

"I will. You bet I will." He kisses me briefly and says, "Wait one minute, don't leave . . . here—" Dialing a number into his phone, he puts it on speaker so I can hear as well.

"Hello?" Felix answers.

"Hey, man, it's Levi."

"Levi!" (I can practically hear his smile.) "I didn't think I'd hear back so soon."

"And I didn't think I'd be calling you so soon. But—" Here Levi pauses, looks up at the house, and back at me, and smiles. "Felix, I found the one."

QUEUED:
PRESSURE SUIT
BY AQUALUNG

O UR WORLD, AND the world of TCP, becomes a vortex. It's sort of what I expected, but bigger and better. As July becomes August (and the heat scorches and the desert reigns supreme), Felix lets us take over the house, even though the sale hasn't been finalized.

After we've sent him a million thank-yous and the promise to have him over once it's done, we begin to strip the house to its bare bones. We're there every day, especially in the almost-cool evenings, tearing out the floors and stripping ugly wallpaper. We spend hours upon hours at Home Depot and Lowe's, picking color schemes and tile flooring. We go to IKEA whenever it's in our budget to buy new furniture. (Thing You Should Know About Me #7: I like playing house with Levi.)

My dad's construction company sends in a few guys to work for free, helping us get things done within our time frame. We supply them with pizza and root beer, and they boss us around and take care of the hard stuff. Eventually, the new flooring is in and the furniture's in boxes in the garage, which leaves us with one more thing on our to-do list: painting.

"We're going to have to work together on this one," Levi says to us, the day after we finish the floors. In the middle-of-August heat, it's so disgusting outside that we've locked all the windows and doors and barricaded ourselves in the main room with three fans. (Mental checklist: Remind Elle to hire an AC company to get a unit in here *immediately*.) Most of us could make it tonight, except Clary-Jane and Nikita.

"I have all the paint," Elle says, going over a list on her phone. "And it's 3:00. We could get a lot done tonight."

Levi looks at me. "What do you think?"

"Let's do it. I can get paint shirts for everyone."

Elle tsks. "Will you bring Tom with you, too? We need more muscly arms."

I personally believe there's another reason for her inviting him, but I say nothing. "Sure, if he's free. Who's on snack duty?"

Suhani raises her hand. "I'll go."

"Can there be glitter?" Albert asks.

Levi's eyes bulge. "No. Absolutely no glitter."

With that finality, we disband. Suhani heads to the store, and I go home. I dig through my dad's old work clothes, coming up with a few torn, already-paint-splattered t-shirts. I also grab some old tank tops from my drawer.

When I get back to TCP, I have the clothes and three siblings in tow. "They all wanted to come," I explain to whoever's listening.

"Oh good!" Elle exclaims, grabbing Tom's hand and dragging him into the house.

Levi accepts the shirt I give him. "Thanks." His smile is strained, a stark contrast to his happiness earlier.

"Is everything okay?" I ask, warily.

"Just . . . " He waves his hand. "It's whatever. My dad." He shrugs and lets me kiss him on the cheek.

"I'm sorry," I say. I almost ask him what's going on, but he looks withdrawn, like he doesn't want to talk about it, so I decide to wait until he does.

He puts one arm around my waist and as we walk into the main room. "If anyone wants a shirt, get it now before you ruin your clothes with paint."

"Thank you," Suhani says, snagging a shirt. "*Mujhe tumhari shakal surat bohot pasand hai.*"

Levi gives her the stink eye. "What does that mean?"

Suhani just giggles, but as soon as Levi turns around to pass out the rest of the shirts, she leans into me. "We only ever compliment him," she whispers. "That first day we met? We'd actually only told him he has beautiful eyes. Today, I told him I love his face."

I laugh.

"Don't tell him," she says. "I'm trusting you."

Then she winks and me, I pretend to zip up my lips. "Not a word."

I turn my attention back to the rest of the group just as Levi gives Missy a shirt. She holds it out between two fingers. "Do I have to?"

Levi shuts her up with a dirty look and turns to me. I reach for him, meeting him in the middle, where he kisses me quick. "Thanks, Bagheera."

I cringe. "Excuse me? You can't call me Bagheera! He's a fictional *panther.*"

"Well, maybe that's why you're so freaked out about your name."

"Do you think my mother would name me Bagheera?"

He thinks for a second. "No?"

"No."

"I still think it was a good guess."

"It was a terrible guess and you know it. You're just grasping at straws." I start to walk away. "Why don't you stop and let me tell you when I'm ready?"

"When will you be ready?"

His voice stops me, as well as his words. I look at him with some difficulty, because I don't know how to answer his question. "It's not a big deal, Levi," I non-answer.

His face changes then: eyebrows drawn, lips set in a line, the sharp contours of his face hard. But it's only a split second, and we're interrupted by Elle shouting for us across the room. We start, glancing at her, but when we look back at each other, his expression has changed again. It's softer.

"You're right," he says, and takes my hand.

Elle waves frantically as we join the group. "You two, help! No one can agree on a pattern."

"What's up?" he asks, like he's coming out of a daze. A small part of me wonders if I did something wrong.

Elle hands us a color wheel. "I want to paint stripes on this wall, horizontally, in four colors. Missy wants diagonal stripes, but that's way too much stimulation for the front room. Suhani thinks we should paint polka-dots. Albert demands glitter."

"No." Levi puts his hand on the back of Albert's neck in an almost threatening way. "I said no glitter."

Elle sighs heavily. "What do you suggest?"

Smiling, Levi puts his hands in his pockets. "All of it."

"What?" This comes from everyone at once as we all stare up at him in shock.

A few minutes later we disband, all of us assigned to different rooms and different patterns and color schemes. We lay out canvas in each room so the new floors aren't ruined, and Levi sets up a music station that blasts too loudly from his portable speakers. After a few minutes of goofing off, and Levi running around getting everyone to hustle, we finally start to work.

In the front room, which has become the main office, Elle and Tom are in charge of painting the walls with blue and green and yellow and pink horizontal stripes, as per Elle's request. She claims it will look fun *and* professional; all we can do is hope.

Suhani takes over the kitchen right away, painting all the cabinets white, letting them dry, and then getting to work on polka-dots every color of the rainbow. Attached to the kitchen is the dining room, which we have turned into our waiting room—Astrid's room. Bless her for putting up with a very annoyed Missy (who is complaining about not wanting to take off her shoes for this). Their job: paint two walls light yellow, and the third wall with chalk paint. (This was also Elle's idea, and she bought every color of chalk pen that she could within our budget to ensure we follow through.)

Millie and Albert have taken over the stairwell, using small brushes and paint cans to tackle the stairs. They've created a pattern: blue, green, orange, pink, yellow, purple, red, repeat. I don't tell Levi, but I see a smattering of glitter mixed in with the wet paint on every step.

Levi and I take the hallway, as well as the bathroom and closet that line the hall. First, we coat the walls and ceiling in a simple, light yellow; then we paint the doors—one blue and one green. When we're happy with this, we lock ourselves into the bathroom with four buckets. (All pastels: blue, orange, yellow, and an extra bucket of white.) Readjusting my tank top, I push aside the funny feeling I still have from earlier, when I saw Levi's expression change. It feels alarmingly close to guilt, but I can't go there right now. So I stand closer to him for comfort.

"I say the bathroom should match the kitchen—white with

polka-dots," I put in, raising my voice so he can hear me over the music blasting just outside the room.

Levi hums in disagreement. "But that's, like . . . weird."

"Levi."

"I don't associate eating with going to the bathroom, okay?"

"Well, neither do I, but it fits. We have cabinets and a sink in here, and the same tile on the counter, and it just matches, okay?"

He hums again and goes back to painting his section of the wall. He gets most of the tall spots, but I brought a stool with me so I can reach higher if necessary. We paint back to back in comfortable silence, our shoulder blades touching every time we turn for more paint or step back to look at our respective walls. At one point he (absently) grabs my hand and squeezes it, making my heart thump at an erratic pace. (Because that's all it takes.)

After a while, when the white is almost finished, Levi stops painting and lifts a finger. "Idea! What if we paint the cabinets like the kitchen and the walls we keep simple with stripes?"

"Hmm." I let my brush drip over the edge of the can before taking it to a new place on the wall. "If we're going to do stripes, I request diagonal stripes."

"Deal."

"Deal," I repeat, whipping around. Before he can react, I smear white paint from his nose to his ear, across his right cheek.

He sputters, blinking hard like he's afraid he'll get it his eyes. "*Beeeeee.*" He raises a hand to touch the paint; his finger comes away white. "You're asking for it."

"What am I asking for?" I bat my eyelashes at him.

Instead of retaliating with his own brush as I'd expected, he grabs me, hands tight on my waist, fingers digging into my skin where my tank top has ridden up from so much bending and reaching. When he kisses me, it's not what I expect: It's slow and agonizing, with Levi taking thorough, gentle care of my mouth, until I'm mad that he won't give me what I want. I let out a frustrated groan, fingers pulling on his hair, and reverse our roles. *I'm* in charge now, and I'm going to kiss him as fast and hard as—

It's my turn to sputter, as my face instantly smashes into all the wet paint dripping off his nose and cheek.

Levi laughs. "Looks good on you."

"Ohmy*gosh*. You're such a jerk." I swipe at him with my brush, and he dodges, but the bathroom is so small that he lands against his freshly painted wall. His arm is covered, down to the tips of his fingers and onto his pants.

"Benette," he hisses, grabbing for me with his wet hand. I screech as his arms snake around me, getting white all over my tank. "We gave *them* the talk about goofing off, and look at us!"

"We don't count," I whisper into his ear. "We are the boss."

This makes him laugh, which of course makes me lose my cool and I'm laughing, too. I stand on the stool, but it only boosts me about six inches, so I'm still shorter. I grab his collar anyway and pull him toward me, sighing as our lips meet, my thumbs brushing the skin by his ears, all my other fingers curving into the hair at the nape of his neck. He wraps one arm around me to pull my waist toward his, both hands running along my spine, elbows keeping me close.

For a split second, I get an image of what we must look like, all painted and messy, locked around each other. And happy— so happy. I don't even try to resist the urge to laugh.

"What's so funny?" he says, lips rubbing over mine as he speaks.

"We're silly," I say.

"You're right. We're very silly." Levi kisses my nose. "Now get back to work."

With everyone working, we finish every room downstairs tonight, our hands blistering from the paintbrushes, our legs sore from doing squats all day. (Who knew bending down to get more paint on your brush could be such hard work?)

We eat pizza late in the evening when everyone is sweaty and exhausted. Elle turns on some kind of techno music to try to get everyone's spirits up, but most of us just want to be lazy and sit on the couch we dragged in from the garage.

That is, until Levi takes my hand and pulls me out of the room when no one's looking.

"What are we doing?" I whisper.

"Hiding," he says, heading toward the stairs. They've been dry for an hour, but we still tiptoe up them, trying to be silent. ("Dammit, Albert," Levi whispers tragically. "He got glitter on the stairs.") Levi leads me across the second floor to the end of the hall, where he pulls the hatch in the ceiling.

"The attic?" I whisper.

He yanks down the ladder. "Uh-huh. It's, like, an old-fashioned attic with a window and everything."

Shrugging, I take the rungs one at a time and Levi follows. Up here, it's exactly like I imagined old-fashioned attics would be. There's a window seat along one wall just below the window, and old boxes stacked in the corner. There's even an old rocking chair (creepy), and the ceiling above my head is vaulted Victorian style.

Levi pulls everything up behind him and claps his hands free of dust. "Last time I was up here, it was dark and creepy, and I was *alone*," he says, looking around.

I dust off the window seat, blowing along the edge, and sit down. It creaks immediately. I jump up, bubbling with nervous laughter. "I can see how that would be kind of freaky." I lean over the window seat and peer out into the backyard. The property is a little over a half acre, and the backyard slopes with the hill behind it.

"You like it?"

Something behind me makes a loud thumping noise, startling me. I glance over to see that Levi has dropped a box, and is waving his hands in the air against the dust. "Spiders," he coughs. "Hey, Bunny, check this out with me."

Something in my heart snaps. Maybe it's from earlier. Or maybe it's been there for a long, long time. "Really, Levi? Bunny?"

He spreads his hands. "I can't help it."

I roll my eyes upward. "You should definitely stop. Your guesses get more and more ridiculous."

"Why can't you just tell me? What's stopping you?" he asks, the words tumbling out of his mouth so fast that I know, instantly, that he's been wanting to ask this for a while. And it's *bothering* him. It's bothering him so much that suddenly he looks irritated, and I wonder how long he's been feeling this way, and if he's been hiding it or if I just missed it.

The biggest problem, however, is that I do not have an answer for him. I open my mouth and close it.

Seeing that I'm not going to say anything, Levi nails it right on the head, and it hurts. "Because," he says, a little breathlessly, like he's starting to get angry, "it's like there's a part of you that you don't want me to see."

I close my eyes. *You don't have to tell me that.*

Everything is closing in on me, so fast, so unexpected. I look at him, and he looks at me, and all I see is disappointment.

I never wanted to disappoint him.

He reaches for me. I let him touch my arm, even though I don't want him to. "Is it not enough that I love you?"

"It is," I whisper. "It *is* enough," I say again, with more conviction.

"No, it's not. It's obviously not." He brushes the tip of his nose along my hairline, breathing in deeply. "What else do I need to do? I'll do anything. God—"

He actually looks pained, as he's begging to *me* to let *him* do more. It's ridiculous, because what have I ever done for him? I look back on everything this summer, and I know—finally—what's so wrong about us: He has loved me more than I have loved him. He has loved me better.

I feel sick. Maybe that's why I don't want to tell him. Maybe it's some part of me that's holding back because I haven't done enough to deserve him.

I swallow and whisper, "You don't need to do anything."

He rubs his face with both hands, as if exhausted. I feel the same, like my body is deflating, like I want to curl up and cry.

Eventually, Levi brings his head up again and says, "Look, downstairs, I said something I don't agree with. You said it wasn't a big deal, your name, and I said you were right. Well, you're not. It *is* a big deal. Is it so hard to believe that I want all of you?"

I do cry now, sniffling, wiping away tears. (Damn you, hormones!) (Oh, who am I kidding? This is completely unrelated to hormones.)

"Bee," he says, and it's as though seeing me cry surprises him. He says my (fake) name again, tenderly, and I don't deny him when he brings me in. "I didn't bring you here to fight with you. I'm sorry." He kisses me, soft and gentle, and I give him everything I can in that kiss, holding his face in my palms, because he loves me and *oh*, I want to do right by him. I want to do more.

My phone rings, startling us both enough that we break off, trying to catch our breath. I quickly pull out my phone. It's 9:00 at night, and it's my mom.

"Hello?" I say, trying to make my voice sound normal.

"Bee." My mom's voice is hushed, despite the fact that it sounds like she's in a place full of loud people. "Bee, are you with your siblings?"

"Yeah," I say, confused. "They're downstairs—we've been painting."

"Good, okay." She takes a deep breath, and I'm almost positive I hear a hiccup. *Like she's been crying.* "Will you . . . will you bring them to the hospital with you?"

"Mom." I feel like everything slows—my heart beating, Levi's arm as it slides around my waist, my lungs that don't want to fill with air. "Mom, what happened?"

"Oh, Baby Bee. Just . . . "

"Mom, please tell me what happened."

She sighs, a light sigh that masks a sob. "Honey, Papa's started having seizures."

chapter 37

QUEUED:
CREATURE FEAR
BY BON IVER

THE DRIVE TO the hospital is the worst in my life. It is quiet and stuffy and Levi-less, Tom keeps fisting his hands around the steering wheel like he's angry, and Millie is sniffling. Worst of all: Astrid has finally lost it.

"Astrid, please don't cry," I say, a little too quietly. "Astrid."

She cries anyway. And it's too damn hard to watch.

All the way there, I hold my phone in my hands, Levi's name pulled up, an empty message waiting for me to fill it with words like *I'm sorry* and *I love you* or even just a heart. Anything. All I can finally manage is, *Please can we talk again soon?*

(He doesn't reply.)

But the driving isn't the worst of it. We have to wait in the lobby for forever because there was a mix-up and we don't know where my dad's room is. It's us and a lot of quiet and upset people who go up and down the elevators and disappear into the hallway to our right and through the sliding glass door to our left.

My heart aches. While we stand there, huddled together, my brain whirrs and jumps like a broken clock. I keep returning to Levi and the way I left him, looking ragged on the steps of the house we made together, and the last words I spoke to him.

I'm sorry I haven't been more, I said. I hear the words on replay, a promise I don't know if I can keep. How stupid of me to say them only because they were what he wanted to hear.

As I tuck these thoughts away, I replace them with thoughts of Mama, and my sisters, and the way we will cry tonight. I think about the way Tom will try *not* to cry, but he'll be shaky. I know there is something more, something Mama hasn't told us. I do know it's going to break me.

Mama comes down the elevator after we've stood there for nearly twenty minutes. She's wearing a baggy sweatshirt over her pajamas, a plaid shirt-and-pants set. (Seeing something that has so much *home* to it in this cold, sad place makes my heart twist.) She starts to cry as soon as she sees us, huddled against the wall, and rushes across the busy foot traffic to get to us. She's shorter than everyone in our family, even Millie, so she's instantly lost in our embrace. She kisses Millie and Astrid, wiping away both of their tears, and takes my face in her hands and smiles a perfectly sad smile. "Baby Bee."

I nod, lip quivering. "Mama."

"You need to know something right now, okay?" she says, taking a deep breath. It's shaky and teary and I hug her tighter. "Papa . . . isn't getting better. His tumor is about the same size, but there are . . . .others . . . now. One on his liver, one on his lung. There is a chance we can operate to remove the new tumors, but it won't change the fact that it's spread."

I'm about to let go and cry—it's been building up—but then I hear Millie's quiet crying and I stop myself. I have to be brave for her, and for Astrid, who's got her head buried in my shoulder. (I was right: Tom's hands are shaking and his breathing is rapid.) I bite my lip and say nothing.

"He's sleeping right now," Mom continues. "We wanted you to come when he was awake, but he just couldn't keep his eyes open. So come see him, give him kisses, and then you have to go back home."

We nod and follow her into the elevator, where it's finally quiet except for Millie's muffled sobs. The floor my Papa is on is even worse; it's as still as death (no pun intended). The nurses' footsteps are like silk on marble—quiet nothingness. They float like ghosts or angels of death, and I want to sink into one of the waiting chairs and cry, cry until my tears are fresh out and I can face my Papa without feeling like someone's just gutted me with a knife.

We enter his room on feet that pitter-patter loudly in the darkness. Papa lies on the bed, hooked up to machinery and an IV, his breathing shallow and broken. He looks skinnier than I remember, just from yesterday. So it can be one of two things: Either I haven't been noticing his slow decline, or it's a trick of the light.

I let Millie and Astrid go ahead of me, their blond heads looking pale and dull in the wan hospital light coming from the corner lamp Mama switches on. They sit on either side of him, fingers lightly touching his arm, his hands, his cheek. I stay back, my heart pounding, and lean into Tom as he wraps his arm around my shoulder.

"You okay, Beef?" he whispers.

"No."

"Neither am I."

I shudder. "I don't understand. Look at him—I've never seen him look so small." Now I'm crying good and hard, drawing deep breaths to try to keep myself stable. Tom tucks me into his arms and whispers something to me through my messy hair, and I'm pretty sure he's telling me it will be okay.

But we both know that's a lie.

I get home, kiss Millie and Astrid goodnight, and lock my door behind me. I kick off my shoes and slide beneath my covers and close my eyes. But while my body is exhausted, my mind is wide awake. I'm imagining the events of today, again and again and again, Levi and painting and fighting and my Papa hooked up to machines like he's dying.

He is *dying*, I remind myself, and the tears come again.

I almost text Levi to beg him to come over or just talk to me on the phone, distract me from my fears. But there are three things that stop me.

First: the memory of his expression, the look of utter disappointment on his face when I wouldn't tell him my name, when I didn't have a reason. When I let fear get the best of me.

Second: He still hasn't replied to my text.

Third: The last time I got news about my papa, I was in Malibu with Levi. I remember the weightless feeling I had that night when I kissed him for the first time—it's the exact same feeling I had when I kissed him tonight for the hundredth time. I also remember what it felt like, afterward, to be told my father was in the hospital because he's dying.

Both times, this happened. The guilt is beginning to plague me. Should I have been here, with my family? What am I missing out on by doing everything with Levi? These could be my papa's last days, and I'm off having a good time with my boyfriend.

I shudder, because I don't want to think about Levi, because thinking about him means thinking about our fight (*oh-God-*

we-had-our-first-fight-and-it-was-terrible) and my guilt and everything I haven't done right.

I shudder a second time because I know what I need to do now.

I dig through my purse for my phone, barely finding it in the dark, and wipe my eyes free of tears as I unlock it.

There she is: her number, her name. Her picture. I waste no time in pressing on it, but my heart still skips several beats inside my chest.

"Hello?" she answers, after so many rings I thought she'd never pick up. Of course, I've woken her from her sleep—it's three in the morning there. But she's answered, and she's here, and that's all that matters.

"Gretchen," I say, barely managing to keep the crying under control. "I have something I need to tell you."

chapter 38

QUEUED:
PIECES
BY ANDREW BELLE

I'M A MESS. An absolute, unprecedented mess.

Gretchen tells me I'm not as I text her throughout the next day, but the facts still stand: I've cried seventeen times in the last twelve hours; I've only eaten gummy bears from the candy bowl at work all day; I dropped a vase in front of a customer; and I charged Velma Hastings, our most frequent and esteemed customer, three times for her arrangement.

But, while all of that is terrible, I keep coming back to one thing: Gretchen forgave me.

That's all that matters, I tell myself gently, sweeping up the glass shards at my feet. *She forgave me and she loves me*, I think, popping another gummy bear into my mouth. *She cried with me on the phone and ate ice cream with me . . . virtually*, I continue to rant to myself, and start crying again.

Eighteen times. Yep, I've been counting.

After work, I head back to the old TCP office. It's weird—I haven't been back since we first visited the new house. It looks the same because we still have two months left on the lease and this is where Levi has his interviews, but I feel like it should be empty and barren.

The back room is packed full of volunteers when I step inside, so loud that I almost put my hands over my ears. Albert and Missy are shouting at each other about some movie that he loved, and she hated, and Elle is laughing, and the twins are whispering in the corner. And Levi—Levi is at the desk in the back, signing some papers, shaking his head. Laughing.

He finally replied to my text earlier this morning, with an *Of course we can talk* and *I love you* and *Can't wait to see you tomorrow.* So I'm not mad at him, except I can't quite get over his laughter in the midst of everything.

I'm still reeling from yesterday's fight, from the news—and from my conversation with Gretchen late last night. In the grand scheme of things, I know Levi and Gretchen love me. But I can't help but think that the world is fragmenting around me (or maybe I'm fragmenting from within), while Levi has enough joy and comfort to *laugh.*

Elle notices me by the door and distracts me from my thoughts by poking me in the arm. Then she wraps me in a hug. "You all right?"

I nod, breaking my stare. "Yeah. I'll be okay." (I hate that I sound weepy.)

"We're here for you," she whispers, swallowing hard.

"Thanks," I whisper back. Then, "Hi, Levi."

He sees me and stands, almost tripping over his chair trying to get to me, consequently making me smile for the first time all day. He huffs, but he still looks happy. "It's not my fault my legs are so long."

I can't talk, so instead I just dive into his welcoming arms because they're there and they're open and I love him.

"Hey, is everything okay?" Levi looks down at me, his eyebrows furrowed with worry.

"No," I whisper.

He grabs my hand and we escape the stuffy room into the hall. (Albert and Missy are *loud*.) "Do you have news?" he asks when the noises are muffled.

I nod, burying my head in his chest. "The cancer spread," is all I say, but obviously that's enough.

Levi's arms tighten around me, locking me in. I can't breathe, but for a minute I don't want to—and then I'm crying, my sobs leaving me gasping. Levi waits patiently, doing all the things a good boyfriend should do, like stroking my hair and rubbing his thumb on my arm and leaving kisses along my hair line. Eventually, he tilts my head back so he can see my face, which I'm sure looks horribly unattractive. (See also: red, blotchy, tear-streaked, puffy.) He runs the pads of his thumbs over my cheeks to wipe away the tears, one at a time. Then over my lips, red from my teeth, which worry away at my mouth constantly.

I remember, suddenly, that once (it seems like too long ago) I was daydreaming about touching *his* lips, and here we are now, tangled up in each other, full of sorrow.

"Ugh, my crying face is gross," I say, and try to hide my face.

"Did you know," Levi begins, voice quiet, "that my dad used to tell my mom that she looked ugly when she cried?" He places a kiss on my cheek, close to the corner of my mouth. "After sixteen years of marriage, he just couldn't bear to see that he'd

made her cry, time and time again, so he insulted her." Another
kiss, on my chin. "I know we haven't been married for sixteen
years, or, um, any years at all, but I can't imagine ... can't
imagine saying that." He shakes his head. "You're so beautiful,
all the time."

"Even right now?" I whisper.

"Even right now."

"Wow. I must be hot stuff."

Levi makes a face. "Are you mocking me?"

"No, shush," I say, and kiss him. (And then I open my mouth
so I can kiss him better.)

"I should get back in there," he says after a minute, when I'm
on my toes and all I want is to keep kissing him.

"Party pooper," I say.

He laughs, wiping away one stray tear. "I love you, and I love
your dad, and I'm so, so sorry, Bee."

Those are the words I needed to hear. I thank him silently,
squeezing his hand too tight. Now that I'm feeling better, I
almost want to bring up what happened yesterday, our fight, the
way he looked at me as if I had disappointed him beyond belief.
But today, all that has been stripped away; there is no trace of
anger or disappointment or fear left between us. Today, I want
to forget what happened.

All of yesterday can go to hell.

I kiss him one more time and take his hand as we head back
inside. (I do my best to leave my doubts behind.)

We walk straight into a war zone. Albert and Missy are still
arguing, but this time, quite bewilderingly, they're on the same
side. This time, they've banded against Elle.

"Give that to me," she gasps, and rushes at the two of them.
They're holding and shaking and tossing around the backpack
she lugs everywhere. Elle's *pissed*.

"Why?" they tease, holding it up between them.

"Don't you dare open that," Elle gasps, and lunges

Albert swings it out of her reach and, swift as the glitter-throwing ninja he is, unzips the backpack and dumps it upside down. Elle's eyes go wide and her cheeks burn red as about twenty books fall out at their feet.

And they're not just any books—they're hot-and-heavy romance novels. Plastered with mostly naked Highlanders and women draped in sheets, bearing long-winded titles like *How To Rescue A Rake From A Marriage of Convenience*, and coming in all shapes and sizes, they lie at Elle's feet in a furious state of disarray.

Of course, that's when the glitter rains down on Elle and her books. "Those covers are rude," Albert states.

Levi's laugh fills the empty space around me like a warm blanket, and I start to feel comfortable here again.

Elle stands up with three books stacked in her arms, nose in the air. "I won't apologize for my taste in literature."

"Literature!" I gasp, feigning horror, and pull up a second chair behind Levi's desk.

Elle's expression turns from embarrassment to relief in a split second. "Come on, don't tell me you haven't wanted to pick up one of these bad boys."

"No, not personally," I say, and a truly happy laugh escapes me.

"Look," Elle exclaims, opening one of the books to a page just after the middle of the book. The title is *To Steal A Demon's Love*. I'm pretty sure the woman on the cover could never actually pretzel herself around a man like that unless she was Elastigirl, but I'm also pretty sure Mr. Beefy-Cover-Model is not Elastigirl's type.

Elle begins reading from her selected scene. I roll my eyes and try to find something to do, while Levi just stands there next to me, grimacing. Albert has his fingers in his ears, muttering to himself. Missy, on the other hand, looks completely enraptured.

After a few minutes, Levi sits in the swivel chair beside me and says, "Well, that was unexpected."

I shake my head in equal disbelief. "I didn't even know she was a reader!"

He whimpers. "If I hear one more thing about glistening chests, heavy breathing, and *clenching* of any kind, I will die."

The amount of disgust on his face makes me laugh, a truly happy laugh, my first in what feels like years. "Don't listen to her, then. Talk to me."

He shudders, stacking some applications. "Want to help with these?"

I nod eagerly. "Distract me."

"Obviously I've been doing that from Day One," he says.

I attempt to laugh at this because he's joking, but it's actually the truth. I see him, in my mind's eye, like it was yesterday: standing by the car, head ducked under the hood, hair gloriously untamed. And later, he believed I was staring at his clothes, when I was really staring at his face.

I poke the side of his neck to get him to look at me, but of course, now I'm exactly what I asked to be: *distracted*. I run my finger up to his jaw, my thumb slipping over the curve of his ear, tracing his sharp cheek bone to his nose—and that's when I realize he's looking at me. His expression makes me shiver, because while I see the adoration that's always there, I see hunger as well, and I realize how I've been touching him and what it's done to both of us.

"What are you doing?" he whispers, as if to remind me that we're surrounded by people. His ears are a little red, but my cheeks are fully aflame.

"I was . . . not . . . doing *anything*," I say, unconvincingly. "You were distracting me."

"Oh, great way to shift the blame."

"I *asked* you to distract me."

"Bee."

I smile innocently. "Just ignore me," I say. "And give me those applications."

Locked in silence, we fall back into work, secluded in our corner of the office while everyone else pretends we don't exist.

chapter 39

QUEUED:
I'll Believe In Anything
by Wolf Parade

Levi

Come rescue me. Elle now openly reads smut in the office. I could cry.

Bee

Tell her to stop polluting the minds of children.

I can't help it: I laugh out loud, the sound echoing in the back of the shop as I slip my phone into my apron pocket. Despite everything going on, I feel somewhat refreshed by the lack of news from the doctor. (No news is better than bad news.) Today is a designing day for me, as Tracy is getting ready for a wedding and needs an extra set of hands, which only adds to my happiness. I have three arrangements left: a simple arrangement to put on display in the cooler, an autumn wreath for someone's front door, and a basket arrangement for a funeral.

I'm starting with the biggest and hardest: the funeral piece. (Tracy thinks I'm ready for this and I hope to prove her right.) I've soaked the oasis already, and now it sits inside the basket, waiting to be filled with stems. I step into the cooler to gather the ordered flowers (a dozen white roses as a base, and white lisianthus, spray roses, stock, and a splash of iris to fill).

I start with the roses, spreading them equally and giving them gradual height toward the back of the basket. Then I weave leather and misty around the edges to create a frame. Within twenty minutes I have filled the in-betweens of the roses with the other flowers and more filler, adjusting it every so often to get the look I want. Finally, I stand back, surveying my work.

"Bee," Tracy calls from the storage room. "Will you open the back door? Ludwig's here! He needs to grab that funeral piece."

I breathe a sigh of relief that I've finished . . . *just* in time. "Yeah!" I call out, heading to the back.

Ludwig, Tracy's funeral delivery man, is just on the other side. I've only seen him a few times, since he works for Tracy at odd hours, but I'd know him anywhere. He has long silver hair, which he always wears down, and he's got on his signature cargo pants and floral button up. "Hey!" he says cheerfully.

"Hi, Ludwig," I say, stepping aside so he can come inside. "It's ready for you on the table."

He nods and approaches the work table. "Phew, Tracy!" he calls out, as if he knows she's hiding somewhere. "This is stupendous work!"

OH MY GOSH, I think, and then I don't know what to think. Tracy laughs—but then comes the sound of crashing.

"You okay?" Ludwig shouts.

Tracy laughs some more. "Yes. Bee made that funeral piece, not me."

Ludwig's expression swiftly changes: a raised eyebrow, one side of his mouth quirking.

I duck my head awkwardly, blushing straight to the roots of my hair. "Thanks?"

He whistles. "It's like you've been doing this for twenty years. Is Tracy teaching you?"

"Yeah." Most of this I picked up from watching her and experimenting on my own, but I don't say that.

"Real talent, this." He waves at the basket arrangement like he doesn't know what to do with it. He walks around the table once to get a three-sixty view.

"Thanks," I say again, cursing the one-word answers sticking to my tongue.

"Ever thought about taking classes?"

His question startles me more than I care to admit. It's not a bad idea. I'd even go so far as to call it a great idea. Why hadn't I thought of it before? "No," I answer slowly. "I haven't."

"You have a lot of talent, Bee."

I shake my head. "It's not—"

"It is," Ludwig says firmly. "I know Tracy. She doesn't put time and energy into people who don't have true talent."

I bite my lip. "Thank you."

"I teach," he announces, as if he's just been *waiting* for this moment. He leans back against the work table. "It's already full for the fall, but I could give you a guaranteed spot in the spring, if you want. And at a discount, for a friend of a friend."

I swallow.

"It's more advanced than what Tracy's teaching you here. More about finding your style and making you the designer only you can be." He laughs. "I sound like the inside of a Hallmark

card, but it's true. Besides, it looks good on your resume and
will be a bonus if you go to school for this later."

I'm not without my doubts (Classes? School? Resume?!) but
I smile at Ludwig and nod. "I'll think about it."

"Let me know by November and I'll have a spot for you." He
turns, grabs the trip sheet on the counter, and hoists the basket
into his arms. "Gotta take this now. See you soon?"

I nod. "Thanks."

He nods, smiling, and disappears out the back door.

My doubts and worries soon fade into general excitement. *I'll
worry about all* that *stuff later*, I argue with myself, and end up
bursting with the news as soon as I get to the hospital and sit
down beside my Papa. "You'll never believe what I just heard
from Ludwig today."

He snorts. "I didn't realize there were any Ludwig's left alive."

"Shh, Papa, I know his name is . . . old fashioned . . . but
you named me Bernice so you can't talk! Besides, he's really
nice." I scoot my chair closer. The room is empty except for us
(Mama went for a walk), and the quiet is kind of nice. I explain
everything to him, hardly taking a breath the whole time. I
heave when I'm done, satisfied with my narrative.

My dad raises an eyebrow and squeezes my hand. "You want
to do it?"

"I don't know . . . I mean . . . yeah?" I clear my throat. "Yeah,
I do."

He nods. "Then you should do it. It's fun for you, and I
think it would make your mother happy. She wants you to find
something you love."

"Me, too, Papa." Our eyes meet, and it is unmistakable—he

is in pain. "What's wrong?" I ask tentatively, hoping his body isn't about to shut down with another seizure. The doctors say the seizures are unpredictable. I never want to see him like that.

Papa squeezes my hand again and swallows hard. That's when I realize he's choking back tears. "I just want to see you accomplish all these things, Baby Bee."

"Papa," I try to say, but my voice cracks.

"Shhh." He brings my head to his chest, patting down my hair. "We have to start preparing for the worst."

I move to the edge of the bed so I can better lean on his shoulder. I'm trying to erase those words, to pretend he never said them, but they are ringing, bouncing off the walls of my mind. It hurts worse with every second, because every second feels closer to the end, and there is no way I can deny this any longer. Not now that he's said it out loud.

Papa falls asleep shortly after, his breathing evening out. I don't move, however, until his door opens and Levi sticks his head around the corner.

"Hey," I whisper, quickly standing up.

"I'm sorry, bad timing," he whispers, crossing the room steadying me as I wobble. "I didn't realize he'd be asleep."

"It's okay. We never know when he's tired." (He's always tired.)

Levi kisses me sweetly (always sweetly), so I bring my hands up to cradle his face. He presses them closer with his own hands, covering mine completely. "How much longer are you going to be here?"

I shrug. "Not sure. My mom's on a walk, and my sisters are with Tom. Maybe until one of them gets back?"

He tugs me toward the window seat, moving aside my mom's magazines and purse so we can sit side by side. I drape my legs across him, and he puts his arm around my shoulders, resting his hand on my ankles. His long fingers play with the laces of my shoes, looping in and out, twisting, knotting. "How was work?"

Sighing, I repeat everything I just told my dad (but with much less flourish). "I don't know what to tell Ludwig," I end with. "It feels so real, like something I could actually do. Something that could make me really happy."

"I think it's a great idea. You get better and better every day."

"Ha." I roll my head against his shoulder, feeling suddenly exhausted. "Thanks."

"Your sarcasm is duly noted and unappreciated."

"Levi?" We both look up as my mom comes into the room, closing the door behind her. She smiles that pixie smile of hers, glancing at my sleeping dad, and lowers her voice. "Good to see you." Levi starts to get up, but she waves her hand at him. "Stay there, don't mind me."

He gives her a broad grin. "Hi, Chloe."

My mom kisses his forehead, and then mine. "Did you get to talk to him?"

"He fell asleep before I got here."

"I'm sure he'll be so bummed when he finds out he missed you."

Levi shrugs. "I can stay as late as you'll let me." Suddenly, he sits up straight and reaches into his pocket. "Hey, before I forget, I brought the check for you."

The envelope that he passes into my mom's hands is white and small, but I can tell it immediately makes her nervous. She glances at me in worry, then back at Levi, and tries to smile. "Thanks."

"What's that?" I ask, uneasy.

Levi glances between us. "Oh." His eyes widen. "I, um, thought she knew?"

My mom sighs. "Bee—" She opens the envelope and takes out the check. It's addressed to my dad.

It's from The Color Project.

Everything in the room slows to a halt as I slide my legs off

Levi's and stand. "What?" I whisper. My blood rushes in my ears, too loudly. "Mom?"

She takes a deep breath in before she says, "Levi has been paying for your dad's treatments."

"What?" I repeat for the third time. I look down at where Levi is sitting, expression confused, like he doesn't know why I'm acting like this. "Why?"

There's a flash of irritation in his eyes. Like he has a few choice words for me that he doesn't want to say in front of my mom. "Bee, come on—"

"There are other people, Levi, who might need this more than we do."

My mom sighs. "We *do* need this. We haven't been able to afford a single treatment."

I look her, with her sadness and stress and worry so plain on her face, and then at Levi, who nods in affirmation. "They applied shortly after we found out that day," he says.

(My heart shatters.) "Why didn't you tell me?" I whisper, willing one of them to answer me. I don't want to cry, but it's a battle I know I'm losing. I'm angry—*so* angry—that I blamed this on Levi, that I assumed he was giving us money without a reason. Why on earth would he do that? Of *course* there was a reason; of *course* my parents applied.

She touches my arm, but I step out of reach. She works her jaw and says, "We didn't want you to worry about anything else. Cancer is a hard burden to bear on its own."

"I could have," I protest, although I'm not sure I'm telling the truth. "I would have been fine! Maybe I could have even helped." I stop, something dawning on me. "Is that why you stopped asking me about college? Because you knew you couldn't afford it?"

She doesn't answer me directly, but her drooping shoulders and the bags under her eyes tell me I'm right. "Baby Bee, we don't want you to help. That's what TCP is for. And if you'd found something you wanted to do, I would have wanted you to go for it without worrying about us. Everything is being taken care of—"

I'm not listening anymore. I *did* find something, but now I can't tell her because she'll insist on paying for the class and whatever college courses I want to take later. I can't let her do that.

(*Papa is dying. Papa is dying. Papa is dying.*)

I take a step back and turn. "I'm going home," I say, grabbing my purse by the foot of the bed. I hear my mom ask Levi if he can follow me home, but I'm gone before I can hear his response.

Because he's Levi, he does follow me home, exactly like my mother asked.

"Wait," he says when I ignore him. He follows me up the path and the steps to the front door. "Bee! Come *on*," he pleads.

"I don't want to talk," I say, and I mean it.

He takes my hand, so unassuming, but I jerk away. "Please, listen to me—"

"I know you didn't know, Levi," I say, and pause fumbling with my keys to turn and look at him. "I'm sorry I blamed you. I should have asked questions."

"That's not the problem."

"Then what is?"

He breathes out. "I can pay for the class, if that's what you're worried about."

"I don't *want* you to pay for the class!" My voice is raised now. My throat hurts. "That's the whole point!"

"You should have told her. She loves you and wants you to be happy. *I* want you to be happy!"

"You can't do everything for me!" I burst, hands closing into fists.

"What?" He rests back on his heels, as if tempted to take a step away from me. He doesn't just look surprised, he looks shocked. "Why would I want to do everything for you? I want to do *one* thing for you. Just one!"

"I don't need help with *that*, not right now. Please, just . . . " I wipe a hand over my face.

"You can't just . . . pull away when things get hard," he tells me, jaw growing hard.

"I'm not—I'm not." (I am, and I know it.)

"I know we still have things we need to work through. I've been trying not to bring it up because there are a lot of other things happening but maybe that's not good for us. Maybe it's getting in the way of . . . us."

I shake my head. "I don't want to talk about *any* of it right now. I'm too tired."

"Why won't you let me comfort you?"

"This is not comforting."

"Not this." He takes a deep breath. "I imagined this going a lot differently."

I wipe my eyes with shaking hands. Everything is falling apart too fast. Everything in me aches for him to understand. "Levi, my dad is *dying*."

"I know he is," he grinds out. "I'm trying to imagine what you're going through, believe me."

"You *know* what I'm going through—your own dad—"

"It's not the same." Levi runs both hands over his hair, jaw locking in what I think might be anger. "I never loved my dad the way you love yours. Hell, I've never loved my dad the way *I* love yours."

"Then you understand!" My voice is raised again. "You know what it's like to watch him wasting away every day, *suffering*. I'm breaking, Levi."

"And I want to help hold you together," he says. "But we have to talk about things—"

"No, we don't! Not right now."

He stops short, his breathing heavy. "That's your problem. You did this before, when the news came out. You didn't want to talk about it with me, you didn't tell Gretchen for a whole week—"

A month, I correct him silently. His words are hitting a mark I didn't even know existed. I know he's right, and I also know that I am angry.

"We have to talk about things. Otherwise, I will never be able to comfort you, because I don't know how," he says. "I can't read your mind."

I don't answer. I don't know how.

"Do you love me?" he asks. The question is sudden and violent, and we both immediately know he's been bursting with this for a long time.

I let out a soft moan. This was exactly what stopped me the other day: I haven't done enough, I haven't loved him enough. "Of course. Of course I love you." I wipe my eyes again.

"Then show me."

Three words. (Three knives.) "I'm trying."

"You're trying." He tries to disguise his scoff, but I hear it. (For a moment, a terrible, unexplainable second, all I feel is fear.). "All right, answer me honestly: Were you ever planning to tell me your name?"

I stare at him, because his question dumbfounds me. I don't know—I actually don't know.

But my silence is answer enough. He laughs, harsh and un-Levi-like, very much like his father, and I want to scream.

"Why?" he asks.

I swallow hard, but there's still a lump. My words come out as hoarse whispers, incomplete, raspy. "At first it was funny, you trying to guess. And then . . . I don't know." I shrug. "I don't know." *I'm breaking. It's not enough. Papa's dying. I love you. I'm hiding. Please, come find me.*

Levi backs up, down the steps, hands in his pockets. His eyes are on me, but they're not *really*, like he can't see me anymore because I'm so small, so invisible. He stops at the bottom and nods once. "See you around, Bee."

That freezes the very blood beneath my skin. The last time he said that there was so much hope and joy in it. Before, it reminded me of an ocean I could float in forever, or eating ice cream sundaes for breakfast, or meteor showers. Now, it reminds me of a promise being broken, and it makes me cry.

And Levi—he sees my tears. He sees my hands shaking at my sides, and the way my chest heaves, and he turns and walks away.

chapter 40

QUEUED:
LIGHTHOUSE
BY PATRICK WATSON

BEING MORE OPEN with Gretchen starts now, when I'm upset.

I'm a lot hurt and a little bit angry, but more at myself than at Levi. He left me alone on the porch when I was begging him for help, bleeding, suffocating—but I realize it was all in my head, that I never asked him to stay, never told him I needed him.

I want to kick myself. I had the chance, and he's Levi: of course he would have helped me. Of course he would have listened. It would have helped him to understand, if I could have gotten the words out right. In fact, the more I look back, the more I understand: He was begging me to talk, and I turned him away.

That night, after a sullen dinner with Astrid and Millie, I grab my phone and pull up Messenger. The app says Gretchen is online, so I take a deep breath and send a message.

Bee

Can I tell you something?

Gretchen

Obviouslyyyyy

Bee

I fought with Levi and it was horrible.

Gretchen

What?!

Bee

We fought a few days ago, but then Mama called about . . . you know.

Levi and I never worked it out, so we fought again today. I remember thinking one thing and saying another, or not saying anything at all.

I don't know how to fix it.

Gretchen

Bee, I'm so sorry. But . . . he knows what you're going through right now. He might need a bit of space, but he'll always come back to you.

Bee

He walked away.

I couldn't talk to him. I didn't want him there, so he left.

Gretchen

Has he ever given you reason to think he'd give up on you all together?

Bee

No.

Gretchen

Exactly. Even if he's upset, he'll come around. He's probably feeling bad right now that he left you earlier.

Bee

Gretchen, he's really mad at me.

I haven't told him my name yet.

Gretchen

WHAT?! Phew. Okay.

Ummm . . . ..

Shit.

I thought you were going to do that ages ago?

Nevermind. There's no time like the present, right?

Bee

Right?

Gretchen

He needs to know you're on his side. He needs to know that you're all in. Telling him will do just that.

I breathe through my teeth; it sounds like a hiss. She's right, for the most part. But what happens if he's no longer all in, like I (and maybe he) once thought he was? I feel cracked, and it's like he's seen everything inside—that I'm barren and empty—and now he knows I have nothing to give him.

Bee

Okay.

Gretchen

You're an idiot. Go talk to him already.

Bee

I can't tonight. I'll go to the shop tomorrow.

Gretchen

You do that. Tell me how it goes?

Bee

Yeah.

Gretchen

I LOVE YOU FOREVER, BERNICE AURORA WESCOTT.

See? It's not that hard to say.

Bee

That's because it's not yours.

Gretchen

sigh I tried.

Well, practice in front of the mirror or something.

I manage a smile and our regular *I think you're crap* before I lie down in bed and dream that the stars haven't gone out over my life.

When I open my eyes again, it's still black as pitch outside.

Someone's knocking on my door.

"Yeah?" I ask, but it's a whisper and I hope whoever's there can hear me. (My throat feels weird, like there's something stuck.)

My mom opens my door and whispers, "Bee, are you awake?"

I'm tempted to not answer, so I compromise: I nod.

"Okay. Do you want to talk?" she asks, a little louder.

I shudder. "No, thanks." Same words I said to Levi. *Haven't I learned?*

She sits on the edge of my bed and runs her hand down my arm. Her fingers are cold. "Bee, it's okay to be scared." I turn around, and instantly her arms encircle me. "We're all scared," she adds, with less confidence, so I can see the side of her that isn't *Mom*. It's the side that's *Wife*, and suddenly my heart is full of secondhand sadness.

"I know," I whisper. Someday I hope to be brave.

"I'm here, Baby Bee. You can always talk to me."

But I still don't want to talk, because that requires walking straight into the pain, willingly, with no guarantee that it will make anything better. I'm not ready to try, not yet, so I just let my mom curl up beside me and cry silently, her tears wetting my pillow.

After psyching myself up, it's more than disappointing to get to Mike's shop the next afternoon and see . . . no one. There are no cars parked out front, and the garages are closed. It's at the last second before I turned back out of the lot that I see the little light in the office (it's too bright out).

I pray Levi's parked around back and pull my car into one of the many free spaces. It's a little strange, being here, after what's happened. I've been by a few times in the past month—usually just to sneak a kiss. But standing here in the empty lot, I'm reminded of that first time Levi spoke to me and I thought I was going to die because I was going to screw up the conversation or stare at him too hard or *something* awful.

And then I kept seeing him everywhere and he liked me and *then*—then he loved me.

I want to go back to that.

My skin practically burning from the sun and my fears, I walk up the steps to the little office, knock on the door, and crack it open. "Hello?"

Someone's standing on a chair in the back, changing a light bulb, but it's not Levi. "Be right with you," Keagan says.

My spirits fall. "It's just me," I say.

"Bee?" Keagan looks over his shoulder at me, wobbles a bit, and laughs as he adjusts his weight. "Good to see you! How've you been?"

Typical, sweet Keagan, always jumping straight into things. Too bad I'm not in the mood. "Oh, um, I'm okay."

"How's your dad?" he asks, turning just enough so he can jump off the chair.

I cringe. "Actually, can we not talk about my dad today?"

His expression dims. "Not good, then? But okay, we don't have to talk." He runs a hand through his wavy hair (it's long now, to his jaw) and gives me that sad smile everyone gives me when they feel bad about my life. "What's up?"

"I was hoping . . . I thought . . . Levi would be working." But now that the words are coming out of my mouth, I'm certain he's not here, and maybe it was silly of me to show up in the first place. The window that looks down into the garage shows only dark and shadowy machinery.

Keagan gives me a look. "He's at a meeting . . . for The Color Project?"

I try not to look surprised, or choke, or feel embarrassed.

Keagan sees all of this anyway. "Did he not tell you?"

I am wordless. I open my mouth to answer, but nothing comes out, so I just spread my hands.

"Shit. You guys are fighting, aren't you? He came in for a makeup shift last night and he looked *horrible*."

I think my knees want to crumble underneath me. "I'm sorry I bugged you, Keagan," I say, and start to go.

"Bee," he says, in a way that makes me stop even though I want to leave right now. I stop because I know he's got something important to say. (Keagan only ever seems to say important things.) "I'm not busy until five." He checks the clock on the wall. "Another hour, at least, so give it to me."

With almost no hesitation, I cave. He doesn't know me, I realize. Not personally, at least, which means he doesn't know the mistakes I've made, the things I'm afraid of. I trust Levi too much to think he'd rat on me and all my issues, so Keagan becomes a clean slate for me to work out all my problems on.

I need this more than anything.

Folding my arms over my chest, I sit beside him on the edge of the desk (*Dear Greg, sorry we made a mess sitting on your neatly organized paperwork. Love, Bee & Keagan*) and give him he watered-down version of everything that happened. I don't tell him about my name; I do tell him about feeling lost. I *try* to tell him that I've shut Levi out and shut myself in; instead, it comes out as *I don't know how to be this person.* But despite how many times I jumble my words and have to repeat myself, he listens. It's so very . . . *Keagan.*

When I'm done, he nods once, as if he expected all this. "You're overthinking this," he says with confidence, crossing his arms, hair tucked behind his ears. "I bet you anything that Levi looked so awful last night because he was thinking of all the ways he was wrong."

"But he wasn't wro—"

Keagan laughs, surprising me, cutting me off. "Levi's a nice guy, really—I told you before that he's the nicest, and I'll always back that—but he hates rocking the boat. It's just his thing, you know?"

I *didn't* know that. And knowing it doesn't exactly make me feel better.

"Don't stress it too much, okay?" Keagan nudges my elbow.

I stand up. "I'm trying not to."

"Hey." Keagan stands with me, looking at me thoughtfully. "I assume you guys are hanging out tomorrow, anyway, right?"

I shiver, but I'm not sure why, because this heat is wretched. "Not . . . no . . . we didn't have plans. Why?"

Keagan rolls his eyes. "Levi's a dumb-ass drama queen. It's his birthday tomorrow."

I can feel my eyes bulging. "What?!"

"Yeah, I know, right? He has this thing about his birthday— he gets shy about celebrating. I found out from Suzie years ago and have been telling everyone since then, getting groups of people together to hang out, watch movies or go out for burgers in OB or something. One year he even tried to trick us and pretend he was out of town, but we soon found out from his mom that he was just trying to avoid the attention."

"That's stupid," I say, drily, because it *is*.

"Yeah, well, we think so, too. I assumed he'd tell his girlfriend, of all people."

I think, *Maybe he was planning to, before*, but I don't say it. (I wonder if Keagan thought it, too.) I have more questions now than before, which makes my head ache. "No, he didn't tell his girlfriend."

"Okay. That settles it. You're joining us tomorrow for dinner. Stop by the shop at five, and we'll all drive to his house together."

I nod, trying to imagine this scenario playing out. It could only be good, right? Maybe this will lighten his spirits, and mine, and we could talk in a civilized manner. This time, I promise myself I won't run from him, and I pray he won't leave me behind.

I pull my purse higher on my shoulder and smile, albeit shakily, and thank Keagan with a hug. "I'll be there."

chapter 41

QUEUED:
STAINACHE
BY EMMA LOUISE

THERE ARE QUITE a few of us on Levi's doorstep: Keagan, Tom, Elle, Nikita, Suhani, Michael, Greg, and some random boys I don't know but assume are from the shop. Elle's carrying two packs of beers, the twins brought non-alcoholic beverages, and Tom's got three bags of chips. One of the boys I don't know is carrying two movies and a video game that he claims is the sequel to Levi's favorite.

I realize, quite gloomily, that I didn't know Levi likes playing video games, that he likes them enough to have a favorite.

The sun's already gone down and Suzie has turned on all the lights. (We waited until later in the evening for two reasons: to not interfere with family dinner plans, and to make him think he's getting out of a birthday surprise this year.) It only takes a few seconds after we knock before Suzie swings open the door, her smile as wide as I expected it to be.

"Oh, he's going to love this, you guys." Suzie hops excitedly (three times exactly) before letting us in. I hang back, letting the others go ahead of me. Suzie shuts the front door and yells, "Hey, birthday boy, come see your present!"

"Mom, you already got me something!" Levi shouts back. A second later, he runs into the room. His bare feet skid on the wood as he sees us and comes to a startled halt. "What. Is. Going. On?"

"Ha!" Keagan shouts. "You thought you were getting out of it this year."

Levi rubs a hand over his face, chuckling. "I shouldn't have gotten my hopes up. What was I thinking?"

"I don't know, man." Keagan clasps his hand and smacks the back of his head. "Happy birthday."

Levi still hasn't seen me, but I know the moment is inevitable. He looks tired, with dark circles under his eyes and his clothes slightly askew, but he also looks relatively happy. He goes through the group, passing out hugs and laughing with each person as they wish him a happy birthday.

It isn't until he reaches for a hug from Elle that he sees me, and my heart flips, and my throat strangles. I hadn't really thought about how this moment would go, just that it would go one of two ways: good or bad. But in reality, it's neither. (Or a little bit of both.) His eyes land on me at the back of the group, and his smile fails us both, and I want to sink into oblivion.

But then he shakes his head and, taking the last few steps toward me, embraces me fully. Sighing, as if he's so happy to have me and so unhappy that we fought, he kisses me full on the mouth.

Of all the things I expected, it was not this. With his arms around my waist, my hands automatically weave through his hair. It doesn't matter that all our friends are watching, or that I feel like I don't deserve something so wonderful.

It doesn't matter that he hasn't smiled at me.

What does matter: that I missed him, that he's holding me like *he* missed *me*, and that we're together. That's it. That's everything.

Tom whistles (I'd be thoroughly pissed if I weren't so preoccupied) and Keagan loudly proclaims, "Well, his first birthday celebration with a girlfriend was bound to be a little different, right?"

And Elle. "That's a little steamy, you guys." (*Oh, Elle, you're one to talk.*)

At that, Levi steps back, tucking me into his side. Then he smiles at them (still not at me), laughs at them, shakes his head like they're funny and he hasn't just jumbled up our already confused hearts.

Elle tosses her blue hair over her shoulder. "I just want a beer. Who's with me?"

Suzie clears her throat by the doorway to the kitchen. "Hello, again," she says, looking closely at Elle (who gives a sheepish smile and hides the beer behind her back) before turning to her son. Everyone stands remarkably still as she crosses over and kisses Levi's cheek. "Drink responsibly, baby. I'll be in my room if you need anything." She waves at us, pressing my hand once before disappearing.

Elle grins. "I mean, she gave her permission, so it's totally legal, yeah?"

Levi rolls his eyes. "At least Albert isn't here to throw glitter on me."

"Actually—" Elle hands the beer to Keagan and reaches into her pockets. "This is from him," she says gleefully, and tosses two handfuls of glitter into the air.

"Happy twentieth, Levi!" Keagan shouts, and Michael and Tom and the rest of the boys join in, with me and Elle and the twins right behind. Then the house goes up in cheers, and

Levi's rubbing glitter out of his hair, laughing. He's so beautiful, standing there with his heart on his sleeve.

(I don't want to break it, but I think I already have.)

We end up on the roof.

One of the boys requested it, so Levi got out the ladder, and we climbed the wobbly thing until we were on the house's slightly angled roof. I laid out a blue and white striped blanket from Suzie's linen closet and all ten of us unceremoniously piled on. The boys and Elle each grabbed a beer while the twins and I popped open Sprite cans.

Now we're on our backs, staring at the sky. Even I (in my uncertain state of being, in my fear and doubt and anger) am enamored with the star patterns visible tonight. After a few minutes of lying beside each other, silently, Levi reaches for my hand. I feel his fingers brush mine, soft and slow, and for a moment I let him grip me. He threads his fingers through mine, squeezing tight like he means it.

But I'm not sure of anything anymore, so I untangle us.

He shifts and lifts his beer as if nothing happened. "Thanks, you guys."

"No," Keagan replies, "thank *you*."

"Shut up," Levi says.

"No," Michael says, sitting up and raising his beer to Levi's. "If there was ever a man who could singlehandedly change the world, it'd be Levi."

"Amen to that!" someone shouts, and another whoops. We all laugh a little.

"Seriously, you guys, shut up," Levi groans out, hand over his face in embarrassment. "You're drunk, Michael."

"Dude," Michael says, in complete control of his faculties, "I've had, like, two sips."

Levi shakes his head. "Thanks. But for real, that's enough."

I want to reach over and smack his arm like I would have before, but I'm frozen, my elbows locked. (I let go of his hand. He walked away. What am I doing here?) My voice is gone, too, so I can't tell him how wrong he is, how it's not enough, how we have so much more to say about him.

Hours pass under the stars. We talk about TCP and Levi and cars and Elle's irrational fear of raccoons. ("There's one living on the roof," Levi tells us, and Elle curls up into a tight ball.) We discuss the stars most of all, with Elle reading off information to us from a constellation app on her phone. It reminds me of a story, a good one that I would read over and over again, and I want to stay like this forever: no cancer, no future, no fear of screwing everything up. I could be happy, forever living in this moment of now.

But then it ends. (Of course it does.) Elle screeches at the slightest sound of scraping on the roof behind us, hurriedly saying her goodbye. Slowly, our friends start to trickle off the roof, telling us to stay, that they'll see themselves out. Sooner than later, it's just Levi and me on the roof, lying still beneath the black expanse. It's like they knew there was something going on, something between us that wasn't quite right, and wanted us to fix it.

Too bad, I think. *I don't know how to fix it.* Keagan said not to overthink it, but all I can *do* is think about it.

I start to stand, to wipe off my jeans, but Levi grabs my hand and tugs me toward him. "I should go," I mutter. I realize, with a terrible pang, that these are the first words I've said directly to him all night.

"Stay," he says simply.

I make a *hmph* noise.

"It's only ten," he adds.

"That's supposed to make me want to stay?" I ask. And then I close my eyes because I did not want to start a fight. It's his birthday and—

"Whatever." He shrugs.

"Levi." I plunk down beside him. "I'm sorry."

"No, you know what? I'm sorry. I spoke out of line the other day." He drinks the last of his beer and balances it beside him so it won't roll off the roof and shatter.

"You didn't really."

"I just . . . for so long, I heard my dad and the way he handled things. He always *had* to say something. He never let anything go, always had to be right. I'm trying so hard not to do that."

"Trying not to rock the boat?" I ask.

He looks at me. (I want to take his pretty face in my hands and kiss away the sadness.) "You talked to Keagan, didn't you? That's his phrase."

I look away. "He was at the shop and you weren't."

"Sorry."

I pull my knees up to my chest and don't say anything.

"I shouldn't have asked you," he says, heaving a breath. "I shouldn't have asked if you love me. I know you love me."

My heart hurts. "How?"

He laughs, a little bitter. The sound goes through skin and bone. "What do you mean, *how*? You love me."

"How?" I repeat, quietly.

"You . . . " He shrugs. "You support me. You laugh at my goofy side. You kissed me—I know you wouldn't kiss just anyone. You're . . . "

"It's not enough." I clear my throat and repeat those words, louder. He looks at me incredulously, like he's going to deny it, but I keep going. "I haven't done enough, okay? I need to, though, I know that. I really want to make this right. What—who—do you want me to be? Because I don't know how to do . . . this." I wave at the air between us. "I don't know how to do this and watch my papa dying and let my mom cry on my pillow and be everything to everyone—"

He catches my hand, fingers tracing mine. "I don't know what you're talking about, Bee. You don't have to be anything, any*one*. You're *you*, and I love you, so quit talking stupid."

"How can you call this stupid? I'm trying to share something with you and you're—"

"I'm not calling *this* stupid!" He raises his hands in exasperation.

I stand up, easing my way toward the ladder. *I can't do this right now*, I think as I lower myself down, taking each rung carefully. Levi doesn't follow me at first, but then I hear his footsteps and the clanking metal and the thump as he lands in his backyard. I'm already inside, already heading for the front door.

"Bee," he says. "Please stop running from me."

I whirl on him, angrily, surprised to see he's standing only a foot behind me. "*I* need to stop running from *you*? You were the one who walked away last time."

"I know, and I'm sorry! I'm sorry I walked away."

"I came here expecting it to make us feel better, to give us some sort of hope that we can work this out. And why didn't you tell me it was your birthday? I don't understand—" It dawns on me at the last second, something I've been missing since yesterday, and it makes my eyes widen and my throat strangle. "You beg me for my name for *months*, but you won't tell me something as simple as your birthday?"

He groans, covering his face with his hands, rubbing his eyes like he isn't seeing me right. "Bee, they're completely different things. I didn't want to make it about me, okay? Your dad is sick, and we've both had a long couple of weeks—I didn't want you to think you had to do anything special for me."

His words make me sick with disgust. Of course. Of *course* that's why he didn't tell me, because he knew I was stressed, because he's forever selfless.

I want to leave, but he's not done. "You, on the other hand," he continues, "are keeping a vital part of yourself from me. *Why*? It's the principle, not the name. I want to know every part of you, inside and out, and you won't give it to me. *I love you.*"

I feel every word, every syllable, each one stopping my heart, slowly shelling me. I'm trying not to curl up, but I feel every inch of me shriveling, retreating.

He must see that I want to leave because he grabs me and pulls me into a hug. I can't resist (despite my persisting fears), letting my arms snake around his waist, my ear pressed to his chest so I can hear his heart beating. I'm crying again.

"I don't know what to do," I say, hiccupping.

"I know. That's okay. I should have been there more, asked more, before it got to this. I'm sorry."

He should have been there more? I cry harder, because now he's apologizing for things he never did. "Please, Levi. Stop." I place a hand on his chest and use it to put space between us. "I think I just need to go home."

Levi looks at me like he can't figure out if he wants to let me go. But then he nods at the last second. "Okay. I understand."

He kisses me without warning, and it's everything I want and not enough—all at once. I gasp a little bit on his mouth, kissing him hard and quick. Our lips drift apart and I'm saying it again—*I just need to go home*—but I haven't had enough of him. That kiss lingers and blurs my vision, until his eyes and hair are out of focus, and all I can see are his lips and his chin and his nose, and I want to kiss every inch of him.

He looks at me, confused, as if waiting for me to actually turn around and leave. But I can't go now. I lift my fingers to trace his bottom lip, which pouts out at me until I replace my fingers with my own lips. He doesn't stop me, doesn't question me, so I pull his head down. His kiss is warm and all-consuming. It becomes me.

"Levi," I breathe.

Then I'm pushing him backward, down the hall, where his bedroom door is slightly ajar. (*Suzie's here*, I think, and then I don't think at all.) He nudges it open with his foot, and then closes it with a fumbling hand and corners me with my back against it.

I wrap my hands around his neck, first with my thumbs brushing the skin around his ears, then his hairline. One hand slides into his hair, the other drifting past the hem of his shirt, skin on skin. His back is warm, strong.

But I am not the only one exploring. His long fingers have escaped the boundary of *my* shirt and now touch *my* skin, at first so softly that it's like a breeze. Then his grip tightens, my shirt falling over his hands on either side. He lingers on the skin at my waist, then travels upward, causing air to whoosh out of my lungs. His nails dig into my ribcage, like he's desperate to go higher but doesn't know if he should.

He's never touched me like his—he's always been good, always held me gently. Knowing this winds me up, suddenly and forcefully. I nudge him backward, not stopping until he's hit the bed, and even then we don't stop, because he's sitting and pulling me down. I roll onto my back, still kissing him, and let him take control. When he does, he moves from my lips to my chin to my neck, where his teeth graze my skin and his lips are so soft and his breath is hot.

I nudge him until his mouth is on mine again and gingerly slip my hands under his shirt. (*New territory!* my mind screams. *Forbiddenforbiddenforbidden*, it warns.) My fingers travel across the expanse of his back, marveling at every tense muscle, every ridge and smooth plane. I linger over a mole beneath his right shoulder blade, and then the tiny scar I find at the waistband of his jeans. He kisses me harder in response, as if I've undone him, just as he's undone me, over and over and over again.

Finally, I think, sighing. I wonder how I could have lived without him, how I could have fought with him or held back at all, because the way we are now is perfect and I never want to go back, never. I slip my hands further up and grab the hem of his shirt and start to tug, wanting it off.

Levi stills, retreating some, lips paused. He's poised above me, our noses touching, his eyes still closed—and then he sighs heavily. He lowers his head so he can kiss my collar bone, but it's chaste and light and leaves everything wanting.

"What—" His voice breaks with a heavy breath. "—are we doing?" he asks. He shakes. His breath and heart and arms and voice. My Levi, my strong, steady fortress: he trembles.

The words tumble through the fog, tripping the alarm in my brain, making me gasp with the understanding of where we're headed. "Oh, my God."

"I thought . . . I thought you wanted to wait."

"I did," I say, clumsily. "I *do*." My cheeks are hot, my body in panic mode, not because we were kissing, but because I grabbed him and pushed him into his bedroom and kissed him on his bed—and almost did everything I said I wasn't going to do.

Still, his skin shivers and his heart pounds, same as mine. "This isn't going to fix anything, Bee." He presses another kiss to my throat, holding on to the moment, as if he's not ready to stop yet. As if he wants to keep going.

I want to keep going. Of course I do.

I wiggle, and he rolls his weight to the side, propping his head up on one hand. He kisses my sleeveless shoulder. "You know, we could have everything we wanted right now, but afterward our problems would still be there. I don't want to do that because I know we'll regret it. I don't want us to be that couple."

"Neither do I," I whisper thinly. I'm feeling two things exactly, and both are sharp. The first is guilt, because I was the weaker one. (Sure, he went along with it, but he also stopped it. He reminded me of everything I've been so careful about, everything I've stood for.) The second is loneliness. I know he loves me, I know he wants me—I felt that in every kiss, in his hands as they explored my skin—but it's over, abruptly, and everything is unfinished, and the hole inside me is wider.

I made it wider.

I roll away and sit up, hands shaking. I grip the edge of the bed to steady myself. "I'm so sorry, Levi."

He sits beside me and reaches out to touch my cheek, moving my hair behind my ear, kissing just next to my eye. "Why are you sorry?"

"This isn't what I wanted."

"But . . . we . . . we didn't . . . "

It doesn't matter, I want to say, but I don't know how to explain it to him because it's not even clear to me. I shake my head, standing. "I need to go home now."

His expression tells me he wants to say something else, but he is also intuitive. He knows I'll break if he breathes another word about it, so he stands with me instead. "I understand," he breathes, his eyes closing briefly with—I can't place it. Is it sorrow? Regret? I try not to think about it; my heart hurts too much already.

Levi walks me to the door, where I squeeze his hand once and start to turn around. When he grabs me and kisses me again, I think I might cry. But instead I let him hold me. I let him take what he can. After a few minutes, when I can't breathe or think clearly, when I'm tempted to go right back to what we just stopped, I disentangle myself.

"Call me soon?" he asks.

"Yeah, of course." I don't give him a final happy birthday, because it feels useless to say anything now. Here his birthday ends on a sad note, on a confused and exhausted note, and I don't want to remind him that I put him there. I drop my hands to my sides and head to my car. This is the third day in a row where we've parted empty-handed, mixed up, broken; where we've come no closer to a conclusion or a solution. This can't keep happening. I've got to do something, or else stop trying altogether.

QUEUED:
TIL KINGDOM COME
BY COLDPLAY

"**A**STRID. *ASTRID.* PASS me the soy sauce, or so help me—" Tom groans, reaching across our makeshift table (okay, it's a blanket) on Papa's hospital room floor.

He's been trying to get the soy sauce from Astrid for at least two minutes.

"Millie," he says, "help me."

Millie raises an eyebrow. "No way, she's scary. Do it yourself."

Astrid grins a terrible grin.

I reach over and smack the back of her head and grab the packet from her hands. "You're not even using it."

"I was going to!" she protests.

"Well, not fast enough. You already had one packet, and Tom had none." I hand the packet to Tom, take a bite of noodles, and look up at the sound of the door opening. My parents went for a walk just before we arrived with Chinese takeout. Or rather, Mom walked, and Dad got pushed around in the wheelchair.

Millie is up in two second flat, running at them in a flurry of flailing hands and arms. "Hi! We got you Chinese food, Mama. And Papa, you can have some of mine if you want." She kisses his cheek and takes the wheelchair from my mom.

"Thanks, M&M, but I already ate before you got here." Papa winks at me. "How's my Baby Bee? And Tom, here with your sisters for a change."

"And me," Astrid mutters.

"And you, Superstar." Papa has Millie roll him up to the bed, and Mama helps him get in, pulling the covers up to his chest. "Guess what? We have some news for you kids."

That's all it takes to get us up, away from our food and crowding around him. My dad takes my mom's hand and looks at us. His blue eyes are round and happier than I've seen for a while. "They're able to get me into surgery this weekend," he says.

Instantly, we all freeze. It's like we don't know what emotion to feel, or how to respond.

Mom squeezes Dad's fingers and smiles sadly. "The surgeon said that while he still can't operate on my brain, he can do his best to remove as much of the other tumors as he can. Of course, that still leaves one or two problems, but we can't be picky-choosey."

I study my father, with his shaved head and thinning face and his breathing that takes more effort. (It's like his lungs are weighted.) He smiles like there's nothing wrong, like he can't wait to get in and out of this surgery—like he has hope. But I don't see it. I don't feel it. The chances he will live are slim, and a surgery that doesn't remove his biggest problem—the cancer on his brain—won't help him. The doctors claim *that* surgery, the one he needs most, will likely end him quicker.

"That's great, Dad," Tom says finally, nodding solemnly, and the girls chime in with hugs and kisses. I only manage to squeeze his fingers, hoping he doesn't notice that I'm hurting. It's not about me right now—it's about him and his future. I won't be selfish, not now.

I sit back down at our makeshift table and set my bowl in my lap. In the last five minutes since I left my phone on the ground, I've missed a call from Levi. I take a few more bites of noodles before calling him back.

"Hi, Bee," he answers, quietly.

I swallow hard. It's been three days since we last saw each other, and a week since his birthday. We haven't discussed the important things yet, but he calls me every day and asks me how I'm doing, and how is my dad, and how are my siblings and mom, and can he come over soon? The only problem with this is that I can never be too thankful—and I have nothing to give in return. I have no questions, no encouraging words for him. He says I support him, but I haven't been to TCP in over a week. Three days ago when he kissed me goodbye, leaning against the side of my car, he looked more exhausted than I've ever seen him. And yet, there we were, saying goodbye, with me realizing it had taken several hours for me to *notice* him.

I never asked him how he was, how I could help.

It doesn't matter that he doesn't seem to mind. *I* mind.

"Hey," I say in response, pushing away my food. "What's up?"

"Just . . . interviews. I'm in between, wanted to check in."

I nod, but then I realize he can't see me. "Thanks," I say. "How are the interviews?"

"Good so far, all things we can work with." He clears his throat. "We miss you here, Bee."

I have to choke back tears. (*Come on, Levi*, I think, but he doesn't know how guilty I feel.) "I know," I whisper. "I miss you guys, too."

"But, of course, we understand," he adds, and sighs. "Any news?"

I take a bite and chase it down with the last of my water. "He's going in for surgery this weekend," I say, trying out the words.

Levi hums tunelessly. "Is that . . . a good thing? A bad thing?"

"Not sure," I say. "Hopefully good."

"Hmm. Can I come see him this week?"

"You can always come see him."

"Is that Levi?" my dad asks from behind me.

I turn around and smile my best. "Yeah."

"Tell him I said hi."

I relay the message. "I think he misses you," I add, a little quieter.

"Dude, I miss everyone—even Tom." He laughs, but it sounds forced, not *the* Levi laugh that makes everything better. "Come see me tomorrow if you can. I've got one interview at four and then maybe we can get donuts or dinner?"

I frown. "I don't think I can. I have the late shift tomorrow, so by the time I get done, it will be after dinner. Plus I have to go to the hospital in the evening."

My dad says, "You don't have to, Bee."

I ignore him. "I'll call you tomorrow night, though."

"Sounds good." He sighs, mumbling something under his breath as he moves around. I hear papers rustling and what sounds like someone knocking. "Hey, I think that's my next interview. Call me, okay?"

"Okay."

He hangs up, and I lock my phone and return to my cold dinner.

(He didn't say he loves me.)

Tracy's shop is in chaos, and it's only one in the afternoon. My shift has just begun, with five hours left on the clock, and our flowery world is falling apart. (Just like everything else. Go figure.)

I check the clock for the billionth time since arriving an hour ago. One-oh-five. Great. It's only been two minutes since I last checked, and it feels like an eternity.

"Beeeeeee," Tracy sings from the back of the shop.

I drop the calculator and receipts I'm holding and bend to her will. "Yes, ma'am?"

She is frazzled, her hair tied back with a loose ribbon (probably from the ribbon rack). She nearly drops a bubble vase as she tries to carry three to the sink with one hand. "Oh, Bee," she says again.

(Did I mention she's crazy?)

"Yes?" I repeat, a little more hesitant.

"I think I've made a grave mistake."

"What?" I ask drily. (The number of times she says this to me every week is innumerable. And it's *always* grave.)

"You remember that funeral I had you book for this week?"

I squint. "Was it the Jameson funeral or the Carlos funeral?"

"Jameson." She sighs. "Well. I forgot that Ludwig is out of the country this week and he won't be back until Saturday. The funeral is *Friday.*"

"We . . . can't take it?"

Tracy grunts, scrubbing away at the vase she nearly broke. "It has to be there at seven in the morning, my dear, and we all know what I'm doing at seven in the morning."

I rub my forehead. "Right. Perusing the flower market."

"And on top of that, I have a wedding on Saturday, which means I can't miss the flower market because they have the dahlias I need or *so help me God* this bride will ruin me."

She's exhausting me just talking about it. "What do you want me to do?"

"Can you take it?" She looks up from the sink and smiles a fake, cheesy smile at me. "I'll pay you overtime. And you'll need someone else to help you because the order is huge. I'll pay an *army* overtime to get this done."

"I, erm . . . " I don't know anyone who would possibly be able to help me except Levi. Fortunately for me, Tracy answers my next question before I have to (awkwardly) ask it.

"If it's your boyfriend you need to bring, that's fine with me. So long as you're not . . . you *know* . . . with him on the job."

I blush. "I don't think that will be a problem."

"Good. He's hired."

"Um. I'll have to ask him, first."

She waves me away, so I pull out my phone and text him. His response is almost immediate, but it's a phone call instead. "What's up early Friday morning?"

I sink back behind the counter and whisper, "Aren't you at work?"

"Yeah, but it's okay. I was missing you anyway." The sounds of the shop around him are loud and metallic, a stark contrast to his soft tone.

"It's work," I say. "Tracy needs me to take an early delivery, but she said I'll need help. She wants to pay you."

"Nah. I'll help for free, as long as I can hang out for an hour after and eat breakfast with you before you open shop."

"That should be fine." I rest my head back against the wall, closing my eyes. "Thanks, Levi."

"Duh, you're welcome."

He sounds a bit more like himself today, which pushes me into a smile. "I love you," I whisper.

"Who, me?"

This time, I full-out laugh. "Yeah, idiot. You."

"Not to be mushy, but I love you more." Somebody at the shop yells his name and laughs like he's making a joke. Levi laughs, too, shouting something back that I can't make out. "Sorry," he says, chuckling. "Are we still on for a phone call tonight?"

"Yeah, of course."

"Call me when you leave the hospital. I won't wait a moment longer."

That night I sit on my bed, legs crossed and my phone to my ear, listening to Levi list off the new applicants he met today. There's a single mom in her thirties who just lost her job but wants to send her son to a good college. Another cancer patient. A woman in her early thirties trying to find her biological father—a long and expensive task. "It's like we're expanding but we're not ready yet, you know?" Levi says at the end, huffing as if he's out of breath.

"Yeah. But what about the new place?"

"It's almost ready. Almost. We've had to slow down a bit, but we'll be ready for a soft opening in a week or so. I can't wait for you to visit."

I want to see it, but I have no idea when I can muster up the time or energy to drive over, plaster on a smile, take a tour, and talk to people—not when every evening is devoted to hospital visits and sleeping off what has now become a recurring headache. (I don't tell Levi this.) "I can't wait to see it. I bet it's amazing."

"Yeah, but only because of all the work we put into it together."

I hear the sound of his keys jangling and his car starting. "Where are you going?" I ask.

"Home. I worked late tonight."

"You been working a lot of late nights lately?" I ask, remembering his drowsy eyes.

"Yeah, but it's going to stop soon. Just have to finish up with this load of applications I got behind on."

"I'm sorry," I say immediately.

I can just see him rolling his eyes. "Why are you sorry?"

"I haven't been there." I scoot down so my legs are under my covers and I turn, facing the wall, phone pressed to my ear.

"I'm going to pretend like you didn't just apologize for something as stupid as that."

"Levi . . . "

"No, come on, Bee. You've been a little preoccupied. You think I can't understand that?"

"It doesn't change the fact that I'm sorry about it. I want to be there and I can't."

The road around him goes quiet for a second, like he's at a stoplight. "Maybe you need to get a different perspective on everything, Bee."

"What do you mean?"

He pauses, his car turning off, the door shutting behind him. It sounds like he's walking up the path to his house as he says, "Hey, can you hold on one second?"

"Sure."

There's the sound of him knocking on his door (I wonder briefly why he doesn't use his keys) and it swinging open and shutting behind him. Except . . . at the same moment, my own front door opens and shuts. And then there are his footsteps in the hallway outside my door, and his gentle knock, nudging it open a few inches. "Everyone decent?" he asks, and then lets himself in.

I hang up, turn, and set my phone on the nightstand. A second later he's there, wrapping his arms around my waist and pulling me in for a kiss. It's slow and warm and exactly the love I need, but also a distraction I *don't* need.

"Bad, bad," I say, with one last kiss, and pull back. "Very dangerous," I whisper, my hand hovering between our mouths.

He kisses my fingers instead. "I'm sorry, I just couldn't resist the opportunity."

"Who let you in?"

"Millie."

"That brat is going to die."

"What?" he asks. "Don't want to see me?"

"I do—I do want to see you." I run my finger along the contours of his jawline and stare at his mouth a little too long. "Okay, I saw you, now you have to leave."

"Oh, no. Not like that." He stands and nudges me over, then rolls onto his stomach next to me, arms under his head, facing me. "This is nice, actually. Great mattress."

"Levi. You could get so busted."

"For doing *literally* nothing?"

I shrug, and I can't resist rolling into him a little bit more. My arm stretches across his back and my hand fiddles with the side of his shirt. "Levi."

"Yes?"

"What did you mean about a different perspective?"

He makes an O with his mouth. "Oh, right. Yeah—I mean that you need to let people do things for you sometimes."

I bite my nails, looking at him closely. "I don't want people to do things for me when I can't do anything in return."

"That's not what we're about."

"But it's not fair."

"Life's not fair." He shrugs. "We move on."

I don't think I can. I close my eyes briefly. "Why did you ask if I loved you, then?"

I know it's not fair to ask this, but I want to bring my point home. He questioned it then, which means he has even more of a right to question it now.

"Are you still hung up over that?" he asks, eyes wandering my face, searching for the answer. "That was weeks ago and I apologized."

"I know you did. But it was the principle of it," I say, using his own words against him. "I already felt like I was doing nothing." I draw my eyebrows together. "That solidified everything I was worried about. I can't be here for you *and* my dad. I just can't."

"You don't have to."

"I need to, in order for this to work."

He must understand the gravity of what I've just said, what I'm implying, because he doesn't respond right away. Instead, he moves to his side and captures my face in his hands, using a thumb on my chin to make me look at him. (I am caught; I have nowhere else to turn.) His eyebrows are raised a fraction and his hair flops over my pillow and I just want to tell him it will be okay.

Instead, I let him speak. "You aren't just a summer fling, you know? You're not a one-summer girlfriend who I'll forget in a month."

I close my eyes.

"You have to know that, Bee."

I nod. "Yes," I whisper, voice cracked.

With my eyes closed, his kiss is unexpected, but I sink into it without question. His lips are slow and tender and I want to cry because I love him so much and we're breaking apart and I can't fix it.

I'm so sorry, Levi.

"I love you," he whispers, kissing the top of my lips one more time, and then my nose, and then my forehead as he tucks me against him.

"I love you most," I say.

With those words, I prepare for the moment when I will walk away so he doesn't have to.

chapter 43

QUEUED:
BIG EYES
BY MATT CORBY

F RIDAY MORNING DAWNS too soon for Levi and me, but at least we get our first taste of fall weather. (After the insane heat of August, everyone is thankful for a few rainclouds hovering on the horizon.)

He meets me at the shop at six-fifteen sharp, grabbing me from behind as I'm unlocking the front door, kissing my cheek. I instantly feel the scruff on his cheek, where I am used to very smooth skin. I raise my hand to brush against his face. "What the heck is this?"

"Five 'o clock shadow, duh." He lets me go into the shop first and then closes the door behind me. I flip on the lights and turn to look at him. He catches me by surprise, because while he looks mostly the same (wild hair, beige pants, bright red sweater), he is different in two ways: the stubble around his mouth and along his jaw, and the glasses that sit on his nose.

"I'm soooo not used to this," I say, raising an eyebrow. (But *gosh-darn-it*, he's still so beautiful.)

"Dude, you've never seen these before?" He seems incredulous.

I shake my head. "When, exactly, did you get them?"

"I've had them forever."

"So, you wear contacts?" I ask. I turn and head for the computer, not wanting to show him that I'm feeling ridiculous. With the weight of everything, with the decision I am slowly inching toward making every single day, missing a detail like this (as small as it is) feels catastrophic.

"Yeah. My eyes are actually blue."

I whirl on him. "WHAT?"

He laughs so hard that it's silent and has him bent at the waist. He heaves. "I'm kidding, my God, I'm kidding. My eyes are most certainly brown. But I *do* wear contacts."

I pull away when he reaches for me. "You're mean," I pout. (I'm only half-joking.)

"Bee," he growls. "I'll make up for it."

"Shut up." I grab the trip sheets and list Tracy left for me on the desk and wave them in his face. "You're not allowed to kiss me until we've finished this task. Tracy said no making out on the job."

"One kiss is not . . . *making out*," he huffs.

I shrug. "Rules are rules." It's a rule I'm making right now, because I feel funny, a little sick to my stomach. *God.* I'm running so hard and so far away, and he can't see it, which means that he can't and won't stop me, which means that I'll just keep running. Fear is at large. My heart hammers and my throat closes off and my ears only hear rushing blood.

Then he's kissing me, and I whimper.

Levi leans his head back, no trace of joy or teasing left in his eyes (that are covered by glasses and look so foreign to me now). "What's wrong with you today?"

I bite my lip, my brain scrambling for something to say. "Um."

He shakes his head, takes a step away from me. "Is there something going on?" He gestures at me, then at himself.

And then I surprise myself. "There *has been* something going on," I answer. Honesty, for once. It's angry honesty.

"For how long?"

Now it's my turn to be incredulous. "That's not an *actual* question, is it? Like, you haven't seen everything that's been going on for the last few weeks?"

Great. Now I'm angry at him for not noticing the things I've been deliberately hiding. Another reason to feel like shit. My stomach twists. Today was not supposed to begin like this.

He shakes his head and draws his eyebrows together. "I'm sorry—" (he's not really sorry at all) "—but you're the one who said 'I don't know' to all my questions last week."

"Can we just—" I realize my hands are raised defensively, and I drop them. "Can we just get to work? We have to be there in thirty minutes, and we have to take separate cars. Yay, we don't have to fight the whole way there."

His expression turns—I see it the second the word *fight* comes out of my mouth. Now he looks angry. Now he looks ready to put up some walls. *Good*, I think. *I'll hurt him less this way.*

Levi curses, a word I don't like and definitely have never heard him say before. Then he rubs his eyes under his glasses and shrugs abruptly. "Fine. What do you want me to do?"

I give him a job (my fingers shake, making the trip sheet bend in my hand) and start grabbing vases from the cooler. He takes the biggest funeral spray and carries it outside, leaving me to stare at the empty space where he was just standing. Then I shake my head and think, *Work, Bee. Focus.*

When I pass him on the way out, he doesn't even look at me.

The church is a ten minute car ride away. Normally I'd need loud music or coffee to keep me awake at this hour, but my blood is still boiling, so I grind my teeth and grip the steering wheel too hard. I feel incredibly alone, because it's me and a stand for the sprays and a few sloshing vases in the back, and Levi is somewhere else, and I can't believe what I've done.

I take a last turn into the church parking lot and park in the loading zone. The building is new, almost modern, but a traditional-looking chapel is built into the back. That's where we're directed to take the sprays, and within a few minutes we've dropped off the first of two trips into a quiet, near-empty hall.

Once we get back to the shop, we load the second half of the vases. It takes longer because they're bigger pieces, and I still don't say a word to him. I'm pretty sure I hear him call my name as I shut the car door, but I pretend I don't hear and start the engine.

We park in the same place as last time and unload in silence. I walk in front of him, my feet hurrying to keep ahead because my legs are so much shorter than his. This time when the doors to the chapel are quietly opened to let us in, however, I'm forced to forget everything for a few seconds, because I hear something completely unexpected.

Singing.

It's as light and beautiful as anything I've ever heard in my life. It echoes perfectly in the stone-walled building, making me want to stand still and bask in it. I hurriedly put down the vases I'm holding and face the stage.

The singer looks to be about fourteen years old, if I'm comparing him to the only other boy I know in his age bracket (Albert). He's a bit pudgy around the middle and his face is round, as if his body is just waiting to grow in height. He's wearing his Sunday best, but his hair is ruffled, out of place amidst all the clean-cut beauty of this chapel. His mouth is wide open in a note that catches my breath right out of me.

"*Pie Jesu,*" he sings. "*Pie Jesu.*"

A little old woman standing in the pews leaves her place to stand beside me. She's frail in a sweet grandmotherly way, a way that makes me want to tuck my arm around hers. She smiles up at me, but her face is sad.

That's when I remember where I am. I come back to earth, pulled into reality with shattering clarity, and I start to see things. The names on the pamphlet the old woman holds, the picture that's set up next to the largest basket of flowers I put on the stage during the first trip.

The way the young, singing boy looks almost exactly like the man in the photograph.

The way the man in the photograph looks like he's nearing forty.

I feel bile in my throat and an ache that tears my heart into shreds. I'd like to never feel my heart again.

"Isn't he lovely?" the old woman beside me asks. (She has tears in her eyes now. Her small hands are trembling.)

"What?" I reply, but it sounds like a gasp.

"He's so young, but he's got the loveliest voice. He and his boys' choir are singing in Carnegie Hall this winter—can you believe it?"

I nod, hoping she thinks my gape is because I'm surprised

about Carnegie Hall. I *am* surprised, but I'm also sickened and angry because this little boy has to sing at his father's funeral.

I'm sick because he gets to sing at Carnegie Hall in the winter—and his father won't be there to witness it.

I'm sick because I'm now thinking of my own father. I'm learning to let go, that I might have to say goodbye. I'm fighting, desperately, my head held under the water as I drown. *Breathe*, I shout at myself, but I have no gills to keep me alive.

(*Papa, you can't leave us.*)

Oh, God. I wipe away tears. I'm too angry to feel embarrassed; warm droplets fall away, onto my neck and shoulder, with the swipe of my hand. "I've got to go," I say quietly, turning. I don't know why I said anything to her; I don't think she heard me.

Levi is setting the last spray, circular and heavy with roses, on its display stand. He looks up when I pass, sees me crying, and immediately follows me. "Bee?"

"Don't."

His hand is on my shoulder, but I shrug it off. I don't want it there. I don't want Levi—*anywhere*, because he only makes it worse. He reminds me of happiness and a summer I can never have back, a time that wasn't marred by the shadow of death. His presence makes me ache.

"Was it the singing?" he asks quietly.

I start to nod, but then I'm shaking my head instead. *More honesty. Way to go, Bee. Just when it's too late.* "Did you see the pictures?" I whisper, the back of my hand against my eyes to block more tears. "I don't want to watch a little boy mourn his father like I'll have to watch my siblings mourn my father." I unlock the company vehicle, swing the door open, and slam it behind me. Levi is still on the sidewalk, keys in hand, staring at me in shock.

I drive away, hoping he knows how to get back to the shop. I have to gun it; I'm going to be sick.

Tracy's in the shop when I get there. I slam the clipboard with the trip sheet onto the counter and, despite her concerned questions, lock myself in the bathroom.

I puke the second I bend over the toilet, grabbing my hair out of the way. I can't breathe for a moment, but then, when I sit back on my heels and start to cry, the gasping sobs become my breath, and my lungs work again. (Just barely.)

"What's wrong?" Tracy asks, outside the door, but she's not talking to me.

I didn't hear Levi come in, but I know he's there. After a moment, he sighs. "She left the funeral crying. Her dad." That's all he says, and I can just imagine him spreading his hands like he doesn't know what else to say, like it's self-explanatory.

"Bee?" she tries. "Sweetheart, are you all right?"

I can't speak yet, so I grab napkins and wet them and drag them across my mouth to get rid of the taste and smell. I suck in the deepest breath I can, getting myself under control, forcing the sobs to stop. My stomach is still clenching in pain and my head is pounding. All I need is to get home.

I open the door to see both my boss and my boyfriend standing outside, mouths pressed grimly. Tracy reaches for me, wrapping her arms around my neck in a hug that calms me more than I expected. "Bee, sweetie, are you okay?"

"I don't know," I answer. My voice shakes.

"You take today off, okay? I'll close the shop for an emergency and do the wedding and wire the deliveries to another florist." She leans away and looks me in the eye, tucking my hair behind my ear.

"Okay," I whisper. "Thanks."

"No need." She waves away my words, pressing my hand tight, and leaves me standing in the dark hall outside the bathroom. The sliver of light from the bathroom lands on Levi, who just looks at me, his eyes a thousand questions. My heart trips, beating a million beats per minute, as he reaches for my shoulder.

I shake my head and step away from him. *Not right now, I can't right now*, I try to say, but my tongue is tied inside my mouth.

So, instead, I run.

chapter 44

QUEUED:
OVER YOU (FEAT. A GREAT BIG WORLD)
BY INGRID MICHAELSON

THE AIR IS chilly from the rain that has started pouring since I left for the shop earlier, and my house is empty. Tom is working late this morning, and when he gets home he'll go straight to bed. Astrid and Millie are at school, and Mom is probably at the hospital, prepping with Dad for the surgery. (Spending time with him, as I should be.)

I message Gretchen, looking to vent, or cry, or something—*anything*—but she isn't there, and she doesn't respond. I wait for thirty minutes, curled into a ball on my bed before I decide it's time to stop waiting around and do exactly what I've been dreading. My stomach hasn't stopped burning, my head is still throbbing, and I know it's not going to get better. In fact, I have this obnoxious feeling it will only get worse until I do what I'm supposed to do.

After another hour of debating, denial, and wishing, I come

to the conclusion that nothing happens unless I make it happen. So I drag myself out of bed and throw on a pair of sweats and a hoodie, putting my hair into a loose bun on the top of my head.

I stand just inside the front door and text Levi to see where he is. Still no response from Gretchen, so I resign myself. Taking a deep, steadying breath in, I run to my car, but the rain is falling so hard that I'm soaked by the time my seatbelt is on. I check again for Levi's response (*I'm at the new office. Come see me.*) and I set my course for the south end of Escondido.

Traffic is terrible because Californians don't know how to drive in the rain, but eventually, ten minutes longer than it usually takes, I arrive in front of TCP's new office. I want to cry because it looks like *home*, a home I that love, with its wide porch and picket fence that they've painted dark blue since I was last here, and the window at the top of the house that lets you see out from the attic.

The attic where we had our first fight.

I swallow and text him again. *Can you come out to the porch?* Then I pull my hood over my face, turn off my car, and make a beeline for the front door.

It swings open as I'm walking up the porch steps, and Levi comes out. I get a tiny glimpse of color and joy behind him before he shuts the door and pulls me tight against him. It breaks me a little, how warm his arms are, how they welcome me back, despite everything.

I can't keep doing this to him.

Then his lips are on mine, suddenly, and my chest aches. I grip his face, fingers coming into contact with the frames of his glasses. I am tempted to slip them off, to make things more familiar, but I'm being stupid—I can't kiss him anymore. Period.

I turn my head.

Levi pauses, then continues along my jaw, making me shiver, guilt pressing into my stomach, rotting it out.

"Levi, stop, please."

Like a good boy (always the good boy) he stops. "I was worried about you," he murmurs.

I close my eyes and drop my head and take a step back. Because I'm the Queen of Bad Moves, I ask, "If you were worried, why didn't you come after me?"

I think he won't have an answer for that (oh, why am I still fighting this?) until he says, "Because I didn't think you wanted me to."

Right. I *didn't.* I hug myself, arms crossing, shoulders sagging.

Moments pass before he breaks the silence. "Bee?"

I'm hardly breathing as I say the words, "I can't do this anymore," through my teeth.

He goes as still as he did the night I told him I couldn't be there for both him and my family. He's smart—and he's equal parts optimist and realist. He understands what I'm saying. "I assume you mean our relationship," he says, voice low, his mouth a grim line.

"I mean our relationship *and* my life right now." I shake my head. There are a few tears on my cheeks. "Every day is a challenge. It takes so much effort to remember to ask you something as simple as how your day has been when all I can think about is my dad dying."

He laughs, harsh and short. There it is again—that word I don't like, coming out of his soft, pretty lips. "Bee, you don't need to ask me something as petty as how my day is."

"But I want to. I care so much about you and everything you do, but I can't give you the time. I can't be who I want to be for you." I pause and sniff, my breath coming out as a wavering sigh. "It is what it is, Levi. I can't run from you anymore." I look up, catching the incredulous expression on his face. "I can't run from anyone."

"There has to be a different way to do this." He swears again.

I cringe. "How? Tell me how, and I'll try. I swear I will."

"How about we don't break up at all. How about we take a break? Or work through it—this. Shit."

I don't have the energy, the emotional capacity, to work through this. Taking a break would be the same as breaking up. The break would last as long as my dad is sick, which could be a short time or a very long time. He knows this, I'm sure of it, because his eyes light up with sudden understanding.

"I'm so tired," I say for the second time. "I can't keep up. I'm weighing you down."

"That's bullshit. Who said that to you?"

I blink slowly. I'm not going to answer that question because he'll only be angry with my answer. "Who do you want me to be for you, Levi?" I ask quietly.

He pushes the sleeves of his sweater up to his elbows, looking like he's ready to fight me for this. "Whoever you are, I want you to be her. You know, the girl who wrinkles her nose at Bon Iver and still listens to him for my sake, the one who plans weddings and sits by my side while I go over applications. The one who laughs too loudly and sometimes doesn't know her glasses are crooked." He shakes his head. "She's not that far off, Bee. Who said you aren't allowed to be lost every once in a while? I love you, lost or found."

He's making this hard, too hard. "I know you do."

"So why can't I have you?"

"Because I'm not ready!" I shout. Then I immediately put my hands over my mouth. That is not what I wanted to say, not *how* I wanted to say it—despite how true it is. "Maybe it's a good thing I never told you my name," I whisper, beneath my shaking fingers.

His jaw locks.

I know, immediately, that I've dealt the fatal blow. (And how I hate myself for it.)

"You were never planning to, were you?" he asks, his voice tinged with disgust.

(He looks so hurt, and I am so broken.) "I'm sorry."

"You gave yourself a way out, just in case things got hard."

He's right again. Blow after blow after blow. "Levi—" I begin.

"I wanted that with you, you know? Hard. I wanted fast and awful and perfect and hard and wonderful and slow and terrible with you."

I try to catch the whimper that is coming up my throat and out of my mouth, but it's bigger and stronger than my willpower. I cry silently, my tears mingling with leftover rain on my cheeks. "I know it's not fair for me to say I love you," I cry, "but I do. I love you so much, but it's not enough because I don't love you as much as you love me. That right there is the biggest reason why I'm not going to drag you through hell."

"That's not—"

I interrupt him. "We haven't talked through a single thing, because every time we're together, something is overshadowing me. We haven't even worked out that first fight—Levi, that was weeks ago. We should have been over that for a long time now, but we're not."

This time, he's quiet. Stunned.

"Please don't make this harder than it has to be," I beg, even though he already has. I wipe the backs of my hands across my eyes.

"Bee," he grinds out, holding out his hand like he's going to grab my shoulder, but because the movement is uncertain, I only have to take a step back. He drops his arm to his side again.

"Don't wait for me," I say. And because it hurts too much to look at him, I turn around and leave him there, alone, on the middle of the porch in front of the house we found, trapped by my words and the rain.

chapter 45

QUEUED:
OUR VOICES
BY MATTHEW BARBER

THIS WEEKEND, I make a new playlist: every Bon Iver album I can find. I listen to them all on shuffle, headphones in my ears every chance I get. The songs go around and around in my head (some surprise me into liking them; others do not), and I can't stop listening because I hope someday, somehow, they will help me heal.

On Saturday I sit and watch movies on my laptop with Papa and Tom while my sisters are at the beach. I offered to take them, but my mom insisted I stay in, claiming I looked a little under-the-weather. I didn't argue with this because, yes, Mother, I'm under-the-weather and no, I won't tell you why. I don't know how to tell them what happened without disappointing them or bringing them grief, so I leave it alone for now. *When* they find out is not important, not with everything looming. I'll tell them when the storm has passed.

The stomach ache I had yesterday hasn't gone away, not really. I don't eat much, either because I'm not hungry or I feel like I'm going to puke again. I'd hoped it would all disappear when I said goodbye to Levi, but in reality, I think I just have a small case of the stomach flu. Otherwise, I was dead wrong.

I wasn't dead wrong.

I *cannot* be dead wrong.

I shuffle Bon Iver again. (I've started calling this playlist The Incredibly Painful Recovery Playlist.) I go into denial, about a lot of things. That I will never kiss Levi again, that he won't look at me with happy, hungry eyes, that I won't go back to TCP when all this is over. Reality hasn't dawned yet.

Like everything else in my life, I'd like to keep it that way. (At least for a little while longer.)

My father's surgery comes on Sunday morning, and I sit impatiently with Tom and my sisters in a waiting room full of equally impatient strangers. My mother paces in front of us, her body taut with stress and fear. But after six hours of waiting, we find out she has no reason to be afraid—none of us do— because the surgery went exactly according to plan. The tumors were removed, the flesh was sewn back together, the body was set to heal.

After another couple of hours, when he is once more awake and cognizant, we're allowed to visit him. He smiles as much as he can, then sleeps until the nurse gives him more pain meds, and then he smiles some more.

After one of his many short naps, he calls me to his bedside with a quiet, "Hey, Baby Bee." He holds out a hand for me, very slowly and carefully, and I take it as gently as I can.

"Daddy." I kiss his forehead.

"Miss you, kiddo."

"I'm right here." It's my turn to whisper, and only because I'm about to start sobbing. With relief, fear, exhaustion—whatever it is, it's taking hold of my sensibilities (if I have any left).

"I know you are." His face twists in pain for a moment, then untwists into ease again. "Ready for me to come home?"

I nod, smiling and teary. "Yeah."

"Good. Me, too."

We set Papa up in the coolest room in our house—the back TV room. It's spacious enough for his hospice bed, with all the amenities: a bathroom close enough to rush to, a kitchen around the corner and a water dispenser close by. We put him close to the couch, which becomes Mama's temporary bed.

It isn't until after a few nights later that I decide I want to sleep there as well. So my mom and I trade off whenever we feel like it, and the nurse who comes daily to check on Papa puts up with all of our belongings trapped inside this makeshift hospital room. (I have to have a *few* books at the ready to keep me company.)

I don't sleep much when I'm out there (the couch is short and my legs get awkwardly propped up or tucked under), but I don't mind. I can hear Dad breathing a few feet away, and that's all that matters.

Breathing is good.

He looks relatively okay, too. I'm not sure what to think about this. Is it a good sign, that he has some color in his cheeks and that his smile is back? Or does it hide the decay underneath that will eventually kill him? I have no choice but to let it be a happy thing, however, because the other option is to sit and worry and never enjoy a single moment with him.

Sometimes, when Tom is about to go to work, and the girls come home from school, and I come home from work early enough, Mama brings home In-N-Out for us. We lay out a blanket over my mom's favorite rug (so we don't destroy it with Special Sauce) and pile on like we used to when we were little. Dad used to make steak dinners on Friday nights, and we would eat our dinner over an indoor picnic. Afterward, we would fold up the blanket and curl up on the couch for a movie, during which my mom would trim my dad's hair. (Thing You Should Know About Me #2183: I'm super nostalgic about these sorts of things.) (Oh, wait . . . you probably knew that already.)

It's during one of these fast food dinners, two weeks after we brought Papa home, that he makes an announcement. I'm just sitting there, enjoying the silence, passing the ketchup to Millie for her fries, when Papa says very loudly, "Bee's going to take a floral design class. Right, Bee?"

I close my eyes, briefly. I'm less than amused, and I make sure he sees the scowl on my face. "Papa . . . "

Everyone is as surprised as I gathered they'd be, which is why I never said anything. I haven't thought about it once since I found out TCP was funding the chemo.

"I'm not doing it," I say, firmly.

Astrid rolls her eyes. "Drama Queen."

"Shh, Ass-trid." I glance at my mom, who's turned her questioning gaze on me. "I, um, don't need to do it. It's expensive."

"Honey, we can cover it," Mom says.

I raise an eyebrow. "Well, I really don't *want* to."

"Why not, Beef?" Tom takes a huge bite out of his burger and says, with his mouth full, "You're really good at it."

Millicent makes a sound of disgust. "*Tom.*" Then she adds, "Bee, I really, really want you to do it. Come on, *please?*"

"It's too expensive, and that's that." I shrug. "I don't know . . . it might be good to keep in mind for next fall, though. Besides, I'd rather be here more, spending time with you guys."

"The class is next semester, Bee," my dad says, like I'm crazy for wanting to hang out at home. "A long way away from now."

"So?" I shrug.

"Your attitude sucks," Papa replies, good-naturedly. "But speaking of spending time with us, when is Levi coming over for dinner again?"

"Um." I choke on a fry.

"Soon, I hope," he says, looking at me closely.

Very closely.

I clear my throat. "Maybe soon?" I say, because I'm a coward.

Papa raises an eyebrow. "Well, he's been nice to stop by this week. He said last week he was so caught up in TCP work that he couldn't make it over. Poor kid. Looked terrible."

"He stopped by?" It takes a lot of work to keep my voice from sounding shrill.

"A couple days ago, and again today. Didn't he tell you?"

I quickly stuff my mouth with fries to avoid Papa's gaze, which tells me he definitely knows something happened. "No, he didn't. Must've forgot."

Tom wipes his hands on a napkin (I'm pretty sure that was *my* napkin) and says, "Well, if Bee doesn't want the spotlight, I'm going to steal it."

Yes, please do. I smile. "As always."

He scowls at me, but his smile is quick to replace it. "I got promoted—I'm a shift leader with a raise. My boss says I'll be manager soon if I keep this up."

Everyone raises their hands to high-five him, raining praises and *good-job*s and *excellent*s. He waits until we calm down before adding, "I'm also going to take classes again next year, maybe transfer to a four-year university if I decide what I want to do. Who knows? Maybe things will go even further at work and I'll never look back."

I clap Tom on the back and fake a smile. "I'm really proud of you."

He beams. "Shut up, stupid."

Mom shushes him. "That's rude. You know the rules—now you have to say ten nice things to Bee."

"Mo-*om*," Tom groans. "How about five?"

My mother considers. "Okay. But make them count."

Tom grunts, counting on his fingers as I wait with a smug expression on my face. "Your hair is long, you have glasses that fit your face right, you sometimes dress cute, your perfume is appealing, and you have a nice boyfriend."

I gasp incredulously at this, trying to pretend like I didn't hear that last one. Like it doesn't cut deep.

Mama sighs, raises an eyebrow, and nods in Tom's direction. "Bee, you can smack him."

I lightly punch his shoulder.

"Harder," my dad puts in.

I hit him again, this time with my palm, feeling the satisfaction that only comes from smacking an annoying older brother. He yelps in pain, which causes my sisters to burst into giggles. I sit back on my heels and smile even though I don't feel like it. My chest hurts. Tom mentioned my boyfriend—the one who hasn't called me, who's been stopping by my house when I'm not around, who, my Papa says, looks terribly stressed. I'm the only one who knows it's not because of TCP.

Ex-boyfriend, I correct myself after a moment of denial.

Ignoring the catastrophe that is my heart, I eat the last of my fries, bring my knees up to my chest as I sit back, and listen to my family's laughter.

chapter 46

QUEUED:
KETTERING
BY THE ANTLERS

Tonight, after we clean up the blanket and trash from dinner, I get ready for my shift on the couch.

Tom heads to work, and my sisters are tucked into bed, and my mom is soaking in a much-needed bath, so I curl up on my uncomfortable makeshift bed. I'm just starting to fall asleep when my dad's voice surprises me awake.

"Hey, Bee," he whispers.

I sit up and scoot toward his chair. "Yeah?"

"Why did you and Levi break up?"

I try to keep my breathing even. "What?"

Papa's eyes are on me, white against his shadowed face. "He came this morning just after you left for work because he didn't want to upset you. He even asked me not to tell you he'd stopped by. I had to pretend like I knew what he was talking about." He clears his throat.

"Daddy." I don't know what to say except, "It was too much, okay? I was dragging him down and I couldn't do it anymore."

"You're not dragging anyone down."

I ignore him. "I wanted to do everything but I couldn't. We were fighting so much."

Papa nods. "He understood, though. He told me he understood why you couldn't work through it right away. He even went as far as to say that he would have gladly fought with you for months if it meant you were together." My dad laughs, but it's a sad laugh. "Then he turned red and apologized, as if he'd said something wrong."

I try to say something, but my words get stuck. The only thing that escapes are my tears. Then, so quietly I hope he can hear it, "I love him, Papa."

"I know."

"I can't do it right now. Not while you're sick."

He snorts a laugh. "Just because I'm sick doesn't mean you get to stop living your life."

"I *haven't*—"

"Have, too." He reaches over, pats my hand. "Bernice, if you deny that class one more time, I'm going to spank you. I don't care that you're almost eighteen."

I can't help a laugh. "Shh, Papa."

"You're a stubborn one. And why you thought it was okay to say goodbye to That Boy is still beyond me."

"It wasn't the right time. I have a lot to figure out," I whisper. For once, the truth—and he seems to recognize that because he doesn't comment for a while.

"You've got to go out there, Bee. Face the wide world," he finally says. "I can't wait for you to do everything, while I'm here *and* while I'm not. You have so much *time*."

I close my eyes. I understand what he's implying: that he doesn't have any time left. "It doesn't feel like it," I cry. I feel like I'm always crying, always wiping away tears, no matter how hard I try to stop it. "It feels like the world's going to end tomorrow and—"

"And what if it does? So what! You should be doing all the things that will make you happy if the world *does* end tomorrow."

I shudder.

"You love him, Bee."

I can't argue (even though I want to) because I just said that yes, I love Levi. I nod, biting my lip so hard I think it might bleed.

"And he loves you—more than any of us expected. Boys are dumb, Bee, but Levi isn't a typical boy." He looks at me pointedly. "You know, your mother told me about how she was certain he was a Precious Heart, all those months ago, and I was skeptical."

I sniffle. I'd forgotten about this, but now that I know him, now that I've been with him and loved him, I know he is one hundred percent a Precious Heart. He is more deserving of that title than anyone else who has ever lived.

Papa continues. "But, darn it, Bee—he's proven himself again and again. What about him makes you worried he won't be enough?"

"What?!" I exclaim. "I'm not worried *he* won't be enough— I'm worried *I* won't be enough."

"Why?" he asks quietly, as if my words have somehow hurt him.

(I don't understand anything.) "I couldn't even tell him my name, Papa. Not once did I actually think about telling him; I was never ready like he was. He loves me so much and I'm scared I won't ever be able to love him equally. I'm such a mess all the time . . . What if, down the road, I'm not worth his time?"

"Bernice." Papa's voice is hushed but commanding. I look up. "Bernice, did I ever teach you to be stupid?"

I practically snort in between sobs. (I am the queen of attractive.) "No."

"Then I don't know why you're saying these things. Who told you that you aren't worth the mess?"

It hurts. "No one, I just—"

"Bee."

I stop.

"You can turn this car around any time you want."

I whisper, "I know."

"He loves you, and you're going to need someone to lean on. Things aren't always going to be as they are right now, Baby Bee."

I cry in earnest again, gripping his hand too tight, but he doesn't seem to mind.

"Hey, hey, don't cry." He pulls me in so that I'm crossing the foot of space between the couch and the recliner. I rest my head on his shoulder and let him stroke my hair. Finally, when I've soaked his shirt through, he says, "Why don't you read *Crime and Punishment* to me tonight? We're almost done with it."

Thankful he's changed the subject, I sniffle. "I think, last I counted, we had one hundred pages left."

"Can we finish tonight?"

Brushing his hand away gently, I stand and retrieve the book. Its pages and cover are bent from being tossed and crushed and moved a thousand times, but I've never been happier to see a book of mine destroyed. "Maybe, if you can keep your eyes open long enough."

"It's a challenge I willingly accept."

I blow my nose via the box of tissues my mom permanently keeps on the coffee table, then turn on the lamp on the opposite end of the couch, turn it on, and open the book. "Ready for this?" I ask.

"So ready," he says.

I start to read.

The words rush from my mouth rapidly, but not so rapid that we can't follow the story. I make sure he's listening ten times before I stop checking and just read. My eyes droop, and my posture slouches, and I adjust my legs over and over so they don't fall asleep, but I do it. I finish that book right there on the couch, with my Papa in the chair next to me.

He made it through most of the end, but even when he started snoring softly, I kept reading. And when I finish and turn off the lamp, I vow to read what he didn't hear over again in the morning. Taking extra care not to make noise, I slip under the blankets and put my feet up. I fall into a deep respite at four in the morning, to the sound of my Papa breathing, his chest rising and falling, gently.

There is, however, a catch about sleeping: You have to wake up.

Matt Wescott doesn't wake up again.

QUEUED:
AMBULANCE
BY EISLEY

THERE IS AN aftermath, but I don't really feel it. I just *see* it, in my mom and sisters, and sometimes in Tom. I see it in the uniformed, faceless humans who come to our house and cover the body and take it away in a brightly lit vehicle. I can't even cry then. I'm just . . . quiet. Everything I do feels wrong, feels like a show, like I'm plastic. Stiff and unwilling.

I have nothing I want to share. Nothing I care to say.

It isn't until a few days after that the world starts to go silent. That's when I cry. The days become one thing, a meshing of tears, a messy daydream that I can't quite grasp. I'm pretty sure the dawn hasn't come since Papa died, but I'm also pretty sure that the sun hasn't set.

The world continues onward, blurry and raw, an endless string of things that don't matter and people who can't possibly understand. It is along this endless string that we prepare for my father's funeral this weekend.

My mother is the strongest of us all, even though she would claim she isn't. She goes forward like a train that can't stop, or maybe she just *won't* stop. I wonder, if she did, would she stop forever? So she goes and goes and goes, and I follow just behind, stumbling.

Millie and Astrid follow just behind me. Astrid pretends she doesn't cry, but I see her swollen eyes and I know she's hiding. Millie never *stops* crying, and every time I see her wet cheeks, I can't help but cry with her.

Sometimes, on the off chance we're both home at the same time, Tom joins me on the couch or my bed or the porch swing out back, and we sit wrapped in each other's arms. I see the tears on his cheeks and running down his chin, and he sees mine, and we don't talk.

(What is there to talk about?)

Every second that I'm not thinking about my father and the night he died, I'm thinking about Levi. Every waking moment is spent wondering, grasping. Everything is wrong, and I don't want it to be my fault, but it is. Fixing my world is impossible, however, because I don't have the strength. It's the same as before: there's not enough energy left in my reserves to make something happen. I can't go to him or talk to him without looking like the bitch who only begs to get a man back when she needs something.

I won't be that girl. Levi deserves infinitely more than who I am.

I go to work again a few days later, but it's hard to get through fifteen minutes without crying. I have a moment of solace before I see the order my mom placed for Papa's funeral, lying on the back counter, and I have to bend over, have to heave to get my breath back.

Ludwig finds me when I've been crying for a full five minutes. He puts a hand on my shaking, wavering shoulder, then helps me to stand up straight again. Sighing, his hands clasping my shoulders, he waits for me to stop crying.

I sniff until I can breathe again, rubbing my puffy face, and put a shaky hand on the table. "Th-thanks," I stutter.

He frowns at me. "What can I do?"

"Nothing." I wave him off, tightening my apron, reaching for the nearest clean vase.

"Hmm." Ludwig takes the vase from me and says, "I think there's something. Can you get me five white roses and three stems of the pale yellow spray roses?"

I don't really have the will-power to say no, so I follow his instructions. When I lay the flowers on the worktable, he asks for filler and light pink stock. I go back inside, fighting tears again, but when I come back, I see he's almost finished the arrangement. It immediately makes me think of flower fields in spring, and life, and happiness.

He's right—he can do something, and he has. I give him a crooked smile, sniffling unattractively once more, as I accept his gift. "It's so beautiful."

He winks. "I like seeing happy Bee. Care to ring me up?"

Ludwig pays for the arrangement, and when I've put it in a box and set it in the back of the cooler to take home later, he calls me back to the work table. "I want you to take my class, Bee."

I shrink inward a little, sitting on the stool beside him. "I know you do. I do, too."

"It's as simple as that, then."

I give him a look.

He shakes his head at me. "It really is. Buy the tools, pay me whatever you and your mom can afford—but I want you at that class every week."

I shake my head. "I can't."

"Accept a gift?"

"I already have—your arrangement." (I'm stubborn sometimes. Real stubborn.)

"That's nothing. Let me give it to you straight: There are people with talent, and there are people with passion. Then, very rarely, there are people who have both. You, Bee, are one of the few. Don't waste it."

I open my mouth—and close it immediately. I have nothing to say to that.

"Now, do I have a volunteer to help me with these orders?" He waves a stack of papers at me. "I have to get through nine in the next two hours."

"Ew. I have nine deliveries today?" I snatch the paperwork from him, smoothing it out on the table. I'm still not happy, but I'm not crying anymore, either. "All right. What do we need?"

"Bee, will you do me a favor?"

I snap out of my trance at the sound of Mama's voice. She stands in my doorway, her hair dragged into a messy bun, her eyelids puffy, her pajamas the same as yesterday's. I nod at her, inviting her in.

"Who made those for you?" she asks, pointing to the vase on my desk. She makes herself comfortable on my bed.

"Ludwig," I say, quietly.

She knows he's doing Papa's flowers. She shudders, her eyes drifting closed for a moment. "They're beautiful."

"Yeah. What's up?" I don't want to talk about flowers.

Mama nods. "Right. Um, I was wondering if you could pick up the last check from TCP?"

Okay, I also don't want to talk about TCP, but there is no way in hell I'm refusing my mom anything right now. "How come?"

"Suzie forgot to drop it off yesterday, and won't be able to come by until Friday. But . . . " She takes a deep breath in. "I need to pay the bills tomorrow."

I try not to cringe. "Okay. I'll go."

She stands up again, nodding. "Thanks, Bee."

As she's about to close my door, I take a deep breath and say, "Mom, Levi and I broke up." They tumble from my mouth, these long overdue words that make my body stiff and my heart burn. Will I never learn?

"You . . . *what*?"

I go quiet again, fighting tears. "I'm sorry I didn't tell you. It was three weeks ago, and it wasn't a good time to say anything."

"Bee," she says softly, and wraps her arms around me. "It's always a good time."

"Not with . . . Papa."

She's crying again. "It's so hard, sweetie, but I don't want you hurting."

"I don't want *you* hurting." Or Astrid or Millie or Tom or anyone else. Especially not Levi. Not on my account.

"That's unavoidable, for me. For *everyone*." She kisses the top of my head, and I sink further into her embrace. "If you don't want to go back, I understand. I can get dressed and run over there."

"No," I say with forced conviction. "I'll be okay. Maybe it's time for me to do this. I can't hide from him forever."

My mom absently strokes my hair, nodding, but I don't think

she really heard me. I'm glad she hasn't asked me why we broke up. We just sit there, holding each other, wrapped in each other's pain and broken hearts, until the world starts to fade away, even if just for a second.

The new office is lit up when I arrive, but there's only one car out front. It's Suzie's, but this does nothing to ease my worry.

Still, I hurry to the front door and let myself in. The place looks like a real office now—an office with a homey touch. The walls are bright, wonderfully finished, with THE COLOR PROJECT splayed across the top in big, black letters to offset the bright stripes.

"Bee?"

I jump, turning toward the stairs. "Suzie."

We look at each other, me by the door, her on the bottom steps, like we don't know what to do, where to start. My heart is about to burst out of my chest, not only because she's there and she looks pained, but because I'm just waiting for the moment when Levi follows her down the stairs and sees me standing here.

Thankfully, that moment never comes. Instead, Suzie walks right over to me and hugs me tight. "I'm so sorry, Bee."

Surprised, I nod into her shoulder. "Me, too."

"We miss you." She pulls back and touches her thumb to my cheek. There is less pain and uncertainty in her eyes now. "Is your mom okay?"

"She's . . . striving."

Suzie sighs. Out of anyone my mom knows, Suzie probably understands this the most. "I assume you're here for the check."

I step away from her. "Yeah."

She moves around some paperwork on the desk and hands me the envelope. "Sorry I couldn't get this to her yesterday."

"It's okay." My voice is still hushed. "Is . . . " I swallow, glancing toward the stairs again. "Is Levi here?"

"No. He hasn't been in for over a week."

"*What?*" I shake my head. "Who's doing interviews?"

"I am." Suzie tilts her head to the side. "He needed some time to . . . process."

I swallow, hard.

Her voice drops to a whisper. "He really misses Matt. He misses *you*."

"He'll get over me," I say, too quickly.

Suzie's expression grows injured at my words. "No, I don't think he will." She raises her eyes to the ceiling, almost like she's saying a silent prayer. "It's been hard for everyone, without you here."

I steel myself. I absolutely *will not cry.* "I'm sorry, Suzie."

She shakes her head. "We all know what you're going through. We just miss you." Here she takes a deep breath, then presses on. "Your mom invited us to the funeral on Saturday, and we said we'd come. I hope you're all right with that."

"Of course," I say, my voice hoarse. "Of course I am. I can't imagine if you weren't there."

Suzie's eyes light up. "You can talk to him, you know. He understands, he wants to be there for you."

I close my eyes. "I'm not ready." But now all I can think about is him kissing me—embracing me until the distance between us is nothing, all of me wrapped up in all of him. "And I . . . " I press on my nose, hard, to ease the pressure building up. One tear escapes my eye, wetting my cheek in a straight line. "I really should be getting back."

"Okay," she whispers. "Okay. Call if you need anything."

I hold up the envelope, my half-smile crooked and stretching my face in ways it doesn't want to be stretched. I want to say *Tell him I'm sorry* and *Tell him I love him* and *Tell him I want him back*. But then I close my mouth, shove the envelope in my purse, and hurry outside. In the warm evening air, everything sparkles by the light of sunset.

I'm almost to my car when I see it, parked a block down the road: Levi's car, freshly washed and glinting dark green. I pause, and it dawns on me what this truly means, that he *is* inside, right now, that he was probably upstairs when I was talking to Suzie.

My stomach twists painfully. I sit in the driver's seat and think about everything Suzie said—about him not getting over me, about how everyone misses me, that I should talk to him. But she also said that he wasn't there. As I slide my key into the ignition and turn into the road, I wonder how much of that was her trying to be nice, and how much of it was a lie to keep him safe.

chapter 48

QUEUED:
THE CRYPT (PART 2)
BY ABEL KORZENIOWSKI

O N SATURDAY MORNING, with lethargic and heavy limbs,
I dress for my father's funeral.

It's an old black dress that I haven't worn since
Christmas last year, but Papa used to compliment me on the
lace sleeves and band around the waist. I took it out of my closet
last night to let it air out, and today I pull it over my head and
zip up the side and slip into some black shoes. I try not to think
too much, try to shut it all out, but I can't. I just end up thinking
about how hard I'm going to cry, how red my face is going to
be when I talk to all those people, all the people who knew him
and loved him but not as much as we did.

When I'm done with my dress, I help Millie zip up the back
of hers, and let Astrid borrow my beige shoes, and fix Tom's
tie. Then I lean against the bathroom counter and smooth out

my mom's makeup, so it looks less like she did it while she was crying.

"Thanks, Bee," she whispers, and blows her nose again, only to have to reapply her lipstick. Then I hold her to me, resting my chin on her shoulder, and let myself cry.

Ludwig's baskets and arrangements look lovely beside the closed casket. I have a perfect view from where I'm sitting in the front row of the church, and they match with the funeral sprays Tracy put together early this morning.

I think we are all crying, every single person in this church. The women who cry for my mother, the big burly men who mourn their coworker, the old college friends who knew him longer than I did. The union of everyone he once knew is terribly beautiful, and I understand, now more than ever, what bittersweet feels like.

Tom gives the eulogy, and that's the worst part of it. I not only hear about my father from the boy who respected him so much, but I also see the man that boy has become. I cry as silently as I can, but it's not enough just to put my hand over my mouth. And by the time Tom gets close to the end of his speech, he is also crying, his lip jutting out. I see him quiver, his shoulders twitching with the effort it takes to stay composed.

"My father had nothing to give the world but himself," he finishes, his voice hoarse and his eyes downcast. But then he briefly raises them to the ceiling above, and we all pretend we didn't hear the single sob on his lips. "To me, to everyone here . . . we understood that that was enough. He was enough. Thank you."

When he joins us again, sitting between me and Astrid,

he leans forward with his elbows on his knees, his face in his hands. I am crying as hard as he is, as hard as my sisters, but we rest against him, arms twining around his waist, faces pressed to his dress coat. I can't even look at my mom for fear of the agony I will see.

At the end of the service, my family stays seated, letting our friends pass our row as they make their way up to the casket. They hug and kiss us, giving their condolences, making sure we know we are not alone. (I have never felt so alone in my life.) Eventually, I am too weak to stand, so I return to my seat and watch legs and torsos as they pass me, and the odd hand that reaches down to squeeze mine.

Then—*Levi*. His legs come into view, long and lean, planted firmly in front of me. I don't look up because I'm afraid to see his face and his pity and his strength. I don't want to think about how he listened to me talking with his mom and didn't come downstairs, that he doesn't want to be with me, that he's trying to move on (despite Suzie's claims, despite my hopes).

But then, he does a very Levi thing: He surprises me. His knees bend, and he squats in front of me and takes my hands and bows his head. His lips brush my fingers, my palms, my wrists. Everywhere.

I am undone.

My mouth opens and a tiny sound comes out—not quite a wail, not quite a whimper. I fold into myself, bending, which means I must lean against him, my face in his neck. He wraps himself around me, arms like twine, a lifeline around my waist. My tears fall harder, and it's only because of his closeness that I know he's crying as well, his body tensing and releasing with each quiet sob.

When he lets me go, I hardly remember where I am. The room suddenly seems too bright and the people too loud, and he is gone, up the stairs to where the casket lies. Soon, too soon,

I lose track of him in the crowd; if he looks back at me, I don't know it. Instead, I use the strength he's given me to stand up again and face the last of the line.

There is darkness, but in that darkness are a million pinpricks of light, and they are all pointing at me.

I've escaped the madness of the after party (the *celebration*, if you want to be positive) where my long-lost grandparents have taken to asking a million questions (as if they cared) and my mom is trying not to cry. Last I saw, Millie and Astrid were lounging sleepily on the couch, so I grabbed Tom's hand and dragged him onto the roof, where we now sit on a spare blanket. His arm is tucked under my neck, his warm body comforting.

He sighs into the silence. "We don't do enough stargazing."

I sigh right back. (I don't tell him that we're here is because it reminds me of Levi.) "I agree."

"I think Dad would have joined us," he says quietly. "Would've pulled out his ladder and climbed up here pretending he wasn't half a century old."

"Tom," I say, "he climbed ladders and stood on roofs for a living."

My brother softly chuckles. His hand wraps around my arm and squeezes, and I get the loveliest feeling of warmth. After the worst day of my life, it's kind of nice.

"That's true," Tom finally says. "He probably would have gotten up here and pretended he was going to push us off, and then pull us back to safety at the last moment to scare the shit out of us."

"Remember how he used to do that when we'd go to national parks? We were on top of Glacier Point in Yosemite—remember that trip?—and he grabbed my arm and pushed me closer to the edge." I'd screamed, even though there was railing and we weren't *that* close. Papa had just scoffed at my fear, pretending he was my savior and that I was silly for being afraid.

Tom laughs loudly this time. "He wasn't the only one who got a kick out of that."

"Hey, shut up."

"I hadn't laughed that hard for, like, a whole year."

I huff. "You're a jerk."

"Whatever. Sometimes I have fun being a jerk."

I elbow him hard in the ribs, laughing at his loud *oof*. "Yeah? Well, so do I."

He grumbles something under his breath, but then his phone rings. I don't catch the name on the screen before he answers, and even then he only mumbles a few *uh-huh*s and *okay*s. When he slides his phone back into his pocket, he nudges me. "You should stand up now."

"Why?"

"Because. You have a person waiting for you on the ground."

I grumble and start to stand, my dress making a static sound as it's pulled away from the shingles. I brush off my butt, glancing over the edge, expecting my mom.

My jaw just about drops to my shoes. "GRETCHEN?!"

She's standing there, her hands on her hips, looking up at me. "In the flesh, you weirdo! Get down here so I can hug you!"

Squealing repeatedly, I climb down the ladder and attack Gretchen, my arms flying around her neck. Now I'm not just squealing—I'm practically screaming. "What. The. Hell. Are. You. Doing. HERE?!"

She laughs, her hand tangled in my hair as she squeezes me closer. But I want to look at her, to make sure she's really here, so I step back and admire her pretty face. She's got the sweetest smile and shoulder-length brown hair with an auburn tint, and she's the most familiar, comforting thing I never expected to see today.

I'm all over the place, so I yank her into another hug. "Oh, my GOD."

Gretchen sighs happily. "I'm so sorry I couldn't make it earlier, you know." Her smile falters. "I'm sorry, *period*, about everything. But I figured me coming at all would make you happy."

"This is amazing! How did you surprise me? Were you in it with Tom? Oh my goodness!"

"Actually, no," she says, and nods her head toward the roundabout in our driveway.

Without even looking, I know. Instantly I understand, and my happiness is drowned by the fact that if I turn, Levi will be *right there*.

I turn anyway.

He stands at the edge of the street, one foot on the curb, the threads of his navy blue suit catching the light from the house. He raises one hand, a half-wave of the pitiful kind. It's like the undercurrent after a wave, the way I'm drawn to him—the way I need to go to him, thank him. I glance at Gretchen, who nods in understanding, and I go.

I see him take a deep breath as I near, but he's bolder than I am—his eyes never leave my face. I, however, am glancing everywhere, trying to blink back tears.

I mean to stop and stand a few feet away from him, but who am I kidding? I let my arms twine around his neck and feel the familiar pull of his arms around me, hands on my waist, the warmth of his breath on my neck.

"Thank you," I whisper, choking on my words. "Thank you for getting her here."

He doesn't answer, but the deep breath he takes in tells me everything—that we're both on the verge of tears, that he doesn't know what to do with me so close, that he's wondering whether I'm breakable.

"Please forgive me," I say. *Now* I'm crying. (Never let it be said that I'm unemotional.) "I'm so sorry, Levi, please forgive me."

His arms tighten, almost too much and not enough. "God, Bee."

"I need more time, I can't just—"

He kisses me, abruptly and beautifully. His lips are the paintbrush and mine are the canvas. My words become muffled and disappear into a soft moan, my fingers drifting down to wind around his arms and . . . I gasp. "*No.*"

Using all my strength, I push him away.

"Shit." He takes a step back, raising a hand to cover his mouth. His sigh is heavy, shuddering.

"We can't do that." (I want to keep doing that.)

"I know. I know, I know, I know." He mumbles the words against his fingers. When he drops his hand back to his sides, I see his jaw tighten and his eyebrows furrow and his Adam's apple bobs with a hard swallow. "You can't give me hope, Bee, if you're not going to follow through."

"I didn't give you—"

"You said you need more time," he interrupted, his voice rough. "You said you're *sorry* and you asked me to *forgive you*. That implies that every bit of hope I have is worth holding on to."

I shudder because he's right. And then I shudder again because, without realizing it, I have shown myself to him. I have been more honest in these last two minutes, without even trying, than I was all summer. "It can't happen today."

He pockets his hands, which are balled into fists. "It doesn't have to happen today. You had to know I'd wait for you."

"That's why I told you not to."

"Well, you're not the boss of me—and it's only been two weeks. I can wait as long as I want."

I try not to smile at his indignant tone but fail miserably. He notices, and his eyes light up, one corner of his mouth quirking.

"Thank you," I say. "For Gretchen, and ... " I spread my hands. "And for earlier. You saved me." *You always save me.*

"Have fun," he exhorts, ignoring that last part. "She's here for two weeks, so you have plenty of time to talk and do everything you want to do. You can heal a little."

I nod, not sure what to say.

He blows out a long and deep breath through pursed lips. "I miss him."

I lift my eyes to his. He's talking about my dad, and it threatens to break me down again. Instead, I draw myself up to my full height. "He really loved you."

"Yeah, well, I really loved him."

This cuts a lot deeper than I expected. I whisper, "I'm sorry we didn't have more time."

"Me, too." He nods at me once, with a certain finality that makes me ache, and turns toward his car parked across the street.

He doesn't say goodbye.

He doesn't have to.

I go back to Gretchen, and the lights, and the people who are celebrating the life my father lived.

chapter 49

QUEUED:
BEGINNINGS
BY HOUSES

G RETCHEN'S ARRIVAL PUTS everything on hold for a day—cleaning my room, hanging up my dress, clearing the mess from the party. Even grieving. I'm here, she's here. We're *together*. And for a full twenty-four hours, I am suspended in a state of blissful denial.

But then, the evening after the funeral, my Papa doesn't come home from work. He doesn't slip off his shoes in the middle of the walkway and shout out, "WHO WANTS TO HUG ME FIRST?" He doesn't go out back to kiss Mama while she waters the plants. He doesn't grab a bowl of cereal and watch the most recent football game he recorded, or kiss my cheek, or make a joke about how Gretchen left our family for her own family and *how rude*. Papa loves Gretchen.

(Scratch that: Papa loved Gretchen.)

I lose it when I walk into my room and see that someone

has placed *Crime and Punishment* atop my clean laundry pile on my bed. The book's spine is useless now, and its front cover bends awkwardly back, the top left corner ripped. It is exactly how I left it last week, when I set it down for the night, when Papa died.

I feel like screaming, but when I open my mouth, no sound escapes. My silent cry becomes me. I grab the book, but I don't know what to do with it because my head feels like it's splitting and my heart no longer exists inside my chest. Before I can stop myself, I chuck the book across the room, where it smashes against my mirror. One edge of the glass cracks in a web where it was hit, and the book thumps to the floor, unharmed.

I try screaming again, but all that escapes is a whimper, barely audible. My chest is about to explode. I lose feeling in my legs for a single moment, but it's just enough for my knees to buckle. I don't fight it; I slide to the floor, curling into myself.

Gretchen's hand is on my shoulder seconds later. She says something soothing to me, fingers drifting through my hair. I don't relax—I can't—but her presence is solid and warm.

"Bee," she whispers.

I catch enough breath to gasp, "Don't say it's okay. Don't tell me it's okay."

She buries her head in my shoulder, arms twining around my shoulders, across my chest, clasping on the other side. "It's not okay, Bee, I'd never say that. But you know what? One day, it will be okay again. It *will*."

And I cry again because I can't imagine an *okay world* where my father doesn't exist.

That night, I leave Gretchen in my bed once she's asleep and climb into my parents' (*mom's*) mostly empty king-size. Her pillow is soaked with tears, and her cheeks are pale from not eating, not sleeping. She takes up a single corner, too short to fit the length. Rolled onto her side, it's like she could disappear if she wanted to. I tuck myself beneath her blanket, and her eyes crack open.

"Bee?" she whispers, yawning.

"Hi," I whisper back. My voice cracks. "I can't sleep . . . "

She reaches out and cradles my head against her chest as soon as she sees my tears. "Neither can I."

"I don't know how he can just . . . not be here." I wipe my face free of tears, but more fall and replace them.

She only shudders, as if trying to contain herself around me. (I don't know how to tell her she can cry.)

"I don't know what to do with that book. That damn book." She knows what I mean. The urge to scream or run or rip something in two comes back. I hold her tighter. "I can never get rid of it, but I don't ever want to see it again."

She shakes her head; her tears wet my forehead. "Put it away for now. It's okay if you don't want to see it."

A voice interrupts at the last word, causing us both to jump. "*Bee,*" Millie whines quietly. "I wanted to sleep with Mommy."

My mom scoots us both over and pats the spot on her other side. "Come here, M&M."

My sister jumps into the bed, shaking it considerably, and rests her head on my mom's other shoulder, looking across at me. "Don't be a hog," she says to me.

I try to laugh, but it comes out as a half-sob. "You sleep in here every night."

"So?" she says—and bursts into tears.

"Seriously?" Astrid asks, entering the room.

We all give pathetic laughs that don't sound much like us, but at least we're laughing. "Get in, Ass-trid," I say, moving closer to Mama.

Astrid makes herself comfortable spooning me, although she scrunches up her nose in distaste. "I want to be next to Mom."

I wiggle. "Everyone wants to sleep by Mom, but we got here first."

My mom actually laughs this time—now *that's* what she sounds like when she's happy. Then she kisses my forehead, and Millie's, and reaches across to kiss Astrid's. "I love my girls," she whispers, almost too quiet to hear. "We can switch around tomorrow night so Astrid can have a turn."

I curl up, bending my knees so our legs entwine, and close my eyes. I like that there's a tomorrow night. I know I'll be here, searching for comfort, finding it sandwiched between sisters and mother.

After that night, I feel like I can't stop crying, not even just for two minutes to brush my teeth or take a shower. The crying doesn't budge for a good forty-eight hours. It takes over my life. The only solace is at night, when Gretchen is sleeping, and I run to my mom's bedroom, trying to be the first to get a spot next to her.

The rest of the time is madness. I can't do anything or touch anything or look at anything without seeing Papa, somehow. I keep finding old things of his in the house, receipts and discarded hats, a single shoe missing its pair (stuffed under the couch). Today, Day Five After the Funeral, I find a t-shirt of Papa's that I forgot I'd borrowed, stacked with all my clean clothes on my bed.

It's only three in the afternoon, but since Astrid is on Mom-duty and Millicent is on watering-plants-duty, I have nothing on the agenda. (Gretchen mentioned she was heading out; I don't remember where because I was crying when she told me.) I strip out of my clothes and throw the shirt on; it comes just to my thighs and is two sizes too big—just comfortable enough for bed. Forsaking everything, I kick my pile of clothes to the ground and curl up under the covers, hugging one of my pillows to my chest.

Gretchen finds me like this an hour later, standing over the bed with a concerned expression. "What's going on?" she murmurs.

I give her a look. How am I supposed to say, *again*, that I've been sobbing? That I've reverse-aged like Benjamin Button and can only function in the fetal position? That my chances of survival seem slim? I'm starting to sound like a broken record.

"Hey," she says, and kicks off her shoes so she can climb into bed with me. Her hair falls over my shoulder as she wraps her arms around my middle. "Want to do something fun?"

I give her another look, accompanied by an atrociously loud sniffle.

"Look, it's going to be hard. I know you," she says. "You like your comfort zone and don't want to step out when things get hard. But when it's easy, sure—heck, you'll plan an entire wedding!"

I groan, throwing my pillow over my face. Her words sting because they're true. *I'm sorry, Levi, that I didn't keep you when I had you.*

I'm waiting for you. It's only been five days since he said those words.

I shake my head beneath the pillow.

Gretchen keeps going, despite my miniature tantrum. "Right

now it's hard, life *sucks*, and despite it all, you and I are going to do something that doesn't consist of wearing pajamas and eating popcorn. Just this once, Bee. Just today."

I *have* been eating a lot of popcorn lately. (And I'm pretty sure I've gained a few pounds.) I throw the pillow to the end of the bed and sit up abruptly. "Know what?" I demand. "You're right and it pisses me off."

Gretchen looks relatively unimpressed. "That's good, I suppose."

"What the hell am I supposed to *do*?" I say, enraged, as I hug my knees to my chest.

"Fight back." Gretchen tugs me closer, so my head rests on her shoulder. "I say we write on the walls."

"Excuse me?"

"You know, like you always wanted to do. Write out your favorite lyrics or something."

I glance at the wall at the head of my bed, empty except for a small map of the world. I'd been meaning to hang up more pictures, maybe buy some art, but now that all seems stupid.

I'm going to write on my walls.

I lean across Gretchen to open my nightstand drawer, where I have a pile of pens and pencils and sharpies. I grab a sharpie and move to my knees, popping the lid off and poising the tip against the wall. I already know what song I'm going to choose. "Gretchen, will you look up the lyrics to 'Michicant'?"

She laughs, incredulously. "You mean the one by Bon Iver? As in, that band you hate?"

"I . . . I don't . . . " I huff. "Ugh. What other Bon Iver is there?"

"I'm just surprised, is all." And then . . . it dawns. "Ohhhh. I see what's going on here."

I glare at her. "Shh, Gretchen. Don't push that button, Jay Gatsby."

"You meant the Levi button?" She roars with laughter as I lob a pillow at her head. "Ready?" she asks, pulling out her phone and holding it up in surrender.

Oh, am I ever. With a nod, she begins to read, and I begin to write.

chapter 50

QUEUED:
THOUSAND MILE RACE
BY A SILENT FILM

IT'S WITH A dull ache that I start to see the world again.

It's not exactly a pretty place, but it's better than the hell I've been in. I see my mother crying ten times a day (I hold her for at least five of those), but I also hear my sisters rapping songs from *Hamilton* at the top of their lungs, and when Tom leaves for work in the evening there's a bit of a smile back in his eyes. I even relieve Gretchen of her job: grocery shopping. (Apparently, *that's* where she's been going every day.)

I'm happy with the song on my wall, except now I think of Levi every time I see it. (As if I'm not already thinking of him every other second that I'm not thinking of Papa.) I don't talk about him out loud, though, as if somehow opening my mouth and saying his name will jinx every ounce of courage I've gained in the last several days.

I don't want to relapse.

Of course, I can't avoid him *at all* when he calls me—calls me!—on Day Eleven After the Funeral. I stare at my phone in agony, so tempted to answer, but I know I can't. I know it's not right.

Gretchen grabs it off the table. "Bernice, answer this phone right now."

"No," I say firmly. "I'm not ready."

"Why not?" she demands, finger hovering over the button.

"I've cried too many times today."

As soon as the phone stops ringing I take it from her. His voicemail alert comes through an eternity later, but hearing his voice is entirely worth the wait.

"Hey." He takes a deep breath in. It sounds shaky. "I know we're not supposed to be talking right now, but I can't help myself. Do you need anything? How's your family? I'm a *mess* over here, Bee." He groans, and there's a shuffling noise. I think I hear Missy complaining in the background. "I know you have Gretchen and I know you need time. I promise I'm not being pushy. Or, erm, I'm trying not to be pushy. I miss you every day, okay? But we don't even have to see each other—just let me know if you want me to drop something off or help with your sisters or . . . anything. Okay. I love you."

He hangs up.

I put the phone on the table, my mouth stretched wide with a smile. Gretchen listens to the message next, lips quirked. *Oh, I'm so done for.*

She clears her throat once before nodding solemnly. "That Boy deserves a medal."

I groan, still smiling, and bury my head in my hands.

"But seriously, Bee, when are you going to get him back?"

"When I stop crying all the time?"

"Hmm. You're not crying right now, though." Gretchen

stands, paces back and forth twice, then raises her finger. "Think about it like this: Do you need me?"

I roll my eyes.

She gasps. "Just . . . answer the question!"

"Yes, yes, okay! I need you."

"So, the reality is . . . I'm not always going to be here. Not physically, anyway. And *he* is. He's going to be here forever because let's face it, he's not going to let you get away. He *loves* you, Bee."

"That doesn't change the fact that I'm not ready." I am, however, tempted to listen to the voicemail again. (And a thousand more times into eternity.)

Gretchen sighs. "You need him. You need him like you need me, and your family, and those smelly boys you're friends with. He makes you laugh, Bee—he makes you smile when you're the saddest you've ever been. That says something—no, I lied, that says *everything*. And he needs *you*, just as badly. He's probably wandering around aimlessly because you're not by his side."

I cringe. "Are you a walking-talking romance novel?" (Elle would be proud.)

"No, shush, I'm just being honest." She tsks, and asks again, "When will you go back to him?"

"I don't know."

"Before you give me all the reasons why you can't, let me say this: You're not allowed to feel guilty about being with Levi because of your dad."

"No, that's not it," I say truthfully. "Not anymore."

"Then what it is? He loves you, you love him, I'm leaving in three days." She smiles. "The list of reasons why you should jump on this—ASAP—is a mile long."

"I know it is. It just . . . has to be at the right moment." I spread my hands. "And I still don't know how to tell him. What to tell him."

"That's simple. Tell him he's a replacement for your bestest friend in the whole world and he'd better do a good job."

I have to laugh at this.

She smiles. "You can also tell him the truth, you know."

A part of me sinks and my mouth quivers. "That's it, though. I don't know what the truth is yet."

"Is it coming together?"

I shrug. "Slowly."

"Then that's all you can ask for." She smacks my arm, shaking us both out of the moment. "Now who's going to show me around San Diego while I'm here? Don't make me call a cab—"

I smack her arm and reach for my purse. "Shut up and get in my car."

Gretchen laughs. "There she is."

I say goodbye to Gretchen three days later on the sidewalk of the airport, my flip flops and tank top not enough warmth in the surprising gust of cold wind coming off the bay. There are a few clouds, too, indicating rain. (At least, that's what the weatherman hopes.)

I shuffle the bottom of my shoes on the ground while I wait for her to gather her purse and suitcase from her side of the car. I start to cry when she turns toward me and her eyes are already brimming with tears and *ohmyGodwhy*. I remember this now, like I remembered it last time, and the time before that. It's not the same—texts, phone calls, Skype. Eventually, though, I'm going to forget that it's better in person. I'll forget for the sake of my sanity, so I can pretend like it's okay that we live so far away.

"I think you're crap," she whispers as she hugs me.

"I think you're the crappiest," I reply.

"That's not how this works, Bernice."

"Yes, it is." I squeeze her tighter. "And stop using my full name."

"Get used to it, will you? Levi's going to think it's sooooo sexy when you tell him."

"Shh, oh my God, *Gretchen*," I hiss.

"What?" Her laugh shakes our hug. "He won't be able to resist its charm." Then she pretends to be Levi, standing on her tiptoes over me, deepening her voice an octave and saying, "Come hither, Bernice. Hubba hubba!"

I poke her side, eliciting a shriek. I'm laughing harder than I have since before Papa died. "That's the dumbest and most un-Levi-like thing I've ever heard." Then I hug her again, to make up for the hug I won't get when I wake up the next morning. "Have a safe flight, okay?"

"I won't die, if that's what you're asking me."

I laugh, but it's also a sob. "See you someday, freak."

She grabs onto her bags, hoisting her purse over her shoulder, and says, "I think you're the *most* crappiest person of all time, ever." Directing her best smile at me over her shoulder, Gretchen disappears into the airport.

I let her win. This time.

The drive home is long, but it isn't lonely. Gretchen calls me while she waits in the security line, effectively proving that we are suckers for each other.

"Indestructible suckers," she protests when I tell her this, and that makes me laugh again.

"Infinite suckers," I say.

But when I pull into my driveway, we're quick to say goodbye.

Not just because her line has gotten shorter, but because there's an unfamiliar car in my driveway. I gather my things and head for the door, only to find my brother and Keagan and *Elle* in the doorway.

Elle whirls around the second she hears me coming up the stairs and throws her arms around my neck. "Beeeee!" she shouts. "You've been away from the office so much lately and we miss you!"

I close my eyes and hug her tight. *She must not know we broke up,* I think, and curse Levi for being such an angel. "I'm sorry . . . "

"Oh, don't be. Levi told us what happened. Gosh, Bee." She shakes her head, squeezing my arm. "I'm so sorry. Your dad must have been amazing, the way everyone talks about him . . . "

"Thanks. We're . . . coping."

She nods. "I'm so glad Tom could come tonight. We invited you but he said you were busy."

I smile. "What did you do?"

"Just went to a movie, us and Levi. It was Keagan's treat." She nods her head to the right, toward Keagan.

Keagan, who is looking at me right this second. Keagan, who is not smiling, who does not look amused, whose jaw is tight like he's trying not to say something. But then the moment passes and he shakes Tom's hand like nothing's wrong. "See you later," he says, and stalks off down the path.

I glare at Tom. "What was that all about?"

He shrugs. "What was what?"

I *know* he knows what I'm talking about. "Keagan looked like he was mad at me. He didn't even say hi." This is *so* not like Keagan. And Elle can only shrug, as confused as I am.

All right, fine then, if that's how it's going to be.

I drop my purse and rush after him, sliding in front of his car door before he can unlock it. "Keagan," I say. "What's wrong?"

His scowl deepens. "Please move."

"Dude, don't lie to me. You're always so nice to me. Did I do something?"

He works his jaw. "Bee," he says. His voice is quiet, thoughtful, a little bit sad. "I don't want to get into this right now."

I raise an eyebrow.

He grunts.

I raise both eyebrows, and say, "You have no choice. I'm staying here."

He shakes his head. "I . . . " Then he sighs. "All right, look. I'm really, really sad about your dad, Bee. And you have one thousand valid reasons to be sad, and angry, and hurt. But you . . . really hurt *him*, and that's a little hard to understand."

"Bee hurt who?" Elle says, huffing as she runs up to us. She looks like a referee waiting for a fight to break out.

I don't look away from Keagan—I can't. I love his honesty. But I do lower my voice when I say, "How bad was it?"

Keagan's eyes darken. "Bad, like . . . really bad. Let me ask you this: Have you ever seen Levi depressed?"

I shake my head no. (It's actually very hard to imagine.)

"Oh, my God." Elle covers her mouth. "Did you break up with Levi?"

Keagan is not amused. "Elle, please."

Elle's eyes widen as if she is starting to understand everything. Scurrying away, she says, "Well, um, I'll . . . be in the car."

Keagan looks at me as Elle shuts her door, his eyes saddened by a weight he's carrying, a burden I don't quite understand. "I hadn't seen him depressed either—until the day after you broke up with him. He came to work and didn't say a word the whole time, didn't even take his break, just plugged in his headphones and listened to music for seven hours. Then he told Michael that he'd need a few days off work because he wasn't feeling well."

I start to say something, but Keagan interrupts me. "And

then," he says, "on top of that, he grabbed all of his work from the TCP office and took it home with him and stayed inside. For *three days.* I don't know if you know how hard that is for Levi to do, but it's *really* hard. He scared the shit out of me—wouldn't even answer his phone for the first day."

I'm appalled, sick to my stomach—the same sensation as before I broke up with him. Like there's unfinished business and I'm standing in the way of getting it done. I wrap my arms around my stomach. "What else?"

Keagan shrugs. "He started answering my texts, told me he was okay, he just needed some time to process, figure out what he was going to do next." He rubs his cheek thoughtfully. "He throws himself into things wholeheartedly, and he thought you did, too, Bee. We all did. That's why you guys were everything. What . . . what happened?"

I shrink back against the car door. I can't blame the cancer, if only because of every conversation I had with Papa before he died—of him pushing me to go places, to be with Levi. No, this was entirely me and my fears.

"I don't know," I answer. And then, more honestly, "I got stuck."

"On what?"

"On the idea that I wasn't good enough for him."

"You know that's bullshit, right?"

I smile at him ruefully. "So people tell me."

Keagan chuckles, but his expression grows serious again, too quickly. "You know there are certain things . . . he hasn't told you. Right?"

I suck in a breath. "No."

He shakes his head.

"Tell me *this instant*, Keagan!"

That's all it takes, thank God. "His dad fought with him about something important, so Mr. Orville took the rent money out from under TCP. Then, about a week before you broke up with him, three sponsors pulled their monthly payments. He was waiting for the storm to pass, waiting for you guys to make up before he said anything."

I bury my head in my hands. Levi wouldn't have told me—not after how I reacted to him paying for Papa's chemo. I would have been unjustly angry at him for making that sacrifice, when that's all TCP is: *sacrifice*. "This is so stupid," I mutter. (I'm once again thinking of ways I could successfully murder AuGUStus!)

"Bee," Keagan says, and I drop my hands so I can look at him. "Levi told me about your conversation, after the funeral. And I have something to say about it. I don't care if you don't get back together with him—although, that would be ideal. Just . . . tell him you're sorry. Tell him all the things you should have told him when you were dating, and move on."

He's right. He's one hundred percent right, and suddenly, I'm pretty sure I have wings. "I don't want it to be just *any* conversation, though," I announce, to both him and me. I've said those words before, however, and they haven't gotten me any closer to the answer.

Suddenly the window behind me rolls down and Elle sticks her head out. "Excuse me, um, I haven't been listening to your conversation or anything—actually, wait, yes, I have. But I have an idea, if you don't mind."

I grab her hand that's hanging out the window and squeeze it hard. "Help me. Help me now," I say, and I'm only half-pretending to be desperate.

She grins slyly. "So, there's, like, this event coming up. You know, the one Felix's friend wanted to set up for Levi?"

I grip her hand so hard, I'm worried I've crushed all her bones. "When is it?"

"Um, it's tomorrow." She clears her throat. "And, well, Levi's having me give this stupid speech that I don't want to give because I'm not a writer or a speaker—not like that anyway. I keep reading over it and it *sucks*. I hate it."

Keagan frowns. "I fail to see how this helps Bee."

Elle rolls her eyes. "*Men*," she mutters. "Obviously, I want Bee to write the speech—and give it. At the event. Tomorrow."

I don't even have to think twice about this—I'm already there, ready for it. "You don't think he'd mind, though, if I show up uninvited?" I ask, just to make sure.

"Bee, you're freaking invited, okay? I have a few extra invitations leftover and one of them has your name on it." She sees my laughing expression and holds up a hand. "I mean it literally has your name on it. Levi had one made and then didn't send it because he kept saying he'd give it to you in person and that you already knew about it." Her expression goes dim, as if she's just now realizing he was lying to her for my sake this whole time. "That little bastard . . . "

I smile, a giddy, ridiculous smile that I'd never admit to in a million years, especially in front of Keagan, but right now—*who freaking cares*. "I'll do it. Elle, I'll do it."

(I already know what I want to say to Levi. I already know how I'm going to say I'm sorry.)

Elle slaps my hand in a high five. "Good. Write your speech tonight, and tomorrow I'll pick you up at ten to go dress shopping."

"What?"

"Yeah, it's a *fancy* event. Like, you know, the kind of fancy only Felix can pull off."

Remembering the event in Malibu, I nod. "Yeah. Okay."

I step away from the car and Keagan opens the driver's door, tossing his keys onto the seat. "I'll see you tomorrow night, then?"

"You'll be there?"

"Obviously." He hesitates, but a second later he reaches for a hug that I willingly give.

"Keagan, thank you."

He pats my back twice, then lets me go. "I know you love him."

"Yeah." I really, really, *really* love him, so much that I could explode, so much that I can't imagine living my life without him. (What was I THINKING?!)

With a nod, Keagan climbs into his car and, after letting Elle squeeze my hand one more time, drives away.

Minutes later I'm in my room, a mug of hot tea on my desk beside me, a blank sheet of paper and a green pen in hand. With a deep breath in and out, I start to write all the words I will say to Levi tomorrow night. All the words I've wanted to say for a while, but just haven't had the courage.

That night, when I've perfected and memorized my speech, I slip into bed with my mom. I'm surprised to find there are no sisters in sight. "Where are the girls?"

My mom, who's looking at something on her phone, laughs and invites me closer. "They decided they missed their own beds. But sweetie, look at this." She tilts the screen toward my face. The text is from Suzie, and it's a picture of—Levi?

I scrunch up my nose. "Oh, my gosh! How old is he there?"

"Seven," my mom says, laughing again.

In the picture, my ex-boyfriend-sort-of-still-boyfriend-will-hopefully-be-my-boyfriend-again-soon is sitting on a park bench with an otter pop in one hand and a skateboard in the other . . . and a full-on Mohawk with blue tips. I mean, I would never put it past his hair to be able to accomplish that height, but *wow*.

"Suzie let him do that?" I zoom in on his cute face, so young, but with that same smirk I love, the same smirk I swooned over the first day I ever saw him.

"Apparently." My mom swipes right. "Oh, look, another one."

Levi's even younger in this picture, probably five, and he's missing his two front teeth, so his smile is not just big, it's dorky, too. I miss that smile. (Suddenly, tomorrow can't come fast enough.) I rest my head on my mom's shoulder. "I'm going to a TCP event tomorrow night, with Elle."

"Good for you, Baby Bee!" she exclaims, surprising me with her enthusiasm.

"I'm going to give the welcome speech, actually."

"Wow. That's an amazing opportunity."

"I'm going to tell him my name," I whisper.

At first, she has no answer except to kiss my forehead. "He's going to love it, the way I did when I named you, the way I still do." She rolls into me, fingers tracing my arm softly. "Do you remember what it means?"

"What? No, actually." (Oops.)

"It means *she who brings victory*."

I close my eyes, starting to drift at the sound of her voice. "Ah, victory. Just within my grasp."

She laughs. "You'll be fine, Bernice. Yours is the only other love I've ever been so sure of."

"Yeah." I embrace her words, along with the meaning of my name, and the surety of her heartbeat. "I think we'll all be just fine."

chapter 51

QUEUED:
THIS IS THE COUNTDOWN
BY MAE

THE AFTERNOON OF the fundraiser, I pull my new dress out of its bag and lay it out on my bed.

The room (filled with my sisters and mother and Elle) gives a collective gasp.

"Bee," Millicent whispers in awe, "you're going to look like a princess in that."

I run my hands over the soft fabric. It's truly charming: shimmering gold, lightly pleated, long enough to drop to my feet. It's beautiful in that Greek-goddess way that requires gold sandals and possibly a shiny, gold wreath crown. (Too bad the crown would be overkill.) "You think?" I ask, grinning.

"Bee," Mama says, "you're going to be so beautiful in this dress, The Boy is not going to know what to do with himself."

I blush. "Mom."

She smiles and brushes my hair away from my eyes. "Astrid, time to tackle these locks."

Astrid holds up a brush and comb and spray bottle full of water. "Yes, ma'am."

Then she squirts a spray of water into my face.

After the hour it takes to do my hair, my mom helps me into the dress, careful to make sure it doesn't snag on my crown braid (adorned with gold pins). I swear I *do* feel like a princess as the soft fabric touches my legs like liquid gold and the straps rest on my shoulders at the perfect length.

I wait until Mama zips the dress in the back before turning to the mirror. I'm assailed by sudden happiness, so strong I can't help the squeak that comes out of my mouth. The dress cinches in the middle, creating a loose-fitting bodice held up by paper-thin straps. The skirt drops straight down, but when I move side to side, it also moves, flowing like it was made for me.

Mama grins behind me, nodding. "I'm glad you got this one."

I tried on seven dresses total, and this was the one I wanted from the beginning. It was pricey but worth it. "Me, too," I say.

"Are you nervous?" she asks, reaching into her jewelry box. She pulls out a gold chain with a leaf pendant and sets it around my neck.

"Not for the speech," I say.

"Levi?"

"Yeah. I'm a wreck." Truth is, I've been rushing with nerves all day, imagining how the evening will go over and over again. It's never perfect in my head; I always manage to screw something up before I have the chance to get it right.

"You'll be fine," Elle says from the closet, where she's trying on her own newly-purchased dress.

"You will be," Mama confirms. "You're not a wreck, Bee." She wraps her arms around me from behind, our cheeks pressing together. We've always looked alike in a sort of distant way, like we could be cousins or niece and aunt. But here we look lovely, a little like angels, with my dress casting golden shadows on our faces through the mirror.

Her embrace starts to ease away my worries. "Thanks, Mama," I whisper.

She kisses my cheek, and I wrap my hands around hers. I glance down at the copy of *Crime and Punishment* lying on my nightstand, the cover torn and abused, flapping in the wind from my ceiling fan. I press my lips, then say, "I wish Papa was here to send me off."

Mama closes her eyes, a tear rolling down her cheek. "Ah." A tiny gasp of a word, and it tears right through me. "He loved Levi so much, Bee. If there's anything you could do to make your dad proud, it'd be this."

I dab my mom's eyes to stop the tears, then kiss her nose, and stand. "Well, then. I should get going."

"Excuse me!" Elle squawks from the closet. "You can't leave without your date!"

chapter 52

QUEUED:
TOMORROW
BY A SILENT FILM

THE HOTEL HOSTING the event is gorgeous, big and marble and fountained, unlike anything I've seen. But I barely get a glimpse of it before Elle (who looks fabulous in her skinny black dress) takes me around to the back door, so we can avoid Levi and other Important People. She deposits me right at the edge of the stage, her blue hair flouncing. "Stay. Here."

I stay there, situated behind a speaker and in the center of a bunch of cords, and wait.

For nearly twenty minutes. The room fills and fills, and everyone is wearing outfits even nicer than mine, and I'm starting to feel queasy, in the best possible way. (*Is there a good way to feel queasy? If there is, I've found it.*) I have a paper full of words in my clutch, words I will say tonight, in front of all these people. I almost get it out to read over it again, but I know that's futile—I was repeating it in my sleep last night.

Apparently, I've been ready for this a lot longer than I realized.

I'm beginning to worry Elle forgot about me when she finally rounds the corner again. "I'm going to introduce you now. Ready?"

"Hell no." I smile. "And hell yes."

"I'm right here, cheering you on." Elle squeezes me in a hug for a split second before hurrying up the steps. The audience claps sparsely when she grabs the microphone and starts to speak. "Welcome, one and all, to what we hope will become the first of many annual banquets!"

More applause. I smile, bouncing from foot to foot. I'm so ready to climb those stairs.

"Levi Orville, our local saint, asked me to give the welcome speech tonight, but as I am highly unprofessional, I asked someone far more capable and deserving of the job to help us out."

(I wish I could see his face right now.)

"I'm not going to introduce her because I think she can do that best for herself." She waves to me. "Come on up."

Letting go of every reservation I could possibly have left, I climb those stairs. I step into the spotlight, squinting for a second before my eyes adjust. The ocean of people makes me briefly dizzy. They are waiting—for *me*.

I take in a lot of faces in a few seconds. Mostly unfamiliar, but some are so wonderfully familiar they give me a touch of heartache. I see Clary-Jane, and Albert, and Missy. (This is the only acceptable place to wear those shoes.) I see Nikita and Suhani, whispering things to each other, smiling, waving at me. I see Keagan, with his dimpled smile and his wild curly hair and his bright eyes that tell me they're happy I'm here.

Then, because he is sitting near the front and I can easily spot him, I meet Levi's gaze and think about how perfect he is in that stupid (gorgeous) suit and that I could stare at him all day. I register his surprise and confusion and his sadness, too.

I smile and take the microphone from Elle.

I put it close to my lips.

I speak.

"Thank you all for coming out here tonight." *Smooth and easy*, I think. *Now continue. Don't look at them directly. Don't make eye contact.*

Actually, make eye contact with Levi. But only sometimes.

I shake my hands out by my sides for a second. When the nerves don't go away, I say, "I'm, um, a tad nervous, so you'll have to excuse me."

This earns an honest trickle of laughter. Confidence surges. I go on.

"Typically, Levi is the one to give speeches at his events. You all know Levi, right? He's super tall—well, to me at least, because I'm really short—and he's probably the nicest person you've ever met. Yeah. Him." I pause, a blush creeping up my neck and down my arms. "He's the reason why you're here. And normally he'd be up here talking about how great and helpful and generous everyone else is. Once, he even stood in front of an audience much like yours and spoke about *me*. But, tonight, I want to focus on Levi."

I catch his expression then: the fleeting pain, the embarrassment. And a smidgeon of joy—I saw that, too.

At the risk of becoming giddy, I continue. "The Color Project is a place of hope. When Levi introduced me to TCP back in June, I had no idea that such a place existed. But it was there, in front of me the whole time, and sooner than later I got sucked in. Who doesn't want to surround themselves with hope? If you don't want or need hope, in any way, shape, or form, you're probably doing something wrong. You probably shouldn't be *here*, of all places."

More laughter. I let out my own breathy huff that I hope passes as a chuckle.

"As it turns out, I was looking for hope. I needed it. I craved it. And TCP gave that to me. I got to watch Levi hand freshly-written checks to struggling, single parents so their kids could go to college, to sickly people who couldn't pay their bills, to practically anyone in need. I was a part of something bigger for the first time, and I've met some of the most amazing people in the entire world. Not only that—I've come to know myself better than ever before. When I first started volunteering, I got to help plan a wedding for two young people from Prague. That wedding, in a roundabout way, led to the realization that I am passionate about floral design."

I shift my weight from foot to foot, still nervous, but I'm starting to get the hang of this. "Everything I've named so far— that's all a part of what Levi does. Pretty spectacular, right? I know," I add, nodding with the audience as there's another trickling applause. "And he's only twenty—can you believe that?"

There is a hoot, and a whistle, and a shout. Levi turns in his seat with an amused expression on his face, but soon his eyes are back on me. He's got his hand by his face, like he's trying to hide. I smirk. *Not tonight, beautiful boy.*

"So, that's what Levi does. Now I want to talk about who he is."

Quiet again. So quiet.

Then, Levi: "Bee, really—"

I cut him off. "A few months ago, when Levi had already become a part of my family, and vice versa, my father was diagnosed with stage 3C brain cancer. The doctors gave him three months to live, which turned out to be a very accurate prognosis, as my father died only a couple of weeks ago." I close my eyes, letting the audience's murmurs dull my pain. "The one person who was there consistently, through it all, was Levi. He visited my father every day he could. He ate with us. He laughed with us. He even shared some moments with me that were the bleakest of my life. He provided a friendship for our entire family that I can say for certain will not die out anytime soon."

Here, I take a deep breath, my heart pounding. "My parents are by no means poor, but they're not wealthy, either. And treatments are, as anyone can guess, very expensive. I thought we were going to make do, going to stick it out till the end . . . until one day I discovered that TCP had been providing for us all along. The bi-monthly checks we were receiving paid for everything, including the funeral. And now, because of Levi, my widowed mother can live the rest of her life debt free. She can provide for us, send us to school, give us a good life."

Levi stands now, and oh, God, I want to hug him. He puts his hands in his pockets and looks up at me, expectant and yet completely uncertain. I realize with a pang in my gut that we are the only two people standing in the entire room.

I take a deep breath—ohmygosh *breathing*—and smile.

I say the thing, the one that will change everything.

"My name is Bernice Wescott," I tell Levi, in front of everyone. He laughs with so much joy and surprise that I'm sure the rest of the audience is confused. But this moment, right now, with our smiles overtaking our faces—this is for us. He knows, without a doubt, that this is an offering. An offering of myself. *Hi, my name is Bernice, and I'm in love with you, so you should take me back.*

"My life has been changed by The Color Project," I continue, working to keep myself under control. "I want to make sure that this ripple effect continues, and never dies out. In light of everything that I've just told you, I hope you will all think hard about your decision here. Actually," I amend quickly, "it's not much of a decision at all. If you have to think twice about where to put your money, you *definitely* shouldn't be here.

"Thank you," I conclude, without flair or any sort of style. Then I hand Elle the microphone and start walking. The stairs seem to wobble under my feet, but I follow them down anyway. That's when I register the (unbelievably loud) applause. I smile, but I'm not going to stop for them.

I'm only going to stop for Levi, if he wants me.

I step through the side door and onto the open patio, where I catch my breath against the railing that follows the steps down into a garden maze. There's a bench there, out of the light, and no trees to block my view of the stars. I make my way down to it, still wobbly; I'm breathing like I've run a mile.

I take the final step, my hand still clutching the rail. I did it. *I really did it.*

I'm about to jump with my fist in the air, to whoop loudly into the night, when I hear his voice. "Bee."

I turn. Seeing him at the top of the stairs makes me turn to Jell-O inside.

"Bernice Aurora Wescott," he begins, drawing out every syllable, marking every vowel and hitting every consonant. The one thing I've been so scared to hear him say and it sounds utterly beautiful on his tongue, like the perfect melody. "Bernice Aurora Wescott, my Delectable Girl, why would you ever think it's okay to say all those nice things and then just *leave*?"

chapter 53

QUEUED:
STORY OF AN IMMIGRANT
BY CIVIL TWILIGHT

I DON'T KNOW WHAT to say to him.

As always, I'm speechless in his presence. *This is going to have to change*, I think.

"Bee?" he inquires of my silence. "You weren't really leaving, were you?"

He's so hopeful. So full of boyish energy and joy. "No, I wasn't," I say, wringing my hands together.

Levi starts down the steps—fifteen of them in rapid succession. He's at the bottom before I can stop him. "You can't!" I exclaim, almost shouting, hurrying out of his reach.

He stops, confused. Then he starts toward me again.

"Don't—*Levi*! I need to talk to you!"

His chuckle is maddening, devilish. "You can't talk to me while I'm holding you in my arms under the moonlight?"

"No, I cannot. No distractions. I'll end up kissing you instead."

"Not if I kiss you first," he growls, and I have never seen him move so fast. His arms are around me and his lips are pressing against my nose, my chin, my neck—and I let him because I've missed this too much. *Talking? What's talking?*

He shakes his head at me, hair bobbing, lips parted. "Bee," he murmurs, then kisses my lips. My small noise of delight fades out as I clutch his shoulders, kissing him back fiercely. I'm pretty sure I'm never going to stop kissing him, not now, not after all that.

GOD, he tastes perfect.

"I'm sorry . . . I never . . . told you . . . my name," I murmur between kisses. I hear his contented sigh, feel it on my lips, and we're a little bit frantic and a lot happy, our arms trapping us inside each other. I have a month of kissing to make up for; he better not think for a second that he's getting out of that.

With a small chuckle, Levi reaches down and grabs my legs and hoists me up, saying, "Now *this* dress I can work with." He sets me on the ledge behind us, so that he can hold me closer, his hands roaming my back, working his way up to my shoulders, squeezing like he can't let go. (I know he won't.) "I'm sorry I never rocked the boat," he whispers. "I wasn't there for you like you needed me to be, and I said so many stupid things that I regret."

"Shh," I say with a finger on his lips. "You were right. Well, mostly."

"It doesn't matter whether I was right or not. I was stupid, and I love you, and I'm sorry."

"Oh, Levi." I rest my forehead on his and, realizing I'm still gripping handfuls of his hair, I trace my fingers down to his shoulders to grasp his lapels. "I should have asked you about your dad. I should have asked you how things were at TCP. You know, the sponsors dropping out."

"How did you—"

"Keagan told me."

Levi grunts. "Bastard."

"He also told me, essentially, that I can't *pretend* to go all-in so I can back out whenever I want to."

"Seriously?"

"*Essentially*," I repeat. "At least, that's how I'm taking it, because it's true. And I don't ever want to back out of this ever again."

"Once again, I assume *this* means *our relationship*."

He's referring to something he said during our breakup, which makes me sad, but it also makes me think of second chances. I like that. "You are correct, sir."

He heaves a sigh. "Thank goodness."

I place my hand over his heart, and my own heart skips a beat when he places his own hand on top. "Come on, you goof. You knew you had it in the bag the second I stood up on that stage."

His eyes twinkle like stars, his smile mischievous. "Duh. Dufus is smart."

I hoot with laughter. "Yes," I say, and I pull him to my chest, where his head rests against me. "Dufus is very smart."

"Did Dufus tell you how great your speech was, by the way? Or how gorgeous your hair is? Or how freaking beautiful this dress is? Or how nice it is to kiss you after all this ti—"

"Shh, be quiet." I can't help it—I kiss him again.

But he's not done yet. Now he's indignant. "I can't *believe* I didn't guess Bernice. Of all the names! That should have been easy!"

"No," I say with equal indignation. "I'm glad you didn't guess, because I got to tell you myself."

His expression turns soft, less teasing, but he adds quietly, "I'm still upset about it."

"You are not." I pat the breast pocket of his suit. "Anyway, shouldn't we be heading back inside now? Won't your adoring fans be looking for you to throw their millions at you?"

He helps me off the ledge, setting me softly on my feet. "Actually, there's an entertainer for the next hour, and drinks and raffle prizes afterward, so . . . "

I look at him. He looks at me. Our hands meet between our bodies. We're so warm, so contained within each other, as if we were never apart.

"We could go for a drive, if you want," he says.

I reach up, my tiptoes barely lifting me to his height, and plant a kiss on the top of his lips. "We could."

Because he knows that is my *yes*, Levi tugs me back up the stairs. We practically run around the building and into the parking lot, where we wait for the valet to bring his car.

"MAXIMILLIAN!" I shout when I see it.

Levi laughs like he's trying not to but he can't help himself. "That horrible name again?"

"What? It's no worse than Bernice." I sit in the passenger seat and close my door, arranging the hem of my dress around my feet.

"Bernice is totally sexy. I really don't know what you're so worked up over."

I roll my eyes. "Exactly what Gretchen thought you'd say."

"Once again, Gretchen is a wonderful human being." He reaches across me to the glove compartment, rummaging around for something, and while he's there I take the opportunity to kiss his beautiful hair. "Pick something," he commands, and pulls back, dropping his iPod in my lap. Then he returns my kiss and puts Maximillian in reverse.

"What if I show you the playlist I listened to every day after we broke up?"

"*We* broke up?" He raises one eyebrow at me, turning out of the lot.

"Fine. After *I* broke up with *you*." I log myself into Spotify and find my playlist, clicking on "Michicant". I cue "Creature Fear" as well, because that's *my* favorite Bon Iver song.

"What? Really? This song? What else is on this playlist?"

"It's literally all Bon Iver." I look sideways at him.

"Well?" he asks, glancing over. "Do you like them now?"

I shrug. "Depends on the song, but yeah, you could say they're no longer deplorable."

"Say it."

"Say what?"

"Say you like them."

You should see my bedroom wall, I almost tell him, but I want to show him that one. So I mumble, "I like Bon Iver."

Levi seems to take this as fair. "Good, excellent. You've conceded. *I win*."

I laugh. "Glory-hog."

He reaches across the console to take my hand, looking very . . . distracted. (I blush.) "Where should we go?"

I smile. "Surprise me."

Levi's expression goes thoughtful as he focuses on the road. Then, without warning, he pulls to the side, turns on the hazards, and . . . starts to take off his tie.

I swallow. "Levi . . . "

He gives me a look before he realizes what I'm thinking. (His slow grin makes my toes curl.) "Calm down, don't jump to conclusions."

My blush runs deeper. "What are you doing?"

"This," he says, and blankets my eyes with the flat side of his tie. When my world is completely dark, and he has tied the two ends behind my head, he takes my hand. "Surprising you."

chapter 54

QUEUED:
ALL MY HEART
BY THE MYNABIRDS

THE WORLD AROUND me changes in a strange new way. One minute I can tell we're in a neighborhood, and the next on a busy road, and then the freeway. But when we exit the freeway and start on the windy roads, I'm entirely confused.

"Okay, I might be sick," I say. "Too much winding."

"Almost there," he assures me, squeezing my hand.

He's right—we park only a minute or two later. I reach up to slip the tie off my head, but he stops me.

"Not yet," he says. "Still not *quite* there."

So I wait. I let him help me from the car, finding myself surrounded by crisp night air. "Where . . ."

"Shh," he whispers, and kisses me.

But before I can wind my arms around him, we're walking again, me in a daze, Levi an explosion of energy. I can feel it in his hand twitching in mine, the way his footsteps sound (frantic and quick) on the dirt. He's quiet, however, and the world around me is quiet, so I don't make a peep. I focus my energy on not tripping, as the ground becomes hard and bumpy. When we go down a hill, I let him carry me on his back; when the grass gets high enough that it's tickling my knees beneath my skirt, I let him pick me up, one arm under my arms and the other under my legs.

When it seems like we'll be walking forever, he finally sets me down on soft, sandy ground. "The beach?" I ask.

"Nope." He reaches up and, in one quick movement, unties the tie and lets it fall across my shoulders.

I can see, suddenly, and while there *is* a vast expanse of water, it's not the ocean. The mountains, dark with night, rise up around the lake on all sides, and above our heads the sky is raw and full of stars.

"I was here the other night," Levi says, as if to fill the silence. "It's so quiet and peaceful and I just needed to think about everything, you know? Well, I ended up just thinking about you, for the most part, because who are we kidding—but anyway. It was relaxing."

I can't speak because I'm choking on my own emotions. The landscape blurs for a second, then clears as the tear drips down my cheek.

"Bee?" he asks uncertainly.

"Oh, Levi." I hang my head, barely managing to keep myself from sobbing loudly. Silent tears drip. "This is beautiful."

"Hey," he says, and puts his arms around me, pressing my back against his chest. His lips touch my neck, then a little higher, and that's when he feels the tears, tasting them as they smear against his lips. "Bee."

"You know beautiful things make me cry," I protest. "Don't be alarmed."

He turns me and tucks me into his embrace so that we're chest to chest. (Erm, well, my chest comes to his stomach. Whatever.) "I'm not. I just want to hold you."

"Oh, in that case . . . " I squeeze his waist, letting the silence of this place overtake me. I could say that's the reason I'm so calm, or maybe the beautiful view, in which thousands of stars are reflected in the smooth lake surface.

But I'd be a fool to claim that. We all know it's Levi.

"How did I ever leave you?" I ask suddenly.

He doesn't respond, just tightens his arms around me.

"Don't let me go," I say.

He bends to kiss me—what I think will just be a peck, but what turns into something lingering, and too precious for me to stop. (Even when I lose my breath.)

"Is it all right that I just want to kiss you all day long?" he breathes.

"Totally fine," I whisper back. "Even better if all day turned into forever."

"That's obviously what I was implying. I proposed already, and we're going to have twelve kids, remember?"

I smile, my palm on his cheek, my thumb brushing the side of his lips. "Are you being serious or . . . "

He blinks twice. "Well, I guess I could go down to ten, if you were persuasive enough."

"Shut up, Levi," I say, putting two fingers over his mouth.

"In reality," he says, ignoring my protests, "I'm actually thinking about moving into the spare bedroom at the new office. And, I dunno, one day maybe you can join me."

"You really are proposing!" I exclaim.

"Only hoping!" he defends, a sheepish grin on his lips. "And promising. You *did* just tell me to never let you go."

An alarm, loud and clear and shrill, echoes across the lake, coming from Levi's pocket. I cringe. "What. Is. That?"

He groans and pulls out his phone. "Time to drive back to the hotel. Sorry."

"It's fine," I say, and I mean it. I just want to be with him.

"My mom wants to see you before she leaves, anyway."

"She's at the event?" We haven't moved to leave yet, so I slide a little closer, savoring these last few moments alone.

Levi grins. "Awesome, huh? My dad's a loser, and Mom always wanted to come anyway. I think everyone's happy with this arrangement." He squeezes my hand, pumping it twice. "Ready?"

I squeeze back. "Thank you for this, Levi."

He kisses me on the nose, murmuring the sweetest, softest "You're welcome" that I feel from the tip of my nose to the bottoms of my feet. And then I let him carry me again: past the reeds, back up the hill, along the path to the parking lot. He helps me in, not letting go of my hand until he has to close the door, but then he's in the driver's seat and holding my hand again.

Once we've started driving again, the silence of the lake behind us, I turn up Bon Iver and let the sounds consume us, louder than the last time. We sing along this time, both of our voices clashing with the music, neither of us caring. He laughs when my voice cracks, but then he forgets an entire verse, and I get to laugh back.

Then Levi pulls up to the stop sign just before the main road, and since there's no one ahead of us or behind us, he looks over at me. When our eyes lock, I reach behind his head and pull him toward me and kiss him. Right there in the middle of the car, in the middle of the road, with the band he loves playing in the background and my heart completely in his hands.

We weave ourselves together. I let him kiss me and kiss me and kiss me, his hands on my arms, our faces so close they could be melded together, our clothes completely out of sorts.

My crown braid swiftly comes out of its bobby pins, and his hair has been so ruined that I know it won't go back to how he had it before.

A familiar ache blooms in my heart. I can't breathe without it spilling out—through my bloodstream, over my bones, into my skin. It isn't just a part of me; it's what makes me alive. It's what makes me *his*. What makes him *mine*.

Approaching headlights startle us back to reality, the car zooming past our hidden road. We sit back in our seats, breathing like we've just run up the mountain. "No more," Levi huffs. "Stop distracting me."

I laugh at him, and he pushes on the accelerator, a little hard, a little excited, which makes me laugh harder. With the mountain road winding ahead and his hand over mine on the console, I have the loveliest thought: Us, driving on forever and ever (him in his blue suit and me in my gold dress), heading straight into the sun, where I imagine the whole world is lit up in glory, and we are at the heart of it all.

The End

ACKNOWLEDGEMENTS

I'LL BE SURPRISED if I can do the thankfulness in my heart any justice on this page, but I'll try my best.

Mama and Papa, thank you for not looking at me like I was crazy the day I told you I wanted to quit school and write full time. I'm here because of that decision, and having you on my team has made it possible. I owe you big. Emmy, Haven, and Timmy – I love you dorks so much. E&H, thanks for lending your personalities to Astrid and Millicent. The book is brighter because of them.

Carlyn, my Parabatai. Thank you for always being the first to hear an idea, the first to read snippets, and the first to get a document with the manuscript in your inbox. Thank you for loving all these crazy ideas I have and pushing me to be a better writer. I love you.

Cassie – I could never ever repay you for the hours you spent walking me through all my spastic freak-outs over this book and all the others. For giving me a million good ideas and listening to me rant about a billion more (good, bad, and ugly). Thank you for being the Ryodan to my Barrons.

Lauz – I don't know what I'd do without you. Why is the pond so big? I miss you painfully much. Thank you for everything you do for me. I'm so glad you found me, Bebby France.

Thank you to the two ladies who edited TCP as we uncovered its final form: Nicolette and Rebecca. You are both queens.

I'm ridiculously blown away by all the hard work that every single one of my 30 beta readers went through to help me get to where I am now. Some of them even read it two and three times to help me get it exactly where I needed it. You were the first people to say, "Hey, you've got something good here." You were the first to cry to me about sad things. The first to tell me what to fix, the first to fight over Levi. The first to say you connected with Bee. Thank you specifically to Marisa, Ellen, Hannah, Amelia, Mika, and Liz for all giving me advice that wildly changed this book for the better.

Thank you to my fellow 2017 debuts who have taken me under their wings and loved on me through thick and thin. I'm so blessed to be in this year with you.

I owe the biggest thanks to all the reviewers who stepped up and said, "Sierra, we're going to make this book happen." *You did this.* You did so much for me and this book and I'm so blessed by you all. Thank you to all of the Glitter Bombs – you seriously took on that name and blew me away with your incredible devotion to spreading the word about this quiet little book baby. I can't name every reviewer, but I do need to name a few (just kidding, a lot) specifically: Jess, Mithila, Nichol, Olivia, Destiny, Pragati, Whitney, Claire, Raneem, Mollie, Helena, Becky, Allison, Andrew, Christy, Danielle, Kathleen, Erika, Shannon, Aly, Kelly, Ivey, Ruzaika, Farhina, Aurora, Mo, Merith, Mariam, Angel, Stephanie, and Katie. Among many, many others.

Thank you to every person who donated to help me cover publishing costs. Your generosity blows my mind daily. I'm also so thankful to everyone who preordered and purchased TCP, and to every library or librarian who made TCP a part of your collection. You all make it possible for me to write more books.

And thank you to my Creator, without whom I would not be here, and neither would this book. Thank You for loving me.

ABOUT THE AUTHOR

A T 7 YEARS old, Sierra Abrams decided that one day she would publish a book. For over a decade, in between exploring other career options, she kept coming back to that very first dream. Now her life consists of writing books of all kinds... Kissing books, angsty books, killing books, whimsical books, and sometimes books that are all of the above. When she's not writing, you can find her reading, traveling, consuming sushi, or daydreaming about Henry Cavill.